Praise fo

"Wow. Calvert really _____ ___ intensity of the drama that our crisis volunteers face out on the streets with cops and firefighters every day. *By Your Side* will be my standard gift this year for every occasion, and even for no occasion."

 —DAVID VINCENT, DIRECTOR OF US CRISIS CARE

"Candace Calvert has created the perfect recipe for medical romance. A tenacious but vulnerable heroine. A dashing but troubled hero. A pulse-pounding story. But most importantly, a generous helping of hope."

 —JORDYN REDWOOD, AUTHOR OF THE BLOODLINE TRILOGY

"[*By Your Side*] is a wonderful love story, a super tribute to emergency workers in general, to chaplains specifically, and an honest portrayal of faith in the lives of hurting people."

 —JANICE CANTORE, AUTHOR OF *CRITICAL PURSUIT* AND *ACCUSED*

"*Life Support* is a fast-moving novel that explores the dynamics of family and faith. Believable and endearing characters alongside family disputes and critical medical crises make this book hard to put down."

 —*ROMANTIC TIMES*

"In *Life Support*, Candace Calvert provides authentic medical thrills from characters so real you miss them when you turn the last page."

—RICHARD L. MABRY, MD, AWARD-WINNING AUTHOR OF *HEART FAILURE* AND *STRESS TEST*

"Calvert's adventuresome story of romance and drama infuses faith into her characters' motivations and makes readers eager for more."

—*BOOKLIST* ON *RESCUE TEAM*

"Candace Calvert makes hearts race, raises anxiety levels, and heightens emotions—all against doctor's orders—but it seems to be an ultimate cure for anyone in need of their reading fix!"

—RELZ REVIEWZ

"Just like an outstanding episode of *Grey's Anatomy*, *Trauma Plan* weaves medical, community, and personal issues with blossoming romance and strands of mystery."

—*BOOKLIST*

"*Trauma Plan* is a humor-filled romance, woven throughout with suspense, medical intrigue, and faith. Readers will look forward to the rest of the Grace Medical series."

—*ROMANTIC TIMES*, 4½ STAR REVIEW

"Calvert . . . infuses her story with detailed medical procedures and terminology along with honest questions about faith that anyone might ask in the face of difficulties. The characters are likable and receive rich and thorough development in this enjoyable 'hope opera' page-turner."

"Candace Calvert has crafted another gut-grabbing medical thriller. *Trauma Plan* kept me engrossed from beginning to end. . . . The faith message was clear, the medical traumas heart-stopping, and the romance heart melting."

"If you need an infusion of hospital drama, *Code Triage* is just the prescription."

"[*Critical Care*] flows well and keeps the reader's attention. . . . Characters find not only psychological healing, but also spiritual renewal."

"If you like *ER* and *House*, you'll love Logan and Claire and their friends at Sierra Mercy [in *Critical Care*]. Give me another dose, and soon!"

CANDACE CALVERT

BY YOUR SIDE

TYNDALE HOUSE PUBLISHERS, INC.
CAROL STREAM, ILLINOIS

Visit Tyndale online at www.tyndale.com.

Visit Candace Calvert's website at www.candacecalvert.com.

TYNDALE and Tyndale's quill logo are registered trademarks of Tyndale House Publishers, Inc.

By Your Side

Designed by Mark Anthony Lane II

Edited by Sarah Mason

Published in association with the literary agency of Natasha Kern Literary Agency, Inc., P.O. Box 1069, White Salmon, WA 98672.

Scripture taken from the Holy Bible, *New International Version,*® *NIV.*® Copyright © 1973, 1978, 1984, 2011 by Biblica, Inc.® Used by permission of Zondervan. All rights reserved worldwide. www.zondervan.com.

By Your Side is a work of fiction. Where real people, events, establishments, organizations, or locales appear, they are used fictitiously. All other elements of the novel are drawn from the author's imagination.

Library of Congress Cataloging-in-Publication Data

Calvert, Candace, date.
    By your side / Candace Calvert.
        pages ; cm. — (Crisis team ; #1)
    Summary: ER nurse Macy Wynn learned essential, gritty lessons in the California foster care system: Land on your feet and trust no one. She's finally located the fellow foster child she loves like a sister, but the girl's in deep trouble. Macy's determined to help, no matter what it takes. Her motto is to "make it happen" in any situation life throws at her—even when she butts heads with an idealistic cop. Deputy Fletcher Holt believes in a higher plan, the fair outcome—and his ability to handle that by himself if necessary. Now he's been yanked from Houston, his mother is battling cancer, and he's attracted to a strong-willed nurse who could be the target of a brutal sniper. When everything goes wrong, where do they put their trust?
    ISBN 978-1-4143-9032-1 (sc)
    I. Title.
    PS3603.A4463B9 2015
    813'.6—dc23   2014033702

Printed in the United States of America

21	20	19	18	17	16	15
7	6	5	4	3	2	1

For the heroes of law enforcement and crisis chaplaincy, whose courage, heart, and selfless dedication offer hope to their communities.

Ask and it will be given to you; seek and you will find;
knock and the door will be opened to you.

MATTHEW 7:7

1

"OFFICER, *HELP*!"

Deputy Fletcher Holt spotted a woman waving her arms overhead, a frantic flash of purple in the crush of idling cars. Sacramento's afternoon rush hour had been brought to a tire-squealing halt by an overturned gravel truck blocking all four southbound lanes. He'd seen it happen in his rearview mirror.

"We need you . . ." The woman's voice strained over a continual, indignant barrage of car horns. "Over here!"

Fletcher signaled back, then broke into a jog, sucking in a breath made acrid by asphalt, car exhaust, and burnt rubber. Sweat trickled beneath his protective vest despite the mild, early June weather. He'd been headed to the Florin substation, end of watch, when the dump truck did its kamikaze dive across the freeway, causing at least a dozen vehicles to skid on gravel and bounce against each other like a Six Flags bumper car ride. It was Highway Patrol's jurisdiction, but there was no way he'd drive on and not help. In the last ten minutes, he'd set out flares, offered his assistance to the arriving CHP officers, and now—

A horn blared: vintage M-class BMW, its driver wearing a business suit, sunglasses, and an openly belligerent look. "What's the deal? When can we get out of here?"

"Hang on. . . . They're working on it," Fletcher huffed, the edge in his voice coming from more than physical exertion. *You're not the only one who's got someplace else to be, buddy.* "Stay with your car—be patient, okay?"

He pushed his stride and covered the last dozen yards, coming to a halt beside the vehicle of the woman who'd waved to him.

"Yes, ma'am," he said, noting that she appeared unharmed. "You called for help?"

"Not for me," she explained, turning to point toward the far lane. "Over there, that van. I think someone's hurt."

Fletcher spotted a clutch of people, phone cameras held aloft. No surprise social media was getting a look before first responders. Tweet-a-wreck.

"Thank you. Stay with your car," Fletcher told the woman, relieved to hear sirens in the distance. Paramedics. Amazingly, the truck driver had climbed from the cab without a scratch. And as far as Fletcher knew, there had been no serious injuries. Hopefully that mercy would continue.

"Cop's here!" someone announced as Fletcher approached the vehicle. Even from several yards away, he saw the shattered window and crumpled side panel. It was an older-model minivan with a faded business stencil. Balloons, kites . . . *kids?*

Yes.

Little faces pressed against the remaining windows. And another child was on the ground beside the van. A young woman knelt alongside, offering aid. A teacher? Probably not, the way she was dressed. Black hair, sort of pulled up in a loose knot, a short blue skirt . . . long stretch of bare leg, high heels. None of it meant for herding kids or crawling around on a gritty freeway.

The young woman turned for a second to gaze across the lanes. Her white top was smeared with blood.

2

FLETCHER DROPPED TO ONE KNEE beside the woman. She was still intently focused on the victim in her care: a girl maybe kindergarten age. Blood trickled from beneath the child's brown bangs, down her cheek, and onto a frilly pink T-shirt. Her eyes were closed.

"Is she unconscious?"

"No, she rouses." The woman, probably in her mid-twenties, tore her attention away from the child and met Fletcher's gaze at last. "Alert enough to tell me her name. Annie Sims. But I suspect she has a concussion at the very least. I phoned 911 right away."

"Medics have already been dispatched, and I just radioed an update," Fletcher confirmed, blindsided by her striking features: inky hair, high cheekbones, dark brows and lashes framing incredible eyes. He'd never seen that color before:

amber, he'd call it. Almost catlike in shape. He realized he was staring and turned toward the van. "The other kids . . . they're okay?"

"Five others. All fine, according to the driver and the two field trip chaperones. I haven't been inside." The woman's capable hands, blotched with blood, cradled the little girl's head, gently stabilizing it. "As soon as I saw the driver carrying her out, I ran over to help, of course." There was something in her tone that said she'd expect nothing less of herself. Or anyone else worth breathing in this world.

"Your vehicle—you—not injured?"

"Oh. Yes, fine." She peered across the freeway lanes as if she'd forgotten how she got here. "We're fine."

We. Her passenger stayed with the car, Fletcher figured.

"The driver said the impact threw Annie sideways against a row of seats," she continued. "The cut on her forehead is from the broken glass. She shouldn't have been moved without stabilizing her neck." The child stirred, whimpered, and the woman gently stroked her temple with a thumb. "That gravel truck hit the van broadside just before it tipped over and went sliding. I saw the whole thing, Deputy—" her eyes found his name tag—"Holt."

"A tire blowout, looked like," Fletcher told her. "CHP's handling things. It's good of you to help, ma'am, but—"

"Macy." The amber eyes met his. "Macy Wynn." Fletcher sensed it was more of a correction than an introduction. She'd offered no smile, only a continuing concern for her young charge. This woman could be the poster child for Good Samaritans.

"Okay. Macy, then," Fletcher acknowledged. "We appreciate your help. But I'll take over now. Go back to your car and—"

"She's at risk for brain injury," Macy interrupted, clearly not good with his plan. "And for neck fractures, spinal complications." Her expression was more than wary. More like something Fletcher had seen on the nature channel. On a growling mother bear. "You're a paramedic too, Mr. Holt?"

"It's Fletcher," he heard himself say, though he rarely offered his first name. He told himself it was to put this woman at ease. "I've had advanced first aid and CP—"

"I'm a trauma nurse," Macy cut him off with a verbal swipe of her paw. "Clinical coordinator at Sacramento Hope ER. And I'm staying right here. You can go."

She's dismissing me?

"I can handle this," Macy insisted as though she'd read his mind. "I'm sure you're needed elsewhere. Go on . . . Do whatever else you need to do."

Fletcher snuffed a flash of anger, lately more common than he cared to admit. He was tired, and getting into a verbal tug-of-war was always a mistake.

"As a matter of fact, I'm end of watch. Or should be. But there was this accident and I came back to help." He connected with the stunning eyes and gave in to the temptation to mimic her: *"Of course."*

"Ah."

A flush rose on her cheeks, but Fletcher felt no sense of vindication. He didn't care anymore. All he wanted was to get out of here. Off this freeway . . . back home to Houston, away from the complicated mess his life had become. He didn't like the kind of man it was turning him into.

"Look," he told her, a jab of guilt summoning his manners, "they'll have the truck cleared soon. Don't worry." He glanced toward the siren yelp that said the medics had arrived. "And here's your qualified help now. It's going to be okay. I promise."

"I . . ." Macy bent low for a moment, whispering something soothing as the child fidgeted. When she gazed up at Fletcher again, her expression was softer. Almost—but not quite—conciliatory. The breeze whisked a tendril of hair across her cheek, shiny as a raven's feather. "I didn't mean to offend you . . . Fletcher. But Annie trusts me now. I promised I'd stay until someone gets in touch with her family. I'm sure you can understand that."

"Uh . . . sure."

He checked with the driver and chaperones—who had the remaining kids busy singing songs and sharing sack-lunch snacks—and waited long enough to make certain the medics didn't need him for anything. Then he gave Macy a quick nod and started back toward his patrol car.

If CHP didn't need him further, he'd get out of here. Take his mother to dinner whether there was something to celebrate or not. She'd been hopeful there would be good news at her doctor's appointment. Charly Holt was a faith-filled optimist. Even when life stomped on her heart.

Cancer . . . After all these months, the word still shook him to the core. Nothing he'd ever chased down, wrestled against—even with gun, badge, body armor—had prepared him for something so evil and merciless. It was wrong, completely unfair. But he'd get his mother through this. Fix it.

No matter what those doctors said, any other outcome was not an option.

By the time he made it back to his patrol car, the tow trucks had arrived and CHP gave him an all clear, along with a grateful thank-you for his assist. The medics were still on scene but would no doubt be leaving soon. All in all, things were much better, though you couldn't tell it by the continuing scowl on the face of Mr. BMW Business Suit. If anything, the man looked more agitated, lifting his designer sunglasses to glare out across the sea of cars.

Fletcher's cell phone signaled a text message. Jessica Barclay, back in Houston. That other thing he had to fix.

3

No one needed to tell Macy Wynn that three-inch heels and her narrow skirt weren't practical for jogging, let alone weaving through cars like a 49er rushing the end zone. She didn't have an option. Barefoot meant risking lacerations from broken glass, and walking guaranteed she wouldn't get back to Annie Sims before the ambulance took off. There was no way she'd abandon that scared kid, especially after learning she'd been placed in foster care. Macy knew far too personally how rugged and confusing that was.

She had tried to explain what she was doing to Elliot on the phone, but he'd long since run out of patience. Once she got to the car, she'd make him understand. If he didn't, it wasn't going to change her mind. She'd tell him to go on without her. Stand her ground the same way she had with that take-charge cop. He probably thought he was doing the right thing, but good intentions didn't guarantee a good outcome. Macy had learned the hard way that she'd be a fool to count on anyone but herself.

She squinted across the lanes, searching for Elliot Rush among the drivers still milling around. The late-afternoon sunlight had gone rosy gold, pretty if it weren't for the exhaust fumes, honking cars, and miserable circumstances. Right now she should be on the deck of her favorite river-view café, tackling a plate of grilled salmon and celebrating. She still had the urge to pinch herself. *My sister.* They'd been reunited after all these years and—

What on earth?

Macy stopped short, wobbling on one heel, to stare at the confusing scene ahead. That same deputy. Standing beside the BMW and shining a penlight into Elliot's eyes. Doing a medical assessment? Not only was he unqualified; it was totally unnecessary. Neither Elliot nor Macy had sustained so much as a scratch.

"Elliot!" She waved her hand, then gave up and yanked off her shoes to run the last dozen yards, arriving beside the car just as he handed his driver's license to Fletcher Holt.

"What's going on? What's wrong?" she asked, starting to get a bad feeling. Elliot's face had gone pale beneath his carefully maintained tan, and perspiration beaded along his thinning hairline. His lips were tense. "Elliot?"

"Please, ma'am." Holt's intense blue eyes met hers, his expression—and the fact that he'd gone back to the more formal *ma'am* thing—clearly ordering Macy to stand down. There was no hint of that earlier gentle assurance: *"It's going to be okay. I promise."*

"This conversation is between Mr. Rush and me," he advised.

Macy frowned. "But we didn't even come close to hitting anyone."

"It's not about that, Macy." Elliot cast an anxious eye skyward as the News 10 helicopter hovered. He suddenly looked a decade older than his forty-seven years. "This officer thinks I've been driving under the influence of alcohol. Of course I informed him we were on our way *to* dinner, not *from*. So . . ." He pocketed his wallet after his license was handed back.

"You didn't consume any alcohol?" Fletcher's gaze flicked to Macy for an instant. "Maybe stop for drinks on the way to your dinner date?"

"Business meeting," Macy corrected, not sure why she needed to make that clear. Except she often found herself explaining her longtime relationship with Elliot Rush and his wife, Ricki. He was a financial adviser, the Hope medical system's retirement plan representative. And because of regrettable circumstances, someone she'd been thrown together with since she was a teenager. Elliot might even have been a father figure, if her life experiences hadn't completely tainted that word. "And," Macy added, "I don't drink alcohol."

"Good to know." Fletcher's barely tolerant expression said otherwise. He glanced toward a slow-moving CHP vehicle, offering her a good glimpse of his profile. Nice nose, strong jaw. With his height, that close-cropped blond hair, the blue eyes, and that intriguing Southern stretch in his voice, Fletcher Holt could be extremely attractive. If he weren't a cop. And so determined to be a royal pain in the—

"No," Elliot answered. "No drinks. We'd very much appreciate it if you'd let us get back in the car now." He nodded toward the wrecker preparing to tow the gravel truck to the shoulder. "It looks like they're going to open the lanes soon." He pulled his dark glasses from his pocket, tapped them against his slacks. "With all due respect, Officer, you're barking up the wrong tree here."

Is he? Macy tried to convince herself Elliot's eyes didn't look any more bloodshot than usual and that she hadn't just noted the slightest bit of nystagmus—sideways jerking of his pupils. They hadn't driven for more than a few minutes before the accident, and she'd done most of the talking. Had she been so absorbed with her sister's situation that she didn't notice the signs he'd been drinking? She bit back a groan, hating that this overeager cop had her second-guessing things. She didn't have time for any of this; she needed to get back to Annie Sims. Elliot was right that this interrogation needed to end. Now.

"You know . . . ," Macy began, slipping her foot into one of her shoes and stepping sideways to locate the other. "I think everyone's just plain tired after all of this mess. I'll bet you are too, Fletcher." She offered him a tentative smile. "Back at the van, you told me you were going off duty. You're probably anxious to get home."

"More than you could possibly know . . . *ma'am.*" The edge in Fletcher's voice said Macy wasn't going to succeed in sending him away a second time. "I was about to do that when Mr. Rush walked over to my car to lodge a strong complaint about the delay in clearing this highway. I detected unsteadiness in his gait and some slurring of speech." The blue eyes held her captive as effectively as a set of hand-cuffs. "As a nurse, you may recognize those symptoms as suspicious for substance abuse or an altered neurological state. Either way, I have an obligation to—"

"What do you plan to do?" Elliot blurted, anger warring with anxiety in his tone. "Make me take a sobriety test? Do your little do-si-do right here on the highway?" He glanced up as the news helicopter churned the sky overhead. "You're new to the department—maybe to this state by your accent. Do you have any idea who I am?"

"Yes, sir," Fletcher answered, not missing a beat. "You're a driver who could be risking the life of his passenger—" his gaze darted toward Macy—"and the lives of other citizens. It's my sworn duty to prevent that tragedy. I think Miss Wynn might agree there have been one too many innocents injured already."

Macy nodded. The man had a good point. And apparently no clue Elliot was the brother-in-law of an influential US senator.

"You have a choice, Mr. Rush," Fletcher continued, raising his voice over a volley of shouts in the distance. "Consent to a PAS—Breathalyzer—right here or—"

"Up there, look!" a voice shouted in the distance.

"What's he doing?" someone else yelled.

There was a return volley of shouts as Fletcher's portable radio roared to life, 900 codes repeating rapid-fire. In an instant, people started to run, point, scream.

"He's got a rifle up there, on the overpass!"

"Sniper!"

"Down!" Fletcher vaulted toward Macy.

Like an echo, his shout was repeated by the CHP officers: "Down, down! Take cover and stay down!"

"A snipe—" Macy's heart lodged in her throat, choking
her words. Her legs went weak. She dropped to a crouch
next to the car in horrified disbelief, fingertips trembling
against its side. She saw Elliot scramble to safety at the rear
of the BMW. The air pulsed with a surreal mix of helicopter
blades, screams, and a sickening *crack-crack-crack*.

"Down!" Fletcher ordered again, grasping Macy's shoulder hard. "All the way down, on the ground."

"But those children—"

His hand flattened against Macy's back, and in an instant
her face met the highway with a sharp sting, lips so close she
tasted the tar. There was another loud crack and the sound
of shattering glass from somewhere far too close. The car
door swung open above her, and Fletcher dropped down
behind it, a gun gripped in his fist.

4

WITHIN MINUTES, the wail of sirens drowned panicked shouts as officers from all surrounding agencies and the sheriff's department SWAT team raced to the scene. STAR, the sheriff's department's helicopter, hovered overhead. Patrol car strobes and near-blinding searchlights pierced the darkening sky, lighting the shrubbery in the direction the shooter had disappeared—vanished as quickly as he'd appeared, with no further shots fired. And now, twenty minutes later, the freeway remained closed, while people in the surrounding neighborhoods were told to "shelter in place" as officers with K-9s conducted yard-to-yard searches.

"Copy that," Fletcher replied to the comm center, acknowledging a radio update. His long day had morphed into night. And he was on a perimeter position, like it or not.

For the first time since the drama began, it was quiet enough to hear the voices of folks still hunkered in and around their vehicles. Whispers and nervous laughter, people on cell phones reassuring family and friends they were safe, and car radios tuned to a jarring blend of insistent news broadcasts. Here and there headlights flicked on. The fear that had bonded the freeway captives was fast giving way to irritable impatience to be done with it.

Fletcher knew the feeling. He'd texted his mother to say he'd be late, sparing her the details.

His radio crackled again and went quiet.

"Is the ambulance leaving?" Macy asked from where she leaned against the BMW's rear fender. She sounded different in the darkness. Less mama bear, more little girl lost. There had been fear in her eyes when he drew his Glock. "I think I see the rig moving," she ventured, pointing at lights in the distance.

"Yes." He watched as she slipped the band from her hair, letting it fall loose around her shoulders. "They're beginning to clear the freeway. In about ten minutes two lanes should open so these remaining cars can start moving southbound again." Someone in the next vehicle hit a flashlight app on his cell phone, just long enough that Fletcher could read the concern on Macy's face. And see the small abrasion on her cheekbone; he felt bad about that. "The last update I heard said Annie Sims was stable and awake," he assured her. "The foster parents are waiting at Sac Hope."

"Daddy . . . ," a child's voice whined from the darkness a few yards away. "I have to go potty."

There was a car door squeak, a rustling sound, then a deep voice giving hasty instructions regarding an alternate use for a paper cup from a fast-food restaurant.

Fletcher had no doubt Elliot Rush's amble toward the shoulder of the highway a few minutes ago had been for similar reasons. Too dark to see if he could walk a straight line.

"Do you have any idea who I am?"

Fletcher smiled at the irony: right now, the self-important Elliot Rush was a mere mortal who'd likely trade his "business meeting" for the discreet convenience offered by a Happy Meal paper cup. There was some small justice in that.

"What did I miss?" Macy leaned closer, enough that he detected a trace of her scent. Like warm almond coffee cake. "You laughed."

"It's nothing." Fletcher shrugged, the movement causing his leather gun belt to creak. "Adrenaline ebb, dinner deprivation. Long day. Same as in the ER."

Macy tipped her head to peer at him in the darkness. She was much taller up close. "Sounds like you know."

Fletcher thought of Houston Grace Hospital. Of Jessica. He pushed the memory down—a little easier every time. "I've darkened the doors of my share of ERs. Cops and hospitals—happens too often."

"Can't argue there."

Somewhere in the distance, a car radio stuttered the latest news update: *". . . search for Highway 99 shooter continues. Authorities believe . . . cause of tire blowout on a city truck during rush-hour traffic. An accident that injured a six-year-old girl. Witnesses spotted the shooter on the . . . There were no other victims, thanks to the fast response of—"*

Fletcher cleared his throat. "I'm sorry I had to shove you to the ground. I hope I didn't hurt you."

Macy lifted her shoulders in a shrug, and he swore it sent a waft of coffee cake directly to his senses. His blood sugar must be hovering at zero.

"I'm okay." Her fingers tested her cheek again. "Better than a gunshot wound." She shivered a little. "No matter how many times I see something like this on the news, I still don't get it. Why would someone do that? Shoot at complete strangers?"

"I don't know," Fletcher admitted. "Thrills, maybe. Same reason kids toss rocks or Coke bottles off an overpass. Malicious sport."

"Sport?" Macy hugged her arms across her blood-smeared shirt. "Huge difference between a Coke bottle and a bullet."

"Maybe not in this shooter's mind," Fletcher ventured, though something about this didn't feel like kids. The shooter had lain low after that first shot, waited, then taken the risk to do it again. Kids ran. "Fortunately he didn't hit people," Fletcher added, not sure if he was assuring Macy or himself. "Only a truck tire and—" he glanced toward Elliot's damaged car—"windshields."

Macy grimaced. When she spoke again, her in-control timbre was back. "I estimate we've been out here for nearly two hours."

"Close enough." He had a hunch where this was headed.

"Enough time to lower a blood alcohol level."

Fletcher's turn to be quiet.

"I'm not saying I think you were right," Macy explained.

"That Elliot wasn't telling the truth. I've known him a long time. If I had to pick somebody to trust completely, it would probably be him. And on top of that, there've been a couple of hours as a safety cushion . . ."

"So I should look the other way," Fletcher deduced, finishing her thought. "Let your friend slide. Are you asking me to do that?"

"Not exactly." She had the decency to squirm. "I only thought maybe—"

"I'd set aside my professional observations, my experience . . . my integrity? Step away and take a chance that it's all good?" There was no way Fletcher could stem the rising anger. Not about a drunk driver—not *ever* about that. "I don't want to believe you'd ask that of me. Because I sure didn't see *you* doing that. Over at the school van, when you dug in your heels and told me there was no way you were leaving Annie Sims. You remember that?"

In the meager light, Fletcher saw Macy swallow, her incredible eyes glancing down. "I remember."

"I thought so." Fletcher scanned the freeway for a moment. The ambulance was moving now, flanked by two county cars. The general exodus would begin soon. "The fact is, we're pretty much the same in that respect, you and I. So you should know there's no way I'll allow an impaired driver to climb behind the wheel of a car. It's no safer than some lunatic aiming a rifle from a freeway overpass."

"But what if he refuses the Breathalyzer? Will you actually arrest—?" She turned as Rush approached.

"Looks like we're making progress, at least," the man observed, pointing his cell phone toward a line of cars inching forward at the direction of police and fire personnel. He drew closer, and his face was partially illuminated by the freeway lights. There was none of the earlier bravado in his expression or posture. "I assume my car will need to move soon. Do you have a plan for that, Deputy Holt?"

Fletcher let a few seconds pass, swearing he heard Macy Wynn's heart ticking like a metronome. He assessed the amazingly orderly progression of cars. There was no time or space to do a field sobriety test now. He didn't carry a PAS. But there was no way he'd let Macy know she was probably right about the clearance of the alcohol. He was certain Rush had been drinking. He wouldn't be surprised if there was a flask somewhere in that BMW.

"Got your keys?"

"Yes, sir." Rush produced them from his pocket. "Right here."

"Good." Fletcher nodded toward Macy. "Toss them to her. She's driving."

5

IT WAS WELL AFTER 8 P.M. when Fletcher finally parked his Jeep in front of his parents' place. Only a few months back, he'd had to squint and search for this porch because of the Sacramento Valley "tule fog," a dense cloud that had chilled him to the bone despite his flannel shirt. Fletcher still couldn't get a grip on humidity that wasn't sauna warm. Sometimes it felt like he'd ventured much farther than the mere two thousand miles from south Texas to northern California. Sometimes—in weather, culture, and politics— it was like walking on the far side of the moon. But his father needed him to be here for his mother, stand in for him while he completed the project in Alaska.

The nondescript Roseville house had been purchased over a year ago when the oil company transferred Fletcher's father to California. Even in the improving economy, builders had been eager to unload inventory, so the Holts bought it as an investment. The job transfer was temporary, three years at most. *Home* would always be the house in Houston, with its thick layers of gray paint and crumbling pink brick facade. A nineties split-level shaded by a giant laurel tree that hosted noisy hordes of summer cicadas and Fletcher's initials surrounded by a boldly carved Superman shield.

"Dinner was supposed to be on me," Fletcher told his mother as she spooned a second helping of corn bread–topped tamale pie onto his plate. A rising curl of steam wafted scents of cumin, chili powder, and simmered-soft onions, like proof of his mother's familiar refrain: *"God's on his throne and Mom's in the kitchen—all's right with the world."* There was nothing Fletcher wanted to trust more than that. He'd been relieved by his mother's report of her doctor's appointment earlier today. Still . . .

"I'll take a rain check for dinner; you're not off the hook," Charly teased, her eyes sparkling despite the faint shadows and new hollows framing them. "I'd rather wait until I feel more like ordering something that will make a respectable dent in that fat county paycheck."

"Fat?" He managed to chuckle around a mouthful of corn bread, watching as his mother brushed her fingers through the tufts of blonde hair she insisted were "growing back like Rapunzel's." But after the chemo, Mrs. John Holt looked more like the baby mockingbird she and her seven-year-old son had rescued from a neighbor's cat. Feather fluff, big eyes, vulnerable. They'd nursed the fledgling for more than a week, kept it in a Kleenex box on top of the dryer, fed it with an eyedropper, and . . . Fletcher let the comparison stop there. They buried that box under a peony bush.

"Besides," his mother added, glancing at the iPad lying next to her open Bible, "I had a Skype date with a hot geologist in Prudhoe Bay." She smiled the smile Fletcher hoped to inspire in a woman someday. Then her sparse brows pinched together. "While you were busy dodging bullets on the interstate. It was all over the news, but of course I had no idea." She pointed the serving spoon at him. "You should have called me, Fletcher."

"Sure." He raised a palm like a cartoon traffic cop. "Everyone, freeze; I've got to phone my ma." For some reason an image of Macy Wynn came to mind. She'd been more than disappointed not to accompany the injured foster child to the ER, almost as frustrated as Elliot Rush having to hand over those Beemer keys. He wasn't going to be a happy passenger. Fletcher hoped Macy knew how to drive a stick shift without grinding the gears.

In the corner of his parents' great room, the TV news continued speculation regarding the sniper's identity. Film from the news chopper and pics from camera phones were being analyzed. Speculation was rampant regarding the shooter's possible motive and current whereabouts. The FBI had taken an interest as well, though Sac County was still in charge. House-to-house searches revealed nothing. The news broadcast kept repeating a taped interview with the driver of the school van.

"It's a miracle there weren't more physical injuries." His mother glanced toward the TV for a moment. Her fingers sought the edge of her well-worn Bible. "It could have been much worse. All those people trying to run, get away. Parents protecting their children."

"There was less panic than I expected," Fletcher assured her, though he was still surprised by that. "When we ordered folks to get down on the ground and take cover, they did. Cooperated for the most part." He had an image of Macy Wynn stretched out, her face against the asphalt.

"With the shooter still at large, people will be worrying—those kids from the van and even children who weren't there will be anxious, sleepless. Parents too, neighbors and families of first responders . . ."

She met his gaze, her concern palpable. But Fletcher knew that it wasn't only for him. She was thinking about her volunteer work as a community chaplain with California Crisis Care. It had become a passion for her—being there for survivors in the aftermath of personal tragedy. She'd taken the training, spent long hours shadowing another more experienced chaplain, and then finally become certified. When Charly Holt talked about the work she was doing, she lit up. She was convinced crisis chaplaincy was her calling, like law enforcement was his. She felt that her life, even the painful challenges—maybe mostly those—had prepared her for exactly this. Fletcher could understand it in theory, but . . .

"Your doctor said it's okay to schedule yourself for activations?" Crisis chaplains could be called out in the middle of the night, subjected to physical and emotional stress. Maybe even danger—sometimes they were needed at crime scenes and disaster sites. "No restrictions?"

"I said I wouldn't take night calls," she told him. A temporary ploy to appease her husband and son, Fletcher would bet. "But it's high time I got out there and started feeling useful again." She rolled her eyes. "Another month at home and I'll start playing Candy Crush on Facebook. And send invites to *you*."

He grimaced. "Can't have that."

"The timing is perfect," she continued, healthy color rising in her cheeks for the first time in weeks. "There's the Crisis Care gala tomorrow night." She shot him a look, brows raised.

"I rented the tux," he assured her, still half-wishing there had been a means of escape. But the evening was important to her. "And set a reminder on my phone."

"Good. After that, I'll make sure my name is back on the schedule. I have a feeling we're going to be busy." She turned to glance at the TV, which showed images from the News 10 helicopter: the overturned county gravel truck, the school van, Highway Patrol, Fletcher's patrol car . . . and the vintage BMW with a shattered windshield. "We'll be needed," his mother continued, "because this kind of event has a ripple effect. You don't have to be hit by a bullet to be a victim of the violence."

———

"Your tetanus is up-to-date? You're sure?"

"Two years ago," Macy promised, trying not to wince as fellow ER nurse Taylor Cabot daubed ointment over the freshly cleaned abrasion on her cheek. "I got one the time I did that impressive kickboxing move and ripped off my toenail." She caught the redhead's immediate grimace. "Sorry. Hard to forget."

"There. All set, tough girl." Taylor stepped back and surveyed Macy's face. "It's going to swell. I'd ice it if I were you." She glanced through the supply room doorway toward the main trauma room. A distant siren blended with the usual sounds of overhead pages, phlegmy coughs, squeaking machinery, moans, and occasional tension-valve laughter of medical staff. She turned back to Macy, her green eyes filled with concern. "You're sure you're okay?"

"Absolutely. Stiff from kneeling on the freeway, then practically kissing it—no fault of my own." She quickly dismissed an image of Fletcher Holt standing over her with a gun. "Little abrasion. Huge regret at missing a free dinner. The hospital grill is not a legitimate trade-off. But I'm fine. No big deal."

Taylor touched her arm. "You were involved in a shooting, Macy. That's a *very* big deal."

A shooting. Macy couldn't stop the intruding image of that shattered windshield, the hole. When she told Taylor she was stopping by the hospital to check on the little girl injured in the incident, her friend had insisted on coming over. Taylor arrived in her exercise tights, a Sac Fire sweatshirt, and flip-flops, hair still wet from her daily swim.

"Is that why you hauled yourself over here?" Macy asked. "To use me as a guinea pig for your chaplain training?"

"Of course not. Not the guinea pig part," Taylor amended. "But I saw the news. They're already profiling the shooter. Tallying up how many people could have been killed." Her eyes swept over Macy's face. "I can only imagine how it would feel to be out there, trying to take cover. Or how frightening it would be to have someone you love in that kind of danger."

Not true. Taylor could do much more than imagine that. Her husband, a firefighter, had been killed just over two years ago. And now she volunteered to throw herself into other people's pain. It was hard to understand. Maybe Macy was missing that altruistic gene. Or maybe her rugged childhood had squashed it, leaving her simply with the skill to land on her feet. Compliment or not, "tough girl" might actually fit.

"I'm okay," Macy assured her. "I promise. No tetanus, no trauma." She gave Taylor a quick hug. "And you are a good person. With really wet hair. You should go home and rest up. We're back here in the morning. I'll check on Annie once more and then I'll go too."

Macy found the little girl in an exam room, ready to be discharged. Her foster mother was at the desk getting instructions from the nurse-practitioner.

Annie Sims had a Dora the Explorer Band-Aid on her forehead and the beginnings of a black eye. A half-empty pudding cup and a carton of milk sat on the tray table beside her. She clutched the plastic belongings bag holding her bloodstained clothes on her lap; her foster mother had brought clean ones.

"I don't have to stay all night," Annie explained as Macy came close. "I thought I was going to have to sleep here." She shrugged her tiny shoulders, expression far too serious for a six-year-old. "I didn't know."

Macy's throat squeezed, the old ache crowding in. "But you get to go with Helen now." She knew better than to say "home"—it could mean so many different things to this child. "She'll be finished talking to the nurse in a few minutes and then you can go."

"You're a nurse too?"

"Yes." Macy smiled, looking down at the jeans and cotton knit hoodie she'd pulled on after shedding her soiled top and skirt. "I don't look like one now, but I work right here at Sacramento Hope."

"My real mom is at a special hospital. She's going to get better. Then she can take care of me. And we can go home." Annie sighed, hugged the hospital tote. "Can I keep this bag?"

"Sure," Macy managed despite so many swirling memories of waiting for her own mother, hoping the way only a child can hope. "That bag is yours now."

"It has handles and could hold a lot. They wrote my name on it too, see?"

"I see that—'Annie Sims,' right there." Macy knew where this was going. *Oh, please . . .*

"If they send me someplace else, I'll use this bag," the little girl explained, running her hands over it as if it were a fine piece of luggage. "My mom said maybe she can come get me this summer. If everybody says that's okay. I don't know for sure."

That was the worst part. Not knowing anything for sure. Where you'd sleep, what you'd eat, who was nice . . . or who might want to hurt you in ways you couldn't even understand. You were never, ever sure. You hung on to hope because it was all you had, but after a while even hope packed up and moved on. You kept your favorite things in a bag you could take with you at a moment's notice. And you only trusted yourself.

"I want to go home," Annie whispered, her chin beginning to tremble and her eyes welling with tears. "Really home this time."

Macy's arms were around her in an instant, lips brushing the Dora Band-Aid as she rocked the shivering child. "I know, sweetheart. I *know*."

6

"LET ME TRY AND GET IN HERE." Macy struggled to squeeze into the car so she could position the patient's head and open her airway. An unresponsive fiftysomething woman, at least two hundred pounds, wedged in the backseat of a two-door Honda. The woman's face was an ominous shade of gray and slick with drool. Macy's fingers pressed against her ample neck, just below her jaw. A pulse, but . . . "She's not breathing. We need to pull her out of here. Where's—?"

"Transport gurney's right behind you," Taylor confirmed. "There's a flat to slide her out on. Ronie's got the tank and an Ambu bag."

"Let's . . . try it." Macy suppressed a groan of exasperation. Car extrication shouldn't have been part of this. Why hadn't the woman's son called 911 instead of screeching to the curb outside the ER and running wild-eyed into the waiting room trying to find a wheelchair?

"Hurry! C'mon—can't you do that faster?" he pleaded, observable anxiety making his deep voice turn shrill. "Are you sure you know what you're doing?"

"Yes, they do, sir," said the familiar, calm voice of one of the ER security guards. "Now please, step back and let these folks do their jobs."

"No! I'm not going anywhere. That's my mother in there. I have to be sure they're doing the right things. I have to—"

"Drop the gurney. Get in close!" Macy shouted over her shoulder to a waiting tech. She grabbed the Ambu bag and leaned back inside the car, ducking her head to avoid the elbow of another tech as an octopus of arms worked frantically to slide the woman onto the transport flat. "Make sure that O_2 is on high flow." Macy positioned the plastic mask and squeezed the Ambu bag, delivering an oxygen-rich breath into the woman's lungs. "Okay now, let's slide her out of here."

"What did they do to her? Why are you giving her oxygen?" the son shouted, eyes wide, as they strapped his mother onto the gurney, jerked it to an upright position, and began hustling toward the ER doors. He lurched forward, jogging alongside them. "She said she had a headache, a bad headache. Not trouble breathing."

"I've got the bag," Taylor told Macy, taking over the rescue breaths. She nodded toward the son. "If you want to get some history . . ."

"Right." Macy was grateful to see the two security guards flanking the coded-entry doors from the ambulance bay to the ER. She'd learned the hard way that people under stress were highly unpredictable. "Mr. . . . ?"

"Harrell," the man puffed, a mix of confusion and horror on his face as the gurney carrying his mother clattered through the open doors. His body tensed. "I need to get in there, not stand here talking."

"Please," Macy told him as gently as she could. "In order to help your mother, we need some infor—"

"Her insurance card's on file. Darlene Harrell—look it up." He stepped close enough that she caught a whiff of panic-induced body odor. His teeth ground together, making his words hiss. "Money. It's always money first." He jabbed a finger toward Macy's face. "You'll get paid, if that's what you're worried about."

"It's not. Not at all." Out of the corner of her eye, she saw one of the security guards move discreetly closer. Macy kept her voice calm. "The only thing I need from you is some basic history of what happened with your mother today. It helps us help her. We're trying to help her, Mr. Harrell."

He pulled his hand back, anguish in his expression. "I'm sorry . . . Oh, man. I'm sorry." He jammed his hands in his pockets, stared at the ambulance bay doors. "I'm worried. That's all."

"Of course." Macy made a mental note to page the hospital chaplain once she got through those doors. "We'll get you in to see your mother as soon as we can. I promise. But right now you can help her best by telling me how this current illness started. Did you say she had a headache?"

"That's right. She gets headaches, but nothing a couple of Tylenol can't handle. Ma's tough. She raised six boys, kept us all fed by driving a correctional facility bus—doesn't take anything off anybody. Doesn't complain either." The man swallowed. "But she called me about an hour ago and said this was the worst headache she ever had in her life."

"I see." Macy nodded, wishing he hadn't just voiced the classic symptom of a catastrophic brain hemorrhage. She gleaned what additional information she could and then jogged back toward the trauma room.

Less than five minutes later, Darlene Harrell's body stiffened with a seizure, and the respiratory therapist moved in with a suction catheter to clear her airway. The ER physician, Andi Carlyle, steadied the woman's twitching face between her gloved hands. The overhead exam light gleamed off her small cross-shaped pendant. Everyone knew Dr. Carlyle's faith was as much a part of her practice of medicine as the stethoscope slung around her neck.

"Seizure's over," Macy noted, relieved.

"Good girl," Dr. Carlyle whispered, giving Mrs. Harrell's cheek a gentle pat. "That's enough of that." She pulled the intubation tray closer and glanced at the nurse near the crash cart. "Let's draw up some Versed—better if we're dealing with elevated intracranial pressure. There's no gag reflex. But if we need to, I'll use etomidate and succinylcholine. I'll want labetalol for that blood pressure. I'll need to talk with the stroke team. But first things first." She nodded to the respiratory therapist. "Hyperventilate her; we need to get this tube in. From the sounds of those lungs, this good woman's aspirated a lot of stomach contents."

"I've got the IV line," Taylor reported. "And the blood for the lab. Chest X-ray and brain CT ordered."

Overhead, the operator paged for a chaplain to come to the ER.

"Blood pressure's 208 over 114," Macy reported, watching the monitor. "Sinus rhythm at 54. Pulse ox on the high flow . . . 96 percent."

"Glucose 92," a tech added. "I've got the Foley cath here when we can do it."

"My tube first, then yours." Dr. Carlyle's smile showed a glimpse of dimples. Those dimples, combined with her eager smile and diminutive stature, plus her penchant for Crocs with brightly patterned socks, contributed to countless questions from patients and family regarding her age and experience. But Andi's enviable skill assuaged every doubt. She lifted Mrs. Harrell's lids gently. "Darlene, I don't like the look of your pupils, my dear."

"Her son wasn't aware she'd stopped breathing," Macy explained, imagining the poor woman's struggle. She'd been too far gone to protect her airway. "Someone said the drive from her house to the hospital must have taken at least fifteen minutes."

"Let's hope she was getting air for most of that time." Andi squinted down her patient's throat, laryngoscope in one small hand, endotracheal tube in the other. "Brain's compromised enough already, and . . . Here we go, folks." She threaded the plastic tube deftly, removed the scope, and then nodded to the respiratory therapist to inflate the balloon that would seal it against the woman's trachea. "Looks good. Let's have a listen to her lungs."

"Don't tell me to wait outside. I need to see her!" a too-familiar voice shouted outside the code room. "What are

they doing to her? Get the doctor out here. I've got to talk
to—"

"Mr. Harrell, sir." The chaplain's voice. "If you'll come
this way . . ."

Taylor shot Macy the dreaded *uh-oh* look. They both
knew that it didn't take long before fear and panic turned
to hostility. They'd seen it countless times. Fortunately Andi
also had great skill when it came to her patients' families.

"All righty then . . ." Andi Carlyle rose on the toes of her
Crocs to stretch farther over the gurney as she finished listening to her patient's lungs. "Let's get that portable chest,"
she said calmly. "I'll write the orders for the labetalol. After
it's onboard—and we slip in that Foley cath—we'll get this
lady down to the CT scanner." She reached for the white
coat she'd hung over an IV pole. "Meanwhile, I'll go out and
talk with Darlene's very worried son."

"Be sure you have security with you," Macy advised,
remembering those few seconds when the man poked his
finger toward her face. He'd apologized, but—"Best to play
it safe."

———

"Good going, Houston. You sure know how to pick 'em."

Fletcher responded with an offhand shrug as a fellow
deputy exited the popular south Sacramento grill. There
was laughter as the man joined his partner outside the door.
This was about the thirtieth time since his shift began that
someone felt the need to point out his obvious stupidity.

"It'll die down. Stay cool."

California Crisis Care chaplain Seth Donovan swiped his

fingers across his lips, catching a stray shred of purple cabbage from his taco. "You're fresh meat, Fletcher. Everyone new starts off as a slab of rump roast in butcher paper. Maybe worse for you, since you're a lateral transfer. Didn't go through the academy here—and didn't get a copy of the local who's who. Not likely you'd know that Elliot Rush is the brother-in-law of a sitting US senator . . . who's tight with the county higher-ups." His brown eyes were warm despite rugged features and a world-weary manner that sometimes belied his age—just nearing his fortieth birthday. "I wouldn't lose sleep over it."

Fletcher shoved his carnitas plate aside. "Rush was drunk behind the wheel. I'd bet my badge. He was a risk. If there hadn't been a sniper on the freeway, I'd have proven it."

"And your sergeant would still have gotten that phone call." Seth reached for his coffee cup. "Look, I believe you. Given the circumstances, I'd probably hand those keys to the nurse too. But our senator has been a big supporter of law enforcement." He raised his hand. "I voted for him. And consumed more thank-you-for-your-service pastries than I care to admit. The man's a good guy. Anyone asks me, I'll say you are too. Bottom line: no formal complaint was lodged. As far as we know, Mr. Rush and the Sacramento Hope ER nurse got home safe and sound. Plus, no one died on that freeway last night. I'd call that a win."

Fletcher thought of Macy, her stubborn defense of Elliot Rush. And her clear dismissal of him. "It doesn't feel like that."

Seth was quiet for a while, then met Fletcher's gaze. "I would think, with your mother's illness and the move from

Texas to California, that you might feel like a fish out of water."

Great. Just what I need today: shrink talk. If Fletcher hadn't already decided that he liked this honest-to-his-core chaplain, he'd make an excuse to get out of here pronto. But the truth was, Seth Donovan was the calm in his storm right now.

"I'm doing okay," Fletcher told him. "Meaning I'm not your next project, Seth. Find someone else."

"Doing okay but living like a monk—never mind the very nice women I've offered to introduce you to." His brow lifted slightly. "From everything you've told me, your girl back home is moving on."

Jessica. He should never have mentioned anything about her.

"Maybe you should too," Seth said gently. "Move on; consider this time in California a new start. Put yourself out there."

"I'm good. Don't worry about me." Fletcher pasted on a smile that he hoped would pass for honesty. "I'm getting out." He shook his head at the laughable irony. "And tonight that's going to require a tuxedo."

"The Crisis Care fund-raiser. I'll be there myself." Seth dropped his napkin onto his plate with a sigh. "Mr. Rush will too, I expect."

"What?"

Seth nodded. "Big donor."

7

TAYLOR PICKED A GOOEY, walnut-studded morsel from her hospital-baked chocolate chip cookie and regarded it for a moment. "Even if it goes straight to my thighs, I deserve this. Really. It's payback for this whole day."

"Go for it." Macy leaned back against the plastic visitors' chair outside the doors to the ER, grateful for the filtered afternoon sun on her face. "You have my permission."

"I don't need to pull the widow card?" The teeniest wince said Taylor Cabot's humor and plucky bravado hadn't conquered her grief.

"No need. It's been a lousy day," Macy agreed, thinking of the ominous CT report on Darlene Harrell. Huge, inoperable bleed with brain stem herniation. Translation: no hope.

"But at least the follow-up phone call to Annie Sims's

foster mother sounded positive," she added, remembering the child holding that hospital belongings bag. "Ronie said she even talked with Annie for a few minutes. Said she sounded upbeat, chatty. That was good to hear."

"And you have good news too." Taylor brightened. "I can only imagine how great it feels to finally find your sister after all these years, have her call you out of the blue like that."

"Yes." Macy felt the familiar mix of elation and pain. Leah was her foster sister, not a blood relative—but maybe no one else could understand that it didn't matter one bit. Didn't matter either that the surprise call was not so much "out of the blue" as out of a Narcotics Anonymous twelve-step requirement. Leah was in rehab. Again.

"It feels good," Macy agreed, taking the piece of cookie Taylor offered and remembering that Fig Newtons were Leah's favorite. She'd wrapped some in a napkin once, hid them in her pillowcase. Ants swarmed, but Leah brushed them off and ate the cookies anyway, saying, *"Ant cooties are too small to count."* Macy smiled, grateful for a happy memory; they'd had too many bad ones together. "It's the best thing that's happened in a long time."

"She's younger, right?"

"Three years—turned twenty-four last month," Macy confirmed. "When I saw her in Tucson, I couldn't get over how much she'd changed." The last time she'd seen her sister, ten years earlier, Leah had been fourteen years old. Barely a month after her innocence had been stolen with such cruelty. The familiar guilt prodded. "She's trying hard to get things together now, build a future."

Taylor nodded, empathy in her eyes. "I can understand that."

"I'll do whatever it takes to help—"

"Macy!" Elliot waved from the parking lot, then pointed to his loaner car with a melodramatic frown. "See you tonight, if not sooner." He flashed a thumbs-up, continued on toward the hospital doors.

Macy lowered her hand, expecting the inquisitive look on Taylor's face. But her friend was too polite to pry. A relief since Macy didn't particularly want to talk about Elliot; the drive home from the freeway incident had been awkward at best.

"Employee benefits fair," she explained to Taylor, ignoring his mention of seeing her tonight. "Open enrollment for the health and retirement plans. Elliot's going to be here all month meeting with the staff."

"Ah, that's right. I should double-check to make sure my beneficiary changes were implemented." Taylor toyed with her cookie. "You told me you've known Elliot for a long time because he manages some other personal investments? I'm only asking," she added hastily, "because I was thinking about finding a new company to handle mine. He was recommended to you?"

"Yes. By a lawyer who was overseeing a financial trust. Sort of an inheritance from . . . an old family friend." The lie tasted like bile.

"Like a godparent."

"Uh . . ." Macy tried not to grimace. "Not exactly."

There was no palatable way to explain the "inheritance." Her biological father wasn't dead. It was just that he wished

Macy had never been born. The trust—her continuing
link to Elliot—was the man's humiliating payoff. A sum of
money Macy never, ever planned to touch.

"I'm sorry," Taylor said. "I didn't mean to intrude."

"No, you didn't. It's just . . ." Macy gathered her long
hair up in both hands, then let it fall against her shoulders.
"Between the whole sniper thing and—" she stopped herself from mentioning Elliot's near arrest—"and this ugly
shift, I'm ready for some R & R."

"What do you have in mind?"

"In a perfect world?"

"Of course." Taylor lifted the last chunk of her cookie. "I
have chocolate in my veins; only perfect will do now."

Macy smiled. "Okay. In a perfect world, I'd toss these
scrubs in the nearest Dumpster. Grab my workout clothes,
punch mitts, and ankle wraps and head to the gym." She
raised her fists like a boxer. "I'd spend an hour with my kickboxing coach, do a little bag work. Sweat this day out of my
pores, get those happy endorphins flowing. Then I'd snag
some Mikuni sushi takeout, watch a Landmark Adventures
video of the John Muir Trail—"

"Whoa, girl!" Taylor raised her palm. "Someone needs to
seriously help you raise the bar on your concept of 'perfect.'"

"Doesn't matter anyway," Macy said, surprised and then
annoyed by a ridiculous memory of Fletcher Holt. "Perfect's
out. Tonight's booked up."

"What does that mean?"

"Strapless gown, heels, so-nice-to-meet-you chitchat.
I'm going with Elliot and his wife to the California Crisis

Care gala." Macy sighed. "Not my kind of evening, but still better than a sniper attack."

———

Fletcher took careful aim, starting high over his target and calculating by experience the perfect trajectory—he hadn't achieved marksman status by his good looks. He slowly lowered his arm, closer, closer, and . . .

"*Rrroww!*"

The cat sprang from her twitchy-eager crouch on the apartment's hardwood floor in a flash of white fluff and leaped at the wall, paws batting at the red laser beam. She chased the light across the wall, head swiveling side to side, yellow eyes wide. Every gyration was heralded by agitated, stuttering chatter.

"There it goes. Grab it!" Fletcher bounced the laser beam over her gray ears, zigzagged it up the wall. "Look, it's over there now." He snorted with laughter at the ensuing antics: scramble, spring, thump, white with gray tabby stripes bouncing off the apartment's pale-blue walls.

"Got away—too bad. That's enough now. You wore me out."

Fletcher clicked off the beam and laughed at the look on the animal's face, perplexed but hopeful, though they'd probably played this game a hundred times before. He scooted backward across the small area rug until his back rested against the gray sleeper sofa. Across the room, the muted TV showed a seemingly endless loop of the darkened and indecipherable images of the freeway sniper. Still nowhere to be found.

"You'll get it next time, Hunter. C'mere, girl."

Fletcher drummed his fingers against the rug, smiling at the cat's wary-but-interested regard. For some reason it made him think of that ER nurse. Stupid, because the only interest Macy Wynn had shown was in escaping Fletcher as fast as possible.

"Ah, you got me," he told the animal as she dove at his hand. He waggled his fingers again, and Hunter rolled onto her back, sparring, with her fuzzy face buried in Fletcher's palm and hind legs kickboxing his forearm.

"Good job. Hey, easy on the teeth! No deadly force. There, that's better." He stroked the cat's silky fur with a finger and felt an immediate rumbling purr. Her warm tongue snagged across his skin like a damp washrag. In mere moments, she'd stretched out next to his cell phone and the TV remote, eyes closed and oversize front paws alternately kneading as she slumbered.

A cat. Fletcher shook his head—it was still embarrassing. He'd never imagined himself a cat owner. Ever. A dog for sure. It had been on his list of plans. A Lab or a German shorthair—something comfortable with a pheasant in its mouth, gunfire, and bumping over a Texas hunting lease in his Jeep. But now . . . Here she was, a six-toed Maine coon mix. Whatever that was. A once-scrawny rescue animal that was, six months later, growing like a 4-H pig project. And confidently—with attitude—taking over his new living space. He'd been guilted into adopting her, she'd been forced to accept him, and neither had a clue they'd soon be traveling across the country. It was one of too many detours lately. His mother's leukemia, the move to California, and the shift to reverse in his relationship with Jessica. If Fletcher hadn't committed to trusting God a long time ago, he'd wonder if the man upstairs didn't have him chasing some sort of cosmic laser beam for pure amusement.

Even this new job felt that way. He'd chosen the sheriff's department because the opportunities in the larger organization were better if he had to stay awhile. But it felt too much like a demotion, having to start off with a stint in the jail, watching over inmates after completing his patrol training with a field training officer. They'd shortened it some because of Fletcher's experience with Houston PD. But even though he was solo for these two weeks, sheriff's department policy would put him back on jail duty after that. . . .

He frowned at a new bleeding scratch in a continuing series of small scabs on his forearm. Maybe he was being toyed with or "tested," as his mother would say. It sure seemed like it. Because right now, nothing was going according to—

Brrrr-ing.

Fletcher grabbed his phone. Jessica. A request for FaceTime. He'd left a half dozen of her texts unanswered today.

He took a breath, activated the screen. "Hey."

"Finally. I haven't heard a word from you in days." Jessica's head tipped, her pale-blonde hair swaying as she peered at him. The dark-lashed gray eyes blinked as her teasing smile spread. The same smile she'd tossed his way since she was six years old. Face like an angel, sass and brass from the get-go. Some things never changed. "You had me thinking I'd done something to get on your you-know-what list."

Like break my heart?

Fletcher erased the thought. That was going too far. Right now he felt mostly . . . cheated. Like all his plans had been stomped with steel-toed boots. "Busy, that's all."

"Houston news covered the freeway sniper. Of course I didn't know you were out there." Jessica's brows puckered. "Charly filled me in. She's right—you should have called us."

Us. Because the two of them had always been the women in Fletcher's life. It occurred to him in a merciless jab that . . . *I could be losing them both.* "So you called to read me the riot act too?"

"No." Her expression softened in a way he'd never seen before, in all the years he'd known her. "I called to tell you that I met someone."

Fletcher's gut twisted. He wanted to hang up. No, he wanted reach through the phone, grab her by the shoulders, finally tell her that—

"It's only been a few months, and I know it sounds so beyond corny," Jessica continued, "but I think he's good for me." Her fingers touched her lips. "And I know it shouldn't be possible, but I'm pretty sure he thinks I'm good for him too. Can you believe it?"

Was he supposed to answer that?

"The strangest part is that he isn't like anybody I've dated before—please don't feel obliged to remind me about all those monumental mistakes. His name's Ben, and . . ." Jessica shook her head, that goofy smile still on her face. "Are you sitting down?"

"Yeah."

"He's a youth pastor."

With no criminal record. Not even a misdemeanor. Fletcher had checked the guy out the moment he showed up on Jessica's Facebook page. He wasn't proud of his disappointment that the former TCU running back wasn't wanted in three states. "Wow."

"I know, I know," Jessica laughed. "But so many things have changed this past year. Because of the counseling, getting back to church, and the medication too, I suppose." She wrinkled her nose. "I still have my issues with that vile stuff. But things are so much better now. It's more than just being 'chemically balanced.' I mean, yeah, I'm not bouncing off the walls or hiding in my bedroom anymore. But it's so much better than that: I'm happy, Fletcher. Way down deep inside, really happy. I never knew what that felt like before." Her smile made his heart ache. "And you're a big part of it. You helped make it all happen. Now, with Ben . . . I don't know how to explain it. But I needed to tell someone or I'll explode. Because he makes me feel so—"

"Shouldn't you be talking to your sister about this? Or your mother?"

"Mom?" Jessica laughed. "You know her. She'd have it in the next community newsletter. Lauren's up to her eyeballs with wedding prep. Besides . . ." She feigned a pout. "Nobody knows me like you, Fletcher. All my life, I barely have any memories without you in them."

It was the same for him. The truth made his throat tighten.

"You were my neighbor, forever," she continued. "You're

the person I've always counted on. Even at my bratty, snotty worst, you were always there. You're my best friend, Fletcher."

I'm the fool who never admitted he was in love with you.

"Jessica . . ." Fletcher's pulse quickened. He had to do this. She was better now. There was no more need to worry that he'd be pressuring, confusing her. If he was ever going to admit the truth, it should be now, before she added *brother* to that growing list of platonic labels she had for him. "It's a long time since we were neighbors. We're not those kids anymore. You've changed. I have too. And . . ."

"And what?"

Fletcher jabbed the button to disconnect the video.

"I can't see you. Fletcher? Can you see me?"

"Looks like we lost the video." He turned the phone facedown. If she was going to laugh at him, he didn't have to see it. "What I was trying to say before was that . . ." Fletcher leaned sideways to get a better glimpse of the muted TV screen. "Hang on a minute. Something's going on." He reached over the cat for the remote and hit the button to restore the sound, taking in the breaking news scene: an FBI spokesman . . .

"Fletcher? What's happening?"

"I'll call you back. Looks like they've recovered a rifle bullet and casing from the shooting scene."

8

"YOU'RE TWITCHY. Can't fool a mother." Charly pointed a manicured finger at Fletcher's tuxedo jacket. "Pull out the cell phone you're hiding in that beautiful pocket and check the news. See if they've found out anything on that shooter." She scoffed at his attempt to assure her it could wait. "Go ahead," she insisted. "A woman who steps out with a man packin' a gun learns to graciously accept these things. Just don't confuse those two objects—cell phone and revolver. I'm not up to that kind of excitement."

"Not going to happen," Fletcher laughed. He slid an arm around his mother's shoulders, draped in a shawl that matched her long blue gown. "Tonight is about you."

Despite his earlier misgivings—and the necessity to rent a tux—Fletcher was glad he was here tonight after all. For his mother and because it was a welcome diversion.

He wasn't so sure that the TV news flash about the new evidence hadn't served the same purpose by delaying his declaration of love to Jessica Barclay. Whether or not he'd dodged a bullet there, he didn't know. He only knew that he didn't want to think about her right now. He was here, and he intended to enjoy it as best he could. A world apart from his everyday life . . .

Fletcher glanced around the luxurious lobby of the Sheraton Grand Sacramento, decorated for the event with huge summer bouquets, brightly colored fabric butterflies, white branches, and strings of lights overhead and wound around the stair railings. His mother had pointed it all out in detail; he just hoped the food would be as impressive. On the floor above, a string quartet played something Fletcher doubted anyone could dance to. Definitely not in cowboy boots. Music selected more to stir memories, touch hearts, and—when combined with the countless glasses of complimentary champagne—open generous checkbooks. There was every opportunity for it; the place was teeming with dressed-to-the-gills people, and the air buzzed with conversation and polite laughter. Fletcher had already spotted the capital city's mayor, as well as one of the Sacramento Kings and his wife.

They walked on, then stopped to view one of several giant easel-mounted posters depicting images and testimonials from the nonprofit California Crisis Care. The photos were in stark and undeniable black-and-white, real and gritty against the colorful lobby decor. Couldn't have been more compelling. This one was an image of *Police Line Do Not Cross* tape across the close-up of a woman whose tearstained face and agonized expression spelled trauma and grief in capital letters. The caption read:

110 volunteer chaplains
   400 annual activations
   900 grieving survivors—just trying to make sense of it all
   California Crisis Care, Sacramento

Below was an excerpt of a letter sent by a survivor of tragedy, thanking a chaplain.

She saw me unravel and didn't judge, only cared. I'm still trying to understand what happened with my father. But there is HOPE and a profound feeling that I am not alone in this. How do you get through a life-altering crisis? With an angel by your side.

Fletcher shook his head, moved. These selfless volunteers were digging deep, giving their all in situations that would make most people shudder and run. If Charly Holt had said it once, she'd said it a thousand times: *"This is God's work. We're out there to offer hope to people who have none. It blesses them and us, too."* He wasn't going to argue with that.

"I'm so glad we came," she said after waving at a couple passing by. Fletcher was struck once again by how pale and fragile she looked now, despite her carefully styled hair, makeup, and the pearls his father had given her on their thirtieth wedding anniversary.

Fletcher assured himself there would be many more celebrations. *Are you hearing me, God?*

Charly patted his tux sleeve. "We'll get someone to snap a picture of us with your cell phone. I promised Jessica."

His stomach did a crash dive even a fancy dinner wouldn't fix. "You talked with her today?"

"This morning."

He'd never said anything openly about his feelings for Jessica. And he sure wasn't going to now.

"She sounded so good—happy," Charly continued. "I'm not sure I've ever heard our little girl sound so hopeful. She mentioned a man several times. A youth pastor at the church."

"Mmm. Yeah, I think she said something like that to me too." Fletcher feigned interest in the quartet above them. Where was one of those distractions when he really needed it? Short of a sniper on the balcony, but . . . *I don't want to talk about this.*

"She didn't say they were dating exactly," Charly went on. "But apparently he offered to help her move into her new apartment. And then volunteered his services as a painter—'Peach Pie' was the shade she picked for the kitchen. Ceiling too. She must have charmed the landlord." His mother laughed. "Heaven knows that girl can't abide boring walls."

Fletcher battled the image of Jessica in those old spattered coveralls, the running back preacher wiping a splash of paint from her cheek. How many times had Fletcher helped Jessica paint, pack and unpack boxes? Made certain she had working smoke detectors, decent dead bolt locks, and food in her fridge? Saved her from herself? It was what he did. What he'd be doing now if—

He stepped sideways, something catching his eye in the distance. The man over by the punch bowl: Elliot Rush. With a red-haired woman wearing a black dress and a necklace that looked like it needed a private security detail. Seth had mentioned they would be here. So no big surprise. He was starting to glance away when a much younger woman in a green gown stepped out from behind the redhead. Shoulders bare, long black hair worn sort of half-up, half-down. Dangling earrings and . . . Fletcher's eyes widened. It was Macy Wynn.

———

"These crab puffs are . . . mmm . . . amazing. Oh, excuse me." Ricki Rush pressed an acrylic nail to her lips and finished swallowing. "If I eat another one, I'll pop—only so much you can ask of Spanx. Appetizers are my downfall."

"Hard to resist," Macy agreed. She fought an intruding memory of sharing a box of congealed Chicken McNuggets with her mother. They'd saved some from the night before to eat for breakfast in the heaped-high car that had recently become their home. Macy was six. Within months her mother would die in an apartment fire, sending Macy to foster care. "I guess they'll be ushering us up to the ballroom soon," she said, hoping her hosts didn't sense her impatience. She wanted this evening to end.

Elliot met Macy's gaze. "Did you get a chance to look at any of the properties on the list I gave you?"

"You're buying a house?" Ricki's sculpted brows rose.

"Rental property," Macy explained, already hating the conversation. "As an investment. Maybe."

"Oh." Ricki reached for another appetizer. "The trust money."

"Elliot thinks it's a good idea," Macy confirmed, rubbing her arms against a chill. There were far worse things than day-old chicken nuggets. "But I haven't had a chance to look."

It wasn't true. She'd driven by a few of the properties. Bank foreclosures with dead lawns, high weeds; some had plywood over windows. One had fresh graffiti and a heap of empty beer bottles on the porch. A mix of neighborhoods, but for the most part, nowhere Macy would want to rent, let alone purchase. Except that little house near Tahoe Park. With all the trees. And the stepping-stone path, brass mailbox, and painted window boxes. . . . Not on Elliot's list because of price no doubt. But the sign said *Bank Owned* too. She'd seen it when she took a wrong turn while looking for the other properties. Then drove back again. And again . . . "I've been too busy to look at properties," Macy finished with a shrug.

"Because of your sister. Of course." Ricki's fingers plucked at her glittering necklace. "I don't want to imagine being separated from mine for so many years. Some things are too sad to bear."

Macy stared at her, wondering how much this woman had bothered to learn about the service organization she'd be writing a check for this evening. She surely wouldn't want to imagine the heartbreak these volunteer crisis chaplains saw every day: survivors impacted by murder, suicide,

serious accidents, child deaths, and other personal tragedies. "Too sad" didn't begin to cover it.

"I'm just grateful that I've found her now." Macy squared
her shoulders. "We'll make up for lost time."

"Of course you will." Elliot gave Macy's elbow a small
squeeze and glanced toward the staircase. "Looks like
people are starting to head up. We should probably—" He
stopped, squinted his eyes, and then signaled overhead as
if trying to catch someone's attention.

Macy turned, saw the couple he was hailing: an elegant
woman in a blue gown and a younger man who was far too
familiar.

9

IT WAS NO USE PRETENDING he hadn't seen Rush; Charly had tugged at his sleeve to bring the man's wave to Fletcher's attention. He forced himself to holster his rising anger about that phone call from the senator brother-in-law, reminding himself again that this was his mother's night. And in moments the Rush party navigated the thinning crowd to arrive beside them. The only thing remotely good about it was the chance to see Macy up close. She nearly took his breath away.

"My mother's a community chaplain," Fletcher continued after the awkward initial introductions. "She's being honored for her service to the victims' families after that nursing home roof collapse last fall."

"I'm sure you're very proud of her," Mrs. Rush offered. "Such a worthy calling."

Charly smiled. "I'm honored to be a part of California Crisis Care."

Elliot Rush slid a finger beneath his tuxedo collar, clearly anxious. Why on earth had he come over here?

"Macy's an ER nurse," Rush said at last, connecting with Charly's gaze. "At Sacramento Hope. Or maybe your son already told you that?"

"No. Or perhaps I've forgotten," Charly added, Southern manners coming to the rescue. She glanced at Fletcher. "Remind me. You know this young lady from—"

"We met on the freeway, Mrs. Holt," Macy interjected. "During the sniper incident." She lifted her chin as if she'd decided to tackle the rhino in the room. Her eyes met Fletcher's, even more of an intriguing color paired with the green of her gown. He saw, too, that the small abrasion was still there on her cheek, despite her modest makeup. "I was giving aid to the child who was injured on the school van."

"And your son . . ." Rush cleared his throat, but his wife jumped in before he could speak.

"Well, it looks like all of that nonsense will be over soon." Mrs. Rush nodded with confidence. "We saw the FBI statement on the news right as we were leaving to come here. They have the bullet now. They'll be able to find that madman."

"A rifle casing and a bullet from the truck tire," Fletcher corrected. "And even then, there's no guarantee it will lead to an ID of the shooter. Right now we just have to wait for word from the crime lab."

Charly patted his arm. "I fully expect Fletcher's cell phone to buzz in the middle of our entrée."

"No need." Rush's wife waved her hand, the movement

making a trio of bracelets glitter. "I can make one quick call and cut through all that boring red tape. My brother is Senator Rob Warrington. Nothing happens that he can't handle fast as that." She snapped her fingers.

Rush stiffened, then made a point of glancing toward the stairs. "We should go to our tables."

"Yes," Charly agreed. "But first . . . Macy, would you please do us a favor and take a picture of—?"

"No time," Fletcher interrupted. He could well imagine his digitalized scowl. "We'll do that later. They may need you inside. Excuse us, please." He nodded at the group, then escorted his mother toward the stairs. But not before he heard Mrs. Rush's indignant mutter of "Wet-behind-the-ears, self-righteous street cop . . ."

Rush caught Fletcher just before they started up.

"May I have a quick word with your son?" he asked, nodding politely at Charly.

"Of course."

Fletcher met the man's gaze, doubting he could keep his temper under control, even for his mother's sake. If this self-important fool thought he could—"What can I do for you?"

"Accept my apology," Rush said, surprising Fletcher. "You were doing your job out there on the freeway. Regardless of my pride, I should have respected that." He cleared his throat. "It's possible that your quick action kept Macy from being harmed. I can't tell you how much that means to me . . . to my wife and me."

Fletcher hesitated, more than wary. "And then you had your brother-in-law phone in a complaint?"

"My wife. Not me." Rush grimaced. "I'm afraid there's nothing she likes better than throwing her brother's weight around. I didn't know until afterward. I've already drafted a letter to your sergeant, which I hope will clear things up."

Fletcher wasn't sure what to say. He should trust this guy about as far as he could throw him. But . . .

"Will you accept my apology?" Rush asked again, extending his hand.

Fletcher held off for a few seconds—long enough to see discomfort in the man's eyes. Then he gripped Rush's hand.

———

"What was that all about?" Macy asked as Elliot rejoined them and they began making their way toward the stairs.

"Unnecessary peacemaking, no doubt," Ricki huffed, shooting her husband a sideways glance. "Why you'd apologize to that underling is beyond me. You did nothing wrong."

"I didn't say he was right about the alcohol. I told him I regretted my attitude out there. And—" Elliot gave his wife a pointed look—"that I appreciated his quick action to keep us safe. He could very well have saved Macy's life, Ricki! The man was doing his job. That didn't warrant an official reprimand."

Macy glanced between them, confused. "Reprimand?"

Ricki lifted the hem of her gown at the stairs. "I had my brother call his superior because I knew you didn't have the backbone to stick up for yourself, Elliot—you never do. What if that boy had his way out there? Made you walk heel-to-toe, touch your nose, or whatever it is that they do.

What if someone caught it on their cell phone?" Her face reddened to a shade that clashed with her hair. "Do you know how many people are humiliated on YouTube every hour? What if that news helicopter got footage? How do you think Rob's constituents might feel about that? You should be thanking me." She shot her husband one last glare and started up the stairs.

Macy followed in the wake of their frosty silence and spotted the ladies' room at the top of the stairs. She told them to go ahead, that she'd meet them at the table.

Moments later she stood at the mirror, thankful for the escape and very certain about two things. First, Elliot Rush with all his flaws didn't deserve the belittling he suffered at the hands—and mouth—of his very spoiled wife. Macy had witnessed it on far too many occasions. And second, even if Ricki was right about Fletcher Holt being self-righteous—and he definitely had an angry chip on that broad shoulder—she'd been wrong to sic her brother on him. After all he'd dealt with, it must have been the crowning blow.

Macy reached into her evening bag, pulled out a compact to pat fresh powder over her road rash. She stopped with the puff midway, remembering what Elliot had said in defense of Fletcher. *"He could very well have saved Macy's life . . ."*

She stared at herself, tasting the tar of the freeway asphalt again, hearing the crack of that rifle and the shattering windshield glass. So close. She saw Fletcher standing over her with his weapon aimed—very different from this man in a tuxedo escorting his mother. Maybe she hadn't wanted to think about it before, maybe it made the whole thing feel too frighteningly real, but . . . *Did he really save my life?*

10

"I HEARD HE'S EXPECTING other family to arrive from out of state," Taylor told Macy after a discreet glance at the table adjacent to theirs in the hospital cafeteria. Mrs. Harrell's son picked at his lunch tray, cell phone to his ear. It looked like he hadn't shaved in days. Or slept either.

"I hope those relatives include someone with a longer fuse." Macy shook her head. "I don't envy the ICU nurses. Bridget said it feels like everyone has a big bull's-eye painted on the back of their scrubs; he questions every move they make. I don't want to think about the conversation that's coming about withdrawing life support."

Someone's pager sounded at an adjacent table and a cook behind the grill announced an order up for a garden burger and sweet potato fries. A trio of student nurses hustled by.

"Yes," Taylor agreed. "I can only imagine how hard that

decision would be, even knowing all I know as a nurse about brain death." Her brows pinched. "As hard as it was with Greg, I'm grateful I was spared the decision to let him go."

Macy met her friend's gaze. "I wish you'd been spared all of it."

"All I wish right now—" Taylor's eyes brightened—"is that you'd give me details about that fancy party. I caught a news clip: way too much of the mayor and local VIPs, no shots of you, and only the teeniest glimpse of Charly."

"Charly?"

"Charlise Holt. One of the chaplains who was recognized last night. Attractive, really short hair right now, in her late fifties I'd say. Accompanied by her son?"

"Yes, Mrs. Holt. I met her," Macy confirmed, an image of son, not mother, coming to mind. She wondered idly if he'd been carrying a gun under that tuxedo jacket. "She seems nice."

"She's great. A natural as a chaplain; I love being mentored by her. We're both on call tomorrow. I'm glad she got the okay to come back from medical leave." Taylor caught the question on Macy's face. "Charly hasn't kept it confidential: she's being treated for leukemia. Acute myeloid. Possibly caused by the aggressive chemo she had for breast cancer several years ago."

Macy winced. The gracious woman had courage beyond her selfless dedication.

"Charly's husband travels for work, so her son came out from Texas to be here for her," Taylor continued. "He's a deputy with Sac County."

"I met him." Macy hoped she hadn't said anything rude

about him to Taylor in the aftermath of the freeway incident. She touched her healing cheek, thinking she'd like to erase that memory altogether. Pretend they'd met for the first time Friday night. Cordial, simple. A lovely woman, her attentive son, and no added ammunition for the Rushes' ongoing battle. Macy looked up, heard Taylor continuing. "I'm sorry, what?"

Taylor laughed. "I said he's good-looking—Fletcher Holt. Agree?"

"Oh." Macy felt her neck flush. "I suppose. I never thought about it."

———

"The rifle bullet and casing . . ." Seth set his coffee down, glanced at his watch. They'd arranged to meet at this café because he had a chaplaincy appointment a few blocks away. "No definite leads?"

"No prints. The casing from the shrubbery at the overpass was a .270 Remington, and the slug pulled from the truck tire looks to be the same caliber," Fletcher explained. "Even though it's pretty deformed, the crime lab says they're from the same gun. They haven't been connected with any other known crimes. Yet."

Seth pressed his finger against the muffin crumbs on his napkin. "So maybe he's out of ammo?"

"Yeah, right. More reasonable to hope that his target practice got whatever it was out of his system. Rough day at work, someone cut him off on the freeway, girlfriend told him to take a hike, or life just ain't fair." Fletcher realized he qualified for at least a couple of those himself.

"No." Seth reached for his coffee. "It isn't fair—but it can still be good. That's what people need to know. What we all have to hang on to."

Though the chaplain tended to keep his personal life to himself, Fletcher suspected he'd seen the unfair side of life up close and personal. Some fifteen years back, Seth had been on his own path to a law enforcement career, scheduled for a slot in the sheriff's academy. Until an "interpersonal conflict" left him with a shattered knee and legal issues. Seth referred to that period in his life only as *"Having the time to find my faith."* Fletcher didn't press him further.

"It's the reason I'm out there," Seth continued. "Running Dad's uniform stores gives me a chance to know a lot of folks—we're equipping first responders. But my crisis care work is much better." A deep chuckle rose, amusement warming his eyes. "Kind of like trading donuts for these bran muffins. I never expected to be ordained as a minister, but that legal confidentiality lets me volunteer with law enforcement and fire too. And maybe stop some people from making the mistakes I did." Seth nodded, hard-won wisdom etched on his face. "I've sold body armor all these years and now I'm looking after the souls behind those vests. Not easy, but feels pretty good."

More than "pretty good," Fletcher figured, considering the countless hours Seth donated to that cause. Not only was he an active crisis chaplain; he operated as shift leader, outreach coordinator to local police and fire agencies, and had also gone through the extra training required to teach new volunteers.

Fletcher smiled. "You don't have to convince me that you're doing something you're excited about."

"I'm guessing your mother has told you that same thing."

"A time or two," Fletcher agreed, crumpling his napkin. "Though I still don't like the idea of her being available for activations tomorrow. It seems too soon."

"And there's a shooter out there?"

"Crossed my mind."

———

"I only have a minute," Macy told Elliot, uncomfortable that he'd tracked her down in the ER supply closet. She pointed to the infusion pump she'd been ready to wheel out before he arrived in the doorway—suit and tie, briefcase, no observable wounds after the sparring round with his wife. "I've got two patients who need fluids, one who'll climb the walls if we don't get some pain medication on board."

"I saw him." Elliot glanced over his shoulder. "The young man with the knit cap and the tattoos. Kidney stone?"

She regarded him for a moment. "You know I can't give out any patient information, Elliot."

"Of course not. I'm sorry." His smile was sheepish. "I had one of those evil things once, that's all. And when I saw him, it's the first thing I thought."

"No problem." Macy decided not to remind him that he shouldn't be here to see anything at all; he was as familiar with HIPAA privacy laws as anyone. He met with employees in an office in the administrative suites, not in patient care areas. "But I do need to get back to work."

"Sure. I wanted to leave some information with you. I

meant to talk with you about it Friday evening, but . . ." His lips twitched. "Anyway, I'll give you this and we'll talk more tomorrow." He slid a color brochure from his briefcase. "I think it's something that could work for you."

Macy squinted at the cover. "Viatical investments?"

"The rates of return are surprisingly good. With comparatively little risk. Plus it's medically related. Right up your alley."

"I've never heard of this. What is it—research, pharmaceuticals . . . ?"

"Life insurance. The purchase of existing plans. As an investor you'd be providing a much-needed service."

"For whom?" Macy asked, suddenly uncomfortable. "Who sells their life insurance policies?"

Elliot raised one palm as if in divine supplication. "People who need funds to pay medical bills, make their remaining time more comfortable. Terminally ill patients who want to ease their—"

"Terminally ill?" Macy grimaced.

"Good people who want to ease—"

"No thanks." She handed the brochure back, then pushed the IV pump forward with a clatter. "You'll need to move so I can get out of here." As if on cue, a deep wail rose from an exam room in the distance. "Out there. Where I can ease pain and *save* lives. That's why I'm here. And you shouldn't be."

———

He didn't belong here, he reminded himself as he warmed his hands over the small campfire. He'd built it close to the water and as far as possible from the other fires that dotted this part of the Sacramento River levee. Homeless people with tarps and cardboard shelters, shopping carts piled high with junk. He heard them out there—talk, laughter, sick-sounding coughs, that out-of-tune guitar. He'd smelled them too: rotten teeth, boozy breath, unwashed armpits and filthy clothes, vomit . . . and worse.

It's why he'd built his fire and hunkered down way out here. Because of the stink and the people who caused it, and because he knew for certain that a sizable number of those people were undercover police and government agents. When everyone was asleep, they'd move through the camp, planting evidence and injecting people with toxic Chinese drugs. The kind of drugs that poisoned dogs and altered people's minds. It would be conveniently explained away as heartworm, schizophrenia, and dementia, but it was really part of an ugly and complex scheme. He was still mapping it out, connecting the dots. But he was on to them. For right now, it was safer out here. And not so bad. It smelled like wet oak leaves and grass, riverbanks and woodsmoke. Better times. When he and his dad would load up the old truck and go hunting.

"Dude . . ."

He whipped around, heart hammering as he yanked the skinning knife from his belt.

"Whoa! Easy, dude." The young man, barely more than a kid, backed off with hands raised. His nose ring glinted in the firelight. "I was only going to bum a smoke. No worries." He forced a smile. "Understand, totally. Everyone's spooked by that sniper. You could, like, come up to main camp, you know?" He pointed toward the largest fire in the distance. "Good people there. You can trust them."

He shifted the knife from one hand to the other, slowly rose to his feet.

"Okay, man. It's cool. I'm out of here."

He watched the young man go, then sank back down on his haunches and fed the rest of the morning newspaper to the fire. The front-page story was about the "Freeway Sniper." The kid was right about that; folks were spooked. But he'd never believe the other thing the kid said. *"Good people there. You can trust them."*

It wasn't true. Anybody ever worth trusting was dead.

He checked his watch: nearly ten. He could head back to the house soon. The neighbors never stayed up much past nine. Even if the front door was being watched, he could get in from the back. Cut through some yards—he knew all those properties. He needed to get there. It was home. And he needed more ammunition.

11

A DEATH NOTIFICATION. Her first time.

Taylor Cabot looked up from her Bible study workbook to check the clock on the painted wood mantel. Charly Holt wouldn't arrive for another ten minutes or so. When the text came in for an activation, Charly had insisted on driving, saying if she was coming back, she'd be back 100 percent.

Taylor smiled, remembering the woman's twangy version of Schwarzenegger's line, *"I'll be baaaack."* The immediate addition of a hearty "Praise God!" was Charly's own twist. Taylor couldn't be more grateful to be shadowing Charly during her hours of field training. Today especially, when they'd walk up to someone's home bearing the worst possible news.

She found herself in front of the flagstone fireplace, gazing once again at the framed photos on the mantel. A brightly enameled frame holding a close-up of her youngest nephew, enormous green eyes and a bit of a blond curl, the rest of his cherub face hidden by full ninja headgear. Her older brother's oldest daughter primly holding a daisy bouquet at grammar school graduation. And the photos of her husband, Greg, newly framed after his death—alive, he would have objected to them as vanity.

Her eyes moved over the collection of random and unrelated images that held so much meaning for her, as if the camera had freeze-framed singular beats of her heart. Her husband as she'd known him, in a journey that had led her to love him more each day. On his college basketball team, caught midair as he went for an impressive dunk shot. Grinning into the camera while steadying his fire helmet on a shy kindergartner's head at a community service event. Asleep on the couch with his fat golden retriever puppy in his arms. Taylor glanced at the old dog, sleeping on his fleece bed beside the couch. Her gaze returned to the photo display. Greg on the day he was finally baptized, hair wet and uncharacteristically solemn. And then . . . their wedding photo.

Taylor touched a fingertip to the etched silver frame as if testing a healing wound. She could finally look at it without crying. She saw the love on their faces, the hope in their eyes, and found the blessings in that. She could do that now without railing against all they'd lost, grieving all they'd never have . . . including children. She was a survivor. Two years of sleeping alone, two sets of major holidays, birthdays, and anniversaries endured. She'd finally finished the endless changes in paperwork and policies. She was working at a career she loved and had found a new calling that spoke to her heart, made her feel alive again.

She checked the clock. A death notification . . .

It had been an ER physician at UCD trauma center who'd offered the official confirmation of Greg's death. He walked into the sequestered "quiet room" with a nurse and a female hospital chaplain. And though Taylor had done that same thing a hundred times—on the other side of the Kleenex box—her mind refused to believe what was coming. Even though she'd seen the tragic expressions on the faces of Greg's fellow firefighters and paramedics, heard their emotion-choked whispered exchanges of "changing a tire . . . never saw the car coming . . . massive head injuries . . . no blood pressure . . . ," she couldn't accept it. Until that hospital chaplain led her to the room where Greg lay. Too pale, too still. . . . She'd stood beside Taylor in silence, then slipped an arm around her as her knees weakened.

"I'm sorry, Mrs. Cabot." The chaplain's whisper had been filled with compassion. "I'm very sorry your husband died."

Only that caring moment had made it real.

Taylor glanced out the window and caught a glimpse of Charly's Suburban at the curb. Today she'd be the one to do that for someone else. She reached for her purse, then stopped for a moment and bowed her head. *Help me to offer comfort and compassion, Lord. Be there with me, please.*

———

"Coconut shrimp?" Andi Carlyle offered one trapped between disposable chopsticks.

"No thanks, I'm good with this egg roll." Macy smiled at the young doctor, glad for the unexpected early lunch. A miracle they'd both been able to ditch the ER for this outside table, even for a few minutes. "Got to love the drug reps. They usually come around with the best goodies on my days off—and this isn't half-bad. Of course it's nothing like what I used to get in San Francisco."

"You worked there?"

"I was born there," Macy explained, instantly wishing she hadn't. "My mother was from the Bay Area."

"Oh, I see." Andi regarded Macy for a moment, curiosity in her expression. "Was she Asian? Your coloring and features, that wonderful hair—I don't mean to be too personal," she added quickly. "But when you're stuck with a Keebler elf face like this—" she gestured to herself—"you can't help but be intrigued by people who look far more interesting."

"Chinese," Macy told her. The truth, but she'd learned how to hedge it. "Not my mom. On the other side of the family." She smiled. "It's okay. Everyone asks eventually."

"Well, then . . ." The doc pointed her chopsticks. "I'm envious. And I'm not kidding; my maiden name was Kuebler. Far too close to the cookies and crackers. You can imagine the teasing in school lunchrooms. I used to pray I'd grow to six feet tall. Instead I got thicker skin. Then traded Kuebler for Carlyle." Elfin dimples framed her grin. "For all the right romantic reasons."

"Of course."

Macy had good reasons for changing her name too. From Wen to Wynn. It had nothing to do with love. She picked the name because it was close enough in sound not to feel so jarring. And . . . changing her name was the closest she could get to erasing her father's DNA. Macy had no doubt that wherever he was now—Hong Kong, Dubai, or some other high-powered foreign business setting—he was okay with that. Mr. Wen had never allowed Macy's mother to take his name. And certainly hadn't meant it to be shared with his unwanted child.

They both looked up as Elliot approached from the parking lot, briefcase swaying. He offered them a quick wave before hurrying on. He was holding lunchtime staff appointments again today, offering retirement plan investment information.

"Hey," Macy said, recalling her last conversation with him. "Ever heard of viatical investments?"

"Sure." Andi reached down to hike up one of her signature socks, a Big Bird pattern today. "Investors purchase life insurance policies from patients with terminal illnesses. The patient receives a lump sum, a percentage of the policy payout. The investor takes over the payments and essentially becomes the beneficiary of the full policy payout."

Macy grimaced. "And what . . . ? Waits for the person to die so they can collect? Isn't that kind of ghoulish?"

"Depends on your perspective. Viaticals started getting attention back when HIV/AIDS first hit the news. Long before there were effective treatment options like we have today. Young people who saw no chance of a future jumped at the chance to sell their life insurance policies." Andi sighed. "Unfortunately their desperation fueled greed and unscrupulous practices. There was a lot of controversy over viaticals. And some major lawsuits."

"That's changed?"

"I'm no expert, and viaticals aren't in my meager port-folio. But I've known a few very ill patients who felt that a viatical policy would make all the difference in their remaining months. Pay the bills, lessen their worries—help their families." Andi tilted her head. "Why do you ask?"

"No real reason," Macy answered, always hesitant to bring up the root of her relationship with Elliot. "I just heard about them and wondered what they were."

"Again," Andi told her, "I'm no expert. I defer to my standard default: google it."

"Thanks." Macy scooped the crumbs of her egg roll into her napkin. "Maybe I'll do that."

They'd gathered their things and were about to leave the table when a man signaled to them from a distance.

Macy squinted. "Is that the son of our stroke patient from a couple of days ago?"

"Bob Harrell," the doctor confirmed with a sigh. "He wants to talk with me about his mother's condition. I think he believes there was something else that could have been done, that maybe I should have been able to save her. He needs someone to blame."

Macy winced, glad once again that she wasn't a physician. "What will you say?"

"That I'm very sorry his mother's condition is so desperate. And I wish there had been something else we could have done. But there wasn't." Her fingers moved to the cross pendant at the neckline of her scrubs. "I'll tell Bob the truth: that his family is in my prayers. And I'll make sure he has the chaplaincy phone numbers."

———

"It's been up there for a long time," the elderly neighbor explained, tapping the *Bank Owned* notice in the front window of the two-story tract home. Her mouth puckered, etching wrinkles like ruler marks into her upper lip. "Too much of this lately. That poor young man was working hard to hang on to this place. His daddy would have been proud. Rest his soul."

Taylor glanced at Charly, then met the neighbor's gaze again. "Mr. Archer—Ned—knew about his father's death? The Stockton authorities have been trying to reach him for almost a week without success. That's why we came."

"Ned knows. He told me last Thursday, I think it was. He didn't let on, but I could tell he was pretty shook up. I can't say anybody in this neighborhood was surprised, though. We've all had a turn bringing Abe home when he wandered off. Sometimes in the middle of the night, wearing nothing but his skivvies and that old hunting cap. He'd get so confused. A blessing, I suppose, that he was taken so quickly." She shook her head. "That old-timer's disease is a terrible thing."

Alzheimer's. Taylor couldn't count how many times she'd heard it said the other way. According to the medical examiner's office, Mr. Archer had died in his sleep. The neighbor was probably right—a blessing.

"The phone numbers they had for Ned don't seem to be working," Charly said gently. "Would you happen to have his work phone or new address? E-mail?"

"I don't have any of that. And he's not working now—he

was laid off a few months back. Couldn't have been worse timing. His dog died not even two weeks before that. The bank wouldn't cut him a break. He got the eviction notice, the utility companies shut things down, now this news about his daddy . . ." The woman sighed. "Ned's never been much of a talker. Even as a little tyke. But I saw it in his eyes; I think he was here to say good-bye to this house. I don't expect we'll see him again."

Too many good-byes—Taylor knew how that felt. "There's no other family?"

"Not that I've ever seen. Abe was a widower. Only the one child."

"Did Ned say where he was going?" Charly asked, resting her hand on the porch post.

"Staying with a friend, he said. Modesto, maybe. I'm not sure." The neighbor's brows drew together. "I'm sorry I don't know more."

"You've been a big help," Taylor assured her. "Really." She handed the woman a Crisis Care card. "If you see Ned again, would you give this to him, please? We'd like to help him in any way we can. It sounds like he's having a tough time."

"Thank you." The neighbor looked from Taylor's face to Charly's as she took the card. "We all need help sometimes."

They watched as the woman made her way across the patch of dying grass to her home next door.

"You did well with that, Taylor. Not exactly what we were expecting, but you handled it nicely." Charly closed her eyes for a moment and then eased herself down to sit on the porch railing.

"Are you all right?" Taylor stepped forward. "You look pale."

"I get a little light-headed standing in one spot too long." Charly managed a laugh, fanned herself with her hand. "Sitting on one's behind for weeks watching *Iron Chef* reruns is not exactly an athletic endeavor. I'm okay."

"I don't know," Taylor told her, noticing a faint sheen of perspiration. "I'll go get that water from the car and—"

"No. Please don't," Charly insisted. "I promise I'll drink the whole bottle once we get out there. I'm perfectly fine, cross my heart. Let's not do anything to alert the watchdog."

"Dog?"

"He just passed by, going really slow. Sheriff's patrol car." Charly gave a withering sigh. "My overprotective son— pretend you don't see."

Taylor started to laugh and then stopped, stared. "Charly, your nose is bleeding."

12

"I'm not sure why," Macy explained, watching Leah's expression on the laptop screen. Her sister had finally been allowed computer privileges at the rehab center. If only Skype would figure out a way to let her hug Leah close. There had been too many years without hugs. "But this little house in Tahoe Park reminds me of Nonni's place. Maybe it's the big tree out front or the window boxes, those stepping stones. The whole feel of it. Sort of welcoming. And happy. You remember." How could Leah forget? It was the one foster home in far too many that had felt like a real home. To both of them.

"I remember." Leah tugged at a strand of her curly auburn hair, closing her eyes for a moment. Maybe it was the video cam, but she looked paler, more drawn. Definitely distracted. "I'm worried about Sean. He isn't sure his boss will hold his job, he's afraid we'll lose the apartment, and—"

"He got you involved in prescription fraud. It's because of him that you got arrested."

"It's my fault, not his," Leah insisted. "I told you that. I'm the one with the drug problem. Sean can take it or leave it. That prescription thing . . . He was doing it for me."

What a guy. Macy took a breath, willing herself to be tolerant and understanding for her sister's sake. Getting angry wasn't going to help. "I'm only saying that depending on Sean might not be your best option."

"But . . ." Leah pressed her fingertips to her forehead. "I love him. He's my everything."

Macy had no clue how to respond. In her whole life, she'd never felt that way about any man. Anyone. Anything. How could someone ever trust that much? "I think," she offered carefully, "you should have a plan B. Just in case."

"I do—I did." Even via video, Leah's tears were visible. "I always said I'd take those classes to become a phlebotomist. To work in a hospital and take blood samples." She wiped her eyes. "After that I thought I could register at the community college and really make something of myself. Maybe even become a nurse like you. But somehow I keep getting off track. You know?"

"Yes," Macy managed, throat squeezing. "But you can do it; I know you can. And this—getting clean, staying that way—it's the way to start. You're beginning a whole new life."

"You sound like Nonni. She was always saying things like that." Leah's smile turned grim. "I'll try to remember it. When I can't sleep and my head's pounding. And I have to make another dash for the toilet."

The hydrocodone withdrawal. "Still pretty bad?"

"Like the stomach flu—while being hit repeatedly by a truck. With a side order of spooky jitters." Leah shrugged, the look in her eyes almost mirroring Annie Sims's as she clutched that hospital tote bag. "I'll be okay. I've been through worse than this."

She had. Living on the streets . . . *rape.*

"I should go." Leah glanced over her shoulder for a moment. "They expect us to show up for lunch. Hungry or not. I'm glad I caught you before you had to go into work, and . . . I'm glad I found you again." She leaned closer to the screen as if she might plant a kiss on Macy's cheek like she had so many times as a kid. "Are you going to buy that house that reminds you of Nonni's?"

Macy's stomach did an elevator drop. "No. I can't afford that. I only told you because I thought remembering might make you feel better."

"Oh." Leah sighed, the distracted expression there again. "I'd better go. Love you, Macy."

"You too."

Macy closed down the screen, struggling with the same mix of feelings she'd had since Leah first called her. Knee-weakening relief, concern for her sister's situation, and a strange, inexplicable sadness. She'd found her sister; she'd always been so sure that would be the key to real happiness. Why wasn't she feeling it now?

She reached for her mug of green tea. *Borrowed* mug—this one belonged to one of her two roommates, both traveling nurses. Splitting the rent was great, but Macy couldn't count the number of times she'd had to dig through heaps of mixed laundry trying to match up a pair of scrubs. Or the countless times she'd found her carton of almond milk sitting empty in the fridge. Hectic, crazy, crowded. But then, living barracks style seemed all too normal after foster care.

"Are you going to buy that house . . . ?"

Leah's question had caught Macy completely off guard. She'd answered with the truth—as much truth as Leah knew. She couldn't afford it. Macy had always lived frugally. Her pre-owned Audi had 200,000 miles on it. She ate a lot of her meals courtesy of hospital sales reps. No pedicures, no Starbucks, no credit card debt. She socked away all she could into her retirement plan, and most of the rest went to paying back her student loans. They were Macy's only encumbrances, and she was counting the time until she was free of them. All the while hearing Elliot cluck his tongue about her stubbornness over monthly—more recently, weekly—lunches and dinners. Free eats for her and Elliot's opportunity to explain, in enthusiastic and glittery-eyed detail, that at the tender age of twenty-seven, Macy's net worth would soon afford her the title of millionaire.

She hated everything about that. Though the years of separation from Leah had been painful, Macy was glad her sister never knew about the day she'd finally met her biological father, Lang Wen, at the famous Yank Sing restaurant in San Francisco. Macy's first taste of dim sum, not that she could actually swallow with her mouth so dry. To finally see him, apart from the few photos she'd found in old newspapers and magazines featuring San Francisco art and fashion events, seemed a dream come true. The wealthy international businessman who'd taken Macy's young mother—a beautiful, struggling runway model—to all those events. And won her trusting heart.

What Macy had expected that day—awkward, under-dressed, petrified—she still wasn't sure. Had she really been naive enough to think a man who'd made no attempt to contact her in eighteen years would suddenly embrace her as his own? In truth, it would have been far more likely that he'd ignore her e-mails, refuse to meet. Except that Lang Wen, impeccable, coolly reserved, and so obviously used to being in control, had apparently anticipated that day. And prepared for it. In hindsight, that was what hurt Macy most.

She reached up, instinctively finding the lock of hair now dyed a rich mahogany shade. It had been a startling white all during her childhood—often a source for teasing—and she remembered her astonishment in seeing the same peculiarity in this man's hair. A patch at his hairline, like a brush-stroke of white paint in his fastidiously cut blue-black hair. An unusual hereditary trait he hadn't missed observing either. His gaze fixed on it almost immediately. Macy's face had flushed. She was glad he couldn't know how she'd struggled over the best way to bring up the subject of DNA testing.

But Lang Wen skipped the paternity denial, in the same dismissive manner he waved the waitress away when she offered the steaming bamboo basket of snow pea dump-lings. He simply paused, chopsticks raised, to remind Macy that, at eighteen, she was no longer a minor. And he had no intention of letting this "regrettable situation" bring shame to his family—especially his wife and children. Certainly she could understand that.

She couldn't. She could barely keep from heaving.

The remaining moments were still a blur. Macy recalled him saying something about her mother being sweet and lovely, her death so unfortunate but not surprising perhaps, considering the risky and unstable manner in which she lived: *". . . understandable that she would prefer to call herself a model rather than an escort."* But that she had very clearly overstepped the boundaries of their special friendship by attempting to link his family to a child she'd named after a department store.

Macy's leap from the table had sent her teacup crashing to the floor and caused a dozen heads to whip around. She ran from the restaurant to the streets . . . and then kept running.

The Wen lawyer contacted her six months later. The trust became payable when she turned nineteen. She wanted nothing to do with it—except for the assistance of his attorney in changing her name from Wen to Wynn. The hair dye she'd managed by herself.

Macy took a sip of her tea, tepid now, then glanced at the clock. Eleven thirty. She was doing a favor for a friend by picking up a few hours in the ER, promising to come in at one o'clock. Even if it was her day off, she was glad she was going in. The only thing she had planned was her kickboxing class, and that wasn't until four thirty. Plus, it meant some extra cash. Working would keep her mind off Leah's situation. She frowned. Her sister was making a mistake in trusting that boyfriend, the same way Macy's mother had with Lang Wen. There was no way she could let this happen.

———

"I'm not going to let you drive yourself there," Fletcher advised his mother. "You just told me you've been feeling dizzy today."

"Light-headed. And only if I stand up too fast." Charly managed a teasing smile. "I'll have to postpone the tango lessons." She reached for her purse and her box of tissues. "The doctor's exchange said he's finishing up a surgery at Sacramento Hope. If I go to the ER, the triage nurse will have him paged."

"Fine. We'll do that, then. I drive; you ride."

"You're stubborn."

"Always." He watched as she tucked a plastic bag into her purse, to handle used tissues, no doubt. "I don't like that you've been having those nosebleeds."

"I've had them before," she assured him. "Way back, even before the leukemia. I'm sure it's this dry air out here; my nose is happier in Houston. And I told you that my last labs were much better. The doctor's probably going to recommend that I buy myself a humidifier and dab some Vaseline up my nose. I think this hospital visit is unnecessary, but I'm following the rules and being cautious."

"Good—I'd hate to have to arrest you."

Fletcher took the box of Kleenex from her hands and led the way to the car, trying to push down his growing concern. He hoped she was right about the dry air. He was fine with blaming one more thing on California.

13

"THERE," TAYLOR TOLD THE GIRL, showing her what looked like a clump of tiny spider legs on a gauze pad. "The stitches are out. Your forehead's good as new."

"Can I touch it and see if it feels the same?" Annie Sims asked, eyes wide.

"Sure." Taylor watched the child raise tentative fingers to her face, exploring the healed wound. The ER had offered to take out the sutures as a courtesy to the child's physician and because Dr. Andi Carlyle hated to say no to anyone. Especially today, when she'd shared such wonderful news: she and her husband were expecting their first child. She'd come prepared for the announcement with a sonogram photo, two bakery boxes filled with cupcakes, and a pair of mismatched polka-dot socks—one pink, one blue. She said that they were going to wait until the birth and be surprised by the baby's gender. For now, she was fondly calling Baby Carlyle "our little elf."

"It feels the same," Annie reported, expression too somber for a six-year-old. "Douglas Barker said maybe there was a bullet in it."

"No, sweetie," Taylor assured. "No bullets. Dr. Andi checked everything—you're okay. And safe." She took hold of the girl's hand, gave her fingers a squeeze. "Remember how we talked about that at your school?"

Annie nodded. "Uh-huh."

The Crisis Care chaplain team had been making visits to those directly affected by the freeway shooting; Annie's school had been first on the list. "If you want to talk about it anymore or have a question, you can ask Helen to call us. Anytime."

Taylor saw the child's gaze dart to the door and her worried expression flick to a smile like someone had found the light switch in a dark room. Macy had arrived.

"Hey, kiddo," she said, striding through the doorway, dark ponytail swinging. "I heard my little pal was here."

"Yep . . . it's me."

Taylor watched their silly knuckle bump turn into a hug, heard Annie's giggle, and then found a reason to excuse herself. She told herself she was giving them a little privacy, that she couldn't resist that cupcake any longer, but the truth was she'd found herself blinking back unexpected tears. She'd experienced the same thing a couple of times since Dr. Carlyle announced her pregnancy today. Sometimes it happened that way. Just when things were going great, when Taylor dared to trust that she was through with the worst of it, the grief would come back and pick at the edges of that wound—whisper that she'd lost too much to ever really heal. There were no sutures for this.

———

Macy found Taylor half an hour later in the triage office. Impossibly, the waiting room had thinned out.

"Annie was certainly happy to see you," Taylor told her as Macy perched on the chair provided for incoming patients.

"I'm glad I got to see her too." Macy smiled, the memory warming her. That alone was worth coming in on a day off. "She was wearing tap shoes. It sounded like a Broadway show when she walked out of here."

Taylor laughed. "I saw that. They were going directly on to a dance class. Pretty special foster mother to provide that experience."

"Yes, she is."

When Macy was thirteen—gangly and self-conscious—Nonni had enrolled her in a church-sponsored ballet class. Macy balked, protesting initially as she did with most things. But eventually the music, the other students, and Nonni's warm encouragement wore down her stubborn resistance. For that short while Macy had actually felt like all the things her foster mother told her she was: graceful—"grace-filled"—special and loved. "Helen seems like one of the good ones."

Taylor met her gaze. "That's how you met your sister, Leah, right?"

"I was twelve, Leah almost nine. It was a place in Pleasanton, this old house fixed up to accommodate as many kids as possible. The garage made into a bedroom, second story added over that, big oak tree with a tree fort, and two picnic tables in the backyard." Macy shook her head, that strange, wistful sadness coming back. "It wasn't big or fancy, but it was sort of great, you know?"

"How long were you there?"

"Three years. Longer than anywhere else. Nonni—our foster mother—was in her late sixties, a widow. No children of her own. I got the sense she spent every penny she had on her foster kids, sort of barely hanging on to that house. She joked that she was like the old woman who lived in a shoe. She said she'd keep making a home for children who had none as long as she could make up a bed and flip a batch of pancakes." Macy's heart cramped. "She collapsed at home one day after driving a van of kids to school—massive pulmonary embolus. Never regained consciousness. We all got sent to different places. I heard that the bank eventually took the house."

"It was a long time before you saw your sister again?"

"Two years. She was in Modesto, just turned fourteen, and . . ." Macy hesitated, wishing she'd never started this conversation. "She'd had a rough time of it. But now I've found her again. And I'm going to see to it that—"

The overhead PA speaker crackled. "Dr. Laureano to the ICU. Dr. Laureano to the ICU, please."

"I'll bet that's for Darlene Harrell." Macy calculated the number of days since the woman had arrived in the ER with a devastating cerebral bleed. "Things can't be going well in there."

"No. Andi said that the son, Bob, tracked her down again

this morning, asking her all the same questions he asked before." Her teeth scraped her lower lip. "So hard to accept losing someone you love. . . ."

"Taylor!" The registration clerk burst through the doorway, eyes wide. "Come quick. There's a man in the waiting room with—"

"Open this door!" a man's voice shouted from the hallway. There was pounding from the door to the waiting room. "We need help!"

"He's carrying a lady," the clerk explained in a rush as she followed Macy and Taylor out of the office and toward the waiting room. "He said she's passing out."

"I'll get the hall gurney," Taylor shouted as Macy grabbed for the doorknob. The frantic pounding came again, a split second before she swung the door inward.

It was Fletcher Holt. He held his mother in his arms, her head sagging back, respirations shallow and rapid, skin pale. Her blouse was saturated with blood.

"She's been having nosebleeds . . . vomited in the car. She's being treated for leukemia."

"This way." Macy pointed toward Taylor and the approaching gurney. "Let's get her lying down and back to the trauma room quickly—follow us. You can fill us in on her history there."

———

Fletcher leaned against the trauma room doorway and peered in. It had all happened so fast. She'd insisted she was fine and that the bleeding had stopped, but . . . *Please, Lord. Help them help her. I'm trusting you with this.*

There was staff everywhere. Dr. Carlyle, Charly's oncologist, all the technicians, and an ear, nose, and throat specialist wearing a bright headlamp that made him look like someone attempting a cave rescue. And Macy Wynn was like a dozen people herself—overseeing things, carrying out the doctors' orders, checking the monitors. Moving around that trauma room in those khaki scrubs like some sort of sleek cat on an African savanna. Protecting her territory, confident in her skills. And his mother *was* starting to look better. Her color, anyway, but there was that thing in her nose, and the oxygen, and the IVs, and—

"You can come back in," Macy called to him, beckoning. "It's okay now."

"Thank you." He hated that his legs felt rubbery. A cop passed out cold on the floor was the last thing this scene needed. Fletcher took a deep breath, cleared his throat. "When I signed her registration, it said she was being treated for 'epistaxis'?"

"That's medical for nosebleed."

"Oh . . . and what's that thing in her nose?"

"Nasal packing," Macy explained. "Anterior and posterior. A sort of small double water balloon designed to hold pressure on the bleeding sites." She read the confusion on his face. "Probably 90 percent of nosebleeds start at the front of the nose—" she touched her fingertip to her nostril—"and those are fairly easy to control. But your mother is also bleeding from the back of her nasal passage, more toward her throat. That's why she swallowed all that blood, the reason she vomited and felt so faint."

"I didn't think it was so bad. If I'd known, I'd have called an ambulance. She was talking—joking even, the way she does—and hadn't even had to wipe her nose until we were maybe two blocks from here. And then . . ." His gaze shifted to his mother. "If her blood pressure's doing okay and the bleeding is stopped, shouldn't she be awake?"

"It's okay." Macy touched his arm. The warm amber eyes connected with his. "She's had some pain medication. The packing isn't comfortable. She's only resting; she'll be able to talk with you. Don't worry."

Fletcher had a sudden memory of saying something similar to her the day of the shooting incident, when she was waiting impatiently for an ambulance for that child. He'd told her not to worry. He wondered if his reassurance had been any more effective than hers was now. "What's next? Will she have to stay in the hospital?"

"At least overnight." Macy's gaze shifted to the monitors for a moment. "A lot will depend on what her labs show. This nosebleed may be a complication of her blood disorder—that's her oncologist's concern."

"I . . ." Fletcher dragged his fingers through his hair, thoughts organizing. "I should call my father. And maybe— should I have her pastor come?"

"Well . . ." Macy tipped her head, and Fletcher noticed for the first time that one small section of her hair was lighter, almost reddish against the black. "If you mean her pastor should be here because she's in critical condition, that's not the case. She's stable. But if you mean she might feel comforted by talking with her pastor . . ." She raised her palm. "That's up to you. When it comes to that sort of thing, I bow out fast and page the hospital chaplain."

"Got it." Fletcher held her gaze for a moment, thinking there was much more to this beautiful woman than met the eye. "Thank you. I really appreciate your help, Macy. Give me a freeway shooter and I'll cope. Do what I have to. But this—when it's family . . . You know."

"Of course." Her brows pinched, expression unreadable. "Look, I need to get some things done. Go to the bedside; let her know you're here. By the way—" a hint of a smile teased her lips—"she's a keeper. Lucky you."

———

He wiped the cloth over the rifle stock again. The cleaning was complete—a ritual he performed step by step, carefully, the same every time—but he wanted to draw the process out. Sit here with his father's old cleaning kit. Run his fingers over its patches, brushes, and the brown glass bottle of solvent, breathe in the scent of the old Parker Hale gun oil. Let it all take him back to those good times . . . His father, the woods, that old canvas Army tent, dumping cans of beef stew in a burnt-black camping pot. And the dogs, they always had their dogs. He closed his eyes, remembering their names, the feel of their noses against his palm, that great smell of gunpowder, wet dog, and fresh-kill pheasant . . .

He brought the rifle to his chest, letting his eyes sweep what he could see of the attic in the dim light of the camp lantern. He'd have to be more careful this time. Be sure he counted the shell casings, kept out of sight. A part of him hated what he was going to do. But they caused it. They'd done the same and more to him. They were to blame.

He'd waited after the freeway, asked himself if that was enough. Taking down the gravel truck, popping some windshields—scaring folks a little. But no, it wasn't enough. He had to make them pay. Really pay.

14

"I'M SORRY," MACY WHISPERED, seeing the phone in Mrs. Holt's hands. She was supposed to be on her way home; why had she come up here? "I wanted to peek in on you. I didn't mean to interrupt."

"No, you're not—I'm finished. Come in, please." She rolled her eyes, pointed at the nasal packing. "Between this thing and the pain medication, Jessica said I sound like an Elmer Fudd cartoon."

Macy smiled, pulling up a chair. The narcotics had definitely added another layer to the woman's Texas accent. "Jessica?"

"Adopted daughter in Houston—or that's how we always think of her." She lifted her phone and pulled up a photo of a couple in costume. Fletcher and a stunning young blonde wearing a glittery tiara. "It was taken at the Tacky Country Christmas Cotillion last year, a benefit for the Make-A-Wish

Foundation." Mrs. Holt smiled. "Those costumes . . . astronaut and princess. It brings back so many memories."

"She's beautiful," Macy admitted with a strange sense of disappointment. Though why she should care that Fletcher Holt had a girlfriend made no sense whatsoever.

"She and her sister, her family, are our neighbors in Houston," Mrs. Holt explained. "Fletcher and the girls grew up together. Jessica Barclay was always a free spirit, a delight—and a complete handful. The girl could whip up chaos like a tornado. Fletcher has always taken his role as a big brother very seriously."

Macy glanced at the photo again, wondering if this mother had missed something. The way her son was looking at his princess . . .

"I think . . ." Mrs. Holt rested the phone against her chest, closing her eyes for a moment. "I think it was because Jessica was three when Fletcher first met her. The same age as his sister when we lost her."

Macy's throat tightened. "Oh, I'm so sorry."

"Thank you." Mrs. Holt shook her head. "And I apologize for rambling on like this. I usually let visitors get a word in; that medicine is playing havoc with my manners." A smile creased the edges of her lavender-blue eyes. "Any minute I expect to give way to a rousing rendition of the University of Houston fight song. Promise you'll stop me."

"I promise." Macy smiled. "But I really should go. You're tired, and I have a kickboxing class to get to."

"Looks like my nurse has a touch of tornado too."

"Probably." Macy rose to her feet. "I'm glad you're feeling better, Mrs. Holt."

"Please, it's Charly." She patted her heart. "And thank you, Macy. You were so kind to me in the emergency department—a blessing, truly. My mother always told me that nurses were angels. You're proof of that." Her lips quirked. "Now go give something a good swift kick."

"Absolutely." Macy offered a hearty thumbs-up and headed for the door. She knew now why she'd climbed the stairs, come up here. Even in their dramatic, messy encounter in the ER, Macy sensed that Charly Holt was someone special. Even if she got it wrong about angels and blessings—an effect of the medication, no doubt. Macy was nothing close to that. She was a tough survivor who'd learned to land on her feet—no angel, for sure. Still, for that moment, from that mother, it had felt good.

———

"No more word on the blood tests. Maybe tomorrow." Fletcher switched his phone to the other hand, shifting position on the chair in the last row of the empty and dimly lit hospital chapel. "She's anemic, but I guess some of that is chronic. From the leukemia. No plans for a blood trans-fusion . . . yet."

"Hang in there, buddy." Seth raised his voice over some background chatter, making Fletcher think he was probably in Starbucks. Between chaplain duties, no doubt. "I can be over there in forty minutes."

"No need. I'm okay."

Seth chuckled. "We all wear that I'm-okay badge. Heavier than it looks. Sometimes we've got to unpin it and let a friend help out."

Fletcher smiled. "Thanks. But I really am okay. Once I made the handoff to the ER staff. She's in good hands here."

"She's always in the best hands. No matter where she is. You can trust that."

"Right." Fletcher glanced toward the chapel's non-denominational altar decorated with a basket of white roses and a trio of candles. He knew what Seth was saying. God's hands. Fletcher had said over and over that he was trusting God with this, with everything. But lately things had been going so wrong. And today he'd carried his unconscious and bleeding mother in his arms.

Are you really listening, Lord?

"Is your father flying in from Alaska?"

"Not yet. Mom's fending him off; it depends on what we hear tomorrow." Fletcher caught a glimpse of someone passing the chapel door and stood. "Hey, Seth, I need to go. I'll give you a call later."

"No problem."

Fletcher jogged to the door and peered down the hallway. "Macy?"

She turned, walked back his way. Once again he was struck by her. Hair down around her shoulders, that confident stride . . .

"Hi. I was just—" he gestured toward the chapel—"sitting for a minute."

"Sure. That's why it's there. Quiet, away from all of this." She glanced around the bustling hospital corridor. "Did you need something?"

"Not really." He tried to remember why he'd run out here to catch her. "I just wanted to say thank you. For opening that door from the waiting room and getting my mother back to the ER so fast. Helping her like you did. And for letting me stay there with her. I know there are rules and you didn't have to do that. Especially since—" He stopped himself.

"Since you pitched me onto a highway and tried to arrest my friend?"

"Yeah." There was nothing coy about this woman. "I don't suppose it helps that your Mr. Rush isn't holding a grudge; in fact, he sent me some basketball tickets."

"That would be Elliot." Macy's expression left no clue if the truce extended to their relationship too.

"Anyway," Fletcher repeated, "thank you for helping my mom. It meant a lot to me. And to her."

A hint of a smile crept across Macy's face. "She's pretty great. I just came from visiting her. She said the pain meds and nasal packing were making her sound like a cartoon character, and she might start singing football songs any minute."

"That's Mom."

"Well . . ." Macy glanced at her watch. "I should go. I have a class."

"And I need to get back upstairs. Thanks again."

"Sure."

He'd started to walk away when Macy called his name.
"Yes?"

"About the freeway . . ." She crossed her arms over her scrubs. "Even with all of that, I should be grateful. That bullet came really close. You might've saved my life. So . . . thank you, Fletcher."

"You're welcome."

He watched her walk away, still not certain where they stood. Maybe they were just even now. If Seth were here, he'd probably say God arranged it: Fletcher kept Macy from harm out there on the freeway so she could be there to open that door for him today. If that was true, then a full truce wasn't necessary. *Even* was more than good enough.

———

It seemed as if Macy's old Audi drove to the little Tahoe Park house on autopilot. One minute she was stowing her hand and ankle wraps in her gym bag, taking a swig of her vitaminwater, and saying good-bye to her coach. Then, before she knew it, her car was picking its way down this street while she held her breath to see if the *For Sale Bank Owned* sign was still pounded into the sparse yard. It was.

Macy sighed and lifted her hair away from her neck; even half an hour after leaving her class and despite the cool evening, she was still perspiring. It had been a good workout: rope work, medicine ball, core work, and the bag work and sparring. She'd felt it, cardio and muscle. All toenails intact. So different from the ballet, but much more fitting to real life. Her current life.

She'd packed away her equipment, and then instead of a hot shower and a homemade veggie burrito—if her roommates hadn't eaten all the ingredients—Macy ended up right here, parked across the street from a house she could in no way afford. Shouldn't even want. But . . .

The porch light must have had a solar sensor because it blinked on in the deepening dusk, giving Macy a better glimpse of the door—painted red. Hadn't she read some-where that a red door meant "welcome"? Maybe even hap-piness . . . protection? She wasn't sure. Nonni's door wasn't red, but her house had been the most welcoming, happy, and protected place Macy had ever known. And it was the first time she'd been given a key to someplace she lived. Been trusted with that.

Macy closed her eyes for a moment. There had always been tricycles on the patchy lawn, stepping stones clut-tered with leaves in every season, and Nonni's battered *Wipe Your Paws* doormat, stenciled with dog prints. Three steps to the porch. The tarnished brass door handle felt cool under her fingers, the latch worn shiny-like-new by the fingers of countless foster kids. There was a soft click when she pressed it down, a small and miraculous signal that always brought Nonni. She could count on that. The same way there would be the scent of oatmeal cookies or maybe shortbread and the sounds of praise music filling the hallway, and Nonni's voice . . . *"Welcome home, Macy girl."*

She wondered now, as she had so many times before, if Nonni's door handle set would fit this door. Then reached into her gym bag and pulled it out: heavy, still tarnished, the lever not so kid-shiny anymore. It had been wrapped in an old kitchen towel for more than a decade. Since the night Macy broke a window in Nonni's vacant house, held a flashlight between her teeth, unscrewed the door set, and took it away. Stole it, people would say. But it hadn't felt that way at the time, in the painful mix of grief and anger that followed her foster mother's death. Macy had imagined standing on the porch, lifting a fist, and boldly telling the bank that they couldn't take the house because she had a key. Because it was the only real home she'd ever known. She'd imagined all that and, in the end, simply stolen the door hardware in the darkness.

She ran her thumb over the lever, heard the familiar click. Did Leah remember this the way she did? Macy had meant to ask her.

Macy's phone rang, startling her. Taylor.

"Did I catch you at a bad time?" she asked.

"No." *You just caught me with stolen goods.* "What's up?"

"Have you seen the news?"

"I've been at the gym. What's going on?"

"Another sniper attack, they're saying—this time he shot a police dog."

15

"FOUR NEWS VANS," TAYLOR REPORTED, peering through the Starbucks window toward the veterinary hospital across the street. "Almost as many as there are patrol cars now. Titus is making national news. I wish it was for a happier reason. Like an amazing litter of puppies."

"Puppies?" Seth peered at her through the steam rising from his Bold Pick of the Day. "The tabloids would chopper in for that one. Our heroic K-9 is a male." His expression sobered. "I'm afraid the odds aren't good that Titus will survive this second surgery."

"I hate the thought of that. It's tough just watching our golden retriever getting old and slow." *Greg's dog, outliving him.* "I can't imagine losing a pet that way."

"Bad enough without imagining what could have happened with all those kids at the grammar school."

Taylor winced. The incident had shaken the whole community. A K-9 officer making a goodwill school visit. Shots ringing out as he walked the veteran German shepherd toward the building. Though the officer had been unharmed, his dog was seriously injured with wounds to his head and jaw. There had been critical blood loss. All the adjacent schools were immediately put on lockdown. And remained closed today. The crisis chaplains would make visits next week. "Have there been any more leads?"

"Not that I'm aware of. Only that report of a suspicious white van seen in the neighborhood. You want to take a guess how many white vans there are in the Sacramento area? My dad owns one. So does the mobile dog groomer who visits half a dozen homes in my neighborhood." Seth patted his breast pocket and pulled out a packet of antacids. He never seemed to be without them. "I don't know the details, but they're saying the probability is high that this is the freeway sniper."

"I heard." Taylor battled a chill despite the warmth of the skinny cinnamon latte in her hands. "I can't understand that. To knowingly inflict such terror and pain . . ."

Seth was quiet for a moment, then met her gaze with compassion in his eyes. "How are you doing, Taylor?"

"Good—better." Her quick smile was followed by a more honest shrug. There was a good reason Seth had been appointed "chaplain to the chaplains"—or C2C, as the senior chaplain liked to say. This coffee date was Seth's way of checking Taylor's emotional pulse. He'd been a rock for her after Greg's death, and many times since. And would occasionally stop by the hospital when he was in the area, prompting one of the high school volunteers—perhaps because Seth's hair had a hint of red too—to ask the chaplain if he was Taylor's father. Ridiculous since he was only seven years older than she was. But he'd handled it with gracious humor.

"I'm hanging in there," she assured him. "Work helps. The chaplain work too."

"I'm glad to hear that."

When she'd applied as a volunteer, Seth expressed concern that she was opening herself up to too much stress. That it was too soon. *There's a big difference between a scab and a scar, Taylor.* From the look in his eyes right now, he still wasn't convinced.

"Really," Taylor assured him. "It keeps my focus off myself. It makes me feel needed. And if I'm busy, I don't worry that something will make me slide back into—" She stopped, swirled the stir stick in her coffee, irked at herself for giving him an opening.

"What does that?" Seth asked gently. "Makes you feel like you're 'sliding back'?"

She wasn't going to cry. "Random things—ridiculous things. I mean, I can look at our wedding photo and be okay with that. But hearing some great news, like a friend who's expecting a baby . . ."

"Those emotional trip wires." Seth nodded. "At home, we know where the land mines are buried. We can avoid them, learn to dismantle them, even. At home we're wearing full body armor. But out here—" he glanced around the Starbucks—"in the real world, we can't control things as well."

We. Meaning me. But then Seth would understand. His wife had died of ovarian cancer several years ago.

"I suppose it's the things that come out of the blue that shake me the most," she admitted. "Like getting that letter from the Sac Fire human resources department last week— addressed to Greg." Her lips tensed. "You know how many times he was in and out of that office over the years? He coached two of those women's sons in Little League. They *knew* him, Seth—they know what happened. How could someone make a thoughtless mistake like that?"

Seth stayed quiet; it wasn't a question that needed an answer.

"And the label," she added with a sigh. "That's hard too."

Seth's brows rose a fraction.

"*Widow.* It's like I'm not Taylor anymore, I'm 'Greg Cabot's widow.' You can't imagine how many times I've been introduced like that at department functions. To the new hires, new spouses. I either need a name badge or an exit strategy." Taylor took a slow breath. "I guess it's time to wean myself away."

"Hard to say good-bye to family. Firefighters, cops, medical people, chaplains—we hold on to each other. Tight knit to the last stitch."

Taylor nodded; words were too much of a risk. It was so true—and another loss.

She was relieved when Seth's phone buzzed with a text.

"Titus is out of surgery," he reported. "The officer's kids are there, and if there's bad news, I should be with them."

"Then you'd better go." Taylor began rising from her chair. "I wanted to check on Charly again anyway."

He stood, waited while she gathered her things.

"Thank you for the coffee," she told him. "And the ear."

"Two ears." Seth tugged at an earlobe. "My knee may be shot for basketball, but God made sure this man is fully equipped for listening."

"I'll remember that."

"And we'll do this again. You're a good excuse to feed my Starbucks habit." Seth's eyes softened. "Greg was a great guy. He's missed by a lot of people. But you'll always be Taylor to me—no labels. Except *friend*."

Taylor made it into her car before the first tear slid down her face. She smacked her palm against the steering wheel, anger warring with sadness. The insensitivity of a letter addressed to Greg had sickened her. Anonymous neglect from trusted "family." And any day now Taylor half expected to log on to her computer and see one of those intrusive Facebook pop-ups prompting her to change her status from "married" to "widowed." The combination of all that—plus what was going on with Charly Holt—had almost made her cancel her coffee with Seth.

No. That wasn't the truth.

Taylor swiped at the tear and stared across the street at the patrol cars parked at the veterinary hospital. The chaplain's SUV was among them now. The reason she'd almost canceled on Seth Donovan was because she was afraid she'd be tempted to revisit the questions that refused to stop replaying in her head, even after two years. Taylor didn't want to press that good man for answers he didn't have, draw him into her . . . obsession? Had it become that?

On the night Greg was killed, he'd told Taylor he was going to help a buddy install a home theater system. In Roseville. Why would she question that? Trust was at the very core of their relationship. But the rural road where he was struck by that car was several miles south of Elk Grove—not even in the same county as Roseville. In the painful aftermath, Taylor had endured raw, guilt-ridden condolences from the family Greg had stopped to help that night—as well as the retired teacher who'd accidentally run him down. She'd struggled to accept it all. But no one ever explained what put Greg in that place at that moment in time. Somewhere he wasn't expected to be. She'd asked and asked—expressed her concern to Seth, too—trying to understand even one small part of her husband's horrific and senseless death. But no one had an answer. Or a new home entertainment system.

———

"It's done." Fletcher rolled his sleeve down over the cotton ball the lab tech had taped to his forearm. "We're good to go. Though they said it could be a couple of weeks before we get the official results from the HLA testing."

"There's no certainty of a match." Charly held his gaze as she smoothed the hospital blanket across her hips. "Even with a parent or sibling, it's only a one in four chance of being a marrow donor, at best." She watched as he settled onto the visitor's chair, close enough to take hold of her hand. There was a small, uncharacteristic quaver in her voice. "You shouldn't count on it, Fletcher."

"We don't even know if you'll need a transplant," he

reminded her, reassuring himself that the tiny red spot—"a superficial hemorrhage"—marring the white of his mother's eye hadn't grown larger. It was a common occurrence, the nurse told him, though he'd found no comfort in that. "I only did this because the doc said it's advisable to have family members tested to stay ahead of the game. There's no evidence you haven't responded to the chemo. And even if that changes, they sometimes start off with a transplant of a patient's own stem cells."

She gave his fingers a squeeze. "Someone's been studying."

"I've been doing some reading." He couldn't let her see how much it disturbed him, every word and each statistic. But the bleeding had responded well to the packing and cautery. His mother's anemia wasn't critical. She'd been given a transfusion of platelets—cells that helped blood to clot. And there had been no new bleeding. She was being discharged home in the morning. All of that was encouraging. "You know me. Got to stay on top of things."

"Yes. I know you, Son. And how hard you try to fix things. I don't want you to pin your hopes on being a match." She wiped an eye, tossed him one of her teasing smiles. "We should leave a few things on that to-do list for God. It's his job, after all."

"Right," he told her, knowing with certainty that his prayer would be answered this time. If his mother needed a transplant, it would come from her son. He hadn't been able to save his sister's life or fix his mother's heartbreak all those years ago. But this time things would go the right way.

Fletcher's cell phone buzzed. He slipped his hand away from hers, read the text. And frowned.

"Something wrong?"

"Good and bad." He slid the phone back into his pocket. "They recovered the bullet from that grammar school. Passed right through the dog and lodged in a fence post."

"And Titus? Wasn't he having another surgery today?"

Fletcher wanted to lie, spare her . . . "He had to be put down."

16

"THE SANE NURSE IS ON HER WAY," Macy assured the
social worker who stood alongside the exam table.

"Good."

Their patient, a fifteen-year-old assault victim—and pre-
sumed runaway—lay faceup and shivering despite a triple
layer of warmed blankets. She'd covered her eyes with a
skinny arm, hand dangling, nail polish a chipped, deso-
late black. Her burgundy hair was littered with leaf debris
from the park bushes where she'd been found by an elderly
woman walking her dog. Since then the girl had breathed
barely a handful of words, each accompanied by uncontrol-
lable shaking. Her lower lip was swollen, split by a small
laceration. One earlobe trickled blood. A hoop earring had
been viciously torn free by her assailant—the least by far of
her traumas. The sexual assault nurse examiner couldn't get

here fast enough as far as Macy was concerned. Everything about this was bringing back memories of Leah's trauma.

"Make sure the hospital chaplain is coming too," Dr. Carlyle told the social worker. She tucked the warmed blankets under her patient's back and bent low to whisper, "We're going to help you get through this, Sonya. You're safe here."

Safe. Macy closed her eyes for a moment, remembering the click of Nonni's door latch.

"Is everything ready?" Andi Carlyle kept her voice low as she glanced at the metal instrument stand. "The exam equipment, evidence kit, and—"

There was a knock at the door.

"Excuse me, Dr. Carlyle." The door opened a crack and a registration clerk's face peeked through. Her expression seemed anxious. "I'm sorry to disturb you."

"Unless it's urgent, I really can't leave right now." Andi took a step toward the door, and Macy noticed that her flowered T-shirt, tucked into the faded-blue scrub pants, made the doctor's blossoming tummy visible. "Is it something PA Koenig can handle?"

"It's that Mr. Harrell," the clerk whispered. "He says it's urgent that he speak with you personally. He's insisting." The look on her face said *demanding* was more accurate.

Their patient turned onto her side with a small groan, exposing a glimpse of an amateurish tattoo on her pale shoulder—a painful and permanent typo: *Beleive.*

"Tell Mr. Harrell—" Andi pressed her fingers to her forehead—"that I'll be with him in five minutes. He can wait in my office. Show him where the coffee is." Discomfort flickered across her face. "This has been a rough day for his family."

"Okay." The clerk's brows pinched. "He doesn't look like he would want coffee. But I'll tell him."

Bob Harrell. Macy thought of the day they'd lifted his unconscious mother from the backseat of his car, how agitated he'd been. She'd hoped that having his brothers here would make it easier for him. But then there was nothing at all easy about losing someone you love. The ICU team had discontinued life support on Darlene Harrell an hour ago. The family was keeping a painful vigil—except for Bob, who apparently handled stress by pacing the halls. Miles of them over the past week. Macy had seen a member of the chaplain staff following a discreet distance behind, just in case he wanted to talk. But it seemed that the only person he wanted to talk with was Andi.

"The SANE nurse is here," the clerk added as she slipped out of the exam room.

"Thank you." The social worker patted their patient's arm. "I'm going to go speak with our nurse specialist for a few minutes before she comes in, Sonya. And then we'll both be back."

"And I think I'll slip out now too. I need to give a status report to the oncoming physician." Andi bent low in an attempt to make eye contact with the girl. Impossible since she'd drawn the blanket up high enough to cover her brows. But at least she'd stopped the terrible trembling. "You're in good hands, Sonya. We're going to do everything we can to help you." She glanced at Macy. "And my nurse is going to wait with you until we're ready to start your exam."

"Absolutely." Macy grabbed a rolling stool, straddled it, and moved close to the exam table. "Not going anywhere."

In a moment it was only the two of them, Sonya lying so still that Macy suspected she'd fallen asleep. Merciful, considering that in a short while she'd need to answer a list of excruciatingly personal questions. Things no fifteen-year-old should have to address. Then give permission for an intimate probing of her body, collecting evidence designed to build a case against her vicious attacker. All of it would be performed by a skilled and caring professional. But to a frightened child, it still might seem far too close to a second assault.

The girl pulled down the blanket, met Macy's gaze. Tears welled in her red-rimmed eyes. Her voice emerged in a husky, raw monotone. "That . . . man . . ."

Oh no. Macy wanted to interrupt, advise her that she should wait to talk to the sexual assault expert or the waiting female detective.

"I heard . . . ," Sonya continued, fighting another involuntary tremble. "That man, that sniper out there . . . shot a dog."

The shooter? Macy's thoughts staggered. This battered and violated child was worried about the dog?

"Is it true?" Sonya asked.

"I'm afraid so." Even if this girl asked, Macy wasn't going to reveal the final outcome of that senseless attack. At least she could spare her that. But Sonya closed her eyes and went quiet again. Macy scooted closer, trying not to imagine Leah's experience in that exam room years back; she'd been even younger than this girl.

"I have . . . I had a dog. Back in Pocatello," the girl whispered, a sad smile teasing her lips. "Tater always liked to sleep at the end of my bed. She'd scratch my quilt and turn and turn . . . like she was making this perfect little nest for herself." Sonya grasped the hospital blanket to her chest, exposing that misspelled tattoo. A tear slid down her face. "Maybe . . . it's not too late. Maybe I could . . ."

Macy waited.

"I want to go home." The girl's eyes found hers. "Can you all help me with that?"

Macy nodded, an ache crowding her throat. "We'll try our best."

A few minutes later, the SANE nurse and the social worker returned, and Macy headed back to the nurses' station. Andi was at the doctors' desk, her homely Keebler elf mug—an anonymous gift from last year's Secret Santa—in one hand. The other hand rested protectively against her growing tummy.

"How was Mr. Harrell?" Macy asked after glancing toward the assignment board.

"Changed his mind apparently. Not in my office or anywhere in the department." Andi shrugged. "I'm hoping that means one of the chaplains got through to him. Truthfully, I'm relieved. Besides prayer, there's not a lot I can do for him at this point. And—" she glanced at her watch—"as soon as I finish this tea, I'm on my way. I'm meeting my guy at Babies & Beyond." Her dimpled smile appeared. "The new date night."

Macy smiled back. She could only imagine what that kind of happy felt like.

Andi drained the last of her tea, reached for her back-pack, then glanced toward the doors to the corridor. "Oh, dear, I forgot." She turned back to Macy. "Did he find you?"

"Who?"

"Fletcher Holt, the deputy. He was waiting outside to talk with you."

———

Clearly Macy was busy, Fletcher told himself as he reached the exit doors to the hospital parking lot. He'd find another opportunity to talk with her. *Excuse?* Yeah, probably. But—

"Fletcher. Hey, wait up."

Macy jogged toward him, stethoscope bouncing around her neck. Different scrubs today, green like that dress at the gala.

"I'm sorry," she told him, coming to a stop. "I didn't get the message until just now that you were out here." Her gaze skimmed his off-duty clothes. "Visiting Charly?"

"Right," Fletcher confirmed, amused to hear his mother's nickname—of course she'd insist. "I was on my way out and thought I'd let you know how she was doing. That's all. I can see that you're busy."

"It's okay. I want to hear about your mother. I'm good for a few minutes." She nodded toward the doors. "Let's step outside. Otherwise I'll start believing it's normal for air to smell like iodine, rubbing alcohol, cold pizza, and things you probably don't want to imagine."

"You're right." Fletcher pushed the door open before Macy could reach for it. He agreed with her completely.

Fresh air, a few minutes' respite . . . some peace. He hadn't realized until just this moment how much he needed that.

"Ah, heaven," Macy said almost immediately. She backed up against the stucco wall, lifted her face toward the sun, and closed her eyes. The breeze, scented by eucalyptus trees, played with her dark ponytail. Then her eyes met his. "So how is your mother doing?"

"Much better. The packing is out—no more bleeding. Doctor thinks I can take her home in the morning."

"And her blood work?" Macy tilted her head. "The leukemia?"

"Better than they expected. I don't know the numbers—how that all goes. But her oncologist said we could still be 'cautiously optimistic.'" He rubbed his fingers against the shirtsleeve where the cotton ball was still taped to his skin. "The lab drew my blood for HLA testing. I'll donate marrow if she needs it."

"Ah . . ."

Fletcher was sure Macy had stopped herself from quoting the same statistics his mother had about the likelihood of a tissue match. The math didn't matter. He'd never been so certain of anything. "So . . . all good."

"I'm glad." Macy glanced toward the parking lot, frowned. "Oh, brother. Looks like Andi didn't get away after all."

Fletcher saw what Macy did: the short woman in scrubs standing in the parking lot, arms crossed over her chest. A huge GMC pickup truck idled beside her. "Dr. Carlyle?"

"Yes." Macy sighed. "We treated that man's mother. Sad outcome. Which reminds me . . ." She turned back to

Fletcher. "The police dog, Titus. Do they have any idea if he was targeted?"

"No clue." The next words slipped out. "Even in my line of work, it's hard to stomach this kind of senseless . . . *stuff*. Lately I've had all I care to take."

"I hear that." Macy studied Fletcher like she was seeing him for the first time. "Looks like we've got something in common after all, Deputy Holt. I wouldn't have guessed that could be possible, but—"

They both turned at a loud engine roar, followed by squealing tires and—

"He hit her!" a voice shouted. "He ran that woman down!"

17

"TELL ME HIS NAME, Macy—just that much." Fletcher sucked in a breath, pulse still hammering; he'd chased the truck to the hospital exit, tried to get a look at the license plate as it peeled away. No luck. And now . . . He stepped aside as yet another hospital employee joined Macy on the asphalt beside Dr. Carlyle. Someone spread a paint-spattered tarp over her for warmth. It looked like she needed so much more. Blood coming from her nostrils, a raw abrasion running from temple to jaw, skin too pasty white. "Macy, I need that driver's name. I've got to relay it to dispatch, get units out there."

"It's Bob." Macy pressed her fingertips against the unconscious doctor's neck, then glanced up at Fletcher, anxiety etched on her face. "Bob Harrell. Robert maybe. I don't know for sure." She repeated the last name, spelled it. "I think he still has family members up in the ICU." Her black ponytail whipped as she turned to shout toward the ER. "C'mon, get that stretcher out here. Backboard, C-collar, *now*!"

"Harrell. Got it." Fletcher jabbed a finger at his speed dial for the comm center.

In seconds, the stretcher clattered alongside and was dropped low to the ground by ER staff. Help swarmed like Texas fire ants: technicians, white-coated MDs, and a couple of paramedics who had a rig parked in the ambulance bay. Macy continued to give the orders, watching every move made and urging people to act carefully but quickly. Probably unnecessary—it was obvious they were giving their fallen teammate every chance possible.

"Okay, let's roll!"

Fletcher followed close behind as the ER team propelled the gurney carrying Dr. Carlyle toward the ambulance bay doors. If he could get in through here, he'd split off toward the ICU, try to confirm an address on Harrell, and—

"Fletcher!" Macy hung back as the stretcher disappeared through the automatic doors. Her lips pressed together in a grim line. "Be sure you get that guy."

"I'm on it," he promised, fighting the urge to climb into his Jeep, gun it out of there, hunt the guy himself. Address or not, it still offered much better odds than finding that lousy dog shooter . . . or fighting blood cancer single-handedly . . . or convincing Jessica Barclay she was choosing the wrong man. A clear win right now would go a long way.

"What's going on?"

Taylor Cabot caught Fletcher as he was about to follow

Macy through the ambulance doors. The redhead was dressed in street clothes, her green eyes anxious, face flushed. "I was on my way up to see your mom when a visitor said there'd been some sort of accident. I saw the gurney . . ."

"A hit-and-run in the parking lot," Fletcher confirmed, wishing there were a gentler way to convey this. He thought of the look on Macy's face as she knelt beside her teammate. "It's Dr. Carlyle."

"No." Taylor's fingers rose to her lips, smothering her gasp. "Andi?"

"A truck ran her down."

"Oh, dear God," she breathed, the color draining from her face. "I'd better get in there."

She punched in the door code for both of them, and they headed in different directions, each dealing with this newest tragedy. Fletcher thought of Macy, those few seconds when she stood enjoying the sun on her face. That moment of peace was cut short for both of them, something that happened far too often in their separate workday worlds. *"Looks like we've got something in common after all, Deputy Holt."*

Right now, he wished it were something entirely different.

"I'm starting that second IV line now, Andi," Taylor explained, despite the fact that the injured doctor had roused only a few seconds at a time since her arrival in the trauma room. And then it was to moan and call for her husband. Taylor prayed they were dealing with a concussion and not a serious brain injury. And that she could do what needed to be done for Andi without battling too many memories of Greg's death. Car versus pedestrian—it was the same set of circumstances. "This is a 16-gauge needle, so it's going to pinch—and you know how we totally fib with that mercy word. Hang in there. Here we go . . ."

"X-ray's here!" a tech shouted over the din of voices and electronic beeps.

"Give me a minute, one more minute." Taylor stretched the skin taut, wishing the first liter of saline had raised Andi's veins more. Too flat. *Oh, please don't let that be from hemorrhage . . .* She tapped the vein with a gloved finger, pierced the skin with a quick thrust, then slid needle and catheter farther. She held her breath until she saw blood rush back into the flash chamber. *In the vein, thank you.* "Got it, Andi. I just have to advance the catheter, tape it down, and start that fluid going."

She'd placed the last of the tape and adjusted the flow on the second liter of saline when Macy slid in beside her, a whiff of her almond lotion mixing with the pervasive scent of disinfectant.

"A 16-gauge," Taylor reported. "Wide-open. X-ray's up next. Point me at anything else you need done."

"You are the best for being here." Macy took a step away from the gurney to be out of earshot. "Pitching in like this."

"It's Andi."

Macy groaned. "Obvious femur fracture. Bruising, no deformity of that forearm. But she'll be lucky if her pelvis isn't broken. That truck was monster size, and Andi is, what?

Five foot two standing on tiptoe?" She glanced to where another nurse was setting up for a Foley catheter. "We need to see if there's blood in her urine—her belly didn't seem distended and there's no obvious bruising, thank goodness. And the baby . . . From what Andi's told people, she's about fourteen weeks along. Her OB ordered an ultrasound; he's on his way here. But no matter how much we want it to be different, fourteen weeks just isn't viable. The only way to protect the pregnancy is to keep Andi oxygenated, stabilize her blood pressure. And—"

"Pray." Taylor took a slow breath, wondering if anyone in that trauma center two years ago had ever considered Greg *viable*. "I called for the hospital chaplain, and I'll try to find out her pastor's name."

"Sure . . ." Macy hesitated. "Good. That will be important to her. While you're praying, be sure to ask that she doesn't bleed out from something we haven't discovered yet. I don't like her color, and—" her gaze swept the monitors—"those numbers aren't even close to where we want them."

"No." Taylor scanned the digital displays: blood pressure 87 over 48, heart rate 128, pulse ox 99 percent on the high-flow oxygen, though her breathing still looked shallow and air hungry. Andi's hand, despite the pain of an injured arm, spread over her lower abdomen. Protecting her baby.

"I've got to check on the rest of the department." There was regret in Macy's voice. "I'll be back in a few. You're staying for a while?"

"Try to kick me out." Taylor found a smile as Macy gave her shoulder a grateful squeeze. "I saw a few deputies heading down the hallway. Going up to question the Harrell family?"

"I'd think so. I heard that Mrs. Harrell was pronounced dead about fifteen minutes ago. I'm guessing the ICU staff is getting pretty jumpy."

"Worried Bob Harrell might come back?"

"It's possible."

Taylor's gaze moved to the woman on the gurney, small and vulnerable. Nothing like the vibrant and dedicated physician who strode through these rooms less than an hour ago. It was still so surreal. The tech who removed Andi's cartoon socks—cutting one with trauma scissors because it was so caked with blood—had been unable to stop her tears. Taylor connected with Macy's gaze. "Our staff's been on edge too, after the freeway shooting and then with the news of the police dog. Now this. We'll all be looking over our shoulders. I hope one of those deputies is planning to hang around the ER until Harrell is found."

"I don't think we need to worry about that." Macy nodded toward the corridor to the ambulance bay. "Looks like we have our own private protection."

"Hospital security?"

"Fletcher Holt."

"I saw him out there. We were on the same mission, I'm sure. I was on my way up to visit Charly."

"Well . . ." Macy squared her shoulders, took one more glance at the monitors. "I'm glad you were both here, whatever the reason."

Taylor watched Macy thread her way through the crowded staff, directing people she thought needed it, being her usual woman in charge—not ready to fully rely on anyone but herself. But then that was Macy.

"Eee . . . f," Andi moaned, eyes snapping wide as her oxygen mask fogged. "Pl . . . ease."

"What?" Taylor moved close again. "I'm not sure what you're saying. Tell me again. Do you need something? Pain meds?"

"No. I'm all right. But . . ." The ER doctor closed her eyes for a moment, a tear sliding from beneath her lids. "Elf . . . our baby. Make sure X-ray knows I'm pregnant." She groaned, pupils dilating with what had to be a cruel wave of pain. Her tongue swept across her pale lips. "I'm afraid I'll lose this baby. Would you . . . pray with me, Taylor?"

"Sure," Taylor managed, tears threatening. "Of course."

She signaled to X-ray that she needed another minute. Then Taylor rested her hand over Andi's and bowed her head, trying her best to carve out a peaceful moment amid the clatter, whirs, and hisses of the trauma room—all necessary. But so was this: a simple prayer for a mother and her unborn child. This couldn't end tragically. Not again. *Not like Greg.*

"Merciful God," Taylor began.

"Thanks for the offer, but no. I'm going to drag myself home and crash on the couch. If my roommate's dog hasn't managed to devour it completely." Macy plucked at the sleeveless purple tunic she'd pulled over a tank and black exercise tights. "I was heading to the gym, but I'm not up to it." She gazed across the hospital parking lot. It was still hard to believe what had happened there. Macy shifted her gym bag to the other hand. "Awful, awful day."

"But you have to eat," Elliot insisted, loosening his tie. "I'll take you to Rio City Café—we'll stop first and you can change into something more appropriate. We'd still be early enough to get a great table." His smile broadened. "You can order that grilled salmon you like. I owe you since we got detoured last time."

By a bullet. If Elliot was expecting to perk her appetite with that walk down memory lane, he was failing utterly. Macy resisted the temptation to check if Fletcher was still talking on his cell phone outside the doors to the ER waiting room. "Another time. I don't have enough energy left to chew."

"You did a great job in there today," Elliot offered, giving her arm a pat. "Quick work getting Dr. Carlyle stabilized and off to surgery to pin the femur fracture. It has to be a huge relief that the ultrasound showed her pregnancy hasn't been affected."

Macy's lips tensed. Elliot had been asking questions. About a woman he barely knew beyond a cordial nod in the hallways. Even if this financial planner was a familiar face around the hospital, there was no way staff should skirt privacy issues. Time for a HIPAA review. "You know I can't discuss patients' medical care."

"I'm not asking." Elliot's smile was warm. "Except about dinner."

"Rain check," Macy assured him, hating that she'd probably sounded abrupt before. The Rushes had been nothing but good to her. Fatigue and stress were obviously taking a toll. "Another time. Promise."

"I'll hold you to it."

She'd made it to the car and was stooping to unlock the door when she heard a voice behind her—close enough to make her jump.

18

"I'm sorry—didn't mean to startle you," Fletcher said. "Not a good day to take anyone by surprise."

"No," Macy agreed, keys pressed to her chest.

"Good reflexes, though," he observed. "You whipped around pretty quick."

Her lips twitched toward a smirk. "You're lucky I'm tired; I could have planted a foot square in the middle of your chest."

"You're probably not threatening ballet."

"Kickboxing." Macy pointed to the black gym bag at her feet. "Gloves, ankle wraps, the works. All I need is a worthy target."

"Right." His turn to smile. Macy Wynn was smart enough—maybe even streetwise enough—to figure Fletcher carried an off-duty weapon. He'd never met a woman this downright gutsy. He liked it. "Anyway, sorry I sneaked up on you. Rough enough day already."

Macy's expression sobered as she looked back toward the hospital. "I'm glad the news vans are gone. Andi's going to have a long road healing from those injuries and . . ." She hesitated. "It's good the press is giving her some space. They're probably digging for news on the hunt for Bob—"

"He's in custody. That's why I came over here," Fletcher interrupted. "To tell you. I just got word: Harrell turned himself in. His brothers drove him downtown."

"No problems?"

"A slew of problems. He had some kind of a breakdown; the family's trying to deal with that."

"And their mother's death," Macy added.

"Right." Fletcher had a sudden image of carrying his own mother, bleeding and unconscious, through this very parking lot. He had no idea how he might have reacted if things had gone south for her. "Bad deal all round," he finished. "But the staff can breathe a little easier now that he's not on the loose."

Macy nudged the gym bag with her shoe. "That just leaves our elusive dog killer."

Fletcher nodded, wishing he could make her smile again. If he was right about Macy being streetwise, he'd guess her streets had more than their fair share of potholes. "I thought you'd want to know about Harrell."

"I did . . . do. I appreciate your letting me know." The late-afternoon sun made her eyes all the more intriguing— the color of caramels people melted onto apples when Houston pretended to have autumn. She swept her fingers through her hair. "I suppose you're headed back up to sit with Charly."

"She kicked me out—FaceTime date with my dad. I told her I'd see her in the morning. I'm working swing shift tomorrow so I'll have time to get her settled at home." He glanced toward his Jeep, parked only three spaces from her car. "Guess I'll go find something to eat." The question slipped out before he could stop it. "Are you hungry?"

"Sort of." The amazing eyes met his. "Is that an invitation?"

"If I say yes, will you kick me in the chest?"

"No." She smiled. "I'm sure you're armed."

He'd pegged her on knowing that. But had no clue where to take it from here. Or even if he should. *What am I doing?*

"It *is* an invitation," he heard himself say. "Have dinner with me."

Macy glanced down at her clothes. "I'm afraid what you see is what you get."

"I don't doubt that for a minute—and I'm not afraid. Grab your bag. My Jeep's right over there."

Fletcher let Macy open her own door, suspecting she'd prefer it. This wasn't the time to wage a war about chivalry. He'd wrangle with that later. If there was a later. He was hungry, and right now that basic need seemed to include the baffling Macy Wynn.

"Okay," she told him, tossing her gym bag onto the back-seat before sliding into the front. "I should warn you: I'm not one of those timid, girlie eaters."

"Still not scaring me." Fletcher settled into the driver's seat. He waited as Macy fastened her seat belt. "Okay then," he told her, backing the Jeep out of the parking space. "Where to?"

"You know Sacramento?"

"I've probably covered most of the county now. Call to call: domestic disputes, barroom brawls, home invasion robberies, loose cattle."

Macy wrinkled her nose. "Where do you eat?"

"Mom's?"

"Must be nice."

Fletcher couldn't read her expression. What was that?

"I usually just grab something fast," he admitted, navigating the busy parking lot. "I haven't had a lot of time to check out this city for recreation. The last time I visited, before Mom got sick, we took off to Hawaii for my parents' thirtieth anniversary, and—"

There was a short horn honk, and a familiar BMW pulled alongside.

"It's Elliot," Macy confirmed.

Fletcher put the Jeep in neutral, lowered the window.

"Deputy Holt." Even with sunglasses in place, the man's posture said he was peering past Fletcher toward the passenger seat. "Macy. I didn't know you needed a ride; I could have done that, no problem. The Audi acting up again?"

"No." Macy leaned across Fletcher to make herself heard; that scent of almonds swirled. "Car's fine."

"Good." Rush's tone was curt. "Glad to hear it."

What was this?

Macy's smile did nothing to dispel the decidedly awkward moment. And Fletcher had no interest in playing detective.

"Grabbing something to eat," he explained to Rush, shifting back into gear after a car inched around them. "Looks like we're holding up traffic."

"Yes." The Beemer's engine edged from its expensive, fluid burble to an impressive whine—Rush's shoe leather goosing the accelerator. "Well then . . . enjoy your evening."

"Same to you."

Macy said nothing more as Fletcher pulled forward and headed toward the hospital exit. She'd crossed her arms, making him wonder if he should be prepared in case she changed her mind about dinner and bailed out of the Jeep.

"Careful," she warned, pointing to a man on a bicycle emerging from the Jeep's blind spot. He looked to be early forties, with a beard, gaunt features, and a knit hat pulled over straw-colored hair. "He's not paying attention. In a hurry to get to the ER."

"How do you know?"

"See the bandage on his arm? Piece of an undershirt tied on with a bandanna, dripping wet from trying to stop the pain. A burn, I'd bet. Second degree. From a car radiator or—"

"A campfire," Fletcher suggested, thinking once again that their work paralleled. Similar encounters and observations, different points of view. "See the bedroll tied to his backpack? All those layers of clothes? Homeless, I'd say."

And there it was again. That enigmatic look on Macy's face. She went quiet.

Fletcher waited for the man to cross to the hospital sidewalk and then continued on to the parking lot exit. He flipped on the Jeep's turn signal.

"Let's go the other way," Macy told him, sitting forward in her seat. "North. And then to I-5. Old Town—the riverfront. Have you been there?"

"A few times. But not to the restaurants."

"I know a place with great salmon."

"Works for me." He was glad to see her start to smile. "Do they bring that to our table already cooked? Or will you have to suit up and kick it into submission?"

———

Taylor exited the elevator at the first floor and checked her watch. Barely four thirty. She'd hoped to have a visit with Charly Holt, but apparently the day's activities—including removal of that miserable but effective nasal packing—had tired her out. Taylor was glad she was getting some rest. Whether that good woman wanted to believe it or not, she'd probably gone back to chaplaincy work too soon after completing her chemo. Taylor thought of that last activation: the death notification. Her first time, and Charly had been more than understanding. She'd even praised Taylor's handling of the situation, though they'd come up empty-handed at that foreclosed home.

"Uh, miss . . . which way is out?"

The bearded, middle-aged man, a tall and rangy blond, appeared from out of nowhere—chest laid half-bare by the hospital gown drooping over one shoulder. He carried a large backpack by one of its straps. His other arm, bicep to wrist, was dressed with thick layers of Kerlix gauze. "Do you know where the doors are?"

"Where do you want to go?" Taylor asked, fairly sure

he was trying to find somewhere to use his phone or sneak a smoke. The Hope hospital sprawl could be a confusing maze to the uninitiated.

"Back outside—by that bike rack. The way I came in." The man groped one-handed for the ties to the gown. His remaining clothes, good-quality hiking boots and cargo pants, were dusty and reeked of woodsmoke. Camper maybe, or tending a burning brush pile on his rural property.

"There's a bike rack outside the emergency department." Taylor started to point in that direction but hesitated. "Is that where you came from? The ER?"

"Yeah. But I'm finished there—bandaged up. Just need my bicycle." His gaze darted down the corridor, expression anxious. "I need to go."

"Did you get your aftercare instructions?" she asked gently, wondering if they'd really discharged him in that gown. Something wasn't right. No obvious odor of alcohol, but . . . "If you want, I'll take you back there so we can check on—"

"No," the man blurted. "You're not listening—never mind! I'm going." He yanked at the hospital gown hard enough to snap the ties. Then flung it to the floor and took off in long, clumping strides down the hallway.

No way Taylor would try to stop him. Maybe he really had been discharged and simply couldn't find the exit. She scooped up the discarded gown and then saw the p.m. clinical coordinator, Beverly, rounding the corner from the ER.

The woman eyed the rumpled gown with an immediate grimace. "Let me guess: my AWOL patient."

"Fortysomething, dirty blond, built like the *Wizard of Oz* scarecrow? With a big dressing on his arm?"

"Yep." Bev sighed, sweeping her fingers through her short, steel-gray hair. "I really don't want to start this shift with a patient elopement report. I'm tempted to let it ride; I already discussed the burn aftercare with him. He thought maybe his last tetanus was less than ten years ago, but . . ." The veteran nurse shook her head. "I think the poor man could use a psych consult."

Taylor glanced down the corridor.

"He said he was camping with his father," Bev explained. "But I got the feeling he's a transient—not that *that* situation makes him crazy. He got really nervous when we were dressing his arm, though, and insisted on reading all the labels: the saline bottle, surgical soap, and then the Silvadene cream. He kept asking where it was all manufactured—if they were US companies. Then he wanted to know who had installed the bedside monitoring equipment. Pretty anxious about that. And when I started to give him the tetanus booster . . ."

"He booked out of there."

"Yep. Mr. Archer took off like . . ." Bev tossed Taylor a grim smile. "Like the *Wizard of Oz* scarecrow being chased with a fire torch."

Taylor sighed. "Maybe the community chaplains can help. Did he leave a phone number or an ad—?" She stopped, eyes widening. "Wait. Did you say his name was Archer?"

"Ned Archer. Have you seen him before?"

"Yes," Taylor told her, amazed. *Small, troubled world.* "I

mean, we tried to see him. There was a crisis chaplaincy call to his home. But he was gone. Evicted."

"Ouch . . . sad."

"It is."

Taylor peered down the hallway where the man had disappeared. It was even sadder than Beverly realized. She didn't know the chaplain visit to Ned Archer's house had been a death notification. This poor man couldn't possibly have been camping with his dad. Her heart cramped at the memory of the confusing and painful fog she'd stumbled around in during the first weeks after Greg's death. "I think we have a phone number for the neighbor. I'll check again to see if she's learned of a forwarding address."

19

"IT'S A GREAT SPOT," Fletcher told Macy, his blue eyes making another sweep of Rio City Café's dining area. High ceilings, casually upscale decor—lots of wood, white linens, warehouse light fixtures, colorful local art—with an open view to the bustling kitchen and a fireplace. He glanced out the window, across a wooden dock and a short expanse of green river to the city's landmark Tower Bridge. Fletcher shook his head. "Painted shiny gold. You folks take that whole California 'mother lode' thing seriously."

"Probably. But I heard it was more to match the dome of the state capitol," Macy recalled, noticing how the ebbing sun lit short strands of Fletcher's hair. Gold as the bridge he was teasing her about. "The bridge lifts in the middle," she added, nearly dropping her last morsel of grilled salmon as she demonstrated with her fork. "To let the bigger ships through. I've watched it from here, and when I'm riding my bicycle, and from below too . . . in a sailboat."

Fletcher's brows rose.

"A friend's boat." She wasn't going to tell him that *Move It Offshore* was the Rushes' sailboat; she didn't want to open up that conversation. Partly because of the uncomfortable moment in the parking lot earlier. There was no excuse for Elliot to go all parental like that. But mostly Macy didn't want to discuss the reason she was involved with the Rushes in the first place. Because it all led back to the disconnected mess her life had been. Still was. She'd never shared all that with anyone and wasn't going to start.

"You were born in Sacramento?" Fletcher asked, spreading some apple-bacon relish over the last bite of his pork loin.

"I've lived here most of my life," she hedged, certain of what she'd suspected only moments after climbing into Fletcher's Jeep: it had been a huge mistake to let her hunger—and admittedly some curiosity—put her in this situation. But she could handle it. Not that different from defending herself at the gym. "But I was born in San Francisco."

"Really? Amazing city. My parents' Hawaii cruise started there."

"Ah." Macy smiled politely, took renewed interest in a dab of sweet corn, all that was left on her plate besides the fork and knife. How would this man react if he knew the only cruises Macy and her mother had shared were moving the car they slept in from parking lot to parking lot? Time to switch topics. "Your parents had a FaceTime visit?"

"Yes. My dad's in Alaska, near Prudhoe Bay. He's a

geologist for an oil company. Hard for him to get back and forth until the job's complete." Fletcher's forehead wrinkled. "That's why I'm here, pinch-hitting for a while. Until Mom's recovered."

"You must miss Houston," Macy mused, sitting back as the waiter cleared their plates. "Your job there. And . . ." She remembered the photo on his mother's phone. Fletcher and the beautiful young blonde. Regardless of what Charly said, that cozy shot looked more than neighborly. "And your friends," she added.

"I guess."

Did his eyes look sad? His shrug too forced?

"Coffee?" Fletcher asked, raising his voice over a chorus of laughter and tinkling glass at the bar, just beyond. "And dessert?"

"No dessert. Just hot tea." Macy's lips quirked. "Being dressed for the gym doesn't mean this girl burned any calories. After we finish, we'll just split the check and—"

"No, ma'am. Not happening. I've got this."

Macy narrowed her eyes. "The last time you called me 'ma'am,' you were flashing a gun."

"You should keep that in mind." Fletcher's smile spread slowly. "Okay then." He nodded for the waiter. "You're dressed for it, and I can't get enough of this not-Houston air, so we'll walk off our dinner. Sound like a plan?"

Macy dabbed the napkin at her mouth. "You're the man with the gun."

"And you have two lethal feet. Neither of us should get too cocky."

Macy smiled. The cop had a point.

———

Fletcher turned up the collar on his light jacket against the cool evening breeze, a miracle that had amazed him from the first week he'd moved to Sacramento. He smiled. The capital city was alternately dubbed Camellia City, River City, or City of Trees—these Californians couldn't make up their minds to save themselves. But he'd take their delta breezes wafting off the Sacramento and American Rivers, sometimes dropping the temperature forty degrees in the heat of summer. It was a mercy that allowed folks to sit on their patios without sweltering and made the night feel crisp, like freshly ironed sheets instead of a wrung-out sponge. Breezes that sifted through a woman's hair . . . like Macy Wynn's right now.

She strode, tall and confident, in a mesmerizing sway of that purple top over the black tights, down the raised boardwalks that lined the cobbled streets. Past the *Delta King*, a huge paddle-wheel steamboat–turned–floating hotel, then an old-fashioned candy store with floor-to-ceiling barrels of sweets, a comedy theater spilling music from its doors, and several touristy T-shirt shops—Macy covered ground like she was intent on creating her own breeze. Even six inches taller, he'd found himself lengthening his stride to match hers.

"I still can't get over it," Fletcher told her as they sidestepped a huge display of Mylar balloons. "This night air you have here. I want to bottle it up and ship it to Houston—the cicadas wouldn't know what to do with it." He smiled at her, enjoying the way the streetlamps and shadows played with the planes of her face. "The people either. It could throw the whole culture into a tailspin. Folks walking and talking faster, like . . ."

"Me?" She peered sideways at him. "Are you teasing me?"

"Just stating the facts, ma'am."

She slowed a bit, shaking her head. "People always say that; I think it's the ER nurse thing. Always moving, watching over everything, ready to manage chaos. It's what I do."

It was. He'd seen it more than once. Out there on the freeway with that injured schoolgirl. With Dr. Carlyle in the parking lot today. And with his mother yesterday, moving like a stealthy cat around the trauma room, making sure things were done just right. "I admire that. You're good at what you do. Even if you give me shin splints."

An old-fashioned carriage carrying several giggling children moved past, the horse's huge feet clopping slowly along the cobblestones. Macy made an observable effort to walk more leisurely, close enough beside him that he caught the scent of almonds again. He fought an implausible and foolish urge to take her hand. It only proved she was right: he missed home . . . and Jessica. Though he could count on one hand the times, beyond childhood, they'd ever held hands. And now all she could talk about was some fool named Ben.

"It's the California State Railroad Museum," Macy was saying. They'd reached the end of Front Street and stood at a large redbrick building.

"My parents have been there a couple of times," Fletcher remembered, glancing up. He squinted into the deepening shadows. "I guess there's part of Old Town that's underground?"

"Taylor and I took the tour last year. This part of the city was originally about ten feet lower, and they raised it back in the 1860s. Lifted the streets up on jacks and rebuilt. Actually diverted the rivers." Macy shook her head. "Amazing they could do that. There's all these old brick walls down there. And storefronts. It was used mostly as storage, but some businesses moved underground after the streets were raised. A few brothels, a Chinese herbalist. The railroad drew lots of Chinese here."

Distant ancestors? Fletcher wondered, not for the first time. Macy's features were definitely intriguing, but she'd never mentioned anything about her family.

"Anyway . . ." She glanced toward the Sacramento River, close enough to smell its viscid green water on the breeze. "During the gold rush this was a busy little city. But too close to the rivers, so flooding was a huge problem."

"You don't need to tell a Houston boy that floods can be wicked. They're as common as cockroaches back home. We had a tropical storm last summer that spawned a small tornado—took my neighbor's roof half-off."

"Jessica's roof?"

"Right. But how did you know about her?"

"Your mother." Macy walked a few steps to a mock-up of a mining cart. Leaned against it. "I saw that cute photo of the two of you on her phone. In costume."

Great. He was glad it was dark enough that Macy couldn't see his face. He couldn't believe they were talking about this. "Jessica and her sister lived next door to us for a lot of years."

"You're close."

"Sure." Fletcher settled against the cart. How could he explain it? "A big reason my folks chose the house was that there were lots of kids in the neighborhood. I don't have any . . ." He hesitated. "My sister was killed about a year before we moved to that house."

Macy cleared her throat. "I'm sorry."

"It was a long time ago."

And sometimes it felt like yesterday. The truck careening out of control, jumping that curb. Beth in the red wagon, the handle yanked from his hand so hard it tore his skin and slammed his chin onto the ground. That awful screech of metal shredding over cement. Beth's single confused cry as she disappeared under the tires. His mother screaming and screaming . . .

"A drunk driver ran up onto the sidewalk. Knocked us down like so many bowling pins."

"Oh no."

"Mom was diagnosed with breast cancer almost five years to the day later." He shook his head. "We were all scared, but it was like she knew if she could handle what happened with Beth—trust God to get her through that— she'd beat cancer. And she did."

"Then she got leukemia."

"Yeah." Fletcher frowned. "And now she has leukemia."

"Lousy deal."

"No kidding," he agreed, "but you don't tell Mom that. She's sure there's a plan for this too."

"You mean God's plan."

"That's right."

"You believe that?" Macy asked, studying his face. "That

the God of the universe has some sort of cosmic spread-sheet with all of us accounted for? Each tiny human speck? Every trajectory?"

Fletcher smiled, not surprised the ever-practical Macy would phrase it that way. "If you're asking, do we matter . . . count? Then, yes, of course I believe that. And I don't ever doubt that there's a master plan—a hopeful one. That's the promise. God, by our side in all things. But . . ." He sighed. "We don't get to see that spreadsheet. Or know the timing. That's where faith steps in."

"I don't know." Macy shifted against the cart, crossed her arms. "How long can you keep that kind of trust before you have to accept that you're banging on the wrong door?"

Fletcher didn't answer. He told himself it was because of that age-old advice about avoiding religion and politics—he'd already tossed far more out there than he'd meant to. But the fact was, he'd give a whole lot to get a look at that divine spreadsheet right now.

"I mean, if you don't even consider the mess this whole world is in," Macy continued, "maybe only look at this last week." She raised her hand to count on her fingers. "The shooter on the freeway, Mrs. Harrell's brain bleed, your mother, the dog today—did you see the photo of that deputy's sobbing kids?"

"No." Fletcher shook his head, thinking it could have just as easily been their father who was killed. Maybe the sniper had been aiming for the K-9 officer. . . .

"And then there's Andi. There's nobody as unselfish as that woman, more caring—about everyone. She never judges. Do you know how many times she sat down with

Bob Harrell to talk with him about his mother, answer questions . . . listen to him? Did you know she *prayed* for that family?" She glanced sideways at Fletcher. "Everyone who knows Dr. Carlyle knows about her faith—if they missed it, it's just a matter of time. God's first on her speed dial. And then today that man runs her down. Never looks back." Macy's breath caught. "She'll be lucky if she's able to walk inside of six months. Of course, that's if she doesn't die from a fat embolus or a clot to her lung."

Fletcher grimaced, torn between ordering her to stop talking and the urge to fold her into his arms.

"Andi's pregnant," Macy added, barely above a whisper. "She told everybody just this week. Brought cupcakes and a copy of the ultrasound. Fourteen weeks along. A kid couldn't be more wanted. Couldn't ask for a better home. But with the surgery and the stress, that baby might not survive." She shivered, hugged her arms around herself. "Where's God in all of that?"

———

"Macy . . ."

"I have a sister," she whispered, not letting Fletcher answer her question. "Her name is Leah." Macy wished she could stop, but she was so tired, and there was something about the kindness in this man's eyes, the way he'd shared all that about his own family. "She's twenty-four now. But before a few weeks ago, the last time I saw her, she was only fourteen."

Fletcher's brows scrunched.

"She's not a blood relative," Macy explained, feeling the

familiar ache in her chest, "but she's still family. We . . . met in foster care. When I was nine."

"In San Francisco?"

"Near there." Macy waited for a moment, listening to a boat's bell somewhere on the river, dull and lonely against the peals of childish laughter on the boardwalk. "My mother died in a fire when I was six. There were a lot of foster homes."

"No other family?" Somehow Fletcher had stepped closer, enough that her elbow brushed his jacket sleeve as she crossed her arms. "Your father . . . ?"

"Not in the picture." Even fatigue couldn't weaken her enough to say more than that. "Only Leah."

"She's here? In Sacramento?"

"In Tucson. I'd been trying to find her for so long and then, sort of out of the blue, she called me."

"That must have felt good."

"Mmm-hmm." Macy nodded, wishing that there were some way to make "good" feel the way it did for people like Fletcher Holt. How could he possibly understand that in her life, good had been only temporary? She knew better than to trust beyond that.

"That's a lot of catching up to do," he said, voice deep and gentle.

"She's thinking she might want to work in the medical field," Macy told him, for no other reason than she wanted to hear how it sounded out loud. Test it. "Maybe become a nurse."

"That's great." Fletcher's jacket brushed Macy's arm again. "She couldn't have a better role model."

Tears gathered without warning. "Leah's always been this sweet, trusting girl. Like a lost, hungry kitten almost. The ones that twine around your legs and want attention so badly . . ." Macy wished she could stop talking or take off running. "Leah's in trouble. Drugs. It's not the first time. I'm trying to help her, but . . ." She was trembling now, and it only got worse as Fletcher's arm slid around her shoulders. It loosed the sob she'd struggled to hold back all day. Tears spilled over. "I'm so sorry. I never cry. But I can't stop—"

"Macy . . . here."

Fletcher drew her to him, held her close against his chest to still her shivers, his stubbled chin brushing her temple and his arms strong and capable. Macy closed her eyes, heard his muffled heartbeat beneath her ear. Whether they stood that way for several minutes or only a few seconds, she didn't know. But it was long enough that she finally relaxed, let Fletcher's caring warmth, if only for a moment, be the "good" in her day.

"It's okay," he told her, lips against her hair. "Don't worry. I've got you."

20

MACY SET THE CELL PHONE beside the student loan documents and reached for her mug of tea. Not her usual green, but cinnamon today. Nonni's favorite. The day begged for it. This morning she'd ridden fifteen miles along the American River bike trail as a small scattering of leaves crunched under her tires. There had been a refreshing nip in the air and an earthy breeze made fragrant by the trees that lined the trail: willows, huge oriental planes with bark that peeled like puzzle pieces, liquidambar, and Chinese pistache— come autumn their leaves would go crimson, orange, and a showstopping gold. Like the paint on Tower Bridge.

"You folks take that whole California 'mother lode' thing seriously."

Macy's stomach shivered without warning. Fletcher Holt.

She would have turned down his invitation, absolutely, if she hadn't been so tired and heart-weary after what had happened with Andi. But she'd turned down Elliot's offer of a dinner, the very same menu. What was it about Fletcher? He was good-looking—very. She'd been aware of it even when he'd made her so furious out there on the freeway. Ordering her to turn over the care of that injured girl and threatening to arrest Elliot for driving under the influence. And then he'd protected her when the sniper sprayed the highway with rifle fire.

Macy sighed. Maybe that explained it: she'd accepted the cop's invitation out of gratitude. Even if he'd beaten her to the check—and spared her from sharing Chipotle leftovers with a mooching Labradoodle.

Macy smiled, thinking of Fletcher's admission about his cat. A six-toed, laser-chasing Maine coon. Mentioning the animal at all was a slip he'd clearly regretted. A cat owner wasn't how he saw himself. Apparently he'd offered to adopt a bird dog, but the pet rescue volunteer had started to quote grim kill statistics and . . . If Macy had to guess, she'd say this man probably saw himself as a rescuer, even beyond the badge and gun. Certainly with his mother; he'd put his life on hold in Houston to come out here, volunteered his bone marrow. Macy knew how that rescuer instinct felt.

She pulled her mug close to her chest. She shouldn't have told Fletcher all those things about Leah, shouldn't have let her guard down and cried. Macy couldn't remember the last time she'd weakened enough to let that happen. Fletcher had felt obligated to comfort her. . . .

Her embarrassment gave way to a memory of how it

had felt to be held close in his arms. His solid strength, the warmth of his breath against her hair as he tried to soothe her tears. *"It's okay. . . . Don't worry. . . ."* He'd said almost the same thing to her on the freeway when she'd been anxious for paramedics to arrive on scene. Maybe it was something he learned at the law enforcement academy, an assurance he uttered by rote now. The way a nurse approaching an anxious patient for an injection might promise, *"I'm going to do this as gently as I can."*

It wasn't personal; she knew that. But what happened between them had kept her awake half the night, thinking. Not about Fletcher—about her sister. About how to really help her this time. Because if Leah was ever going to have that future she dreamed of, it wasn't going to happen by parroting a list of twelve-step pledges or pinning her hopes on the man who got them both arrested. And though Nonni, Andi Carlyle, Taylor, and Charly Holt and her son would disagree, Leah's happily ever after wasn't going to be assured by a divine and hopeful plan. Macy meant exactly what she said to Fletcher last night: at some point you had to accept that putting all your trust in God was like knocking on the wrong door. That point was long past for Macy. She trusted herself, period. And now *she* had a plan.

She reached for her phone, refreshed the screen still displaying the calculator she'd used to check and recheck her finances. Figuring remaining debt, her frugal expenses—where they could be cut additionally—savings to date, an estimate of what she could earn in overtime, plus a loan from her 403(b) account . . .

Macy's pulse quickened. It would take all she had. But this was for Leah. She owed her that much.

She closed the calculator app, brought up her list of contacts, tapped the number. Waited as it rang.

"Macy!" Elliot laughed. "You read my mind. I was just going to—"

"I want to buy a house, Elliot. Right away."

"Well, that's . . . great." There was no hiding the surprise in his voice. "Glad to hear it. That's a smart decision. We'll talk about it over lunch. I'll bring the newest property listings from my broker and—"

"I don't need a list," she interrupted. "I know the house I want. It's a foreclosure. Vacant." Macy glanced toward the well-worn brass latch set lying on the table beside her mug of tea. It was going to fit perfectly; she had never been so sure of anything. It was the right door. She could already imagine Leah crossing the threshold.

"Where's it located?" Elliot asked.

"In Tahoe Park."

———

"It's a fine balance—and a risk," Andi told them. She adjusted the oxygen cannula in her nostrils, grimacing as it rubbed against the raw and weeping abrasions on her cheek. "Thinning the blood to prevent clots while not endangering my pregnancy." Her brave smile hinted at the familiar dimples. "I'm glad I'm not the doc on this mess. But I have to trust that it's going to be all right." She glanced between Taylor and Seth Donovan. "How is Bob? Have you heard?"

"Still at behavioral health," Taylor told her, thinking this doctor looked no more than twelve years old lying in the ICU bed. Face and forehead shiny with antibiotic ointment, one eye swollen partially shut. Her left arm lay swathed in bandages and a sling, though there had been no bone fractures. The staff was monitoring several deep puncture wounds for signs of infection. Investigators estimated the big truck's grille had caught her there, at the same instant the bumper shattered her leg and flung her—

Taylor fought a wave of dizziness, forced herself to concentrate on Andi's question, not memories of Greg's accident. "The only real information I've heard about Bob Harrell is what the media is reporting."

"Speculating," Seth countered, his expression saying he was far too familiar with that. His voice, however, was filled with gentle concern. "At least in here you're not subjected to all that. Do you remember much of what happened before you were struck?"

"More of it now." Andi shook her head. "It's so silly, but I remember drinking tea from my Keebler mug. And being selfishly relieved that Bob decided not to wait in my office after all. Matt and I were going to shop for a crib."

Taylor's heart tugged. "And then Bob found you in the parking lot."

"They'd made the decision to take his mother off life support. His family did—I don't think Bob was on board. He didn't trust doctors. I got that from the first day in the ER; he didn't believe I'd done all I could. I went over it with him on at least a half-dozen separate occasions. I know Dr. Laureano did too—we all tried."

"There was nothing you could say that would have

changed things," Taylor offered. "He had issues none of us were aware of." For some reason she thought of that burn patient, Ned Archer, who bolted from the ER. She made a mental note to call his neighbor today. "Sometimes a situation just sets people off."

"And then it's a matter of proximity. Lucky me." Andi glanced between them, tears springing to her eyes. "I'm more than lucky—I'm blessed. Family and friends. How's my team doing down in the ER?"

"Hanging in there as best we can." Taylor glanced at Seth. "The director's asked a crisis team to meet with the staff. Sort of touch bases." She hesitated. The last thing she wanted was to burden Andi with any of this. "Folks are a little edgy with all the sniper news coverage. And now . . . this."

"Now me." Andi wiped at her eye. "I think it's good what you're doing. Let them know they're being supported and encourage them to keep an eye on each other. Safety-wise and emotionally too. Medical people . . . we want to believe we're immune. Unbreakable."

Taylor and Seth excused themselves when two sheriff's department detectives arrived to interview Andi, promising they'd reassure the ER staff that she was hanging in there. They walked toward the emergency department, each saying very little. Taylor was certain Seth was going over the plan for their meeting with the staff. She was more focused on tamping down her reaction to seeing Andi like that, knowing she'd been mowed down by that truck on purpose.

Seth came to a halt along the ER corridor. "Are you going to be okay with this? Being part of the staff debriefing?"

"I think so. I've taken part in a few now. So . . ."

He met her gaze. "I meant personally. Andi's in that ICU because of a car-versus-pedestrian incident. Maybe too much like Greg's death."

"Did Charly say that? Earlier, when you went up to visit her?"

Seth's lips twitched. "We might have shared some mutual concern."

"I think I'm okay with it. It's just . . ."

Seth stepped closer. "What is it, Taylor?"

"What I said to Andi. That nothing she could have said to Bob Harrell would have changed what happened out there in the parking lot. Maybe . . ." Taylor's voice cracked.

Seth waited.

"Maybe there *was* something I could have said—should have said—to keep Greg from being out there that night."

———

"What the—?" Fletcher sputtered, avoiding a mouthful of fur as Hunter's tail feather-dusted his face. A final flourish in her perfect-ten Olympic vault from breakfast bar to stool to a perch atop his leather recliner. He laughed as a six-toed paw batted his cheek. "Okay, I'm impressed. C'mere, bird dog."

He lifted the cat into his lap, heard her immediate rumbling purr. Then checked his coffee for stray hairs. He'd never intended to mention this crazy animal to Macy, but he was glad the story made her laugh—they'd shared more than a few laughs last night. He smiled, remembering their evening, from her playful threat to plant a foot in the center of his chest, to the way she'd savored every flaky bite of the grilled salmon, to how the setting sun seemed to set fire to that crazy cherry-cola stripe in her long, black hair. She probably didn't notice the heads turning as they walked to their table, admiring the tall, long-limbed woman with compelling, even exotic, features. An obvious athlete; he'd have guessed that even without her mention of the gym and bicycle. That confident stride, air of competence and strength. Yet . . .

Fletcher scraped his fingers along his jaw, recalling their conversation in front of the train museum. The talk had turned so unexpectedly from history and weather to his sister's death, his mother's cancer, and Charly's strong faith even in the face of all of that. Then to his own personal belief. It was obvious Macy had doubts, questions when it came to faith. *"How long can you keep that kind of trust before you have to accept that you're banging on the wrong door?"* How could she not have doubts? After being raised in foster care, having an absent father, and still all that turmoil with her sister . . .

Macy's tears had taken Fletcher by surprise. His reaction, pulling her close, attempting to comfort her, had been purely instinctive. The same way he'd block a punch, draw his duty weapon. A necessary response, no thinking. Except in hindsight. He'd turned the scene over and over in his mind until late last night. How she'd felt in his arms—much softer than she appeared—the scent of her hair, and the smooth warmth of her skin against his. But mostly he'd found himself recalling how quiet she'd been after she stepped away from him, so distant afterward though they'd walked close together to his Jeep. He doubted Macy said more than a few sentences on the drive back to the hospital parking lot. Even then, it was only to speculate on the weather for her morning bike ride and make a polite remark about his mother. It was clear Macy regretted confiding in him. And that his instinct to hold her had been all wrong. But what did it really matter? It wasn't as if he was interested in—

Hunter twitched as Fletcher's phone buzzed on the arm of the recliner. Fletcher grabbed for it before she could pounce.

"Macy, hi." The uptick in his pulse made him a liar. *She does matter.*

"Did I catch you at a bad time?"

"Talking myself into getting ready for work. What's up?"

"I wanted to ask how it went. Your mother's hospital discharge and getting her home."

"Fine. But I had to make her promise she'd rest and not start baking cookies for the hospital staff."

It sounded like Macy sighed. "What kind of cookies?"

"Oatmeal probably. With pecans. When I was a kid, I'd know it as soon as I opened the door."

"Sounds . . . great." Macy's voice was funny. "Well, I'd better get going. I just wanted to check on your mother. And . . . thank you again for dinner."

"You're welcome." The awkwardness was back. On both sides, he guessed. Fletcher kept his voice casual. "Are you heading out for that bike ride?"

"No. Did fifteen miles before breakfast. I'm running errands. And then I have an appointment at my bank."

———

He inched forward on his belly, over the old Buick's ripped-apart backseat and down into the dark trunk space. Then pointed the rifle barrel toward the four-inch hole he'd cut, resting the stock on an old Amazon box. It was exactly the right height to steady his aim from this distance. He shouldn't have worried so much about parking; the cops were tracking white vans. He'd counted seven on his way here. No one was looking for a 1992 LeSabre. But he'd switched out the license plates anyway.

He shifted position, wincing as his arm bumped a stack of ammo boxes crammed between two gas cans. The fumes made his eyes water. Crowded in here and lying downhill on his belly was more than uncomfortable. He groaned, remembering his father's words as they crawled over buck-brush and through blackberry thickets that bit into skin like barbed wire. *"Quit your whining, Son. Man up. You want your shot or don't you?"*

He needed this shot.

It took patience, but he'd do it. Lie here, wait. Make sure he had everything right. He shifted the box a quarter of an inch to the left, slid the barrel forward, and squinted through the scope. Perfect. Even from across the street, the sign looked close enough to trace a finger over the letters: *Southside Bank.*

21

"THIS CHECKLIST WILL HELP YOU gather the few remaining items we'll need," the loan officer explained. "Does that help?"

"Yes, I think so."

Macy would bet her next paycheck this bank employee wasn't much older than she was. Though her classic gray suit, perfectly cut hair, and pearls—who had real pearls that young?—made her seem older, far more accomplished. And made Macy wish she had more than two decent outfits beyond hospital scrubs. She wasn't sure she'd been successful in cleaning the stains off the knit top she was wearing right now. Annie Sims's blood, from the freeway shooting incident. But great clothes had never been a priority—couldn't be. It was month to month, pay the bills, and save for the future. And now the future was here, not-quite-white blouse or not.

"Because your checking and savings accounts are here at Southside Bank, it will make things a bit easier," the woman explained. "Maybe cut some time off the process. I understand you're eager to make an offer on that house." Her smile was whiter than her pearls. "Your first home. Such a big step. I'm excited for you."

Macy struggled to quell her shaking insides. "I'll get the prequalification letter, then?"

"I can't say officially. We need the rest of those items on the list. Including that employment verification from Sacramento Hope. But . . ." The young woman glanced at the printout of Elliot's latest e-statement. The trust set up by Lang Wen. "But I would think your income, credit rating, and *very* substantial assets are more than enough to obtain a loan of this size."

What would happen to that pearly smile if Macy confessed she had no intention whatsoever of using a dime of the trust money? If she told this loan officer that, despite what it said on that paper, Macy Wynn—not Wen—refused to be seen as an almost millionaire? The very idea made her ill. What Southside Bank saw right now was what they'd get: a nurse in a tainted blouse, willing to spend all of her savings, take a loan on her retirement account, and commit to working bruising overtime . . . *because I love my sister. And she needs a home.*

"Great," Macy managed, watching as the loan officer slid the paperwork into a folder embellished with the bank's logo. "I'll get that back to you."

"Fax or e-mail is fine. The contact information is on my card. In the folder."

"Good—thanks." Macy picked up her cell phone and stood, grateful her knees weren't as wobbly as they felt.

The loan officer came around the desk and offered her hand. "Thank you, Miss Wynn. I'll look forward to—"

"Help!" An elderly man with a cane lurched through a side door of the bank, expression frantic. "Get some help. A woman collapsed in the parking lot. She's on the ground. Out cold."

"Call 911," Macy instructed, pointing her finger at the loan officer, "and watch my purse—I'll go see what I can do to help." She took off at a jog, dodging customers and personnel already moving toward the door. "Let me through. I'm a nurse."

"She's over there." The man hobbled back through the open door, pointed his cane. "On the ground in the employee parking lot. It's right next to the handicapped spaces."

"Right behind you, miss," a balding security guard rasped, hurrying forward. "That's the lot to your right."

In moments, Macy saw her. A young woman sprawled on her side on the asphalt, motionless. Fainting episode? Seizure? Possible diagnoses tumbled through Macy's brain as she closed the distance. She dropped to her knees.

"Ma'am . . . hey." Macy grasped the woman's shoulder, her concerns doubling. Too pale—far too pale. Eyes open, ominously vacant . . . *Is she even breathing?*

"Make sure an ambulance is on its way!" Macy shouted to the security guard as she hurried to cradle the woman's head, open her airway, and—*blood?* Macy pulled her hand back, stared. Her palm was dripping with bright-red blood. The back of this woman's head, her scalp, was gushing. How could that—?

There was a sharp cracking sound. The security guard crumpled to the asphalt.

A man shouted in the distance. "Someone's shooting!"

No.

Everything happened in a blur—people running, screaming. *What should I do? What . . . ?* Macy crouched lower, heart pounding her senseless as her gaze darted toward the distance, then back to the bleeding woman next to her and the downed guard.

"Leave us, miss," the security guard pleaded, eyes intense as they gripped Macy's. He coughed, blood speckling his lips. "Go hide. . . . Save yourself. *Go!*"

There was another sharp crack, and Macy's vision tunneled down to survival circumference, its periphery as black as the asphalt tearing into her palms and knees as she belly-crawled, gulping at the air in terrified gasps, toward the thick shrubbery ahead. Closer cover than the nearest car. *Stay low. Keep moving.* Odds said she had a better chance to survive than those people on the ground. But the shooter wouldn't stop until—

I won't let you kill me.

Macy's knuckles smacked the curb, and she heaved herself onto her knees, then flung her body shoulder-first at a shrub. Branches tore at her face, yanked her hair as she struggled to disappear inside its foliage, hide herself. Finally, teeth chattering but determined to her core, she grasped the thick, peeling trunk and hauled herself in. Then she drew her legs up and hugged them tight, head down. A fetus in a hostile womb. No, a warrior—she'd do this. Had to. For herself and for Leah. But . . . Macy thought of that poor woman, the guard, and fought back a surge of bile. There was nothing she could do for them now. And if she didn't stop trembling, she'd shake this entire shrub. The shooter would see that. And she'd be a goner too. She was too tough to be that stupid.

Macy ignored her cramping muscles, talked herself out of making a run for it half a dozen times . . . waited endlessly, straining to hear more bullets or sounds of rescue. She lost track of time, had no idea how long she'd been there. Only that—

Her phone buzzed in her pocket, bringing another vicious wave of trembling. She didn't want to imagine what could have happened if it wasn't muted. . . . Was anyone coming to help?

Someone laid on a car horn. Sirens wailed. The air thrummed. A helicopter?

"Stay inside. Stay under cover—nobody move!"

Boots thudding. Coming her way? Macy's heart had wedged so tightly in her throat she could barely breathe. *Is it him? The shooter?* She'd fight. She had to. She raised a fist close to her lips, then recoiled when she tasted the coppery salt of the dead woman's blood on her fingers.

More boots. Voices.

"Two down. Bank employees. Looks like at least one fatality. Ambulance is standing by, but we can't let them in until—"

Cops. Macy's chin sagged to her chest, a rush of relief making her physically weak.

Another set of boots. "It came in as a medical aid call. Fire got here ahead of the first patrol car. Then dispatch got flooded with reports about a shooter and a car speeding away. They moved civilians from the parking lot into the bank through the side door . . . the injured guard, too."

"What about that nurse? The one who ran outside to help—did anyone find her?"

"Here." Macy shoved against the shrub's trunk, swept the branches aside. "I'm here," she called out in a voice she barely recognized. "I'm coming out."

———

Fletcher's heart stalled as Macy entered the side door of the bank, escorted by two officers. He'd heard on his radio that they'd found her but couldn't let himself believe it until he saw her with his own eyes. *She's okay. Thank you, Lord.*

"It's the nurse," a deputy said, nodding in that direction. "The one the loan officer was talking about. Looks like we won't have to add kidnapping to this sorry scenario."

"No." A hostage situation had been Fletcher's first thought after recognizing Macy's Audi in the parking lot, then hearing she was missing.

No, his first thought had been that this courageous, take-charge nurse had been hit, and they'd find her body under one of the parked cars. He'd called her cell phone but gotten no answer. The last fifteen minutes had felt like hours.

"She looks okay, considering." Fletcher watched as Macy declined the offer of a blanket from one of the firefighters.

If they tried to check her over, they wouldn't have an easy task. But then none of this was easy for anyone.

He glanced around the bank; the building had become a temporary shelter until people could be safely moved to another building—once it was determined this was no longer an active shooter scenario. It had been so chaotic, the incident morphing from a call for medical aid to a possible bank robbery to what now appeared to be a third sniper episode. Officers from every agency had raced to the scene. The dead woman, still outside, was thirty-two and had recently been promoted to a management position . . .

"Command post is set up two blocks north," the other deputy advised. "SWAT's en route. If we can't get that ambulance in here in the next few minutes, we'll need to load that security guard into one of our cars and drive him out to meet it."

"I'm parked right outside the doors," Fletcher said.

His gaze moved to the area manned by county fire, where a lone paramedic accompanying the fire truck was kneeling on the carpet beside the security guard. The man had a bullet wound in his upper chest. With a collapsed lung, someone had heard, and maybe spinal cord injuries. Getting him to a level II trauma center was critical. If they wanted to load him into Fletcher's car, it was fine with him.

The big-screen TV mounted to pacify waiting customers had been switched from the Food Channel to local news.

"Residences and businesses immediately surrounding the bank," the anchor was saying, "remain on lockdown. Traffic continues to be diverted, only emergency vehicles allowed in or out. The identities of the shooting victims are being withheld at this time. We have word that a bank customer, a local nurse, attempted to give aid to the victims and—"

"One lucky nurse," the other deputy opined. "Medic said that bank employee was probably dead before she hit the ground."

"Yeah . . . lucky nurse." Fletcher's pulse quickened as Macy's eyes connected with his across the room. "I'm going over there."

He tried not to wince at her appearance as he got closer: multiple scratches on her face, mussed hair littered with leaves, blood smears on her hands and down the front of her shirt. There was that anxious look in her eyes, the same as before, on the freeway. Fletcher forced a grim smile. "We should stop meeting like this."

"We should." Macy reached a shaky hand toward her hair, then stopped, staring at her fingers. "I need to wash. Where's the—?"

"I'll take you there," he offered, resisting a strong urge to scoop Macy up in his arms, carry her out of here . . . save her from all this. He caught the eye of a firefighter instead. "I'm going to show Miss Wynn to the ladies' room."

"Fine by me."

If he'd thought Macy was quiet on that walk to the car last night, it was nothing in comparison to this. His mother would say it was traumatic shock. And she'd probably be right, though he would expect Macy to deny it to the bitter end. "A chaplain team will be available when we get folks to the other building," he heard himself say.

She stretched a stained hand toward the door and turned

to look at him. "I'm fine. But I should call my sister. In case my name gets out—I guess it's possible. Tucson news might cover this."

"Might." Fletcher decided no good would come from telling her the news had already gone national, maybe even international by now. US shootings, especially involving a sniper still at large, incited a media feeding frenzy. Macy would be hounded without mercy.

"I got my purse back, but I can't find my cell phone. I think I must have dropped it when I was crawling out of the bushes."

"Don't worry," Fletcher said, seeing in her expression a first glimpse of the vulnerable and lost child she'd been. "We'll get you connected with your sister."

"Thank you." Her beautiful eyes shone with unshed tears.

Somehow he was going to find a way to make this better for Macy.

When she emerged from the restroom five minutes later, the leaves were gone from her hair. She'd cleaned the scratches on her face and rid herself of the blood on her hands—as well as that earlier look of vulnerability. Now he saw hints of the kickboxer.

"Better," Macy told him. Then frowned as one of the other officers beckoned to her. "I guess I'm going to have to answer a lot of questions. Even if I know absolutely nothing."

"We're ready to move folks out of the bank," Fletcher explained, glad to see additional paramedics coming through the door; the ambulance had been allowed in. "You'll be sequestered at another site, a restaurant across the street.

Witnesses will be interviewed by detectives and probably the FBI, too. It's important. Sometimes when you retell an incident, new details come to mind. And that could be very helpful to the investigation." He caught her gaze. "After all that, when they let you go home, will your roommate be there?"

"Roommates. Two. But one is in Colorado visiting family and the other works weekends in Fresno; she stays over with a friend. I babysit her dog." Macy rubbed the side of her neck. "I'm comfortable being alone, if that's what you're asking."

"I was only going to say that I'm working swings, but I could drop by." He hoped his shrug was casual. "Check on things and see if you need anything."

"I'm sure I won't. Thank you, but no."

———

It wasn't until Macy got home and switched on the TV news that the horror of it really struck her. The full-color, HD reality: aerial footage of the bank and the church parking lot across the street. With a fuzzy, distant image of what was apparently a fresh oil stain on the church asphalt—perhaps, investigators speculated, where the shooter's vehicle had sat as he lay in wait.

Then came photos of the victims. That young accounts manager, her résumé photo and a candid shot taken on a beach vacation with her husband and two small children. The security guard was a grandfather to eight. He'd survived surgery for the chest wound but would likely live the rest of his life as a paraplegic. One news channel even showed a photo of the dead police dog and several shots from the initial freeway incident, including a close-up of a cracked windshield that looked a lot like the bullet damage to Elliot's BMW.

"We should stop meeting like this."

Fletcher had tried to offer her comfort today. Like he had last night in Old Town. That seemed so long ago now. But his grim cliché had been true. One of the TV reporters implied the same thing when they flashed a publicity photo of Macy taken at the chaplaincy gala. "This Sacramento Hope emergency department nurse offered aid at two of the three sniper incidents. What are the chances of that?"

Macy didn't believe for a moment that she was some sort of target, though theories on the shooter's motives were coming fast and furious. FBI profilers would eventually put the puzzle together. Meanwhile, she was left to face the very real fact that she'd come close to death twice in the past ten days. It only served to reinforce what Macy had always believed: there was no certainty in this life. She could only count on herself. And that made it all the more important to—

She reached for her phone, returned by the sheriff's department. Tapping Leah's contact listing, she waited while it rang . . . and rang. Then went to voice mail. Again. Macy caught sight of the bank folder she'd set on the table next to the old brass door set. "Hey, sis," she began after taking a slow breath. "I'm still fine, just like I told you in my message earlier. But give me a call back. I want to tell you something else. Something I know you're going to like. Love you."

Macy disconnected. She took a sip of her tea, then hugged her arms around herself as tightly as when she hid in that awful bush today. She tested the words out loud for the first time.

"I'm buying that house, Leah. We're finally going to have a home."

22

Fletcher pulled off Florin Road into an empty parking lot and let the patrol car idle as he lowered the driver's window. The chaplain pulled alongside, angling his SUV so they were as near to face-to-face as they could be—without a couple of Starbucks cups. A much better idea, except Fletcher had no time. Between shift trades and overtime, he'd missed church too.

"Swing shift yesterday and here you are back again." Seth shook his head, reaching into his pocket for his ever-present antacids. "You'll be asleep before the Giants' seventh-inning stretch."

"Fully caffeinated." Fletcher lifted his gas station paper cup. "Had to be downtown early for a big multiagency briefing."

"The shooter." Seth's forehead wrinkled. "He's directing my day too. Taylor and I are doing a debriefing with the

Sacramento Hope ER staff, and then I'll be talking with the bank employees this afternoon." He turned his head to glance toward the road. "You notice how light the traffic is? Even for a Sunday. Freeway too. Folks are afraid to go out. Good night to be in the pizza business—unless you're the nervous delivery guy."

"That fits the scattered MO as well as everything else: gravel trucks, German shepherds, bank employees . . ."

"I saw a clip of Macy Wynn on the morning news."

"That photo from the gala." Fletcher had seen it too. Macy with Elliot Rush. Probably the only photo they could get; she wasn't posing for the media.

"And a new video clip—short one. Some eager-beaver reporter caught her on a bike trail this morning and tried to get an eyewitness statement." Seth smiled. "What he almost got was tire marks on his back."

"Can't say I'm surprised."

"I'm glad to see she's out there riding. Physical exercise, resuming normal routines, eating right . . . it's all helpful after a traumatic incident."

"Sounds like you're practicing your debriefing spiel."

"Maybe. And that goes for you too, pal. It wasn't only Macy who's been on scene at two of these shooting episodes. But then I'm sure Charly has offered you a full list of the signs of critical stress."

Fletcher smiled. "Enough to know that if I try the 'It's my job; I'm fine' line, you'll come over here and lay hands on me."

"Count on it. Too many folks need you healthy and happy." Seth lifted a brow. "How's that young woman in Houston?"

"She's . . ." Fletcher realized he hadn't thought of Jessica since his dinner with Macy. Maybe there was an upside to critical stress. "Jessica's fine. Busy. We both are, I guess."

Seth regarded him for a moment, then put the SUV in gear. "I'm outta here. Promised Taylor I'd do a follow-up on one of her chaplain visits. One she did with your mom, as a matter of fact. A no-contact situation with a death notification. He'd moved away. And then this same guy went AWOL from the ER a couple of days ago without his tetanus injection. Phone number didn't work. Since we're involved already, I said I'd try to get new contact information from the neighbor."

"Maybe this guy doesn't like shots. I'm not exactly excited about a stranger coming at me with a needle."

"I hear you." Seth stroked his chin, his tell that he was about to philosophize. "Hard to find somewhere to put your trust these days, with all that's going on in the world, in the government, and right here in our community. Who are you gonna believe, some politician stumping for office? A 24-7 news channel trying to boost ratings? Or maybe that infomercial guy selling the stuff that cleans the pet stains off my carpet . . . and leaves me with six-pack abs."

Fletcher smiled, shaking his head. Seth on his soapbox.

"Everybody's looking for something they can trust," the chaplain continued. "In all the wrong places. Sometimes I just tell them to pull a buck from their wallets. Turn it over and read the line that's printed right there between the eyeball pyramid and the eagle." He smiled at Fletcher. "You know what I mean."

"'In God we trust.'"

"Absolutely. 'Knock and the door will be opened . . .' I learned it the hard way." Seth glanced at his watch. "And now I'd better go see if I can hook a man up with a tetanus booster."

"Catch you later."

Fletcher watched as the chaplain popped his antacids and drove away. Then he thought about what the man had said. And about what Macy told Fletcher at the bank when he offered to come by and check on her. *"I'm comfortable being alone."*

He'd bet it was because she'd never found someone she trusted. *Including me.*

———

Macy glanced up as Taylor joined her at the table she'd chosen. Back of the Starbucks, away from the window. "I'm glad you could meet me."

"I almost didn't recognize you. Sunglasses, hair tucked up in that ball cap—all your disguise needs is one of those fake mustaches." Taylor slid onto her chair and regarded Macy over her latte. There was concern on her face. "Those reporters can be a pain."

Macy warmed her fingers on her mug of Calm brewed tea. "I'll trade you one special agent for three reporters. The Feds kept me for three hours."

"To see if you could recall any details that might identify the shooter?"

Macy's short silence was filled with the steamy hiss of the cappuccino machine and baristas calling out orders. "Yes.

That and making sure I have no connection to him. Three shootings and I'm lucky enough to be at two."

Taylor's eyes widened. "They don't really believe these incidents have something to do with you?"

"I don't think so. Even if the media vampires seem to." Macy lifted her sunglasses, met Taylor's gaze. She had to ask. It was one of the reasons she'd asked Taylor to meet her here. "Does the Sacramento Hope staff think that? Is that why they 'strongly suggested' I take a few days off? Afraid I'm making the hospital a target?"

"No." Taylor sighed. "At least no one said it openly. And several people expressed concern for you, Macy. They love you. We're like a family. You know that."

Macy's throat tightened. She raised her tea to her lips.

"Everyone's edgy. Anxious. It's understandable. After what happened to Andi and now this. All of the shootings happened within a five-mile radius. The hospital's in there too." Taylor nodded. "Seth and I had that debriefing with the staff. I was hoping you'd come."

"I'm banished, and I'm not big on those kinds of things. I do better dealing with stuff on my own. It's nothing personal against you. Really. How'd it go?"

Taylor frowned. "It turned into a major gripe session about hospital security or the chronic lack of it. Nobody feels safe. Seth and I tried to offer coping tips for stress but finally walked away thinking what would help most right now is a thick perimeter of cops." She raised her brows. "Charly mentioned you had dinner with Fletcher."

Heat crept up Macy's neck—she blamed it on the hot tea. "You know I never turn down a free meal. I promise it's

not my personal attempt at a law enforcement perimeter."
She smirked. "I'd be smarter than to choose a cop who's also
been at two of those shootings."

"True." Taylor's expression said she hadn't bought the
whole story. "I won't say another thing—except I like him.
What are you going to do with three days off?"

"I'm getting some paperwork together." Macy's stomach
did a flip-flop. "To buy a house." She'd expected Taylor's
surprise. "That's why I was at the bank. I know it doesn't
sound like me. The girl who can't even commit to a cell
phone plan. I'm not doing it for myself—you know I'm not
choosy about where I live. I'm doing it for Leah. So she'll
finally have some stability in her life. I want that for her."

Taylor pressed her fingers to her chest. "That's so
wonderful."

"We haven't worked out the details yet." Hard to do when
Leah didn't answer her messages. "But Elliot works with
a Realtor, and they're getting the ball rolling. We should
have an offer in by Tuesday. It's . . . it's a great little place. I
haven't even seen the inside yet, but I can tell that it's right."

Taylor smiled. "I know the feeling."

"So anyway . . ." Macy slid her sunglasses back into place
and glanced toward the door. "I thought I'd do another
drive-by. Want to see it?"

Taylor reached for her coffee cup. "Let's go."

———

He crumpled more pages of the newspaper and fed them
into the campfire, making certain the front pages had been
totally consumed. People might come snooping, find the

ashes, and wonder if this homeless person had more than an ordinary interest in the freeway sniper. He frowned; he wasn't sure if he was okay with that name. But maybe it was better than dog murderer or . . . woman killer. His gut roiled. Partly from those frozen burritos he'd tried to cook over the fire and also because this was about so much more than killing a dog or some woman with two kids. No one got that.

He poked at the fire with a piece of river driftwood, remembering what he'd read in the newspaper articles. Those government agents were trying to put it together. But it wouldn't happen. He'd be safe as long as he kept a low profile and didn't do anything dumb again. Like dropping that bullet casing at the freeway.

He lifted a newspaper sheet, saw the photo of that nurse again. It was hard to tell for sure, but she looked Asian . . . or partly. Wynn wasn't a Chinese name. But it didn't mean she didn't have connections overseas. Everybody had connections these days. Everybody was watching. He'd be a fool to trust anyone.

He'd seen the nurse at the bank—through his rifle scope. They said she was at the freeway, too. Speculated that he was stalking her. Only maybe . . . maybe Macy Wynn was following *him*. Knew what he was doing. She worked at Sacramento Hope.

Idiot! This isn't about hospitals . . .

He dropped the stick, cursed. Then pressed his fingers hard against his temples to stop the hissing whispers. And those electric hums that sliced through his brain . . . like his bullet hitting that bank woman. A kill shot. The same as deer hunting. *"Hit him just below the ear, Son; you'll drop him in one shot."* He'd missed with the guard because that Chinese nurse distracted him.

He pressed harder to try to stop the whispers, in a foreign language now. Cursing him? Yes. Branding him a failure. He deserved it.

"I'm sorry, Dad," he whispered into the smoky darkness. "I'll do better next time."

23

"IT NEEDS WORK," Elliot told Macy, frowning at the bare wires hanging from the ceiling in the small foyer. A missing chandelier. He stooped, picked up a single cut-crystal pendant left behind on the scratched hardwood floor. "Have to expect that with a foreclosure. Emotions run high in the months following a loan default—even worse when the sheriff's department finally delivers an eviction notice. Some owners haul off whatever they think they can sell. Sinks, stoves, bathroom vanities . . . doors, fixtures." He pointed at the enameled red door. "Like right there: You can tell the original hardware is gone. The bank just slapped on a cheap door handle and a good dead bolt."

"Hmm . . ." Macy tried to swallow down the ache that had risen the moment the door swung inward. Emotions running high? Elliot didn't know the half of it.

"Hopefully we won't see out-and-out vandalism. It happens too often." He shook his head. "Graffiti on walls, 'surprises' in toilets. I don't get it. That's animal behavior. I suppose they feel they have the right to take things out of the home and don't consider it stealing per se."

Stealing. Macy tasted the metal of that flashlight between her teeth, heard the grating as she unscrewed the brass lock set from Nonni's door. Felt that bittersweet mix of victory and loss as it slid free at last, heavy in her hands. And heart.

"It's not as if the banks can hire security guards on what amounts to thousands of foreclosures. Or rent guard dogs to—"

"I'm going to walk around," Macy said, cutting him off. "See the rest of the house."

"Of course. Let's—"

"By myself." Macy met his gaze. "I want to walk through it alone."

"Sure." Elliot cleared his throat. "Go on ahead. I have a couple of calls to make. Let me know if you have questions."

"I will."

She walked the short hallway to the kitchen, holding her breath. Peered in and then entered. The stove was missing; she could see greasy scrape marks where it had been dragged across the aged tile floor. And the faucets were gone from the stainless-steel sink. But there was a small brick fireplace in the kitchen that hinted at a pizza oven. Someone had lacquered the cabinets in sage green and installed manufactured stone countertops. They were a sort of speckled oatmeal color, plain but clean-looking. And somehow, probably in order of rushed priority, a couple of tall stools had been left at the breakfast bar. With straw seats and painted green to match the cabinets.

Macy closed her eyes, imagining it: Leah laughing around a mouthful of homemade pizza. Macy quizzing her for an upcoming physiology exam. A dog maybe and—*oh, that yard!*

She struggled with the door for a moment, pulled hard, and then stepped outside at last. Her breath caught. Neglected but so beautiful. Morning glory vines climbing the weathered redwood fence. Roses in lush, branch-bending bloom. Trees—an evergreen and several others that cast leafy shadows on the sparse lawn. Macy explored the yard further, spotting empty hummingbird feeders, a wooden frame for a raised garden, a dog run. And there, against the fence: a rusted red wagon, a turtle-shaped sandbox, a pink scooter thick with peeling Barbie stickers . . . In an instant, she felt the brass door latch under her fingers. Smelled those cookies, heard the soft strains of gospel music. *"You're home, Macy girl."*

There was no need to see any more.

She found Elliot back in the living room. Down on his hands and knees, sniffing at a piece of carpet.

"Ah, that was fast," he said, rising quickly. He searched her face. "You seem a little overwhelmed. That's understandable. But try to overlook the flaws, Macy. I know some great, cheap contractors. A few gallons of generic beige paint, definitely some new carpet. I think I smell dog. Replace those missing fixtures, weed-whack the yard, and you'll be surprised at how—"

"Can I put in an offer?"

"Well . . . sure. You've been preapproved. We'll have to get inspections. But I think you're right that it's best to move quickly. This is a desirable neighborhood and the schools—"

"Make the offer today," Macy insisted. "I don't want to lose it."

Elliot smiled, stepped forward, and gave her arm a squeeze. "There's my budding entrepreneur. This will be a good first real estate investment. I'll run the figures, but I'm thinking you might even get a positive cash flow from the rental."

"No." Macy glanced toward the front door, seeing the warm gleam of polished brass. "This won't be a rental. I'm living here. With my sister."

———

"I'm glad Aunt Thena's coming." Fletcher watched from the table as his mother waved a Swiffer duster over the kitchen hutch. Her sister was attending a writers' conference in San Diego and planned to spend a couple of days here before heading back to Texas. Charly insisted that a pesky nosebleed wasn't going to keep her from enjoying the company of the most interesting person in their family.

Fletcher smiled. Thena was a published poet. He hadn't had a birthday he could remember—to date—when he didn't receive a targeted verse or two. Or a single visit when she didn't proudly proclaim, "I speak in rhyme . . . but not all the time." Jessica had a giggle fit the first time she heard it.

"Thena did ask if I thought it was safe." His mother paused, duster in midair. "She heard some theory that since the first two shootings were on Thursdays and the bank incident was on a Saturday, maybe the sniper would 'go dormant' until the weekend. Because it's a pattern."

Fletcher groaned.

"I thought you'd react like that."

"Look, I wish it were true. I hope he, or she, is finished with this shooting spree altogether. But we can't go under either assumption. A woman is dead. That guard is paralyzed. We have to find this guy. Trust me: there's a lot of manpower dedicated to doing exactly that. But . . ."

"But what?"

"What do you and Aunt Thena have planned for while she's here?"

"Nothing definite yet. She's going to help me go through some family photos and work up ideas for a scrapbook." Charly smiled. "I know. I've been saying that for years. But this time I mean it. Beyond that, I'm not sure yet what we'll want to do."

Fletcher tried to make his tone casual. "I'd feel better if you didn't play tourist. Maybe stick closer to home."

His mother pulled up a chair at the table beside him. She reached for her iPad. Her wallpaper image was the photo of Jessica and him—the same one Macy had seen on her phone.

"Do you think it's true," she asked, "that the shooter is staying within a certain target area?"

"The freeway, the school where the dog was shot, and the bank are all within a five- to six-mile radius. Sacramento Hope is in there too."

Charly's eyes met his. "I've been thinking about Macy. Two encounters. She ran to aid victims both times. Such a strong and selfless young woman. But I wish she'd shown up for the staff debriefing with Seth and Taylor."

"She said she does fine alone," Fletcher recalled, knowing as soon as the words left his lips that he was sounding a crisis team alert.

"Macy held that bank manager's bleeding head in her hands. And saw the guard fall." His mother winced. "She had to hide in the bushes to protect herself. Even a strong person feels that. She'd benefit from a listening ear, whether she thinks she needs it or not."

Twenty minutes later, Fletcher told his mother good-bye. Promised he'd stop by in the next day or two for a dose of family poetry. Promised, too, that he'd keep Charly apprised of any major changes in the investigation of the shooter. She was champing at the bit to be out there helping the families of the victims and offering relief to a community becoming increasingly stressed. Even with a flak jacket and a Glock, Fletcher felt the anxiety this situation provoked. There was no way Macy could be immune to it.

Halfway down the street, he pulled over to the curb, picked up his cell, and tapped the contact number.

"Fletcher?" Macy's voice was a little breathless.

"Hey." He reminded himself that this was simply what a friend would do. *Whether she thinks she needs it or not.*

"What's up?"

"I'm on my way to Starbucks," he told her, keeping his voice as casual as it should be. "Needed some coffee. Maybe some company. I'll buy. What do you think?"

Fletcher was sure he heard her brain ticking.

"I'd need you to bring it here. I'm sort of involved in something—can't stop."

"Sure," he told her, surprised she hadn't turned him down. "Tea?"

"Green."

———

"Roommates," Macy said by way of apology for the usual state of the rental house. In truth, she'd done a quick tidying. This would teach her to say yes without thinking. "Three nurses with crazy schedules," she continued, leading Fletcher down the hall toward a small combination family room/kitchen. "So there's always scrub jackets tossed on chairs, a box of Grape-Nuts on an end table, magazines everywhere. I almost sat on a pair of bandage scissors on the couch once, so be careful if you—oh, dear, heads up. Here he comes!"

The Labradoodle shoved past her in the narrow hallway, yipping with unbridled excitement. Macy made a grab for his collar, missed. "No . . . stop!"

"Hey, whoops—whoa there," Fletcher managed as the huge, white, curly-haired animal lunged, rose up on hind legs, tail wagging frantically. "Easy now." He raised the Starbucks tray and paper sack as high as he could to protect them while the dog tried to lap at his chin. "Foot in the middle of my chest—I've been threatened with this before."

"Off!" Macy's face warmed with embarrassment as she hauled at the dog's collar. "I'm so sorry. Come on, Dood. Be good. Down, Dood!"

"What *is* he?"

"Labrador . . . and poodle. Labradoodle." Macy shook her head.

"Okay then. Here, take these." Fletcher handed off the drinks and sack, then gave the dog a vigorous head scratch while easing him down to the floor. He was still wriggling and whining, but at least finally on all four paws. "There you go, guy. Good to meet you, too." He met Macy's gaze, laughed. "What's his name?"

"Dood." Macy sighed, then spelled it aloud. "Like in—"

"Labra*dood*le." Fletcher's blue eyes crinkled at the edges, doing something truly ridiculous to Macy's stomach. "Good one."

The dog pushed past her again, a furry host leading them on. She walked ahead of Fletcher, carrying the things he brought to the coffee table, catching a whiff of something sweet—and willing her pulse to return to normal. Why on earth had she invited this man over here?

"I brought cookies. Oatmeal," Fletcher told her, settling onto an ottoman that looked like Barbie furniture under him. Somehow he managed to seem comfortable. Maybe it was the clothes: worn-soft Levi's, cowboy boots, and a blue cotton shirt, sleeves rolled back over tanned forearms. He wore the shirt untucked. To cover his gun, she'd bet. "And I didn't know if you like sugar or—"

"Black. I mean green. No sugar. And thank you." She settled onto the couch, taking the tea and a cookie from the tray. "This was nice of you."

"No problem—glad to." Fletcher lifted his own cup from the tray and removed the lid, releasing the scent of something dark, rich. He glanced at the array of clothing and hiking gear she'd stacked on the table inches from where he sat. "Yours?"

"Mm-hm. I'm going hiking," she confirmed, blowing on her tea before taking a sip. She wished suddenly that she'd bothered to brush some powder over the scratches on her face. The last time she'd seen him, she'd just emerged from Southside Bank's landscaping. "I had a couple of extra days off," she explained, hoping he wouldn't guess she'd been asked to stay home. "So I thought I'd grab a getaway—tomorrow."

"Mosquito repellent, sunscreen, backpack, Camelbak water bottle," Fletcher noted. "GPS, trekking poles, some *serious* boots . . ." He glanced sideways for a quick glimpse at Macy's bare feet. There was no good reason for her face to warm. "Sleeping bag. And is that bear spray?"

"Yep." She smiled, enjoying the look on his face. A triumph after that faint smirk when he peeked at her feet. "It is. I like to be prepared." She glanced at Dood resting his furry chin on Fletcher's boot. "Although apparently I need Labradoodle protection too."

"Looks like you're not planning to walk around Capitol Park."

"No," Macy told him around a bite of cookie. She could never eat an oatmeal cookie without thinking of Nonni. "I'm hiking a good 150 miles southeast of here. Three hours in the Audi. Or maybe two and a half if . . ." She smiled. "If I manage to evade the highway patrol."

"Let me guess: radar detector app on your phone."

"I'm kidding," Macy assured him. "Seat belt and legal

speed limit—I'm an ER nurse. You and I have seen too much tragedy to take that kind of risk." Without warning, the pale face of the young accounts manager rose. Along with a memory of her sticky-warm blood on Macy's hands. "I needed to get away," she heard herself admit. "The waterfalls in Yosemite are perfect now."

"Yosemite?"

"National Park. It's—"

"I know what it is, where it is." Fletcher smiled. "We've heard of Yosemite in Texas, too. It's just that it's on my bucket list. I've read about it, seen videos . . ."

"It's better. Nothing can do it justice. You have to see it, feel it. Be there." Macy shook her head, feeling the goose-bumpy awe already. "You can't imagine the scope—sheer granite cliffs so high they make your neck hurt to search for their tops. And the smell of the air, with those huge pines and redwoods. And there are incredible waterfalls . . . At least once in your life, you *have* to see it." The invitation popped out, surprising her. "Come with me."

Fletcher lowered his coffee. "Seriously?"

"Sure." Macy's heart began to tap-dance in her ears. Needlessly—this was a casual, spur-of-the-moment thing. The guy hadn't seen Yosemite. What could she do? "Come along. If you want."

Fletcher rested his hand on her sleeping bag. "I . . ."

Was he hesitating? She felt like an idiot.

"I'm off work tomorrow," he told her, obviously thinking it over as carefully as she had her packing list. "And my mother—"

"No problem," Macy said quickly, refusing to debate if

her wave of dizziness was from relief or disappointment. "I only threw it out there because—"

"I meant, sure, I can come. My aunt's arriving in the morning and staying for a few days. Mom's been doing fine, anyway." His brows drew together. "I have to work day shift on Wednesday . . ."

"We'll leave early. Have the whole day to hike. And we would be back by—" Macy's face flushed furiously as Fletcher tugged the drawstring on her sleeping bag cover. Oh no. What on earth did he think?

"It's a *day* trip," she said more emphatically than necessary. "The sleeping bag was only because—"

"You like to be prepared," he finished. "I figured that. Bear spray and all."

"Right." She told herself it didn't matter if he said no thanks. It would be far from the first time she'd reached out and been turned down.

"How early is 'early'?" Fletcher leaned down to scratch Dood's ear.

"I have this thing about watching the sunrise," she admitted, realizing the tap dancers in her ears had moved down to her stomach. "I plan to leave Sacramento by two o'clock."

"Zero-two-hundred?"

"Pitch-black outside."

Macy told herself if Fletcher bailed, it was probably the best thing anyway.

"I'm a cop." He smiled. "We have great flashlights."

24

"It's . . ." Fletcher stared out from the Tunnel View overlook, struggling for words.

"That's El Capitan on your left. About three thousand feet bottom to top." Macy pointed at the impossible expanse of towering granite peaks rising above the lush green forests and meadows of Yosemite Valley. "Then Half Dome—elevation's close to nine thousand feet at the top. And that's Bridalveil Fall on the right, about a six-hundred-foot vertical drop. When the wind gets blowing, it almost seems like the water's falling sideways." She hugged her sweatshirt close against the chill breeze, and Fletcher wanted to yank her back from the low railing. "There's a lot of old tribal lore about Bridalveil. Curses and evil spirits, of course." A smile tugged Macy's lips. "And a legend that breathing in the mist would improve your chances at finding someone to marry. Leah loved that one."

"You came here together?" Fletcher asked, noticing the glint of the day's first golden rays on her black hair. It picked out that shiny cherry-cola stripe, making it look like a little girl's satin ribbon. Or a hidden waterfall.

"We visited Yosemite once. With our foster mother Nonni. She brought seven kids up on a church trip—first time any of us had camped. In the mountains, that is. We were more the downtown shelter sleeping bag crowd. And car camping—parked beside the Safeway Dumpsters." Macy nodded toward the vista. "Not nearly the same view."

Fletcher hunted for words again. But Macy's careless shrug was accompanied by a blossoming smile.

"I can't count the number of times I've been here since," she continued. "I even worked a summer in their medical clinic. Ask me anything about new-boot blisters, altitude sickness, and hantavirus symptoms." She took a deep breath, eyes on the valley below. Her voice hushed to a near whisper. "There's something about this place. I feel . . . different here."

You are. Fletcher had to stop himself from saying it aloud. But it was true. He'd never met anyone like this woman. Streetwise, gutsy, competent, and capable for sure. But wary. And still so tenderhearted and sort of vulnerable deep down. Especially when it came to her sister. Her patients. And this place.

His eyes swept the breathtaking panorama again. A mist had begun to rise from the floor of the valley, a soft contrast to the sheer granite cliffs lit by pale sunlight. Macy had surprised him with her invitation to come along, even more with the raw honesty in that comment a few moments ago.

Maybe she felt "different" in this place because it softened her defenses. It made him wonder if the day would bring more surprises.

"We should head on to Yosemite Village. Catch the shuttle."

"Shuttle?"

"To Happy Isles. If we pick up the trail there, it will shave a little time off our hike. Not a bad idea, since it's easy to spend a lot of extra time ogling the views on the way up there."

"Up where?"

"Vernal Fall . . . the Mist Trail." She pointed to the massive peak she'd identified as Half Dome. "I'm going to get you a lot closer to that puppy." Macy's lips twitched. "And maybe some marmots."

"Marmots?" Fletcher shot her a look. "What is that? Some kind of . . . bear?"

Macy smothered a laugh. "I think I'll let you be surprised."

Surprises. He'd predicted that.

———

Taylor told herself to turn the TV news off; this was too painful to watch. But what would that say about her ability to work with crisis victims? That Charly Holt and Seth were right to be concerned?

"There's a big difference between a scab and a scar, Taylor." Seth was wrong. It had been two years; Taylor was fine now.

She reached for the remote and turned up the volume

on an interview with the husband of the accounts manager killed at the bank.

"You and your wife had—have two small children," the reporter amended, extending the microphone.

"Yes. Three years and almost six. Boys." The man swallowed and shoved his hands into his pockets. He looked like he hadn't had more than a few hours' sleep.

"That must be so difficult," the reporter continued. "How are the boys taking the loss of their mother?"

Taylor cringed. *Who asks that kind of question?*

"How . . . ?" The young widower's brows pinched together as if he didn't understand. He closed his eyes for a moment before speaking. "They . . . miss her. They keep asking when she'll be back. If she's away on a business trip. I've tried to explain, their grandparents have, our pastor . . ." His voice broke. "They don't understand how she could go to work and not come back. How this could happen. None of us do."

Taylor switched the TV off, closing her eyes against a familiar ache. *"How this could happen . . ."* That was the worst of it right there. Trying to make sense of something that should never have happened. Making it fit into a suck-it-up-and-deal-with-it, stuff-happens sort of box. The kind of platitude that softens the blow of being passed over for a job, dealing with a costly fender bender, flooding your kitchen, burning a Thanksgiving turkey. There was no box for this kind of tragedy. The shattering of a soul-deep trust that allowed you to kiss a loved one good-bye with assurance that . . . *he'll come back.*

Taylor closed her Bible and reached for the printed list of phone records. Papers she'd promised herself at least a dozen times to toss. She'd finally emptied Greg's clothes closet and donated his tools to the church's Mexico outreach ministry. She'd even stopped sleeping in his old shirts. But these stupid papers . . . Why couldn't she let them go?

Taylor traced her finger down the list of cell phone calls. The ones Greg made in the week before his death. She stopped at the number she'd highlighted with a yellow marker. Three calls to that number the day he died, the last one made an hour before the accident. It was a landline belonging to a friend he played basketball with. Not a close buddy, just one of a loose group. His fiancée was a flight nurse; Taylor had met her a few times during transports. They'd both been at Greg's funeral.

Taylor set the paper down, angry with herself. What was the point of this? She'd already asked the basketball buddy about the calls—if he'd seen Greg that night. He hadn't. Hadn't even been home. He guessed Greg didn't have his cell number, and he'd insisted he knew nothing about his friend's plan to help someone install a home theater system. There was no point in asking again. It would simply spotlight Taylor as the widow who couldn't move on. A woman with a scab, not a scar.

"*. . . don't understand how she could go to work and not come back. How this could happen.*" The young widower's words. The beginning of his battle to accept the unimaginable and still . . . trust God?

Taylor touched her Bible, stunned by the thought. Of course she trusted God. It wasn't that. That wasn't why these questions kept turning in her head. It was . . . *that I don't trust my husband?*

Her stomach roiled. Enough of this.

She carried the remains of her breakfast to the kitchen, dumped it into the garbage. Then reached for the nursing magazine she'd left on the breakfast bar alongside her coffee cup. It was folded open to a page she'd highlighted with that same yellow marker: a recruiter's ad for a traveling nurse position in San Diego.

———

"How's it going?" Macy cupped her hand around her mouth, shouting over the tumultuous roar of the Merced River. "Doing okay?"

"You mean . . . can I still breathe?" Fletcher puffed, pausing with one hand on the metal rail that ran along the sheer, staggering drop down a granite cliff to the river. He grinned, a flash of white against tanned skin flushed by exertion. He was literally soaked with water, drenched. Hair, face, shoulders, broad chest . . . "Or are you checking to be sure I haven't drowned?" He glanced down at the frothy white torrent rushing over endless boulders, some nearly the size of a house. His expression was clearly awestruck. "This is a whole new definition of humidity," he shouted back. "I'm inhaling melted snow!"

"Exactly." Macy nodded, impressed with Fletcher's ability to keep up with her. He was obviously fit, but the elevation here was nearly six thousand feet, with a total heart-slamming gain of nineteen hundred feet once they reached the top of Nevada Fall. Jogging in Houston or even some of the rugged hiking he'd done on hunting trips wouldn't be training enough for the Sierra Nevada mountain range. She glanced up the trailhead, slabs of shiny-wet granite fashioned into crude steps, pitted with residual jackhammer marks from the volunteer crews who'd painstakingly carved them. Six hundred steps to scale this last half mile. Condensing mist from the waterfalls sluiced downward from step to step.

She turned to look at Fletcher again. "We're more than halfway," she shouted against the deafening roar of the river. "Maybe another two hundred steps to the top. Watch your footing." She blinked as water streamed into her eye. "Slippery."

"I'm doomed." Fletcher shook his head.

"Just grab the rail. You're doing great."

He grinned, blue eyes teasing. "No. I meant my single days are numbered."

"What?" Macy asked, not sure she was hearing him correctly.

"That legend about the mist . . . and marriage. I've breathed in a gallon of this stuff."

"Oh." Macy laughed. "Wrong waterfall—you're safe. Two hundred more steps, Holt. Let's do this!"

25

By the time they reached the top, Fletcher's lungs were heaving. He followed Macy to the spot she said was best for viewing, and when he turned to take in the panorama, he nearly lost the last of his breath. He widened his stance, momentarily dizzy. And completely awed: Morning sun and clear-blue sky, distant snowcapped mountains studded with green pines. Unbelievably immense granite peaks with that cascade of white water, Nevada Fall, in its endless free fall down the boulders, before finally disappearing from sight.

"Pretty amazing?" Macy spread her arms wide and turned in a slow circle, a beautiful hostess enjoying the obvious delight of her guest. "Worth the climb?"

"Absolutely. I . . . Wow." He'd never seen anything like it, doubted he ever would again. He raised a thumb. "I'm impressed."

Fletcher watched as several people reached the top and joined them; the glut of hikers had thinned after Vernal Fall, where the climb got considerably more strenuous. He was glad Macy insisted they come early. The crowds were evident the moment they entered the valley, and based on the group that had shared their shuttle, these people came from all over the world. Fletcher had already heard Japanese, German, French, Portuguese, and Russian. There were cyclists, parents with children in backpack carriers, senior citizens, photographers with huge lenses, people pointing cell phones—and countless people simply pointing fingers, mouths agape. Why wouldn't they be? *Impressive* was far too small a word.

"Pull up a rock." Macy sat down and slid her arms from her backpack. She retrieved sunglasses from one of the pockets and slid them on. Then she lifted her face toward the sun and sighed. "Ahh. This will dry our clothes faster than you think."

Fletcher sat down beside her, sneaking a peek at her as he pulled out his own glasses. Following Macy up the trail had been a great view in itself. Those long legs, nicely muscled calves showing below quick-dry hiking pants, the sway of that long ponytail. And the way she looked right now, with the morning sun on her face . . .

"That's Liberty Cap," she told him, pointing again, "just beyond the waterfall. Mount Broderick is the smaller bump in the middle. And over there, Half Dome again—the back side of it this time. The cables just went up last week."

"Cables?"

"For the hike up Half Dome. You have to apply for a

permit—access is very protected now. Then it's about ten hours up to the top," Macy explained, hugging her arms around her knees. "The last nine hundred feet is really a rock climb; you have to pull yourself up the rest of the way—sometimes sort of hanging out away from the cliff—using steel cables. There have been more than a few people who fell to their deaths. The whole first time, I didn't want to trust those cables."

"You . . ." Fletcher stared at her. "You climbed that thing?"

"Four times." Macy lifted her glasses, smiled. "And when you finally get up on top, you're in serious danger of lightning strikes."

Fletcher scraped his hand across his jaw. "Obviously you didn't need me out there on that freeway."

Macy's smile eclipsed. "That's not true. That was . . . a whole different thing."

Aagh. Fletcher wanted to take back the words. Only a few days ago this woman had faced that shooter again, held his victim in her arms.

"I'm sorry, Macy. That was a lame attempt at a compliment. I should have known—"

"No problem," she said quickly. "I think it's time to dig into these packs and find food. You brought some too, right?"

"Sure did." He unzipped his pack, hoping he hadn't crushed what he'd brought. And wishing there was something he could say or do to bring back Macy's smile. Maybe—

"Well," she said, her lips quirking toward a smile after all. "Right on cue. We have company." She pointed.

CUT

Fletcher turned his head, saw them. A troop of furry creatures standing on their hind legs. Inching closer, rising again. With the obvious mission of getting their paws on the contents of the backpacks. Fletcher squinted at the leader. A gopher face, but much bigger, more like an oversize groundhog. Or a beaver out of water—with a fuzzy tail. "What are they?"

"Yellow-bellied marmots."

———

"Good sandwich," Macy told him ten minutes later, wondering if Fletcher had noticed the hunk of roast beef she'd tossed to the marmots. He'd politely insisted on sharing the food from his pack. Admitting she was a pescatarian—ate fish, but no other meats—might seem ungrateful. Besides, he'd probably think she meant Presbyterian or some other religious affiliation. Why on earth had she mentioned that her first trip to Yosemite had been with a church group? She swore she saw hope in the man's eyes. Going to church had been more about pleasing Nonni than trusting God, but that's the last thing she wanted to discuss right now. "How are you doing with that veggie wrap?"

"It's . . . great." Fletcher wiped a stray alfalfa sprout from the corner of his mouth. "Grilled tofu and seeing Half Dome—a day of firsts."

"You're a good sport," Macy told him, meaning it.

"So are you." He glanced at a trio of begging marmots. "After that taste of your roast beef, Larry, Curly, and Moe will be craving Texas brisket."

Macy's face warmed.

Fletcher raised his barely nibbled wrap, smiled. "I should have guessed we might like different things."

Macy returned his smile and shrugged. "But we're in total agreement on—" she swept her arm across the amazing view—"all of this."

"We are." The sun was drying his clothes, but the awe in Fletcher's expression looked like it was there to stay. He laughed.

"What's funny?"

"I don't know. I was thinking about those last six hundred steps up here." He glanced toward the steps. A young couple had just reached the top. "I kept hoping I wouldn't embarrass myself by coughing up a lung. And then I noticed how those steps, with all the mist, seemed to rise up and disappear into a cloud. It was like Moses climbing the Mount." Fletcher's eyes crinkled at the edges again. "Only a miracle would keep a bush burning anywhere near that waterfall."

Macy smiled. "Only *you* would bring God up the Mist Trail."

"Nah . . ." Fletcher looked out toward the expanse of towering granite. "I'm sure he was here first."

And I'm sure we couldn't be more different.

"It's like what we were talking about the other night," he continued, reverence in his deep voice. "You can't see something like this without trusting in a plan way beyond human design."

Faith. Again.

Macy searched for a way to change the subject, but Fletcher did first.

"So . . . how many guys have died trying to follow you up here?"

Macy laughed. "None yet. I mean, you're the first person I've hiked it with. I've always gone alone."

His eyes held hers for a moment. "I'm honored then."

"No problem," Macy told him, embarrassed. She shouldn't have admitted that. Shouldn't have given in to the foolish urge to invite him. *A man who packs roast beef and God.* "I sort of owed you for the dinner, anyway."

"You don't owe me. I enjoyed it. It's not every day I get to see a vegetarian attack a salmon like a grizzly bear."

"Pescatarian," Macy corrected, lifting her chin. "That's someone who—"

"I know what it means." There was teasing in Fletcher's eyes. "We have a few in Texas—keep 'em up in Austin."

———

Fortunately the hike back down was much easier. But still as wet. Fletcher was glad that his off-duty firearm had been sufficiently protected from the water. And that Macy had suggested he carry a fresh pair of socks in his pack. *"A hiker's only as good as his feet."*

He smiled to himself. This pescatarian was nothing like the women he knew in Houston. Though Jessica had managed to get herself into some reckless and irresponsible situations, she generally turned her nose up at any venue that didn't require a manicure and completely impractical shoes. Yet somehow Macy Wynn could make a pair of cargo pants and REI hiking boots look—

Fletcher stopped himself. What was he doing? Comparing? That was stupid. It was bad enough Macy had seen their embarrassing costume photo on his mom's phone—and asked him about her. The last thing Fletcher wanted was the subject of Jessica to come up again.

"It's—" Macy glanced at her phone—"almost three. With traffic, we could have a four-hour drive back."

Fletcher was surprised by a stab of disappointment. They'd been here since dawn. Hiked the Mist Trail, seen three waterfalls—including the staggering Yosemite Falls, plunging more than two thousand feet—watched crazy ant-size climbers ascending the face of El Capitan, and ogled the impressive stone-and-glass Ahwahnee Hotel. They'd done so much. Still, he wasn't ready to leave this place.

"Want to see the Grizzly Giant?" she asked.

"Does that involve your bear spray?"

"No." Macy's eyes half closed with her laugh. "It's a giant sequoia tree. About two thousand years old."

"Great . . . sure," Fletcher told her, noticing how, despite Macy's judicious use of sunscreen, her skin had gone sort of rosy. Lips too. The intriguing stripe in her hair had slipped from that Giants ball cap to hang loosely along her jaw. It occurred to him that it wasn't only Yosemite Park he was reluctant to leave.

Fletcher cleared his throat. "Big ol' tree. I'm game. Let's see it."

26

"THERE I GO AGAIN," Macy continued as they hiked along the shady crushed-granite path, "ticking off numbers: elevations, heights, diameters . . ." She had to be boring him to tears. "I sound like the Discovery Channel. Just stop me."

"No way. If you didn't tell me, I'd be asking." Fletcher smiled at her. "You must have memorized the park brochures. Back when you worked here at the clinic."

"I like to know what I'm seeing, and—" she shrugged—"I sort of dated a park ranger for a while. Till he remembered he had a fiancée in Salt Lake City." Macy cringed at the slip. This wasn't the time, place, or *person* to engage in a conversation about her lack of trust when it came to relationships. Safer to stick to facts and figures. She took a deep breath of air pungent with pine and redwood bark. "We're almost to the Grizzly," she added, grateful he'd made no comment. "How're you doing?"

"Great. Much easier than the StairMaster Trail." Fletcher gazed at the scenery: pines of every size, ferns, strewn pinecones and bark, and downed trees lying like a child's scattered Lincoln Logs. "Can't believe all this. The green, the trees. It's like hiking through a Christmas tree lot." He stopped and stared upward, jaw sagging. "Is that it?"

"Sure is," Macy confirmed as they stepped aside to let a man and his dog pass by. "Giant sequoia, one of the oldest living things."

"I can't even see the top." Fletcher stepped back, craning his neck. "Go ahead: hit me with the numbers."

"Most estimates put it at around two thousand years old," she started, resisting the urge to say she'd googled these facts long before she met the cheating ranger. "The tree is 209 feet tall. About 96 feet around at the base. That bark's like two feet thick." She pointed up the tree's massive, vertically grooved and cinnamon-red trunk. "See that branch way up there, sticking out from the trunk?"

"Yeah."

"Over six feet in diameter. That one branch is bigger than most trees here."

He gave a low whistle, stepped sideways enough that their shoulders brushed. "I'm feeling short."

"I remember reading once," Macy continued, suddenly too aware of Fletcher's physical closeness, "an estimate of the number of pinecones the Grizzly's produced. Like two million. Because of its age, you can figure this tree has seen 700,000 sunsets. That always gives me goose bumps." She rubbed her arms. Fletcher was watching her now, not the tree. Her pulse skittered. "And it's probably been hit by lightning thousands and thousands of times."

"Whoa." He glanced back at the tree. "Amazing it's still standing."

Amazing that I am . . . Macy took a safe step away, shielded her eyes, and gazed up at the giant tree again. "They're resistant to fire. In fact, it's important to them—helps the cones open, clears away fallen debris, and makes them stronger."

"Hmm, trial by fire . . ." Fletcher's expression sobered. "It works for people too, I hear. Gotta hope it's true."

Macy checked the trail behind them. "It's going to get crowded. Looks like the tram off-loaded. Have you seen enough?"

"I want to get a few pictures." He pointed into the distance. "Maybe if we go down there, off the trail, I can get more of the height." He shook his head. "Up this close everyone in Houston will think I took a dozen shots of a huge redwood barn."

"Good idea. It's out of the crowd too."

Fletcher led the way and Macy followed behind, using the opportunity to check her phone—cell reception was hit-and-miss out here, but maybe a text had come in when they were near Curry Village. She stepped off the trail, feeling the crunch of bark under her feet and the soft brush of pine seedlings against her ankles. She walked behind Fletcher, scrolling through the messages.

"Hey, Macy, watch out for—"

Her shin connected with a fallen log and she pitched forward, stumbled, and fell to one knee.

Fletcher was there in an instant.

"Here, I've got you." He grasped her hand, slid an arm around her waist. Then eased her up to a standing position. "Are you okay?" he asked, still holding her hand.

"Fine. I guess there needs to be a law against hiking and texting. And—" her fingers moved inside his—"I dropped my phone. It's probably over . . . Oh, I see it."

"Stay put. I've got it." Fletcher leaned down and managed to grab the phone without releasing her hand. "Your leg's scraped. There's a bench over there. Let's sit down a minute."

"I'm okay. Really."

"Don't make me flash the badge, ma'am. You're coming with me."

"But I'm fine," she told him as he began to lead her in that direction. The truth was her shin *was* fine. Her knees were the problem now . . . weak as a fifteen-year-old's with a crush. Fletcher's hand was warm, strong, and . . . This was ridiculous.

"It's nothing," she told him, sliding her hand away as she sat. "Minor scrape. Soap and water, Band-Aid. My tetanus shot is up-to-date. I had to trot that information out after . . ." Her hand rose to her cheek as she remembered.

He sat beside her. "After I pushed you down on the freeway."

"You already apologized." She managed a smile. "And I already—"

"Thanked me." The blue eyes did a number on Macy's knees again. "We do have a strange history."

"We do." She took a breath, sighed.

"Well . . ." Fletcher glanced upward to where the sky, visible through the canopy of trees, had changed from golden to a lavender pink. "Looks like the Giant is about to see another sunset."

"It does." Her capacity for words was setting as fast as the sun.

Fletcher pointed to her phone, lying beside her on the bench. "Important message?"

"No. I . . ." She met his gaze and found it impossible not to tell him. "That's not true. I've been waiting for a text from Elliot—he's helping me buy a house." Macy saw the surprise on his face. "Taylor reacted the same way."

"No. I mean . . . It's great. Because you're tired of renting?"

"To help my sister. She's never had that stability. I think if I bring her to Sacramento, help her to find a job and register for school, I can give Leah a real sense of family. Permanence." Saying it, Macy felt Nonni's door latch under her fingers. "It's what she's always wanted. What she needs."

"How's she doing with the rehab?"

"I haven't talked with her in a couple of days," Macy admitted. "But she's doing the program, trying. I guess the withdrawal symptoms from hydrocodone are tough. She's having trouble sleeping. And a lot of vomiting."

"It is tough." Fletcher nodded as if he had experience with it. He'd probably arrested countless people for drug violations. "My . . . neighbor went through rehab for that same problem. She said it was the hardest thing she's ever done."

"Jessica?"

"Yes." There was obvious discomfort on Fletcher's face.

"I don't want to pry."

"No. It's okay. She's very open about it. In fact, she wants to use her experience to help kids—adolescents. She's a psychology major."

"So Jessica did well in rehab?" Macy asked, more curious about the play of emotions across Fletcher's face.

"She did. Even though her treatment was complicated by a diagnosis of bipolar disorder."

Macy winced. "Ouch."

"I've known Jessica so long that I saw it all evolve. You don't want to know what she put her parents through. How hard it was on everyone who loves her."

Including you? Was that what Macy saw in Fletcher's eyes?

"But even with that, she did great," he continued. "She completed rehab, clean and sober. She's back to work. Doing great in college . . . Moving on with her life." Unless Macy was imagining it, there was something in Fletcher's eyes that said she was moving on without him.

"That's good to hear," Macy told him. "Thank you. It makes me feel encouraged. Leah's had such a hard life. I tried my best to be a good sister, protect her, but . . ." Her throat tightened enough to choke her. But the kindness in Fletcher's eyes prodded her on. "When she was fourteen, she was raped. It was my fault."

27

BLAMING HERSELF FOR HER SISTER'S ASSAULT? Fletcher didn't know what to say. Or do. But he didn't like that Macy had gone quiet. "Want to walk a little? Is your leg okay for that?"

"Sure." Her eyes met Fletcher's. The gratitude in their sad depths said he was doing the right thing after all. "I'd like that."

"Let's go."

They continued along the path leading toward yet another giant sequoia. The crowds had thinned considerably; folks were heading back before darkness encroached. They'd have to do that too, but right now—

"I think I told you that my mother died when I was six," Macy said, her voice blending with their soft footfalls on the path. "I sort of pieced some things together later and found out she was a fashion model. She did a lot of runway work on the West Coast. A few top magazines too. One of them called her 'spectacularly Nordic.' I had no clue what that meant. But she was amazingly beautiful."

Fletcher noticed how the sunset glow highlighted the planes of Macy's face. He wasn't at all amazed her mother had been beautiful too.

"It was important to me, made me feel important, I guess—back then. That stack of old fashion magazines and some newspaper clippings were all I had. I read them to Leah like they were bedtime stories. And filled in the huge gaps with fiction. I told her she could be a model too. I must have said it a hundred times. She was about ten then and ate it up. She loved to pretend . . ." Macy's breath escaped in a groan. "I shouldn't have done it. It feels like I set her up."

"What do you mean?"

Macy stopped walking. "This man stopped her in a mall. . . . He told her she was special and that he'd see to it everyone in the world knew it too. He said he represented a Los Angeles modeling agency and that he could arrange to have her photos taken for free. Because she was that 'special.' Leah wanted to believe it. She trusted him." Macy squeezed her eyes shut. "They found her in an abandoned warehouse in Modesto. Incoherent from drugs. Her jaw was fractured. The police figured there were three men—" She shuddered.

"Hey . . ." Fletcher reached out, grasped Macy's hand, and drew her to him, hugging her close. "Shh," he whispered into her hair, desperate to still her shivering and stop her pain. "Shh. It's okay."

"But it's not," she insisted, her voice cracking. "It was never okay after that. Leah ran away. Started drinking, got involved with drugs. I tried so hard to find her."

"And you did." Fletcher cradled the back of Macy's head in his palm. "You've found her, Macy. And you're helping her. That's huge. Like a second chance." He thought of his sister. "That doesn't always happen. Trust me."

She'd stopped shivering. Her sigh warmed his skin.

"All right, then." Fletcher stepped back a little and searched her eyes. "Tell me about this house you've found."

———

They'd started to walk again. Fletcher was still holding her hand. Macy wasn't going to overthink it. Right now it felt okay—more than that, really. She knew it was probably this place as much as it was Fletcher Holt, but for the first time, it felt better to talk than to keep all this stuff bottled up inside.

"It's a little house," she explained. "A bank foreclosure. But you can feel that it was a real home for a long time. You know, with kids. And dogs probably." Macy remembered Elliot down on his hands and knees checking the carpet with observable disgust. "Dogs definitely. And trees in the yard. It's been empty awhile and the previous occupants took some things. Like the stove, a few faucets, and even the front door hardware." Macy dared to smile. "But I can fix that."

"Hiking boots . . . and a tool belt, too?"

"I'm more determined than handy, I'd say. I never thought I'd be doing this at all. But . . ."

Fletcher gave her fingers a squeeze. "But you want a second chance with your sister."

"Yes."

"I can understand that," Fletcher said with a sigh.

"Because you lost your sister."

"Yeah." He tugged Macy aside as a trio of kids raced toward them, heading the other way. A beleaguered mother followed behind, shrieking at them to slow down and be quiet.

The boisterous family disappeared in the distance, leaving Macy and Fletcher alone in the quiet again. They stood alongside the path, shadows beginning to deepen around them. "Did you say your sister was three? At the time of the accident?" Macy asked as gently as she could.

"Right." Fletcher looked up the trail. "'Bout the same size as that feisty one in the lead just now. Beth was like that—no one could stop her."

Except a drunk driver. It was Macy's turn to give Fletcher's fingers a squeeze. "Were you injured?"

"Mom's ankle was broken in three places. I had a gash in my chin. The impact threw us. But I was still able to get up and try to—" Fletcher's grimace said it first. "I tried to haul Beth out from under the car; she was whimpering and fighting to get her breath. Choking. I kept trying, but she was pinned tight."

Macy stepped close. Fletcher's eyes looked smoky dark in the shadows, his expression somber. She reached up, rested her palm against his jaw. "I'm so sorry."

"Long time ago." He swallowed and took a slow breath. "But this thing with my mother . . . the cancer. She's been through too much, Macy. I'm going to make sure she gets past this. If it's the last thing I ever do."

"She's lucky to have you," Macy managed, barely above a whisper. Somehow she'd moved closer until there was no measurable space between them. Her fingers brushed the stubbled warmth of his cheek. "And Charly's strong. Really strong."

His eyes held hers. "You are too. Strong, caring. Beautiful inside and out."

"Fletcher . . ." Macy wasn't sure if she'd risen on tiptoes or if he'd leaned lower. But somehow her arms were around his neck and his lips found her cheek. A tentative kiss. Warm and gentle, but more than enough to make her heart flutter like a captured bird. She breathed in the clean, masculine scent of him: skin-warmed cotton flannel, a hint of musky soap. The perfect mix with mountain air and redwoods . . .

"Thank you," Fletcher told her, his lips brushing her brow. "For inviting me along. I didn't know how much I needed a day like this."

"You're welcome." Macy leaned back, leaving her hands exactly where they were—fingers sifting the soft hair at the nape of his neck. "I needed today too. And . . ." She decided to risk it. Trust the moment, even in this uncharted territory. "I'm glad that the first person I invited here was you."

Even in the dark, Macy saw the crinkles at the corners of Fletcher's eyes. He held her gaze long enough for her knees to feel wobbly again—if she'd been on the cables of Half Dome, she'd be a grim statistic. Then he leaned in a fraction of an inch closer . . .

"It's all right," Macy whispered, hearing her heart in her ears. "I want you to kiss me."

"I'm glad." Fletcher chuckled, hitching her closer against him. She felt his heartbeat through his shirt. "Are you always this direct?"

"With most things." She smiled at him. "I have no map for this."

"My turn, then." He slid his pack from his shoulders. Dropped it. "That's better."

Macy's skin shivered as Fletcher swept his fingers along her face, then cradled it in both hands. He leaned lower, touching his lips to the corner of her mouth. Brushed her lips very lightly, more of a nibble than a kiss. He took a breath before capturing her mouth again, slowly and more deliberately this time . . . warm and still gentle. A lingering kiss that hinted at passion held respectfully in check. It sent Macy's pulse racing nevertheless. She twined her arms more securely around his neck, responding to his kiss, and—

"Marmots!" a youthful voice shouted. Far too close.

"What?" Fletcher drew back, confusion in his voice and hands still knuckle-deep in Macy's hair.

A flashlight beam blinded them.

"Oops, sorry, sir, ma'am. A bunch of marmots are all over your pack. I think I scared 'em. No, there's still one—see?"

"I . . . We . . ." Macy laughed, fighting a breathless wave of giddiness. She stepped away from Fletcher, catching sight of the remaining animal bandit. "Thank you for letting us know. We appreciate it."

"Right," Fletcher added. A frustrated lie was never more painfully obvious. "Thanks, buddy."

"No problem." The boy pointed. "I think he was trying to steal a treat."

Fletcher's lips twitched. "I can relate."

"We should probably get headed back too," Macy told him after the boy bounded away. "The last tram leaves in less than fifteen minutes." She read pure reluctance in his eyes. She'd been right earlier: she had no map for this part of their day.

"We walked up here." He hefted his pack. "We could hike back out—no reason to wedge ourselves into a tram with a crowd of people."

"Except that it's getting dark."

"Flashlight." He patted his pack. "I think we covered that point when we first planned this adventure."

She smiled. "We still have a long drive home. You have to work in the morning."

"And you don't." Fletcher reached for Macy's hand as though it was a given. "Did you take those extra days because of what you have going with Rush? The house purchase?"

"It worked out that way." Macy decided she liked that they were walking hand in hand, almost as if they were a couple. She decided, too, that honesty was still in the air. "I was at the bank because of the house. But I didn't plan to take extra days off. My boss, the ED director, suggested I take a little time. Because of what happened there."

"Not a bad idea." Fletcher's fingers tightened very slightly over hers. "Seth Donovan, the law enforcement chaplain—you know him—met with the bank employees. He did one of his not-so-subtle checks on me too."

"He and Taylor talked with the hospital staff. About Andi Carlyle and now the shooter. I didn't go."

"Because you handle things fine alone."

"Yes. And it's not like I'm having any issues." A single nightmare—so real it had sent Macy to the bathroom to wash the horrifying sensation of blood from her hands—didn't mean she was suffering from critical stress. This mountain getaway was all she needed to get things back on track.

"You probably heard the speculation that your being at two of the scenes wasn't a coincidence," Fletcher said. "The reporters are reading a lot into it."

"Sharks. Sense a little blood in the water . . ." Macy regretted the analogy immediately.

Fletcher nodded. "Keeping things stirred up. Whatever it takes."

Macy decided not to mention her conversation with Taylor. The hint that some of the hospital staff might share the media's absurd fantasy. Probably the same people who refused to say the word *quiet* in the ER for fear it would conjure up a horrific bus crash. "There's no reason for that sniper to target me."

———

He ran his fingers down his jaw, surprised once again by the feel of his skin. Plucked smooth like the carcass of a pintail duck—minus the buckshot holes. *Shoot 'em through the wing, Son; makes the dry plucking a lot easier.*

He closed his eyes, remembering the primal smell of singed feathers and congealing blood.

He'd shaved the beard. Had to. The same way he'd

changed the plates on the Buick. Twice now. You couldn't be too careful. He told himself it was why he was here right now. Caution, not curiosity or . . .

"They say you've got a case of the paranoia, boy. And these pills will keep your brain trackin' up better . . . stop you from imagining things that aren't real."

His teeth ground together. He was here out of caution. Period.

He'd arrived in the parking lot around six fifteen, still light, and parked near the administrative annex. His second trip here today. Twice as much risk, but he'd had to do it that way because there were eight-hour shifts and twelve-hour shifts. The twelve-hour graveyard shift started at seven. But maybe they didn't call it graves here.

The women had come and gone. Dozens, dressed in all different colors of scrubs. All ages, shapes, and sizes of women. He ignored the old ones, the short ones, the fat ones . . . the blondes. He'd waited in the gazebo out by the staff parking lot and watched for her. Tall, he thought from the photos in the paper, with long black hair, light skin, and eyes like—

That.

He stared at a photo in the glass case in the hallway outside the hospital cafeteria.

Macy Wynn, RN—Emergency Department
Hope Health Care Nurse Excellence Award 2014

He'd found it by accident when hunger made him risk the open, unwatched door at the loading dock, drawing him to the food machines outside the basement cafeteria. He'd snagged some peanut butter–filled cheese crackers—packaged in the US—and a paper cup of coffee, tongue-scalding hot, dispensed as he watched. He'd skipped the creamer; no information on its origin. He burned his tongue, downed two crackers. And then found the award case. Found . . . *her*.

Chinese—or part. Definitely. He stared at the small photo, memorizing her face.

They couldn't have predicted he'd come down here. See this. But even so, it wasn't positive proof she was really a nurse. Even if she was, she could be working for them. The police, Sacramento County, the FBI . . . or a foreign government. Undercover deep enough that even the hospital didn't know. She'd been on the freeway. At the bank. Maybe she'd been there at the school, too. He didn't trust coincidence.

He scraped his tongue between his teeth, testing the coffee scald. Then headed back toward the loading dock. It was dark now; he'd go home. Not to the river camp. To the house.

And make a new plan.

28

"I'M NOT AT ALL SURPRISED the bank countered our offer," Elliot told her, setting his e-notebook on the visitors' table. "They have a rock-bottom figure in mind. And they know we do too. They'll test us to see how far we'll go. It's to be expected."

"Maybe for you," Macy told him, noticing that there were now two off-duty deputies posted near the ER entrance. A temporary beef-up in security demanded by hospital staff threatening to take their concerns to their respective unions. She turned her attention back to Elliot. "I've never made a real estate offer. I have no clue *what* to expect. I only know I need that house."

"I hear you." Elliot reached across the table, gave her hand a quick pat. "You can trust me with this, Macy. We'll counter back. Increase our offer to five thousand below what they've asked here. We didn't lose any traction because I was out of town yesterday; it's good to let them sweat a little. We'll get the house."

"Okay." Macy forced a smile, not sure what was causing her more discomfort—Elliot's overly paternal hand pat and the way he kept saying *our* and *we* or the financial issue. Her stomach churned, proving it: the money talk was scaring her spitless. "If the Audi lasts another three years and I pick up as much overtime as I possibly can, I could make it work."

"Macy." Elliot pinned her with the stop-being-stubborn-and-listen-to-me look he'd employed since she was a teenager. "You have close to a million dollars at your fingertips. I've presented options that can grow it upward from there. There is no reason for you to be—"

"No. I won't tap the trust. We've gone over this a thousand times."

Elliot adjusted the frame of his glasses, a familiar lip twitch saying he was humoring her. "We agreed to disagree. And you—" the gray eyes warmed—"are a force to be reckoned with, Macy Wynn. I don't doubt your determination for a moment. We'll counter the offer today. Jump through the bank's hoops—make this happen. Trust me. And answer my calls, for pete's sake."

She sighed. "I'm sorry. Out of cell range, I guess. I should have told you I was going to the mountains."

"Yes. Well, I admit it confused me when I swung by your house and saw the Jeep in your driveway. It took me a moment to recognize it."

Fletcher's Jeep. She'd insisted on taking the Audi, driving them herself.

"You usually go hiking alone." If Elliot was attempting to look casual, he wasn't pulling it off.

"Spur-of-the-moment thing." Macy shrugged, ashamed of her ungrateful urge to tell Elliot to back off. He'd always watched out for her. He and Ricki both. "Yosemite was on Fletcher's bucket list."

"I can imagine. More than a few great places to visit while he's here in California." Elliot's brows rose. "It's not a permanent move?"

"No. Houston's home." Macy was surprised by a wave of sadness. "He's helping his parents out for a while. His father travels for his work, and his mother's had some health problems."

"Ah, right. Ricki heard something about that. In regards to the chaplaincy gala, since Mrs. Holt was being honored. I guess it was touch and go whether or not she would be able to attend. A blood cancer, she heard."

"AML . . . leukemia," Macy clarified, remembering what Taylor said: Charly was quite open about her diagnosis.

"Did I hear that she was an ER patient recently?"

Macy met his gaze. "You know I can't—"

"Sorry." Elliot threw his hands up. "I was putting myself in Fletcher's shoes. I watched my grandmother lose a battle with cancer. Sad for everyone. No guarantees even with top-notch treatment."

"No." Macy thought of Fletcher's offer to be a marrow donor and his vow to get his mother through this cancer . . . *"if it's the last thing I ever do."*

"Well then, we'll hold the good thoughts that the compassionate Mrs. Holt beats all statistics. And that her son can return to his life in Texas." Elliot's lips edged toward a tolerant smile. "With our Yosemite National Park crossed off his bucket list."

Our offer, our house . . . our park? Elliot Rush was in no danger of anemic self-esteem.

"I should go back inside," Macy told him, checking her watch. "I need to make sure everyone gets their lunch breaks."

"Okay then." He stood. "I'll get together with my broker and we'll e-mail the counteroffer over right away. I'll stop by your place later. We can grab a bite to eat while I fill you in on the next steps. Once we get the offer accepted, we'll need to move on with the appraisal, inspections . . ." He smiled at Macy's anxious grimace. "I'll explain it all. Give you a checklist. When's a good time to stop by?"

"I don't know . . . Could you e-mail it to me?" Macy glanced toward the ER waiting room doors. One of the deputies was talking on his radio, gesturing to the other. "If it's a list, I could go over it. And if we get a green light, we could get together later with your broker. The three of us. That way, I can ask you both—"

"You have plans tonight?" Elliot interrupted.

"Not really. It's just . . ." Macy's lips tensed. She'd finally arranged for a FaceTime call with Leah. But there was no reason she needed to discuss that with Elliot.

"Well, speak of the devil," he muttered as Fletcher walked their way.

———

"I'm not quite sure how to take that guy," Fletcher admitted after Rush offered him a curt greeting and strode away. "I've met javelinas with more predictable temperaments."

"Hava . . . ?" Macy's nose wrinkled.

Fletcher smiled. "Wild animal—Texas game. I shouldn't take it further since Elliot's your friend. But he was sure in a hurry to get out of here."

"Probably concerned about his national parks." Macy chuckled. "Never mind."

The faintest hint of color rose in her cheeks as she held Fletcher's gaze. It hiked his heart rate more than it should. His gun belt creaked as he shifted his stance.

"How was your visit with your aunt?" she inquired.

"Good. We took her to Roseville. Galleria mall and Fountains." He groaned. "Nothing I like more than pretending to be interested in useless shoes and kitchen gadgets. But they liked it, and it was far enough away from—" Fletcher stopped himself, but Macy caught what he was about to say.

"It was out of the shooter's target area." She glanced toward the officers at the ER doors.

"Yeah. But mostly Aunt Thena helped Mom organize family photos for scrapbooks." Fletcher shook his head. "There are at least two decades of Holt family photos in ziplock bags—heavier than a load of marijuana bundled to smuggle across the border. And 75 percent of them are humiliating photos of me."

Macy smiled. "Let me guess: first lost tooth, first fishing trip, first prom . . ."

He hadn't gone to his prom but ended up at Jessica's senior ball by default. When the boy she invited made some lame excuse. Fletcher was her pinch hitter. It said a lot about his track record with women. One of the reasons he hadn't attempted more than a quick text to Macy yesterday. Assuming she'd expect—or want—anything more was probably a mistake.

"Mom thinks it's time she finally did something with all the photos," Fletcher continued, still uncomfortable with what his mother had really said: the scrapbook was for her grandchildren. He'd laughed, reminding her he didn't even have a serious girlfriend. Then realized with a shock that this new interest was prompted by the leukemia. Because she'd accepted that she might not be around to see them.

"I think," Macy told him, a wistful expression on her face, "that it's a good thing. Passing down those keepsakes. You'll be glad to have them."

"What did you end up doing yesterday?" Fletcher asked, changing the subject. "Bike ride?"

"Only ten miles." Macy plucked at a few hair strands straying across her cheek. "I shouldn't admit it, but I'm a little sore after our climb."

"Really? I'm fine," Fletcher teased. "Until I have to slide behind the wheel of that patrol car or chase down a perp on foot. It was a good workout."

"And I conned you into driving home."

"You did."

She'd put up weak resistance to his offer to drive the Audi back. And had been asleep by the time they'd reached Merced, curled up against the passenger door, using his jacket as a pillow. He'd caught glimpses of her when freeway lights softly illuminated her face. She'd seemed childlike almost, a vulnerability at odds with her usual manner. Kickboxer with her guard down. He'd found himself thinking of what she'd said about her first trip to Yosemite, a church trip with a group of foster kids whose experience of camping was sleeping in cars in parking lots. Had she been talking about herself? He didn't want to imagine that.

"Then I conked out and left you with a long, silent drive. Sorry," Macy said.

"No problem. Plenty of things to think about—work stuff," Fletcher amended quickly.

Partially true. He'd spent more than a few minutes of the three hours imagining scenarios where he pulled out his handgun and drew down on the marmots, scattering them so he could kiss Macy again. Which led to wondering if she'd ended up in his arms because he told her about Beth. Classic pity kiss. By the time he got Macy home, met the roommate who owned Dood, and said a quick good-bye, Fletcher had successfully convinced himself that those few minutes in the redwoods had been an enjoyable aberration. And there was no point in thinking about it anymore. Then he ended up here, now.

"Macy!"

Elliot raised his hand, calling out from several yards away. He switched his briefcase from one hand to the other, jerked his head toward the parking lot. "I'm on my way to the office. I'll give you a call after I finish that business we talked about."

"Fine. Good." Macy's brows puckered for a moment, and then she turned to Fletcher. "I need to get back to work."

"Same here." Fletcher's shoulder mic crackled with static. "I just thought I'd stop by and let you know we may have come up with a lead on the sniper. It's probably already public; there was a press conference planned for a few minutes ago."

"What? What did they find?"

"A piece of video surveillance from one of the businesses near the bank, maybe showing the vehicle that leaked oil in that parking lot across the street."

"At the church?"

"Right," Fletcher confirmed, wondering if he should have brought it up at all. The color was disappearing from Macy's cheeks. But she'd see it on the news. "Not the best film quality. And no proof that the vehicle belongs to the shooter. But it's fairly close to some of the descriptions from witnesses in the bank parking lot. And it's something to work with. We've already started to canvass neighborhoods."

"The car . . . It's that white van someone saw at the freeway?"

"No. This one's an older-model sedan, dark blue or gray."

———

"No problem," Macy assured Taylor after her friend returned to the exam room. "Mr. Chan's been sleeping the whole time."

"Great. He was in such pain when he arrived." Taylor shook her head. "Said he knows how his wife felt when she was in labor. The Toradol didn't touch it. Did you repeat it?"

"Half dose. And then we added some morphine. He was snoring after 3 mgs." Macy glanced at the middle-aged attorney, distinguished-looking despite the hospital gown and some remaining pallor. She hated that something about him made her think of that awful dim sum lunch with her father. This man looked nothing like Lang Wen. What brought that on?

"You hung a second liter of saline?" Taylor asked after glancing at her patient's vital signs.

"Yes. He's had that first bag and what you see gone from this one." Macy eyeballed the bag hanging overhead.

Taylor slid the plastic urinal along the bed rail until it was within closer reach of her patient. "He's going to need this."

"Labs were normal except for the blood in the urine," Macy reported. "No obstruction on the films. Uncomplicated kidney stone. As soon as he's awake and recycles that saline, he'll be out of here."

"Great." Taylor looked toward the doorway. "Did his daughter leave?"

"Out in the waiting room. She needed to make some calls," Macy explained, thinking of the girl—pretty face, incredibly worried expression. "Mrs. Chan's at the airport picking up some relatives."

"For the daughter's high school graduation tonight." Taylor smiled at her sleeping patient. "That's one proud father."

"I . . ." Macy's throat squeezed without warning. "He told me that too. At least twice." *And that's why it hit home.*

"Your other two patients were discharged," she continued,

eager to leave the room. "So if you're up to speed, I think I'll get back to the desk."

"Go." Taylor reached up for the IV bag. "Thanks again for letting me take a few minutes longer. I wanted a chance to pop upstairs to see Andi and—"

"Whoops, what's that?" Macy asked, pointing to a dark stain on Taylor's scrub top. "Betadine?"

"No. It's why I'm wearing these stupid shoe covers." Taylor lifted a foot, displaying a blue-paper surgical bootie. "I had to run over to the HR office during lunch. And I stepped right in it."

"In what?"

"Motor oil. Big puddle."

The video . . . the vehicle that leaked oil in the parking lot across from the bank.

"Of course they've got kitty litter soaking it up now," Taylor continued, "but it's just my luck to—" She stopped, studying Macy's face. "Are you okay?"

"Sure." Macy smiled despite her queasy stomach. "Fine."

There was nothing wrong with Mr. Chan being proud of his daughter. A puddle of oil in the parking lot didn't mean that ruthless sniper had been to Sacramento Hope. None of this had anything to do with Macy. After she called Leah, she'd take a long bike ride.

Clearly she needed to put things back into perspective.

29

"RAT . . . what?"

Fletcher laughed into the phone, imagining his father's expression. "Ratatouille. It's a French recipe. Mom's taking it to her Bible study potluck tonight. Near as I can figure, it's got a chunk of everything she bought at the Cesar Chavez farmers' market. Plus some of the neighbors' lawn clippings, maybe." He glanced down the short hallway toward the kitchen, the epicenter of a rich, garlicky-tomato aroma. "She's got this new thing about going meatless two days a week. It's healthier, she says. If this keeps up, I see Thanksgiving Tofurky in your future." Fletcher thought of Macy's grilled veggie wrap and smiled.

"Your mother sounds . . . good." There was a deep sigh. "You can't know how much I appreciate your being there, Fletcher. The weight it takes off. If it was anybody else telling me to hold my horses and not jump on a jet when she had that bleeding spell . . . But I trust you, Son."

"I know that, sir. And she is good. I promise. Aunt Thena's visit helped keep her mind off things." He decided not to mention the scrapbooks his mother was making; the thought was still too unsettling. "And like you said, you're at a critical point in your work there. Taking time off now might extend the project and keep you away longer. None of us wants that."

"I wish I didn't need to travel at all, but with these new medical expenses . . ." His father's voice trailed off; Fletcher was sure he'd decided to shield his son from his concerns. The man would heft a Yosemite boulder to spare the people he loved. "I know we can't expect to understand these things, but when Charlise passed that five-year mark after the first cancer, I thought we had it licked."

"Yeah." Fletcher remembered something one of his teachers had said all those years ago when Beth was killed. About "why bad things happen to good people." An attempt, no doubt, to comfort and explain away the inexplicable—with harmless if unhelpful clichés. Now, in the throes of his mother's suffering and his father's worry, it made Fletcher want to shoot somebody. "I'm not going to let anything happen to her, Dad," he heard himself say. "You can count on me." *Right down to my bone marrow.*

"I know I can." There was a bear hug in John Holt's voice. "So . . . French lawn clippings?"

Fletcher chuckled. "We'll put some in the freezer for you."

They said their good-byes and Fletcher ambled back to

the kitchen. He found his mother standing in taste mode over the simmering stainless-steel pot, wooden spoon to her lips, eyes closed.

"Praying for a slab of chuck roast?" Fletcher teased as she lowered the spoon. "I could still run out and—"

"Cloves," she instructed, pointing toward the granite counter. "That brown powder. Right there next to the salt. Hand me the bottle, then convince me that your father's not fretting himself into a head of hair the color of a polar bear."

"He's good," Fletcher assured as he gave her the spice container, wondering once again if he'd ever have the kind of committed and loving relationship his parents had. He was surprised that on the heels of that thought came a memory of Macy Wynn in his arms. "Dad said you didn't tell him I got the HLA testing."

"No. I didn't." Charly took a slow breath, brushed the remnants of spice from her hands. Her eyes met Fletcher's. "There are too many ifs to that, Fletcher. I can't have your father—or you—hanging on to scientific hope that could be flimsy at best."

"Are you talking about statistics again?" His frown deepened as he caught sight of the scrapbook paraphernalia she'd left on the kitchen table. "Where's that faith you've always talked about?" Fletcher hated the edge in his tone, but he had to make her understand. "I'm not supposed to trust that God would want me to be a tissue match?"

His mother swept her fingers through her hair, released a small sigh. "Do you remember your swimming lessons?"

"Swimming?" He watched as she crossed to the table

and sat, gesturing for him to do the same. Fletcher settled opposite her, wishing the fatalistic scrapbook wasn't inches away. "What's that got to do with anything?"

"You were four," Charly recalled, a smile teasing her lips. "I was seven months pregnant with Beth, and between the scent of chlorine and that wicked Houston heat, sitting on the bleachers at the community pool was the last place I wanted to be. But Elaine Ford's grandson had drowned the month before . . ." Her brows pinched together. "You had a Superman bathing suit and a death grip on the side of the pool."

The memory of chlorine made his nose sting. He had no clue where she was going with this.

"You took the guppy course twice. The instructor advised waiting another year. Because you were still so anxious. Then your dad and I drove you to Grandma's house in Corpus Christi. Her next-door neighbor had a shallow lap pool. I carried you into it. We must have looked like a mother whale and calf." Charly smiled. "You learned. You stopped trying to clutch on to the water and finally understood that thrashing only made you sink. You learned to trust, Son. To loosen up and float." His mother's eyes held his. "Faith is like that."

Fletcher waited, knowing she hadn't finished.

"We can't know what will happen with my cancer," his mother continued. "Whether the chemo has caught it. If I'll need that marrow transplant—if you'd be a tissue match. Or even if I'd survive if you were that selfless. We. Can't. Know. We simply have to relax as best we can and trust God. Float on the beautiful hope in that."

"But . . ." Fletcher tried to swallow the angry knot in his throat. "It isn't fair."

"No." Charly reached across the table to grasp his hand, tears shimmering in her eyes. "A 'fair' outcome isn't promised. Despite that, faith requires trust."

"I do," Fletcher managed, mostly for her sake. "I always have. But this, when it's *you* . . ."

His mother nodded. "Now is the tough part. When you're forced to ask yourself that hard question: Do you fully trust God, or do you simply trust him not to let something bad happen?"

"The bank accepted my counteroffer. We signed the papers! Can you even believe it?" Macy straddled the gym's locker room bench and smiled at her sister's image on the iPad, feeling breathless though she'd finished her workout ten minutes earlier. Elliot's triumphant news had hit her like a defibrillator zap, and Macy was still reeling. She'd sent Fletcher a text, all caps, while waiting to hear back from her sister. Then finally got Leah's request for video chat. "I'm going to be a homeowner, Sis!"

"That's . . . amazing." Leah's teeth scraped across her lower lip. "I know how much you wanted that, Macy. It's all done then?"

"Not completely." Macy tried to tell herself that her sister didn't look as pale and drawn as she had last week. And that she'd be smiling—as over the moon as Macy was—if she weren't still in rehab. Hard to happy dance in that grim situation. "Elliot pulled strings to get the inspection done today; the contractor is probably there right now. Checking the roof, looking for pests, all that stuff."

"Oh."

Just "oh"?

"The bank requires the inspections for the loan," Macy continued, noticing how distracted her sister seemed. "I'm on such a learning curve here. But Elliot thinks it will be fine. He says I should have the keys in my hand by the end of next month. The actual *keys*! And then—" Macy stopped short as Leah closed her eyes. "What's wrong?"

"Nothing." Leah forced a smile, failing utterly. "It's just . . . I can't think about all of this right now. The landlord told Sean he can't hold our apartment much longer."

"You won't need the apartment." Macy struggled to keep the impatience out of her voice as she watched her sister press fingers to her forehead. "We talked about this. You'll come here, stay with me until you get back on your feet. Sean's going to be in jail, Leah."

"We don't know that. Not for sure." Leah's lips tightened into a thin line, her eyes huge, sad. "He called me today. Even after all that with the landlord, Sean sounded better, more sort of . . . hopeful. I haven't heard him sound like that in a long time. He's been talking with one of his friends."

Macy almost rolled her eyes.

"This guy he hung around with in school. He's a pastor now, or an assistant pastor, I guess." Leah bit at her fingernail. "It's been helping Sean, talking with him like that."

"Well . . . that's good." What was Macy supposed to say?

"They talk about it here too."

"About what?"

"A higher power." Leah's brows pinched. "The twelve-step thing. Something like 'Follow the dictates of a higher power and you will . . . live in a new, wonderful world, no matter what your present circumstances.'"

"Leah . . ." Macy wanted to reach through the screen and take her sister by the shoulders. She wanted to make her come to her senses and understand that there *was* a wonderful new world; it was exactly what Macy was working so hard to make. In just over a month, she'd have the keys to that new world and—

"Nonni trusted God," her sister whispered. "She always said that it was the most important thing you could do. And if you trusted him with all your heart and soul, everything would be okay."

Right. And then Nonni dropped dead, the bank stole her house . . . and you were raped, Leah. Have you forgotten that?

"I have to go." Leah looked over her shoulder. "They're having a special meeting for those of us who are being discharged." She offered Macy a small smile. "Not much longer until I'm free."

"Right." Macy smiled back at her, aching to give her sister a reassuring hug. "And everything *is* going to be okay now. I promise."

"Gotta go . . . good-bye."

"Bye. Love you."

The iPad screen went black, but Macy sat there for a moment, her fingertips gently touching the glass. She'd so hoped to see joy on her sister's face, excitement at the news about their house. She'd ached to talk about bedrooms and paint colors, the rose garden . . . a puppy maybe. And most of all, seeing that beloved brass door latch on their very own home. Dreams finally coming true. But instead their conversation had taken such a different turn. To Sean— not unexpected—and then more surprisingly to God. Faith. Trust?

Macy winced, remembering Leah's sad eyes, her obvious pain. How could she tell her sister that Nonni, for all her loving-kindness, had been so very wrong? Leah would be as much a fool to trust God with her future as she would be to count on a boyfriend facing jail time for prescription fraud. Right now they could only trust that Elliot had everything in order. So that next month they'd be stepping across the threshold of their very own home. Right now it was their hope, the only real reason to smile, and—

Macy reached into the pocket of her knit hoodie as her cell phone buzzed. Then traced her fingertip across the screen to connect. *Fletcher.*

"Where are you?" he asked.

"The gym. What's up?"

"I've got good news," he said, his voice warming her ear. "I called in a favor and have tonight off. So that means . . ."

"What?" She was fairly certain her heart rate was faster now than when she'd performed that stellar cross power punch with her trainer. This man was a cardio workout even over the phone. "What does that mean?"

"Dinner. On the river—Scott's Seafood. Any kind of fish you want." He chuckled low in his throat. "So you won't have to toss your plate to the wildlife."

Macy feigned an indignant groan.

"I thought," Fletcher continued, "that your great news about the house deserved some celebrating. We could drive by Tahoe Park on the way. Then over dinner you can tell me what you plan to do with it. Carpet, paint, landscaping . . . that kind of stuff. What do you think?"

"I think . . ." Macy blinked against a foolish prickle of tears. "I think that's exactly what I needed tonight."

"Good. Pick you up at seven?"

"I'll be ready."

Macy disconnected, shook her head. She'd been wrong: there was definitely another reason to smile.

———

There she was. He watched as she pushed open the glass doors, hiked the strap of her gym bag more securely over her shoulder. Broad shoulders for a woman, but proportional to her height—she looked to be at least five foot nine. Maybe taller. Strong, obviously. A fighter. Not easy to take down. He'd expected that, of course. The sign in the gym's window said they offered kickboxing and tae kwon do. He wasn't surprised by any of it; they wouldn't send a fluffy ballerina to follow him.

He smiled grimly behind the wheel of the Buick. Who was following who now? From the hospital to the gym. And to her house, if she was going there next. He'd told himself it was worth the risk. If he could believe what he saw on the news, they hadn't identified the Buick LeSabre from that photo. Not exactly. He'd changed the plates again this morning—down to his last set. He needed to know for sure if Macy Wynn was part of it all. He couldn't let her screw things up before he finished what he needed to do.

He watched her climb into the older-model Audi and then started his engine.

30

"BUT . . ." The woman's red-rimmed eyes searched Taylor's and she hugged herself as if the air-conditioning in her comfortable home were suddenly running dangerously cold. Seth had settled a knit blanket around her shoulders, but it didn't seem to matter.

"Howard was fine this morning," she insisted. "I packed him a lunch—salami and cheese with those little pepperoncinis he loves. Only a few. I always watch that because of his acid stomach. And he promised me he'd use sunscreen. SPF 30. And a hat. He was only going to fish until three at the latest, so he could shower and change. We have to be at our grandson's baseball game at . . ." She shuddered and grasped Taylor's arm as if it were a life preserver. "The man they found out there on the lake? They're sure it's him? That it's my Howard?"

"Yes."

It was the third time in twenty minutes the poor woman had asked Taylor that question. She was clearly clinging to any hope that she hadn't just become a widow. Taylor knew the same desperation firsthand. She took the woman's cold, shaky hands gently in her own. "The deputies are certain, Mrs. Emick. It's your husband."

"He was wearing his fishing license around his neck," Seth added, his deep voice managing to sound both caring and professional. Once again, Taylor was beyond grateful he was by her side for this chaplaincy call. "His wallet was in his pocket," Seth continued, "and the boat is registered in his name. The *Bonnie Mae*."

"After me . . ." A tear slid down Mrs. Emick's cheek. "What should I do? I need to let our family know but—"

"That's why we're here," Taylor assured her quickly. "To help you with the things that must be done. We'll explain all that. And make the calls, assist you with the arrangements. We'll do anything you need us to, Mrs. Emick. Seth and I are here to . . . to help."

Oh, please. Taylor drew in a slow breath. Was she floundering here? Could she trust herself to remember even one little thing she'd learned in chaplain training? She'd almost told this suffering woman that they were here "to make things easier." *Easier?* There would be nothing easy about any of it. Taylor knew that as well as she knew her own name. This woman's husband grabbed his lunch, waved from the driveway, and was found slumped in his boat three hours later, the victim of a probable heart attack. Dead. Gone. With no good-bye.

"I should call our daughter." Mrs. Emick slid her hand

from Taylor's and glanced at the elegant grandfather clock across the room. "They'll be leaving for Jordy's ball game in an hour. I should call, but I'm not sure how to . . . or if I can . . ."

"We could do that for you," Seth offered, pushing up his sleeves and reaching for a pad of paper. "Taylor can call your daughter and ask her to come here. That might be the best place to start." His expression said she was his only priority and that nothing mattered in this world more than helping her. "Would that be all right? If Taylor calls your daughter, while you and I put our heads together about things we need to do after that?"

"I . . ." Mrs. Emick looked from Seth to Taylor and took in a deep breath. She closed her eyes for a moment, her hands clasped in her lap. "Yes," she said finally, meeting Taylor's gaze. "Please call my daughter. Cynthia—Cyndy. You'll do that better than I can right now. I know you'll be careful not to frighten her too much. . . . I trust you."

"Thank you." Taylor nodded, swallowing against tears. "I'll do my very best, Mrs. Emick. I promise."

The new widow looked away and dabbed at her eyes. Seth took the opportunity to capture Taylor's gaze. This time his concern was for her alone.

Please, Lord. Help me do my best for this family . . . and help me survive it too.

———

"What do you think, Dood?" Macy laughed as the eager Labradoodle inspected the bedroom closet, hoping, no doubt, that there was a tennis ball or rawhide bone hidden somewhere among her meager collection of hangers. "Dinner date attire. Not that we have much choice." Macy sighed. She was standing here in her underwear, thirty minutes from zero hour, with no clue what she was going to wear. It was beyond pathetic.

The Yosemite trip with Fletcher had been a wardrobe no-brainer. Hiking boots, quick-dry capris, shirt layers, sunscreen, a little dab of almond lotion that simply stirred her senses with no practical purpose. Her usual uniform—that's what her closet offered. Hiking clothes plus biking gear. And scrubs, of course. Macy had loads of scrubs—nothing too trendy or cutesy; she didn't go that far. It wasn't like she was looking to snag some eligible surgeon.

Macy smiled, thinking of what she'd told Fletcher about the Bridalveil Fall legend. Marriage was the furthest thing from her mind. Along with home ownership. Which she was actually accomplishing. It was the reason for tonight's celebratory date. She stared at her closet. What on earth could she wear? This dog had more collar options than she had choices of—

"*Grrrr—ooof!*"

Dood's low growl became a bark as he took off toward the living room.

"Nobody there," Macy called out to him in complete futility. "We checked three times already. Nobody on the porch, nobody in the yard." The poor dog was a curly hero aching for a cause. If there were more time, she'd snap on his leash, take him for a run down the—

There. Macy snatched a hanger wedged between her ski parka and the oversize denim shirt she'd worn to paint all the apartments she'd ever lived in. She retrieved the dress with a smile: sleeveless summer linen, purple and white, a color-block design that highlighted the bodice and sort of nipped the waist. Short enough to show some leg, but still modest, tasteful. The dress had been a birthday gift from Ricki Rush; Macy had forgotten all about it. She just needed to snip off the tags. Her sling-back espadrilles would work fine with it.

Dood's barks rose to a crescendo.

"Easy, boy," she shouted, pulling the dress over her head and her hair away from the zipper. "We don't have time for playing burglar. I keep telling you that there's nobody out—"

Thudding knocks echoed down the hallway. The front door.

"Oh, great." Macy struggled with the last few inches of the zipper, wiggled the dress down over her hips, and took off at a trot toward the living room. Fletcher was half an hour early, her hair was still damp from the shower, and—

Elliot?

She stopped short, stunned to see him in the room. "Why are you—?"

"I'm sorry," he apologized, managing to close the door behind him and pat the wriggling Labradoodle at the same time. "The door wasn't locked, so I . . ."

Walked right in?

She reminded herself that she'd always given the Rushes her extra key; they were practically guardians.

"That dress." Elliot's gaze moved upward from her bare feet with obvious appreciation. "As soon as I saw it, I knew it would be perfect for you. I described your build and coloring to the personal shopper at Neiman's—*Ricki* did," he amended quickly. "And we found—"

"Why are you here?"

"I just came from the Tahoe Park house," Elliot explained, striding toward the couch. He brushed at one of the cushions and perched on its edge, beckoning for Macy to join him. She smoothed the dress and settled on the ottoman across from him, very aware she had no time for chitchat. "I wanted to catch the inspector before he left." Elliot's well-groomed brows scrunched as Macy sneaked a peek at the wall clock. "You're going out?"

"Yes. Is there some problem with the house?"

"I'm afraid so." Elliot bridged his fingers. "The report won't be filed for a few days, but there's a big problem, Macy. Mold—substantial mold. I saw it myself."

"You mean like the shower grout?"

"No, far worse. It's in the subfloor, inside the walls. Clearly there was a water leak at some point. It's extensive. With a bank-owned house, this would be an as-is sale. And your lender wouldn't touch a moldy structure with a ten-foot pole. I'd say pinch your pretty nose and run away as fast as you can. There are plenty of other homes, even an auction coming up on a house not far from where you're living. That inspection . . . it's a deal breaker."

It's my home. Our hope. "There's no way to repair it? Get rid of the mold?"

"Macy . . ." Elliot shook his head, sighed. "It's a huge process. Very expensive. I'll find you another house. We can start looking tomorrow."

"How much?" Macy's mouth had gone dry. "To fix it?"

"That's foolish thinking. I understand your disappointment but—"

"You couldn't possibly understand," Macy blurted, crossing her arms. "And I don't need you to judge my thought processes, Elliot. I need you to tell me what it would cost to make this problem go away."

He brushed at the couch cushion again. "A ballpark estimate could be upward of thirty thousand dollars."

She fought a wave of nausea. "And then . . . after it was fixed, we could go ahead with the purchase?"

"Yes. The inspector didn't see any other issues. The preliminary title report looks clear. But, Macy—"

"Use the trust money." She squeezed her eyes shut against the humiliating memory of her father's face across that San Francisco table. *This is about a home for Leah.* "Withdraw what we need to fix the house. And then make whatever investments necessary to ensure that the principal is replaced as quickly as possible. Put it all back—every penny. Whatever it takes."

"Free rein?" Elliot's expression brightened. "Those higher-return investment vehicles I've been trying to discuss with you? Like the viaticals and—"

"Just get it done, Elliot. Please. Work your magic. I trust you."

"And I appreciate that. I've always done my best to look out for your interests, Macy. It's my privilege and—"

"I'm sorry." She glanced at the clock, stood. "I need to finish getting ready. Fletcher will be here any minute."

"Of course." Elliot's lips compressed. "Don't forget to cut the tags off that dress."

————

"I guess I'm not sure how to handle it. If I'm ready for something like this." Jessica leaned closer to her tablet monitor, making her gray eyes look even more beautiful. And little-girl vulnerable. She sighed and Fletcher swore he could feel the warmth of her breath. "Ben and I have only been dating like four months. Isn't that too early to say he loves me?"

Yeah. He should have the decency to wait like I did. Couple of decades.

"And then there's this mood disorder thing. The meds and all," she continued without waiting for his answer. "I mean, I know I'm so much better. School, work, spending. I'm doing my own pedicures now, and I'm wearing the same dress to the Summer Symphony as I wore when he took me out for Valentine's Day." Her lips puckered into that teasing smile that had fueled so many of his adolescent daydreams. "Mostly because Ben loves it on me. Really, I am better now, Fletcher. But this love thing . . ."

"Big step," he agreed, carrying his phone with him as he pulled his sport coat from underneath Hunter. Cat fur. Great. He was picking Macy up in twenty minutes. Even if that hadn't been the case—even if he were sitting around watching paint dry—he didn't want to have this conversation with Jessica. "If it makes you uncomfortable, maybe it is too soon, Jessica. I think you have to trust your feelings with something like that, right?"

"That's just it." Her brows pinched. "I'm not totally sure how I feel. Ben's great, so great. But I've never really loved any guy but my dad and my grandpa . . . and you, Fletcher."

His breath stuck.

"I miss you." Jessica's voice sounded choked and raw, like when she was ten and had strep throat right before Christmas. "When are you coming home?"

"I don't know." He thought of his mother's pile of scrapbook photos; Jessica would be in a number of them. "I'm here as long as my parents need me."

"And I'm being selfish."

Fletcher shook his head. She *was* better. That insight alone was proof.

"I miss you too," he told her, switching the phone to his other hand as he slipped into his jacket. "There's a lot to like about California, but Houston is home."

"Hey . . ." Jessica peered into the phone the same way she used to do through the Holts' front door sidelights. The perspective made her face look like a pampered, mooching spaniel's. "Is that a sport coat you're wearing?"

"Sort of."

"There's no sort of about it. You're dressed up, Holt."

"I'm going out to dinner."

"A date?"

"I guess you'd call it that."

"Oh." Jessica was quiet for a moment, turning her head away just enough that he couldn't make out her expression. "She's . . . one of those things to like about California?"

"Yeah." Fletcher nodded. "I think so."

31

"I REALLY WASN'T, you know, checking out your legs," Fletcher explained, feeling like an idiot for saying anything at all. Great choice for after-dinner conversation. "But when you slid into the Jeep earlier, I couldn't help but notice your ankle."

"It's okay." Macy leaned forward enough that the candle on the outdoor table was reflected in her eyes. She lowered her voice like a conspirator. "If I've accepted that you have a handgun under that jacket, then you can know that I have a tattoo. Temporarily—I have an appointment to get rid of it."

"Ballet shoes?" Fletcher asked, failing a second glance at her ankle in the dim lighting. Her crossed legs were lightly tanned, summer-bare. The heels on her sandals would make her tall enough to look directly into his eyes. If he was lucky enough to draw her that close . . . "It's such a small design that it's hard to tell, but it looks like the dancing shoes my cousin had. With those sort of ribbon ties."

"Good eye. The other day, this guy at the gym asked me if they were pinto beans. Seriously. Beans." Macy sighed. "I was sixteen when I agreed to be a tattoo guinea pig for the big brother of one of the other foster kids. Not my brightest idea. Though I heard he developed quite a following later—" she rolled her eyes—"in prison."

"Why ballet?" Fletcher asked, remembering her teasing threat to plant a combative foot square in the middle of his chest. No tutu there.

"I . . ." Macy reached for her cup again, hesitated. "One of my foster moms—the same one who took us to Yosemite—paid for me to take ballet lessons for a while. They were sponsored by her church."

Church . . . That connection again. It had been there, once.

"She . . . Nonni was pretty special." Macy glanced over the deck railing toward the small marina. The delta breeze blew a wisp of hair across her face. Somewhere, beyond the soft burble of conversation at the adjacent tables and the *tinkle-chink-clatter* of wineglasses and silverware, a single gull's cry repeated over and over. A lonely sound. "I was thirteen," Macy continued, "and skinny. Bad hair—worse attitude. I didn't even trust the sun to come up in the morning. But Nonni kept after me, doing all these little things. She made me feel special—safe, too, I guess—maybe for the first time in my whole life." That faraway look came into Macy's eyes. "For a while I believed it all: I'd dance *Swan*

Lake with the San Francisco Ballet, grow up beautiful like my mother, and have a family, a real home . . ."

Fletcher waited. There had to be more. She'd made an appointment to have that tattoo removed.

Her wistful expression closed down. "Nonni died, no warning. The house was auctioned off. The kids . . . We all went different places. Then Leah . . ."

Was brutally raped. And you took up kickboxing.

"Well." She gave a short laugh, waved her hand as if to erase the pain of what she'd shared. "Guess that will teach you to ask a girl about a tat, Deputy Holt."

"Sir." The waiter set their check down and Macy immediately reached for it.

"Oh no, you don't," Fletcher warned, entering into what became a small tug-of-war. "I invited you."

"Too many times," she insisted, adjusting her grip.

"You're complaining?"

"No." The amber eyes met his, making it nearly impossible to continue to wrestle—good thing she wasn't a perp going for his gun. "I meant that you're too generous, Fletcher. I'd like to get this, do that this time." Macy shot him a look. "If you're worried my credit card will be denied and you'll have to wash dishes, relax. I'm packing cash. Tons."

"Win the lottery?" he teased. "Secret heiress?"

"Maybe. Something like that." Her expression was unreadable. "Let me do this, Fletcher. Please."

"I don't know . . ." He stayed quiet for a moment as one of the restaurant staff lit the small stone fireplace nearest them; flames rose and warmed the cool breeze. He was reminded once again that he was far, far from humid and sultry south Texas. Reminded, too, that Macy Wynn was unlike any woman he'd known. So independent, self-assured. He admired it, but pay for the check? That was going too far.

"If it helps my case," she wrangled, leaning back toward the heat, "I ordered more food than you did—remember the oyster sampler?"

Raw on the half shell, barbecue, and smoked. Macy had enjoyed them like a California otter cracking an abalone over its belly. She'd followed that with a Dungeness crab Louis, then the macadamia nut–crusted Alaskan halibut. A pescatarian fantasy, no doubt. She'd discreetly checked the right-hand column of the Scott's Seafood menu and then savored every single bite of her order. It had been a beautiful sight. He smiled. "I remember the oysters."

"So . . . ?" Macy held up the check.

"Sorry. Can't let it happen."

She tilted her head. "I buy dessert?"

"Well . . . sure," Fletcher conceded, impressed she had room for it. "I'll call the waiter back and—"

"No. Not here," Macy interrupted with a slow smile. "We'll go to Midtown. Rick's Dessert Diner. Great, funky, retro spot—glass display cases, checkerboard floor, vinyl upholstered booths—with like *two hundred* or more desserts." The tip of her tongue sneaked across her lower lip. "Chocolate strawberry fudge cake, toasted pecan coconut cake, fudge fantasy. And pies: key lime, apple blackberry, chocolate peanut butter . . . Cheesecakes, tarts, brûlées, cobblers . . . The air reeks of buttercream."

Fletcher smiled, enjoying the uncensored bliss on her face. He slid the dinner check from her fingers. "What are we waiting for? You're on."

———

Taylor daubed a sweet potato fry in ketchup, then met Seth's gaze across the vinyl-top table. She raised her voice above the summer evening chatter of the café crowd. "Thank you. I needed to dilute that painful situation with comfort food gluttony."

Seth's smile was kind, his brown eyes as warm as the molten fudge brownie she was tempted to add to her order. "I thought a little comfort was in order. Care for the caregivers. How are you doing now?"

There was no skirting the truth with Chaplain Donovan.

"Better, I think. It was hard not to cry in front of that poor woman," Taylor admitted, remembering the pain in the new widow's eyes.

"There's no rule against that," Seth reminded her gently. "We're only human."

"I know." Taylor sighed. "It's just that . . . her husband dying out there on that lake, no warning and no chance to say good-bye. It was almost like . . ." She lowered her gaze, toyed with a fry.

"It was too much like what happened with Greg."

She met Seth's gaze, nodding. Words weren't an option.

"I'd be surprised if it didn't bring that back, Taylor. There's no way around it." He set his coffee down and released a sigh. "August will be almost five years since my wife passed, and I've probably been on a couple hundred activations since. Community situations and tragedies within the law enforcement and fire family. Drownings, crib deaths, officer-involved shootings, teen suicides. I'm a seasoned volunteer. But to this day, whenever I'm called to make a hospital visit, I get one whiff of that antiseptic smell and I'm right back there in Camille's room. I'm watching her fight that cruel cancer pain—and feeling so blasted helpless to fix it." He reached into his jacket pocket, pulling out the familiar package of Kleenex stamped with the chaplaincy logo. "These things will work for us too, Taylor. Trust me on that."

Taylor would bet there were few people more worthy of trust than this man. People felt comfortable with him, like he had wide enough shoulders to share anybody's burden. It's what made him such a great crisis chaplain, why officers and firefighters hung around his family's uniform store long after they'd purchased their pair of pants or that new flashlight. Seth Donovan invited folks' confidences because he listened without judging.

"You did great out there," he told her. "And now that we've slid that heart on your sleeve—" he pointed toward the front of her shirt—"back up where it's safer, you get to be proud of yourself for getting through your very first death notification. You made a difference today, Taylor. That's good." He peeled the wrapper from an antacid tablet. "Your call will be added to the monthly debriefing, of course. But informally, can I answer any questions or concerns?"

"I . . . May I ask something personal?"

"Sure." He set the tablet on his plate. "Ask away."

"It's just . . ." Taylor's breath snagged. "How long did it take?"

"For what?"

"To stop feeling so lost . . . alone?" She heard the pain in her voice, knew there was no way Seth could miss it either. "After your wife died. How long did it take until things got better?"

His smile was like a hug. "I think everyone's different, Taylor. I leaned pretty heavily on God. I've let him pick me up and throw me over his shoulder more than a few times— still do. And time does help. It will get better." He nodded. "Friends are good medicine."

"Yes." She wrinkled her nose. "And they can be a pain too. All the 'You should get out more' hints and those awkward 'At least you're still young; you'll find someone else' lines that are supposed to be hopeful." She groaned. "Someone even e-mailed me a link to widow's etiquette. When to stop wearing your wedding ring and how soon is too soon to date." Taylor shook her head.

"All that 'help' that feels so insensitive."

"Exactly." She met Seth's gaze, grateful. And wondered if he too had struggled over that ridiculously painful decision to change his Facebook status from married to single. He kept his personal life pretty private, but she'd heard he was dating a forensic tech. "I'm determined to move on," Taylor added, "but I guess I resent being told how and when."

"Well . . ." Seth's eyes held hers. "No worries. I'm not the kind of friend who's going to preach grief etiquette. And I'm only going to make one important suggestion."

Taylor lifted her brows.

"The molten fudge brownie."

———

"I can't believe you actually *knew* the counter girl at the Dessert Diner." Macy studied Fletcher as he maneuvered the Jeep Wrangler into the turn lane that would bring them closer to her neighborhood. They'd passed the Southside Bank a mile or so back and she'd purposely found something to look at on the other side of the street. "And don't try to convince me that your pie slice wasn't half again bigger than mine. I thought she was going to strain a muscle lifting it."

"Coincidence on all counts," he insisted, smile lines creasing his rugged profile. "Like she said, I met her once at her son's school when we responded to a bomb threat. A prank fortunately. We only talked a little, but I guess she remembered me."

Who wouldn't? Macy was grateful her memories had moved from the realm of sniper incidents to . . . this. Whatever this was.

"*If* my pie slice was bigger," he conceded, "it's because most business owners appreciate having law enforcement officers on-site. Simple as that."

"Makes sense." Macy glanced at the badge and weapon secured to his belt, more visible now that he'd slung his jacket over the seat. "You never know when a layer cake heist will go down." She laughed at Fletcher's groan. "Seriously, you always carry that gun when you're not working?"

"Bad guys don't take days off."

"Good point."

Macy pushed down the nagging sense of foreboding that had been dogging her for several days. It made little sense since there had been no news regarding the freeway sniper. Only coverage of the bank employee's funeral service and an interview with the paralyzed security guard. She'd muted the TV for both.

"One of my roommates is away doing her insane weekend work marathon. And Sally's probably sleeping before her night shift," Macy told him, noticing that they were about to turn onto her street. She couldn't deny she was reluctant for the evening to end. It had been great, and there was something so nice about the way he'd taken hold of her hand as they walked to the car from the dessert place. "You'd have to put up with the Dood, but I have some good organic coffee beans. And clean cups—a minor miracle. It's not really that late. . . ."

"Thanks. I'd like—" Fletcher suddenly braked the Jeep four houses down from hers. He hunched forward, staring into the shadows between the streetlights. "See that car?"

"Where?"

"There, across the street. With the running lights—no headlights?"

"Yeah." The foolish foreboding came back. "Why?"

"Recognize it?" Fletcher inched the car forward, his gaze never leaving the vehicle across from them. "Older-model dark sedan—Buick, looks like. Have you seen it before?"

"No. I mean, I don't think so. Not that I remember." Macy's words escaped in a confused stagger. "Why? Do you think there's something wrong with—?"

"Wait." Fletcher stiffened, reached for the window button as the sedan's headlights came on. "You have your house key?"

"Yes. But what's going on?"

Fletcher stuck his head out the window, craning his neck. "I need to check the guy out. I don't like the way this feels." He unfastened his seat belt and reached down to touch his holster.

Macy's breath sucked inward.

"He's pulling away," Fletcher told her, stepping on the gas. "Be ready to get out. I'll drive to your porch. You're safe. Go straight into the house, lock the door." He roared up her driveway, hit the brakes. "Go, Macy!"

She threw off her seat belt and jumped from the car. Once she hit the porch, she turned to look over her shoulder—as Fletcher whipped the Jeep around, tires squealing in pursuit.

32

"I'M SORRY," Fletcher told her, settling onto the couch. "I got caught up with things and lost track of time." He noticed she'd changed her clothes, the dress replaced by those pants she'd worn at Yosemite and a sort of thin, lacy pink sweater and flip-flops. Her hair was pulled into a loose knot. "Am I keeping you up?"

"No. It's fine." Macy sat beside him, drew one long leg up. "I wouldn't be able to sleep anyway after all that happened with that car." She tried for a casual shrug. Didn't pull it off very well. "I mean, I wasn't sure where you'd gone or what was happening."

"I'm sorry," Fletcher repeated, recognizing the look in her eyes. Worry, even fear maybe. Though she'd try to hide that like a champ; he was sure of it. He should have come back here sooner. "I wish I hadn't put you through that. But

I can't promise it won't happen again. It's that whole thing we talked about earlier—bad guys not taking a day off. And cops needing to be prepared."

"Like ER nurses. There's a CPR face shield and a pocket mask in my glove compartment. Somewhere under an avalanche of energy bars and hair bands." Macy met Fletcher's gaze. "Was it him, the shooter?"

"We don't know yet." Fletcher knew he could only say so much, though she was obviously worried. For good reason. "The fact that he took off like a bat out of—folks don't do that for no reason. The headlights off. No bulb on the rear license plate. I got close enough to hit the plate with my headlights and got a partial. And I snapped a couple of decent pics with my phone. Then I lost him in traffic when I was calling it in to the comm center." He frowned. "But it's something to work on. The car fits the general description. And this location . . ." Fletcher stopped himself.

"My neighborhood." The pink sweater sagged to expose a bare shoulder as Macy hugged her arms across herself. "My bank . . ." She glanced toward the door. "It's all in his target area. Should I be expecting detectives again?"

"No. Not tonight," Fletcher said gently. "I told them I'd be here. But I'm sure your neighbors are fielding some questions right about now."

"What do *you* think? Do you think it was him?"

"I think it's very possible. The description and partial plate information went out to all units." He couldn't tell her that the FBI had expressed keen interest in his photos, especially the one that seemed to show a defect in the Buick's trunk—a round hole. More than large enough for a rifle barrel. When the media got ahold of that, there would be immediate and endless comparisons to the 2003 West Virginia shootings. "We'll know more soon. I really don't have anything more than that, Macy."

She was quiet for a moment, arms still hugged across her sweater. When she finally spoke, it was barely over a whisper. "Where the car was parked . . . did they find oil?"

"Yes."

———

It took her a few minutes to put together the coffee she'd promised earlier, and meanwhile she heard Fletcher occupying himself with Dood. Macy had banished the dog to a bedroom after arriving home, for fear he'd wake Sally. She didn't want him to go completely bonkers, barking again like he had when she was getting dressed for dinner. Long before Elliot showed up.

Was the shooter out there then? Her stomach shuddered. And then there was the oil. That puddle at the church across from the bank, then at the hospital . . . and here now, on her street. It could still all be coincidence. But it was far too close for comfort. And explained the nagging and dark sense of foreboding plaguing her for days.

Stop it.

Macy poured the richly scented coffee into her roommate's *Seriously?* mug, grabbed her own cup of green tea, and carried them toward the living room, reminding herself of what Fletcher said: they didn't know if the car tonight belonged to the shooter. It was possible, but not certain. There was no reason for her to be paranoid. Prior to Fletcher's action-movie stunt, she'd had a great evening and anticipated a far different ending. More along the lines of quiet conversation and a little more hand-holding. All of which might still be possible. Even with detectives grilling her neighbors.

And the fact that her very good-looking date . . . just set a gun holster on the coffee table?

"I hope you don't mind," Fletcher told her, moving the weapon aside so she could put the cups down. "This couch sort of sinks."

"Not a problem," Macy managed, despite a rising laugh. "What's funny?"

"This." She shook her head. "Me, with you."

"Meaning?"

"Police officers were part of my early education." She dunked her tea bag a few times, decided the story was more entertaining than pitiful. "When I was six—that last year with my mother—we spent a lot of time sleeping in our car." Macy saw Fletcher wince. "It wasn't so bad. It was a big gas-guzzler, had a working radio, and was roomy. We didn't have a lot of stuff. Mom . . . she knew how to make any situation feel like a Disneyland commercial. And a life lesson. The cops were part of acting improv."

"Acting?" He regarded her over the coffee mug.

"That's right. Mom taught me the drill when it came to dealing with law enforcement. She always said, 'If you need your life saved, trust them with that, Macy. But with anything else, you have to remember the cops are all about doing their jobs—upholding the law. So if we find ourselves a teeny bit on the other side of that line, we need to put on our show faces.'" Macy sighed as a high-gloss magazine image of her mother came to mind. Spectacularly Nordic.

Fletcher met her gaze, waiting.

"If we were sleeping in the car and a cop rapped on the window or shone his flashlight, it was my cue. I talked first. I did it exactly the way Mom coached me—two scenarios. First, if the officer was kind-looking, I'd roll down the window, sit up straight—" Macy pulled her shoulders back—"smile, and say, 'We're moving to Grandma's house in Tiburon. I brought my clothes and all my toys . . .' But if the officer was grouchy-looking, I'd clutch my little hands to my chest, make my eyes as wide as I could, and say, 'My uncle Bob is a policeman too. In Wyoming. He catches the bad guys and makes sure all the children are safe.'"

"And that worked?"

"Like a charm." Macy knew she should stop there. But Fletcher's trustworthy eyes lured her on. "I remember we had a blue plastic bucket in the trunk that was for a bathroom when we didn't have access to one. And a white one for water. To wash the car with," she explained, recalling her mother's counsel: *A dirty car is a huge clue that people are living in it.* She shrugged, making herself smile. "I was a pretty good actor. And car washer. If your Jeep ever needs—"

"Hey." Fletcher took hold of her hand. "You don't have to pretend with me. Having to live like that must have been awful. How . . . ? Did you say your mother died in a fire?"

"An apartment fire." Fletcher's fingers tightened around hers, gentle, warm. "We were living in the car and I'd been sick, I guess. Mom left me sleeping in the backseat one night while she ran into a convenience store. They said she stole some Tylenol. The clerk called the police. They called Child Protective Services." Macy shook her head. "The 'moving to Grandma's in Tiburon' doesn't fly with those folks, I guess."

"They took you into protective custody?"

"Emergency foster care. Mom said it was only for a few days; she'd met some nice people who had a place." Fletcher's arm slid around her shoulders. He probably thought she was going to cry. "They think it started with the curtains. A candle maybe . . ."

"I'm sorry," he said softly. "It's not something you ever really get over."

Macy met his gaze, certain he was thinking of his sister. Then a smile began to tease his lips.

"So—" his fingertips brushed her hair—"you couldn't imagine yourself with a cop?"

"Never," she admitted, relaxing against him a bit. She wondered about the statute of limitations on breaking and entering, stealing door hardware. "I never thought it was possible. Not like this."

"And this, us . . ." Fletcher's eyes held hers. "You're good with it?"

"I think, yes. Maybe." Her pulse danced as his lips touched her forehead.

"Only 'maybe'?"

Her chuckle was breathless. "Considering that you knocked me to the ground the first time we met, you all but threw me out of your car tonight, and—" She stopped as his big hands cradled her face.

"I think . . . I'm very good with the idea of us, Macy

Wynn." That small hint of an accent stretched his words. "You're an amazing woman. Smart and gutsy, generous . . . and beautiful. From that stripe in your hair right down to your pinto bean tattoo."

She started to laugh, but his lips had found the corner of her mouth.

"You are special, Macy," he told her, drawing back a little to look in her eyes again. "You should believe that. Ballet or not, regardless of where you came from—because of that probably. I've never known anyone like you."

Macy blinked, determined not to cry as she wove her arms around Fletcher's neck. "Well . . ." She smiled, an achy-good sensation making her dizzy. "Since you put it that way, Deputy . . ."

Fletcher's lips met hers, lightly at first, then more completely as he wrapped her in his arms. Warm, secure. Macy's eager response stirred the kiss to deepen, until she wasn't sure she could still breathe, but . . . it was worth the risk. He'd buried his hands in her hair, leaned over her enough that she slid back against the sofa arm, not at all confident the timeworn piece of furniture could tolerate the weight of two people at one end without tipping or—

"Grr—oooof!"

The Dood leaped to his feet and began trotting down the hallway, toenails clicking on the wood floor. Music erupted from somewhere in that direction.

"Sally . . . ," Macy breathed, rising to a more upright angle on the couch. She glanced at the wall clock. "Her shift starts at eleven and—" She laughed as Fletcher's handsome features morphed into an adolescent pout.

"Great." He shook his head. "If it's not a kid stalking marmots, it's a night nurse. I'm batting zero."

"Hardly." Macy's skin warmed as he lifted her hand to his lips. "But . . ." She glanced in the direction of what sounded like the shower starting up. "You don't want to talk to Sally until she's had at least three cups of coffee. She's half the reason I own bear repellent. And if she spots a gun on the furniture . . ."

"Got it." He reached for his holster. "Maybe I'll give the sergeant a call, see if they've found anything out yet."

Macy's stomach tensed. "You don't think he'd come back here tonight?"

He studied her face. "You're worried?"

"I'm not. I'm just—"

"Acting." Fletcher finished fastening his holster, met Macy's gaze. "I see it in your eyes. You're worried."

"Maybe a little. But I'll move Dood's bed to the living room and . . ."

"No need. I've got it covered." Fletcher reached out and traced his fingers along her cheek. "Your own surveillance detail. All night."

"Uh, I appreciate that, but—" her face warmed—"you can't stay here, Fletcher. We have a house rule about men. And I really can't, wouldn't . . ."

"Whoa." Fletcher caught her hand. "Hold on. Take a breath. I wasn't suggesting I'd be sleeping here—even on your couch." He laughed. "I'm sorry, but that look on your face . . . What I meant was that one of the graveyard units will do some drive-bys. Keep an eye on this street and your house."

She stared at him, embarrassed and touched too. "You arranged for that?"

"Sure." He stood, reaching out a hand to help her up. "I made a call while you were in there getting the coffee."

"Because it's really more dangerous than you've said?"

"Because . . ." Fletcher drew Macy into his arms. "I want you to be able to sleep. I don't want you to worry." He hugged her close. "And because I care a lot about you."

Macy closed her eyes, feeling the solid warmth of his back beneath her palms. And a strange and sort of wonderful sense of safety she hadn't felt in a long, long time.

Down the hallway, Sally grumbled something to Dood about offensive dog breath. And that no one better have eaten the last bagel.

"I should leave," Fletcher told Macy, leaning away. "Before you pull out the bear spray and I get caught in the cross fire." He bent low, gave her a last, lingering kiss. "Mmm. Sure worth risking it, though."

"Thank you," Macy whispered, realizing that her knees were trying their best to tremble. Her kickboxing coach would have her dropping down for twenty push-ups. "For dinner . . . and for everything."

"I'll call you in the morning," Fletcher promised. "My buddy's name is Jason Gormley. This is his patrol area anyway, but he'll make some extra passes down the street. Till about seven in the morning. He'll slow down when he passes your house, take a good look around. Maybe shine a light in the shrubbery. You're okay with that?"

"Sure." Macy feigned an innocent smile. "My uncle Bob is a policeman. In Wyoming."

33

"I COULD PROBABLY DO IT." Andi maneuvered her wheelchair forward and back, leg extended, to prove her new expertise. The sling was gone, and her crutches had been propped against the corridor wall beside her. "Half shifts, run the department right from this chair." She peered past Taylor toward the trauma rooms. "Doesn't look too challenging in there. Grab me some scrubs."

"No way." Taylor shook her head, noticing that the plucky physician had paired her hospital robe with red-yellow-and-blue Wonder Woman slipper socks. "Physical therapy will be here in a flash to take you and the little elf back upstairs. They weren't too thrilled that you conned the transporter into a detour over here."

"I know." Andi smiled, spread a palm across her pregnant tummy. "We'll be good." She glanced through the department doors again and sighed. "I know it's going to take time to heal and feel normal, but it's . . . harder than I thought."

"I'm sure," Taylor empathized, remembering her conversation with Seth last night when they'd talked about healing from grief and she questioned him about his personal experience.

"Taylor?"

Seth Donovan was suddenly beside them. His face was grayish pale and his expression pained, anxious. He glanced between Andi and Taylor. "I'm sorry to interrupt . . ."

"What is it?" Taylor asked, concern growing as she noted the perspiration dotting his forehead. "What's wrong?"

"I was upstairs with a patient and . . ." Seth pressed his palm against his lower sternum, closed his eyes, and groaned. "Half a roll of antacids hasn't touched it this time."

"Get him to an exam room," Andi ordered, reaching for the crutches. "Take this wheelchair."

"No," Seth insisted despite his obviously increasing distress. "It's just my stomach. And you're hurt, Dr. Carlyle. I can't let you—"

"No arguments." Andi set the brakes and hoisted herself onto one superhero slipper sock. She waved away Taylor's attempt at assistance. "I see the transporter right down the hall; he'll grab me another chair." She stared at Seth, her expression a mix of steely resolve and compassion. "What we *can't* have, Mr. Donovan, is one of the good guys risking a cardiac event in our hallway."

"She's right, Seth." Like it or not, Taylor was thinking the same thing.

"But—"

"Right in that chair," Andi ordered, armpit over one crutch. She nodded with approval as Taylor made a quick call to give Macy a heads-up in the ER. "You'll get your chance to prove it's your stomach. After you meet MONA."

"Mona?" Seth grimaced, settling with reluctance into the vacated chair. "Who's Mona?"

"What, not who. It's a mnemonic for chest pain protocols," Taylor explained, seeing with relief that the transporter had already retrieved a second chair for Andi. *MONA: morphine, oxygen, nitroglycerin, aspirin.* It wasn't etched in stone, but it was a great guideline to remember the cardiac treatment basics. "As in, 'MONA greets all patients.'"

"I'll have to trust you on that," Seth told her, closing his eyes against the pain.

"Good." Taylor put the wheelchair in motion, saying a quick prayer for her chaplain friend. "That's what we're here for."

———

"Got all the blood for labs?" Macy asked as Taylor stepped away from Seth's gurney, carrying several filled tubes.

"Chemistry, blood count, PT and PTT . . . Troponin's already running." Taylor glanced back toward their patient, the concern in her green eyes obvious. "He was popping antacids last night—I didn't even think about it."

They'd been teamed on a death notification, Taylor had said. Gone out for a bite to eat afterward. Probably about the same time Macy and Fletcher were having their meal. She knew he'd be concerned about Seth. "The EKG didn't show any ST elevation," Macy reminded Taylor. "Seth's still under forty, with no previous cardiac history or big risk factors."

"If you don't count job stress. And life stress."

"If you're going to count that, then you'd better tell the chaplain to scooch over—we'll all have to climb up on that gurney." She met Taylor's gaze. "You okay? Want me to ask someone else to take over with him?"

"No. I'm okay." Taylor found a smile. "It's just that Andi was right. Out there in the hallway, when she was trying to muscle him into the wheelchair. She called him 'one of the good guys.'"

"Yes." Macy looked back at Seth, lying beneath a web of monitoring wires and oxygen tubing. He'd been at the hospital visiting the family of a child who'd suffered a near drowning; the mother was a 911 operator and had taken the unimaginable call. Seth Donovan was absolutely one of the good guys. The same way Fletcher was.

"I have to trust that he'll be okay," Taylor added softly. "He has to be."

Macy wanted to say something reassuring. But that had always been Taylor's role. It was the perfect moment to say something supportive about hope . . . or faith? When had she started to factor that into any equation? For the first time Macy could remember, she was tempted to try that. But climbing Half Dome seemed far less daunting. Better to stick to what she trusted most: facts.

"Look," Macy said at last, "so far so good. Seth's vital signs are stable. The EKG and chest X-ray are good. He's not a smoker or a diabetic, no high blood pressure. Even with the troponin pending, the docs are betting on gastric reflux." She raised her brows. "The man admitted to chili cheese fries."

"And a molten fudge brownie."

"See?" Macy nodded, relieved to see Taylor's lips tug toward a smile. "Plus, Andi's up on crutches and wearing Wonder Woman socks. All signs that the Earth is shifting back to its normal axis."

———

"You're sure you're okay to do this?" Fletcher asked, opening the car door for his mother. He glanced at the doors to the Sacramento Hope ER, trying to shake the sense of déjà vu; last time they'd been here together, he was carrying her in his arms. "Seth tried to talk you out of coming."

His mother snorted. "A snowball's chance in Houston."

Fletcher smiled. That about said it.

"He told Taylor it was okay to call me," she continued as Fletcher tapped in the code for the ambulance entrance doors—it had been cleared with security. "And you know how many times that good man has been there for me. And a thousand other folks." His mother tossed him a knowing look. "Plus, I didn't think you'd mind coming with me to the hospital."

Macy was working. They'd texted well into the night and talked on the phone before breakfast. She was working days and Fletcher had taken a swing shift. They wouldn't have seen each other. After learning Seth was out of immediate danger, he almost thanked his friend for the excuse to come over here. Even if it would take all his willpower not to haul the beautiful nurse into his arms.

She was in the corridor outside the emergency department when they got inside. Nobody should look that good in baggy scrubs.

"Seth is being watched in the CPAU. Our chest pain assessment unit," Macy explained after greeting his mother. "It's a precaution; he's really very stable." Her eyes met Fletcher's at last, breath drawing softly inward. "He'll be glad to see you both, I'm sure."

Fletcher was only sure that his feet were cemented right where they were.

"I should go on ahead," Charly insisted with uncanny mercy. "Seth may want to fill me in on that sad situation with the child in ICU."

Fletcher waited until his mother was three strides away, then reached for Macy's hand. "I missed you."

"Same here." She smiled at him but slid her fingers from his as a pair of lab technicians came around the corner. "Work," she said with a small frown. "No getting around it."

"Nope." Fletcher glanced toward the overhead speaker as a stat page went out for the obstetrics resident. "Seth said he's okay and that it's not his heart. Maybe it's stomach-related, from stress?"

"It looks that way. I can't say officially . . ." Macy was guarding his friend's privacy; Fletcher admired her for that. "I guess you know he was here visiting the family of the police dispatcher?"

"Yeah. And now my mother's making a chaplain visit to the chaplain." He shook his head. "A regular compassion pile-on."

"You can add two more to that hero huddle: Taylor

was the one who coerced Seth from the corridor onto our gurney . . . after Andi climbed out of her wheelchair and offered it up."

"Andi Carlyle?" Fletcher's eyes widened. "The ER doctor from the hit-and-run?"

"Yep. Triaged Seth, leaning on her crutches. Everyone's pitching in. Not so different from your team." Macy's eyes held Fletcher's. "I appreciate the extra patrol in my neighborhood last night. And how the detectives worked around my schedule today."

They'd questioned her, of course. "You okay with all of that?"

"Creepy coincidence, not a target. There's no reason for that maniac to follow me." Macy's chin rose. "That's my story and I'm sticking to it." Her forehead puckered as the OB resident was paged a second time. "I caught some of the news on the nurses' lounge TV. They were showing those photos you took with your phone last night. They're saying it's the best lead they've had toward catching the shooter."

"Maybe. But none of it is certain. Identifying that Buick—even ruling it out—would be a help. We'll be going door-to-door in the communities again tonight."

"And you have that partial license plate; you got a look at it."

"Right."

They were fairly certain they'd traced it to a vehicle with a nonoperational registration. An old Honda Civic—not a Buick—parked in a trash-heaped carport in Stockton, almost an hour's drive from the shooting locations. The owner, an elderly gentleman housebound by deteriorating health, had no clue the plates were missing. Detectives were circulating photos of the Buick and making inquiries regarding any strangers seen on or near the property. Rumor had it that one of the CSI officers required treatment for a spider bite after attempts to dust the Honda for prints.

"Oh no." Macy grimaced as yet another physician page sounded overhead, this time including a room number. "That's Andi."

"What? But . . . she's a patient."

"That's what I mean. Those pages for OB assistance are for Andi's room up on the surgical floor. She must be having trouble with the baby." Macy grabbed her phone from her scrubs pocket as it buzzed with a text. Her face paled as she scanned it. "It's Taylor. Andi's bleeding." She winced, met his gaze. "I shouldn't have said that."

"I didn't hear it." Fletcher gave Macy's hand a quick squeeze.

"I should get back to the ER. See if Taylor knows anything else."

"Go. I'll be up with Seth and—"

She was gone before he could finish.

Fletcher remembered what Macy had said about Andi Carlyle. How she'd given up her wheelchair to help Seth. Probably one of hundreds of selfless acts she'd done without thinking. Maybe all her life. And then some guy deliberately mowed her down with his truck. Fletcher couldn't forget the image of that doctor lying in the parking lot, broken and bloodied. Too much like his sister under the wheels of the drunk driver.

His jaw tightened. Where was the sense in any of it? His

sister, his mother, Dr. Carlyle . . . that dead bank manager, the paralyzed guard? And now what—a dead baby too? All too often lately, it was getting harder to pray, to put things in God's hands. Maybe there came a point when faith wasn't enough, prayers went unanswered. He shifted his weight, felt the bulk of his holster on his belt. Maybe the only true mercy was justice.

———

He rested his bicycle against the tree, glanced toward the river. A new camp. Couldn't risk going back to the other. Too many prying eyes. People who knew his face. Last night was a big mistake. If he hadn't felt it in his gut when that Jeep took off after him, he would have been smacked upside the head for sure this morning by the *Sacramento Bee* headline: "Possible Lead in Freeway Sniper Investigation."

Fuzzy photos, but they'd nailed it like a kill shot. Make and model of his father's Buick, within a year. They probably had the plate too, one of those he'd lifted from abandoned cars. He glanced back toward the river. There were a thousand other old plates down there. Rusting, cluttering up the river bottom, maybe even poisoning the fish—who could trust it wasn't true? He'd tossed the plate in the river before dawn, after stowing the car away; no one had seen him. He was sure of that. Still . . .

"Homeowners are being asked to identify the car in the photos . . ."

They'd started by going door-to-door in the neighborhood of that nurse. Not close enough to be risky. But with the information on TV and in the papers, it was possible someone might remember.

He examined the Hostess snack cake package, making certain of the manufacturer's trademark and location: Missouri. Then he washed a mouthful of the cream-filled chocolate down with the bottled water he'd bought at the mini-mart. Lousy breakfast. If they caught him today, it would be a humiliating last meal. And his own fault.

He'd taken too much of a chance parking in her neighborhood. Gone off on some fool tangent, like his father always said he did, about that nurse with Asian eyes. Stupid. Same thing with the oil leak; how could he miss that? They were probably tracking all sales of motor oil now and—

Didn't matter. He jabbed his finger into the side of the second cupcake. Hooked out a glob of cream the same way he'd learned to gut a bluegill. He sucked the filling from his finger as his gaze swept the river once again. The license plates were gone. The Buick out of sight. He didn't need it anymore. What he was going to do next wouldn't require a car. Just timing.

34

"DID THEY PAT YOU DOWN FOR CHILI CHEESE FRIES?"

"Nah." Fletcher shook his head, sliding the visitor's chair closer to Seth's hospital bed. "Just sprayed me with that special luminol for chocolate fudge."

The chaplain tossed him a sheepish look. "So much for medical privacy."

"Well . . ." Fletcher's gaze moved over the array of equipment: heart monitor, blood pressure and oxygen readings, an IV port taped to his friend's arm. "At least you had the good sense to chow down in the company of an ER nurse." He watched as Seth's eyes did a quick scan of his digital heart tracing. It had to be rough lying there like that. Helpless. The worst feeling in the world. "Seriously, I'm glad it wasn't worse. We all are. How're you dealing with this?"

Seth's eyes wrinkled with obvious amusement. "Are we switching roles here?" He chuckled at Fletcher's grimace. "I'm okay. I don't like hospitals; I admit that. The smells, the sounds, and these blasted fluorescent lights. But I have to think there's some good reason I'm forced to deal with this, beyond the incentive to lose a couple of pounds, get a little more exercise and some decent sleep. Maybe I needed to get a feel for this side of the stethoscope, you know? To help me deal with crisis survivors. Maybe that's the plan."

"'The plan'? I suppose you're talkin' divine, not Blue Cross."

Seth smiled. "Gotta trust it."

Do I? Fletcher glanced toward the sound of voices outside the doorway; his mother and Taylor were still talking out there.

Seth reached for his water glass. "Word has it those photos of that suspicious car were yours."

"For what they're worth. The plate was stolen. Everyone's grandmother owns that car."

"Not with a barrel-size cutout through the trunk."

Fletcher wasn't surprised Seth knew that detail; his connection to law enforcement went way back. "Probably a new add. It's doubtful anyone noticed."

"You did."

"Right place. Right time." Fletcher caught Seth's smile. "If it was divine, we'd have that crazy felon scheduled for arraignment."

And Dr. Carlyle wouldn't have been run down, his mother wouldn't have to battle cancer a second time . . .

Fletcher reminded himself to check on those blood test results. Being a donor was something he could handle all by himself.

"I also heard that you spotted the car near Macy Wynn's place?" Seth's brows rose.

"A few houses down. The detectives questioned her again, but I think she's right that it's a coincidence and—" Fletcher read the look on his friend's face. "Okay. I've been seeing her."

"I didn't ask."

"The same way you didn't stuff your face with chili fries." Fletcher shrugged, warmth crawling up his neck. "Macy's . . . great. I don't know. Real, I guess. Different from other women I've known." He laughed. "Right down to the hiking boots and bear spray."

Seth raised his hands. "Not asking. It's good, though, to see you moving on."

Jessica. He'd never returned her call. After cutting short her concerns about her new relationship, he'd been too eager to get to Macy's house. "I guess I am," Fletcher said finally. "Moving on."

———

"If I didn't need to sign anything, couldn't we have done this over the phone?" Macy set the sheaf of paperwork down on Elliot's cherrywood desk. Stopping by his home office hadn't been in her plan. "You could have e-mailed me these contractors' bids. Saved paper . . . and time." She hated how that had come out, far too much like he'd wasted *her* time. But her sister was calling tonight.

"I'm not worried about the price of paper, Macy." Elliot waved his arm, indicating she should sit in one of a matching pair of tastefully upholstered wing chairs, then waited until she complied. "Besides—" a smile tweaked his lips—"I've always found it impossible to attach the food. And I knew you'd be hungry. You're always hungry."

There was no point denying it. The first time Macy set foot in this office—formerly a mother-in-law quarters down a lush, camellia-lined brick path from the main residence—she'd been accompanied by Lang Wen's San Francisco attorney. She'd been a few weeks past her nineteenth birthday and about as friendly as a dogcatcher's nightmare. If there had been a larger window in the office bathroom, Macy would have hoisted herself through it. But in a rare motherly gesture, Ricki Rush had thought to order food. Blissful food. Macy's first-ever margherita pizza: wood-fired with summer-sweet heirloom tomato slices and snipped basil. In mere minutes, it had softened her prickly edges like melting mozzarella. And set a precedent that had held for eight years now: distasteful business meetings made palatable by great food. Elliot knew Macy's weakness. And her father's money kept it all going.

"Thank you," Macy told him as Elliot approached with a small tray of appetizers. She noticed as he came close that he smelled of alcohol, no doubt from the small bar he kept for clients. The black-lacquered cabinet with pewter hardware held an array of bottles and crystal glasses that glittered in the recessed ceiling lights. She'd never bothered to inspect it and had said, "No thank you" enough times that Elliot finally stopped offering. It occurred to her, as she selected a cracker with fruit-topped Brie, that she'd probably saved him hundreds of dollars in alcohol over the years. She chuckled around the appetizer.

"What?" Elliot settled into the chair beside her. "What's so amusing?"

"Nothing, really." Macy shook her head, glanced around the redwood-paneled room hung with an array of Ricki's ever-fickle art purchases. "Except the usual. Me . . . here." She plucked at her scrub top. "Eating Brie cheese and talking about money." She almost added, *"When we both know where I come from."* She'd talked very little about her past with Elliot but suspected he'd heard plenty from the Wen attorney. "It's . . . a funny fit. That's all."

"That's not true." He leaned forward, an almost-disturbing intensity in his expression. She noticed, definitely now, that there was a slur in his voice. "You fit. You more than fit, Macy." Elliot's eyes squeezed closed like he'd had a stab of pain, but before she could ask, he met her gaze again. "You're a breath of fresh air. You have been since the first night you stomped in here with that wild black hair . . . holes in your jeans and looking like you were willing to gnaw your arm off to get away. Or bite mine if I was fool enough to try to stop you."

Macy shook her head. He'd nailed it.

"You weren't going to take anything from anybody—charity money or bull," Elliot continued. "But you listened; you sifted the facts. Sized it all up. And then you took those street smarts to college—on your own dime—and grabbed your future by the throat. You made it happen. I can't tell you how much I admire that. How highly I think of you. Smart and honest and so very—"

"Elliot, please." Macy squirmed in her chair, wondering if she'd really evolved that far beyond arm gnawing. He was simply saying he respected her. Paying a compliment. But still, this was far too uncomfortable. "There's no need for this. I appreciate your confidence in me. And the great food. But I should go."

His lips pinched.

"My sister's calling in about an hour. I need to talk with her." Macy stood. "I'll review the bids for the mold cleanup. But I trust you with the decision. I always have."

He stood and took a step toward her.

It was a hug moment if there ever was one. He'd known Macy since she was a wild orphan kid. Helped her, absolutely. But they'd never had a hug history. It wasn't starting now. She took a step back. "Thanks for the Brie. I'll get back to you."

"Don't make a mistake, Macy."

"I'm not. I need this house. For my sister. It's the only reason I'm tapping the trust."

His eyes captured hers. "I mean Fletcher Holt. Don't get involved with him."

Macy's lower lip sagged.

Elliot's eyes narrowed. "He's only here until his mother dies."

Her stomach lurched. "Elliot . . ."

"He'll go back to Texas. Back to some pliant woman who themes her nail color to every national holiday. Who owns a full set of her grandmother's china and has the Holy Bible downloaded to her iPad." He crossed his arms, swayed in place. "Don't trust him, Macy. You don't fit with that. And he's not even close to being worthy of you."

"This is way out of line, Elliot. And you're drunk." Macy was surprised by a sudden prickle of tears. Their history might not have included hugs, but it shouldn't dissolve to this. "I'm cutting you some slack because of that. But my personal relationships are none of your business. I trust you with my money, but that's as far as it goes. I'm not looking for a father. Please don't try to be one."

"Macy—"

"I'm going."

In her adolescent world, she would have thrown a punch at Elliot Rush's head. But in the end, Macy simply turned and strode back down that elegant camellia-lined path, climbed into her Audi, and left him behind.

"It's eased up. No more cramping at all." Andi's small smile revealed a single dimple. She smoothed the cotton blanket across her abdomen. "They've scheduled daily ultrasounds. And I won't be perfecting my crutch aerobics anytime soon."

"No." If Taylor could do it over again, she'd insist Andi stay in that wheelchair. Or better yet, go straight from PT to her room with no detour to the ER. But Andi was as stubborn as any member of the team. It was nearly impossible not to offer help in an urgent situation. "It must be hard to be in the middle like that. Itching to be up and making progress and knowing you need to do what's best for . . ." Her heart tugged. "Elf."

"It is." Andi took a breath, exhaled softly. "But I'm determined not to worry. Or slip into heaping blame on Bob Harrell. That's too easy to do. It doesn't serve any good purpose." Her fingers moved to her cross pendant. "His brother came to visit me last week. Not to try to explain away Bob's actions or press for mercy—as if that could even be up to me. He wanted me to know his family is praying for me, that I'm on their church prayer list. The baby too." She swallowed. "He said his brother's finally getting the mental health help he's needed for a long time. They're relieved but sad it came this way. I felt good about that. It helps."

"I'm not sure if I could do that. Put aside the blame, not obsess over why it had to happen at all."

It wasn't true; Taylor knew for a fact she *couldn't* put it aside. Two years after Greg's death, the unanswered questions still ate at her.

"We can't live in this world very long, certainly not in these careers of ours, without running up against a boatload of things that are painful and feel just plain wrong," Andi told her. "Far beyond our ability to understand—I don't have to tell *you* that." Her eyes filled with compassion. "We can only wait. And place our trust right where it belongs."

"Absolutely." Taylor nodded in agreement, putting on what she'd come to think of as her "chaplain face." Nonjudgmental, caring, faith-driven. While deep down—maybe not as deep as she'd like—she wasn't at all sure that waiting and trusting were helping. She needed to put Greg's death behind her. She had to regain control of her life.

———

"But we'll get it fixed, no problem," Macy promised, watching Leah's face on the phone screen. "Elliot has bids from like six contractors." She pushed aside a memory of his intrusive and controlling diatribe. She'd made herself clear; he'd back off. They'd pretend it never happened. "The mold will be gone, and it's a good excuse to change the paint colors anyway. Neither of us are the basic beige type. What do you think about—?"

"I can't. I can't think about that. Not now."

Pink. I was hoping you'd say pink and giggle like a little girl whose dream is coming true. It's finally happening, sis. Happily ever after . . .

"It's okay," Macy assured her. "You need more time. I get that. We'll have fun with those details later; no rush. The contractors will be busy for a few weeks. You just need to finish up there. Get healthy." Her eyes swept the phone screen. "You do look better, sweetie. More rested. The withdrawal symptoms have eased up?"

"I guess so. Yes. And I'm trying to eat better now. Take good care of myself." Leah twisted a hank of her curly hair, tipped a little closer to the screen. Her wide eyes looked painfully vulnerable like those puppies peering from cages on the SPCA commercials. "Sean thinks he might get his time reduced to sixty days. And he talked the landlord into holding the apartment for a while. He had to sell his truck for the money. But he did it."

Great. What was Macy supposed to do, hang a banner? This was ridiculous. Sean the Forger figured nowhere in the equation. He was the regrettable past. The Tahoe Park house, mold-free and freshly painted, was the future. Leah's bright future. Then nursing school and—

Her sister cleared her throat. "Macy?"

"Yes?"

"I'm pregnant."

35

"YOU COULD HAVE SLEPT IN. Should I feel guilty?"

"Absolutely—*mmph*—not. 'Scuse me," Macy mumbled around her last mouthful of an Adalberto's Mexican Food breakfast burrito. Fletcher must have been at their window before dawn. She grabbed for her paper napkin, noticing how the pale sunlight from the window played over his sleep-mussed hair. Her pulse ticked upward at his smile. "I'm always hungry." She hated that saying it made her think of Elliot. At least they'd smoothed things over when he called late last night.

"And I thought you'd be getting ready for work."

"Last-minute change." She'd asked for the day off, claiming a family emergency. It was the truth. Leah's news had hit her like an undefended gut kick.

"So you can go to Tucson."

"My flight leaves at ten thirty." Macy hadn't mentioned the pregnancy. Or that awkward meeting with Elliot. Fletcher was a fixer, and these were Macy's thorns. "My sister's only a few days from finishing up with rehab. We need some real face time."

"I get that."

They were speaking in stage whispers to keep from waking Sally. The Dood had already mooched a good portion of Fletcher's second taco.

Macy pushed up the sleeves of the baggy sweatshirt she'd yanked on over her pajamas. "And while I'm gone, you'll be working overtime."

"Looks like it." Fletcher stuffed their paper trash into the take-out sack. "If that new information pans out—the old Buick seen parked at the Stockton nursing home over the past few months—it won't take long to put together a list of possible suspects."

"Good." Macy fought an involuntary chill. "I'm so done with all of this."

Fletcher's eyes held hers. "As long as that doesn't include me."

"You?"

Her skin warmed as he slid closer on the couch.

"You're not done with me?" he whispered, watching Macy's eyes.

"No." She smiled slowly, very aware of the effect his closeness was having on her senses. "It's not every day you meet a guy who can find a good burrito before sunrise."

"Ah." He smacked a fist against his chest. "Bold kick to the heart—score for the lady."

"And . . ." Macy was surprised by the sudden quaver in her voice. "Someone who's willing to take the time to get me. Maybe even be okay with who I am."

Fletcher was silent for a while, watching her eyes. "It's more than *maybe*," he said finally, a mercy that allowed Macy to exhale. "I think you're amazing." He took hold of her hand, lifted it to kiss her fingertips. "And I think I'll probably offer to paint that old house you're buying—lug all your sister's boxes in."

"Fletcher . . ." Macy's voice choked. He couldn't have said anything more perfect. How could she tell him that? Let him know that, impossibly, he'd begun to make her feel hopeful about things in a way she'd never known before?

He crooked a finger under her chin. "When do you get back from Tucson?"

"I'm staying overnight; there's a family apartment at the center. I arranged for it," Macy whispered, realizing that almost as much as she felt the need to see Leah, she was already missing this man. "My return flight arrives in Sac tomorrow at 4:10."

He kissed her forehead. "I don't start work till three today. I can drive you to the airport. And I'm off tomorrow. So when I pick you up, we'll go out to—"

"Elliot already hired an airport van. He has some sort of arrangement with the owner of the company." He'd also insisted on using his air miles to purchase her flight. He'd been profusely apologetic and never once mentioned Fletcher's name. She saw no point in rebuffing his kindness. Or provoking the issue by canceling on him now. "But I should be back here by five thirty at the latest. And—"

"You'll be hungry." His thumb traced her jaw very gently.

"A woman can't live on airline pretzels." She sighed as his lips touched her cheek.

"Can't risk it then," Fletcher whispered, the faint stubble of his beard tickling her skin. "I'll make reservations. One of the guys told me about a great place overlooking Lake Tahoe."

"Really?" she asked, leaning away. "Tahoe?"

He chuckled. "You can wear hiking boots with your skirt."

She wouldn't. But Fletcher seemed very okay with that idea, which was staggeringly wonderful. "Sounds perfect."

"Great. That's settled. And now . . ." Fletcher dipped his head low, and in less than a heartbeat his lips found hers. His hands slid to the back of her head, drawing her closer as the kiss deepened. Tender, warm . . . dizzying.

Macy didn't care. Dizzy was fine—she only wanted the moment to go on and on. She needed to trust that happiness could really happen, that her heart was safe. She wanted to dare to hope, finally, that everything could be okay.

She stretched her arms around him, felt the warmth of his broad back through his shirt. And returned his ardent kiss measure for measure.

―――――

"They're kicking me out," Seth told Taylor, leaning against the doorframe of the triage office. "I talked the transporter into letting me out of the wheelchair in the lobby. I wasn't going to risk a flashback to the last time I was in your fine department." He grimaced and rubbed the front of his powder-blue polo shirt. "That cardiac monitor left some pitiful divots in my chest hair."

"Ouch," Taylor said, wrinkling her nose. It was good to see Seth upright again. Beyond the stubble of auburn-brown beard growth and some shadowy lines of fatigue around his eyes, he looked no worse for wear. Downright handsome, according to several floor nurses. Taylor would tend to agree. And Seth's humor was intact, always a positive sign. "Can I assume this means you passed your treadmill test?"

"Flying colors. Well, more lumbering than flying." He scraped his big palm across his hair, lifting a thatch that left him looking disarmingly boyish for a man pushing forty. "Finding my running shoes—and making some time to fill them—is on my new to-do list." He flexed his knee. "You probably wouldn't believe it, but for an old guy with a limp, I used to log some serious miles."

"I believe it. I think you'd accomplish anything you set your mind to." Taylor smiled, meaning it sincerely. "All the while giving everyone else the credit."

"Well . . ." He shook his head, then met her gaze. "That's why I stopped by here. To say thanks for all you did for me yesterday. I probably gave you a hard time, but I appreciate it, Taylor."

"I . . . You're welcome," she told him, knowing he'd call her on it if she pulled the modesty card. The man practically read minds. "Even though I was a contributing factor, since you ate that molten fudge brownie just to make me feel better."

"Don't flatter yourself." His laugh ended in a groan. "I should know better. Half of what we tell our crisis survivors about dealing with stress has to do with taking care of themselves. You know the drill: eat right, get enough sleep, exercise . . . do the things that make you feel good."

"A case of 'Chaplain, heal thyself'?"

"Can't just talk the talk." He glanced out toward the hallway to the waiting room. "Am I holding you up with triage?"

"No worries; they'll signal me."

"So yeah," Seth continued, "I'm going to pay better attention to things, make a list of where I can cut back." He caught the reflex pinch of her brows. "Not with California Crisis Care. That's too important to me. In fact . . . I've been asked to head up some training in San Diego."

Taylor stared at him. There was no way he could know she'd been considering—

"It could work; it's not like Donovan's Uniforms can't run without me. I've got an assistant manager at the Midtown store who's been shouldering a lot of extra work since Dad was forced to cut back."

"Because of his emphysema." Taylor had seen the man visiting Seth, carrying a portable oxygen concentrator over his shoulder. Similar coloring as Seth's, same dark eyes. But thin, barrel-chested, with a grayish cast to his skin—the textbook picture of a COPD patient.

"Dad's stubborn, but he's doing his best to follow his doctors' recommendations to ease up a little," Seth confirmed. "Anyway, this Midtown assistant should have been promoted to manager a long time ago—doesn't need me breathing down his neck. I could go to San Diego." Seth's eyes wrinkled at the edges. "Beach jogging . . . easier on the knees."

"You're going to move?"

"I'm going to commit to thinking about the teaching situation. It wouldn't require a move, at least not outright."

Taylor could only guess that his father's health was a big factor. And maybe that alleged relationship with the CSI staffer? She wasn't about to ask.

"I have family near La Jolla, not far from there."

"Small world."

The triage light flashed overhead.

"That's my cue to make an exit." Seth extended his hand. "Thanks. You're good people, Taylor Cabot."

She returned his warm handshake. "You too."

———

He'd have to talk with her again about locking the front door; his mother had always been far too trusting. Fletcher halted at the doorway to the kitchen, the distant voices confusing him for a moment. Then he smiled: his mother and father on Skype, their voices blending together in that warm, laugh-peppered burble he'd heard all his life. He peeked in.

"Halibut," she was saying. "In fish tacos, with cilantro, guacamole, and shredded cabbage, the way you like it. From the frozen fillets you sent." She shook her head. "The doctor said more protein; he wouldn't buy my suggestion that Thena's pecan brittle was just as good."

"Those blood tests . . . When is our next round?"

Our. Fletcher caught the thinly veiled worry in his father's strong voice.

"I have blood drawn next week, I think. I'd have to check.

I'll let you know, John—I promise." She touched the frame of the laptop gently with her fingertips, the way Fletcher had seen her touch his father's face a thousand times. "We'll be okay. I'm sure of it." She chuckled softly, tipped her head like a flirting teenager. "Getting you back here is the best medicine. Even pecan candy is no substitute."

Fletcher waited until they said good-bye and walked in as she was closing the laptop.

"Burglar," he said, pointing to the front of his uniform. "Walked right in—the TV and Grandma's silver are already in my van."

"I didn't . . . I did?"

"Practically wide-open." He sighed, thinking there was no way he could take a hard line with this woman. "Working on that scrapbook again?" he asked after crossing the room to give her a kiss on the cheek. Stacks of photos, scissors, pens, indecipherable bits of artsy stuff. Fletcher picked up a photo and laughed. "Does Dad know you're immortalizing his epic fail at ballroom dancing?"

"It was worth my broken toe. He tried it for *me*. It says a lot about the kind of man your father is."

"What's this?" Fletcher asked as Charly went to fill a coffee mug. He lifted a thin, stapled sheaf of papers from a stack of mail and read the first lines. "Reverse mortgage?"

"People do it," she said, carrying the mug back to him. "Helen in our Houston neighborhood, Granny Astrid at church, and—"

"Old people," Fletcher interrupted. "Widows and . . . You're not really looking into this?"

"I don't know." She attempted a casual shrug that was

about as successful as his father's fox-trot. "Our real equity is in the Houston house, so we'd have to be living there to qualify."

"Dad has at least another six months with this project. And your medical care is here, Mom. You couldn't move back to Texas until—" His heart froze. "You're not giving up on the treatment?"

"Of course not. I'm only being realistic, Fletcher." Something in her voice sounded too much like the day they knew that baby mockingbird they'd rescued was dying. "I'm only considering options."

"Like this, too?" Fletcher snatched an informational brochure from the mail pile. A glossy photo of an elderly couple in each other's arms, under the heading *Viatical Settlements: Selling your life insurance can buy you peace, comfort.* He stared at his mother, confused. "What the . . . ?"

"It came in the mail. I thought I'd look it over." She met his gaze. "It's a way of collecting on an insurance policy early. A lump-sum payoff. And then an investor takes over the payments and becomes the new beneficiary." His mother seemed to read the confusion on Fletcher's face. "It's a benefit that's offered to people who are terminally ill."

His stomach lurched. "Wait—no one's said that. Right?"

"No." She touched his arm. "No, the doctors haven't said that. The information came in the mail. Right along with my *Southern Living* magazine. I simply thought there's no harm in checking it out. It seemed . . . hopeful." She glanced toward the laptop. "*If* things get worse, it might mean your father could be home. We wouldn't have to burden you or—"

"Stop." Fletcher raised his hand. "You're doing okay—you've beaten this thing once. You'll do it again. If it comes down to a bone marrow transplant, I'll be set up to do that. No problem." He turned the brochure over, anger rising. "Who sends this morbid stuff out, anyway? The doctor's office, hospital . . . ?" His gaze dropped to the ink-stamp logo at the bottom of the page:

Elliot Rush Financial Services

36

MACY SHOOK HER HEAD, still surprised at the turn of events. "I expected that I'd be visiting you at the rehab center again. Not at . . . this apartment." She refused to say "your apartment" or to bring up the boyfriend's name. Even if his presence was everywhere in sight: Photos of the young couple on a shelf above the TV—he was cute, of course, sort of clumsy-puppy endearing. An acoustic guitar leaning against the futon where Macy had slept. Close to a dozen baseball trophies. Plus that pair of huge Nikes lined up next to Leah's dainty sequined flip-flops. "You weren't supposed to be discharged until Thursday, right?"

"I told them I had an appointment with a nurse-practitioner in the ob-gyn office." Leah blinked up at Macy from where she'd sunk into a red plush beanbag chair. Her willowy and too-thin limbs, in a black tee and leggings, made her look like an upended ladybug. She nibbled at her dry breakfast toast. "I fudged a little. The appointment's not until Wednesday." Her eyes held Macy's. "I guess I just needed to be back here. To think about it all, you know?"

"The counselors . . . they think you're okay now?" Macy asked carefully. "On your own here?"

Leah planted her bare feet, pushed herself up higher, and set her toast on the coffee table. "Because I could have a stash of Lortabs in my sock drawer?"

"No. Of course not. I wasn't thinking that," Macy said quickly, hating herself.

"You were." Leah's pallor made her little-girl dusting of freckles even more apparent. "I would be thinking that if I were you. But don't worry. They let me go because I did the program and earned their trust. It's weird," she said, voice suddenly soft. "I think I even trust myself now. I know I won't do anything that hurts this baby." Her fingers, nails polished a pale shell pink, brushed her flat belly as gently as if there were a kitten curled in her lap. Her eyes shone with tears. "I'm going to be someone's mother, Macy."

Oh, Leah. Macy slid from the futon to the floor, wrapped her arms around her sister.

"Remember when we talked before," Leah whispered, drawing back a little, "and I asked you if you believed in a higher power?"

"I think so . . . sure," Macy acquiesced, thinking only of the Southwest Airlines gift card in her purse. Getting Leah to Sacramento was even more important now.

"I've been thinking about it," Leah continued. "A lot. And about Nonni. She was the closest thing to a mother I ever had, you know?"

"I know."

"And she and God, they were tight." A faraway look came into Leah's sleepy eyes. "Once she told me that God knew me before I was born. And he even knew the exact number of hairs on my head." Her fingers traced a tiny circle on her belly. "The exact number. She said he loved me that much because I'm his child. We all are. Do you believe that?"

An ache rose in Macy's throat. She wasn't sure if it was because of the question or because they were talking about Nonni; right now, it seemed one and the same. "I think . . . it must feel really good to believe that."

Leah was quiet for a few beats. "I want to believe my baby will be loved like that. That it can be different this time . . . starting there."

Macy stayed silent, though with every fiber of her being, she wanted to shout that it *was* going to be different. Starting when Leah boarded that jetliner. And then walked onto the porch of their house, saw Nonni's brass door handle and the backyard with the trees and roses. A real home—a place to study, laugh, and plan a future. A home that would soon be filled with childish squeals, bedtime stories, giggly games of peekaboo . . . and the scent of oven-warm oatmeal cookies. And there would absolutely be love.

Macy smiled, remembering her impromptu breakfast with Fletcher and his offer to paint rooms and tote boxes. "Leah?"

"Yes?"

"It is going to be different, better. I promise."

Macy wanted so badly to talk about Fletcher. Explain how she was beginning to feel about him, the hope it was bringing her. She ached to share that wonderful news with her sister. But how could she do that when her most critical goal was moving Leah far away from the man she loved?

———

Taylor checked the time on the triage computer: 3:20. The p.m. shift would be getting assignments from the clinical coordinator, a substitute today. Macy had asked for the day off, something to do with her sister. No one knew better than Taylor how readily family problems could demand priority. And make a person sleepless, even physically sick. Thank heaven Taylor was past that now. Despite her lingering questions about Greg's death, she was long past the crippling effects of grief that interfered with work and—

"I'm here to set you free," the p.m. nurse announced, arriving in the doorway. She hiked a thumb in the direction of the waiting room. "It looks fairly decent out there; nobody vomiting in a wastebasket or waving a weapon." She raked her fingers through her hair, grimacing. "Probably not a good thing to joke about these days."

"Probably not. But I'm going to trust you're right." Taylor offered her a smile, thinking that the nurse looked familiar somehow. Nearly as petite as Andi, but with burgundy-brown hair worn in short, soft spikes. Lavender scrubs with a Velcro tourniquet and a roll of tape hanging from her lime-green stethoscope. Despite her dark humor, she seemed a little anxious. Taylor glanced at her registry name badge. "You've worked here before, Ronda? Familiar with the setup?"

"Couple of times." The nurse glanced back down the hall. "I'll be okay."

"Great." Taylor smiled. "I'm caught up. Have a seat—" *stop hovering, for goodness' sake*—"and I'll fill you in on who we have out there. In a few minutes we'll both be good to go."

"Sure." The petite nurse sat at last and met Taylor's gaze. Her dramatic dark-fringed blue eyes prompted Taylor's sense of déjà vu once again. "Go ahead. Fill me in."

"Okay." Taylor scrolled down the registration screen. "Our only priority patient was roomed ten minutes ago. That leaves you a two-year-old with a croupy cough per Mom; he hasn't made a peep since they arrived. A woman, seven weeks pregnant, spotting this morning. Her OB's been called. A retired dentist, seventy-six, with ear pain. Looked uncomfortable when he arrived but says it settled down. He and his wife just got off a plane from—"

Taylor stopped, remembering suddenly. She turned, met the nurse's gaze. "You're a flight nurse, right?"

"I was." The nurse swallowed, the anxious look returning. "We've met. I usually go by my middle name, Sloane."

"Sloane Wilder. You're Paul Stryker's fiancée."

"Was." Her lips compressed. "We broke up . . . six months now."

Taylor's stomach sank. Paul Stryker. Greg's basketball buddy, a volunteer firefighter. The number he'd called the night of the accident. The man who had no idea why Greg would have been driving in that area and—"You live near Elk Grove."

"Not anymore." Discomfort flickered across Sloane's face. "New job, new hair, new zip code . . . Lots of changes."

"I . . ." Taylor kept her voice steady. The last time she'd seen this woman was at Greg's funeral. "I understand that."

"I figured you would. Considering . . ."

Don't make me cry. . . . I'm past crying.

Taylor shifted her gaze back to the computer, trying to ignore the sound of her heart pounding in her ears. "Now let's see . . . Yes, you're all set here. That's it. Triage is officially yours."

In less than two minutes she was out of the office, down the corridor, and inside the ladies' room. She held herself together until the cleaning lady finished wiping down the mirror and clattered her cart back through the door. Then Taylor sank back against the sink. Her throat ached with unshed tears and her stomach was dangerously queasy. The strange thing was that all of it had less to do with Greg's death than it had to do with her own life. Her continued failure. Wasn't it only minutes ago that she'd applauded herself for being past the effects of grief? And then a simple encounter with a woman she barely knew sent her tumbling back down that rabbit hole?

Taylor closed her eyes, remembering the nurse's words. *"New job . . . new zip code . . ."* Sloane Wilder had moved on by moving away. Maybe that's what it took.

———

"That artist's sketch is about as helpful as the one they had for the Unabomber," the older deputy complained. Hank had caught Fletcher as he exited the briefing room. He grinned, waiting as Fletcher grabbed a shotgun from the armory. "You going to bring him down, Houston? Hog-tied and branded?"

Fletcher smiled. "Maybe."

"I'll watch for the YouTube video." The man's grin faded. "Seth says the kids of that bank manager sent a letter to Vince's kids saying they felt bad about Titus."

The slain K-9. Fletcher shook his head.

"Say . . ." Hank met Fletcher's gaze as they walked on toward the parking lot. "How's your mother doing?"

"Good. A little stir-crazy; they haven't cleared her to get back to her volunteer work yet. But she's keeping busy. And waiting for the next lab tests."

"My sister was like a pincushion with all those tests."

"That about says it," Fletcher agreed, grateful once again for what this man had shared regarding his sister's gastric cancer treatment. Surgery, radiation, chemo. Three years a survivor. She and her husband were "birding" in Copper Canyon, Mexico, right now, another annual celebration of her continuing health. "Hey, when she was going through all of that, did she get hounded by folks trying to sell her insurance? Financial assistance? That sort of thing?"

"Not that she said." Hank's graying brows drew together. "But medical information is confidential: HIPAA laws. It's not like the hospitals bring vendors in and give them a list of potential clients. Heads would roll." The man mimed a football move. "Because the Feds would be drop-kicking them from here to DC."

"Bet on it," Fletcher agreed.

"Why do you ask?"

"No reason. Something someone said."

"Well—" Hank tossed him a salute—"strap on those spurs and go find yourself an old Buick, Houston."

"Yessir."

Fletcher hefted his pursuit bag and headed toward his assigned patrol car, thinking about what Hank had said. The police artist sketch, obtained from witnesses who'd seen a stranger in the Stockton neighborhood where the plates were stolen, was minimally helpful. A white male, early forties maybe, tall and lanky build, thin face, knit cap pulled low. Glasses. Maybe. Beard. Maybe. Hank had been right: it was about as useful as that hoodie sketch of the infamous bomber. Hank had also been right about federal privacy laws. The hospital or doctor's office wouldn't have divulged his mother's AML diagnosis to a financial planner.

Elliot Rush was also the Sacramento Hope employee retirement adviser. He was on-site frequently. How difficult would it be to obtain patient information? Would he actually do that? Fletcher's jaw tensed at the image of Rush the day they'd met. Out on the freeway the day of the first shooting. Defending his expensive car and his bloated ego. Even if he'd gone out of his way to be conciliatory since, something smelled very bad about this situation. Fletcher wasn't going to let it rest.

He slid into the car, secured the shotgun. He'd called Rush's office twice and left messages. Didn't give details but requested an appointment later today regarding "some personal business." Fletcher had almost mentioned his concern to Macy but decided not to bother her with it. Her priority was her sister. He could understand that.

His was protecting his mother from vultures.

37

"I SHOULD KNOW BETTER than to eat the pretzels," the sixtysomething passenger told Macy, vigorously wiping her tray table. "Makes my fingers puffy." A deep chuckle made the skin around her dark eyes wrinkle like California raisins. "Sausage fingers—that's what my littlest grandson calls them. I think he's a spy for my internist." She glanced at Macy's iPad, pulled up to the ER nursing staff shift schedules. "Was it business that took you to Tucson?"

"No." Macy watched the woman's bracelet dangle as she cleaned the table, small silver discs with multicolored stones and engraved names. Her grandchildren in Sacramento, probably. "I was visiting my sister. She's pregnant," Macy added, figuring she'd better get used to saying it.

"How wonderful!" The woman's face lit. "First baby?"

"Yes." Though *wonderful* hardly factored into these

circumstances. Leah's oft-repeated and pitiful death grip on the toilet bowl just after dawn this morning hadn't been so terrific either. "First baby."

"Nothing like it." The woman touched a fingertip to her bracelet. "Except the second, third, fourth . . ." She chuckled again. "Though I have to admit grandchildren are easier. Haven't had a single stretch mark this go-round."

Macy smiled despite a crowding ache. She'd never known grandparents; neither had Leah. This baby wouldn't either. No birthstone charms. But . . . "My first time being an auntie too," she added, sending the new truth out there like fragile soap bubbles from a child's plastic wand. Leah had agreed to move to Sacramento "for a while." That this had been settled only after another racking bout of morning sickness—and some tears over Sean's uncertain future—didn't dilute Macy's relief. Leah was coming. It was a reality now. "They're going to live with me."

"Ah." There was a knowing look in the woman's kind eyes, but not one speck of judgment. "A blessing for all of you."

"Yes." Macy blinked against tears. Something about this stranger's gentle manner encouraged her on. "I wasn't sure she'd agree, but she needs help. And now that it's all settled, I'm . . ." A deep sigh escaped her lips. "So relieved. And really happy."

Their impending arrival in Sacramento was announced overhead. Macy dutifully switched off her electronic device.

"Then I'm happy for you," the woman said, patting her jacket sleeve. "After such good news, I'd say a celebration is in order."

"I think so too." A wave of giddy warmth buoyed Macy far beyond childish soap bubbles. More like champagne and—"Actually, I have a dinner date tonight."

"With someone special." The woman smiled. "I can see that on your face."

"Yes," Macy agreed, telling herself she'd never see this woman again. There was no risk in being crazy honest. Right this minute she trusted her feelings more than she ever remembered. "He's really special . . . like no one I've ever met before."

Like someone I could love.

Twenty minutes later, Macy had traversed the Southwest Airlines concourse, caught the Terminal B tram—passing beneath the airport's iconic fifty-six-foot-long fiberglass red rabbit sculpture suspended on cables from the ceiling. Before she could begin looking for the contracted transport van, the driver magically appeared. He was carrying a Starbucks cup of her favorite chai tea.

Leave it to Elliot to think of everything.

———

"Thank you, but no," Fletcher said, passing on Rush's offer of coffee or "something stronger." There was a well-stocked bar in this man's home office, an unpleasant reminder of how they'd met. Even more so was the obvious odor of alcohol on his breath right now. When they'd finally stopped playing message tag, Rush made a point of how he'd squeezed Fletcher in for this short afternoon appointment despite his daunting schedule. As a favor, he'd said.

And now Fletcher had used up half the time wandering this expansive East Sacramento property trying to locate the office. Which ended up being down a brick walkway as narrow as a deer path, through a jungle of bushes, behind the pool. Fletcher had seen Texas wild game blinds not nearly as well camouflaged. He shifted on the upholstered chair.

"Well then, how can I help you today? Some information on investments?" Rush's tone suggested he doubted the paltry commission would be worth his time.

"Not exactly," Fletcher began, noticing a framed photo by the desk: a casual shot of the Rushes on the deck of a sailboat along with a tanned young woman in a swimsuit. Macy? He pulled his gaze away, set the viatical brochure on the shiny desktop. "You sent this to my mother, Mrs. John Holt?"

"I'm not sure." Rush's leather chair squeaked as he leaned back into it. "I have a variety of investment packets. With brochures from several vendors. It would be hard to know if—"

"There." Fletcher turned it over, pointed to the inked logo at the bottom. "Your name, this address. Same as on the envelope."

Rush looked at his watch. Then met Fletcher's gaze, a so-what expression on his face. "Evidently, then, we did."

We. As if there were a half-dozen assistants in this hidden art gallery and bar masquerading as an office. Fletcher let it pass. "Why did you send it?"

"My discussions with clients are confidential, Mr. Holt. So I couldn't possibly—"

"She's not a client. And she did *not* request this information." Fletcher tensed as the financial adviser checked his watch a second time. If the man made a move to stand and dismiss him, he swore he would—"It says, right here, that this information is only offered to people with terminal illnesses. And you mailed it to my mother? You solicited her?"

"I'm under no obligation to explain my marketing plan." Rush had the decency to show the smallest hint of nervousness. The slight slur in his voice had become more apparent. "What's your point?"

"Never mind my point, how about *federal law*?" Fletcher challenged, enjoying the faint sheen of perspiration appearing at the man's thin hairline. "My mother's diagnosis and care are confidential, protected." He wanted to punch this man for even suggesting his mother's illness was terminal. "Even if your alliance with Sacramento Hope allowed you access to patient records—which it doesn't—it would be completely unethical to use that information for personal profit. You *did* that!"

Rush's eyes narrowed. But he said nothing.

Bile rose in Fletcher's throat. For the first time in his career, he questioned the wisdom of carrying an off-duty weapon. If the man didn't wipe that smirk off his face . . . He aimed his finger instead. "What are you doing, scouting the hospital for clients on your lunch break? Just who do you think you are?"

"Who?" Elliot stood, planted his hands on his desk. "I'll tell you who I am." He pointed to the wall behind his desk: College diplomas, certifications, and what could be twenty various plaques. Rotary symbols, awards with brass so shiny the engravings weren't even discernible, sponsorship plaques from local Little League teams . . . and even a photo of himself sharing a cigar with Governor Schwarzenegger. "I'm the man people trust with their futures. I'm who they come to. I have the answers. I make success happen. People trust me to do that."

"To break the law? Invade privacy?" Fletcher rose to his feet, stared at Rush, a hairbreadth away from reaching over the desk to grab him by the throat. "People trust you to offer odds on human life? How many decent people would be okay with that?"

Elliot smiled. "Maybe . . . people like Macy Wynn?"

Fletcher's breath stuck. "What's Macy got to do with it?"

"Plenty. Her portfolio includes viaticals—and she'll get a nice return. I'll see to that."

Fletcher shook his head, trying to make sense of it. The man had to be lying. It couldn't be—

"A woman her tender age doesn't approach a million dollars' net worth without maximizing her returns, even with trust fund seed money. Macy's sharp. She trusts me—always has. We'll see that million mark, together, before the year ends." His lips twisted. "With all the right investments. And her valuable input, of course."

Input?

"But Macy wouldn't . . . You're not saying . . . ," Fletcher flailed, trying to wrap his mind around it. There was no way Macy would divulge his mother's medical information.

"All I'm saying, Mr. Holt—" Rush tapped his Rolex—"is that I have another appointment. I'm sure you can find your way out."

Macy stooped down, cupping the Labradoodle's face between her palms. "You fuzzy mutt, have I told you lately that I love you?" She giggled, squeezing her eyes shut as the dog tried to lick her nose. "You have to promise Deputy Holt you've been a good guard dog. The man is pretty serious about my welfare." That ridiculous champagne-bubbly feeling came back. It was true—Fletcher cared about keeping her safe . . . *cares about me. A lot.*

He'd just returned the text she'd sent to say she was home. **On my way over**—short, to the point. And much earlier than she'd expected him to arrive. Macy's face warmed. Fletcher didn't want to waste any time either; he was as eager as she was to start their evening together. Dinner overlooking Lake Tahoe. Pine-scented summer air, the Sierra sky glittering with stars . . . What had that woman on the plane said? *"A celebration is in order."* Yes, it was going to be perfect.

She glanced in the full-length mirror the three roommates had struggled to install on the door of the hall closet. Not the best lighting, but . . . Macy did a little turn, almost a dancer's pirouette. She smiled at herself. Not half-bad—the twirl and the choice of outfit: white cotton-and-lace tee, modestly clingy and soft, under a short denim jacket topping the same slim navy skirt and heels she'd been wearing the afternoon they first met. On Highway 99. It seemed so long ago now, like it had been some other cop and nurse butting heads out there. So much had happened, changed, since then. Good things in the aftermath of tragedy, sun slanting through rain clouds: finding that amazing house, Leah's determination to stay clean and sober, her willingness to move to Sacramento, and . . . *Fletcher.* The bubbly feeling made Macy deliciously dizzy. Fletcher was definitely a good thing. She'd never felt this way before. Happy, hopeful . . .

Was it possible, what he'd said about God? That he had a hopeful plan for every single person? Goose bumps rose as she thought of Leah remembering Nonni's assurances: *"God knew me before I was born. And he even knew the exact number of hairs on my head. . . . Loved me . . . because I'm his child."*

Macy stared at her reflection, reached up to touch the carefully dyed strands in her hair. God, the loving Father? She thought of her answer to Leah's question about faith. *"I think . . . it must feel really good to believe that."* It had been a half answer, a hedge. But right now it felt like the truth. Maybe she did want to believe. Maybe she finally would. Could she trust that finding Leah and meeting Fletcher was part of a bigger plan to—?

A text message buzzed:

Roommates there?

Only me, she typed back quickly.

Macy's skin tingled, imagining Fletcher preplanning how he'd sweep her into his arms. She couldn't wait to tell him about Leah and the baby and about how good she'd started to feel about so many unexpected things.

The doorbell rang. Dood lurched.

"No way! I get him first," Macy laughed, scrambling close behind. She grabbed for his collar with one hand, fumbled at the lock with the other, and flung the door open at last, her heart racing like a rabbit.

"Macy."

"Hey," she blurted, ridiculously breathless. "What on earth took you so long? What's a girl supposed to—?" She stopped short, her runaway heart hitting a wall. Fletcher looked agitated, undone. "What's wrong? More news about the shoot—?"

"My mother," Fletcher interrupted. "I need to talk with you."

"Of course. Sure—come in," Macy told him, fear creeping in as she stepped back. "Dood, down."

She reached for Fletcher's hand. "Has something happened?"

"Maybe." He drew his hand away from hers. His eyes seemed more stormy gray than blue. "I just came from Elliot Rush's office. He said something about you being a millionaire."

She grimaced, hunted for words, but Fletcher kept talking.

"He said you're investing in buying life insurance policies from people who have terminal illnesses."

What?

Macy's brows scrunched as she struggled to understand. "Look. I can explain about the money. I should have— would have. Only it's so complicated . . ." Her knees weakened without warning. "What does this have to do with your mother?"

"She got a letter from his office. A brochure about viatical investments. When I asked Rush about it, he implied—*rubbed my nose in it*—that you'd shared medical information about Mom's cancer diagnosis. And about her . . ." His voice choked. "Her projected prognosis. So you could add her life insurance policy to your investment portfolio."

Oh no . . . "Wait—"

"No. I won't wait; I need to know. *Right now.*" Fletcher's lips were a grim line. "Is it true? Did you do that, Macy?"

38

PLEASE, LORD . . . Fletcher's gut twisted as he sat on the edge of the couch, waiting for Macy to return from closing the dog in her bedroom. He'd nearly heaved into Rush's jungle of landscaping as he headed back to his Jeep. Then prayed all the way over here that the pompous little man had lied. It had to be a lie. But that look on Macy's face . . .

"He's contained," she reported, taking a seat next to Fletcher. "We're safe."

He wished that were true.

"Talk to me." Fletcher captured her gaze, confirmed the guilt on her face; he hadn't imagined it. "I'm going crazy here, Macy. Explain this."

"The money . . ." She closed her eyes for a moment. "That part's true. There's this fund that my . . . biological father set up through a lawyer. I never wanted it. But . . ."

"You let Rush manage it," Fletcher finished, remembering what she'd said that day on the freeway. She'd said that her interrupted dinner with Elliot Rush was a business meeting. "He invested your money under your direction."

"No. I didn't even want to talk about it. I just wanted him to handle things. Do what he thought was best."

"Like viatical investments." Fletcher's jaw tensed. "Because there's such a 'good return' on the investment."

Macy looked almost as sick as he felt. "He only mentioned viaticals a few weeks back. I told him I didn't like the idea. On principle—I'm a nurse. I took an oath to help save lives." She hugged her arms around herself, rocked forward. "In all these years, I've never even touched that money, Fletcher. Not a dime. I hated the thought of it. It was a humiliating payoff from a man who wished I'd never been born." Macy trembled. "But then they found mold in the house I'm buying. I didn't have the money to fix it. So I borrowed it from the trust. I told Elliot to work his magic with investments to replace what I used."

"'Magic'?" Fletcher asked, disgust stomping on any empathy he felt for her story. "You mean trading on people's lives? Making yourself a beneficiary to life insurance policies and then—what? Gambling that those people die fast? So you don't have to make more monthly premium payments?"

"No." Macy's face paled. "That's not what—"

"Did you tell him to make those investments?"

"I . . . Maybe." Her voice dropped to a halting whisper. "I'm not sure. I think I just gave him free rein. All I was thinking about was getting the house. I didn't ask for any details."

"But you offered some. Plenty. Information about my mother's cancer."

"No." Macy's eyes held his. "I swear, if Elliot did that— approached Charly—I didn't know anything about it."

"But you talked to him about her condition. That's how he knew?"

"In conversation maybe. Your mom didn't hide the fact that she had AML. I might have said that I felt bad for her . . . for you. I didn't say anything about her prognosis or *ever* imply her condition was terminal." Macy touched his arm, wincing when he recoiled. "I swear, Fletcher, I'd never give Elliot the go-ahead for something like that. I'd never consider trying to benefit from your mother's situation."

"But it's okay to gamble on the lives of strangers. Buy anonymous life insurance policies and cash in. You think that's fair." Fletcher wanted to shake her. No, he wanted to get as far away from her as he could. "A house is more important than human life? You're fine with . . . betting against hope?"

"I can't look at it like that." Macy lifted her chin, blinked against gathering tears. "I need this house. For my sister. Elliot's making it happen. I have to trust him."

"Great." Fletcher shoved himself up from the couch. "I'm going."

"Wait, Fletcher. Please." Macy began to rise. "You need to understand—"

"No." He raised his palm. "I don't understand. I don't even begin to get you, Macy."

"Please . . . wait."

He jogged to his Jeep, gunned the engine, and sped away without looking back.

———

Macy glanced toward the window, shadowy now as the sun dipped toward the horizon. She swallowed a mouthful of green tea; it might as well have been used bathwater. She couldn't taste and wasn't all that sure about breathing, either. It had been two hours since Fletcher's Jeep roared off, and she'd sent a minimum of six texts to his phone. All unanswered. She took another sip from her cup, trying to ease the ache in her throat. Elliot hadn't responded to her voice mail either. He probably thought her tone sounded accusing. And didn't want to deal with her questions so soon after butting heads with Fletcher.

Macy could well imagine that ugly scene in Elliot's office. Why on earth had he said those things to Fletcher—done all of that? Was it payback for the embarrassing confrontation on the freeway? Elliot had been humiliated, beyond furious. Plus, it was clear he wasn't happy with the fact that she'd been seeing Fletcher socially. But neither was an excuse for revealing Macy's private financial information. And for telling Fletcher she'd violated his mother's privacy—breached confidentiality. Illegal and heartless. She'd never knowingly do something like that. But the way Fletcher had looked at her . . .

Tears welled again. It seemed impossible that only short hours ago she'd been happy, practically overcome with cheesy bliss. So much so that she'd been willing to risk telling Fletcher how she felt about him. How she loved the way he made her feel, happy and hopeful and—

"You're fine with . . . betting against hope?"

Macy set her cup down, swiped at a tear. She had to buck up, get a grip. Even if she'd had a chance to tell Fletcher about her sister's pregnancy, she wouldn't have made him understand that owning the house was even more important because of that. He wouldn't see that Leah needed a home, a real home. Fletcher Holt couldn't understand because he'd always had those things. A home and a family who loved him. Things that were almost unimaginable to people like Macy and Leah. Someone like Fletcher couldn't know what it felt like to never really belong *anywhere*.

"I don't even begin to get you, Macy."

It was true. She'd been a fool to hope for anything else. And to start to believe . . . *what?* Macy scraped her teeth across her lower lip, feeling the ache in her throat return with a vengeance. It was true. She'd almost fallen for it all: a man who could love her for who she was, and maybe even a God who wanted what was best for her. She reached up, once again found the dyed stripe in her hair. She'd almost bought into the fairy tale. What a fool. The fact was, God didn't get Macy either. He wanted as much to do with her as Lang Wen did. Her hard-knocks life had proven it over and over, taught Macy the most valuable lesson of all: the only thing she could fully count on was herself. Period. And despite what had happened today, her own plan was still moving forward.

Before Fletcher arrived, she'd contacted Elliot's associate, the real estate broker. They'd made an appointment to meet at the Tahoe Park house tomorrow. She'd signed the papers to get the mold removal started. He'd agreed to give her an opportunity to take some photos of the house— from the little brick oven in the kitchen to the bedroom that could be Leah's and the tree in the backyard that would be a perfect spot for a child's swing. Macy already had her sister's promise she was coming to Sacramento, but the photos would help Leah get it on a heart-deep level. She'd see that she and her baby would have a real home.

Macy reached for the brass door set she'd brought out from her bedroom. She would ask the contractor to install it. It had been as much a part of their foster mother's home as the scent of warm oatmeal cookies. Nonni might have been gullible about a loving God who knew all of his children down to the number of hairs on their heads, but she knew everything there was about making a lost and lonely child feel wanted.

"Welcome home, Macy girl."

Macy nodded. It was time to pay it forward.

She lifted her phone from the coffee table, checked once more for messages that weren't there. And then reached for her tea again. She'd finish it, then work on her to-do list— things to accomplish as escrow ticked forward and preparations for Leah's move to Sacramento. It all needed to be done, and without Fletcher it would be easier to stay focused.

Without him. Macy's heart cramped. Right now they should be together at Lake Tahoe . . .

———

"No. Thanks," Fletcher told the waiter, raising his voice over shouts from a raucous darts tournament that drifted onto the brewery's deck each time the doors opened. "I'm good here." He nudged a half-eaten potato skin, frowned at the beer he'd ordered—flat, untouched. "You can take this away. The beer too. Bring me some coffee. Black."

Fletcher couldn't remember the last time he'd had a beer. Never much liked the stuff. But it seemed like a good idea tonight, the same way driving to Tahoe City had. He'd been wrong on both counts. Thin air combined with a little beer buzz should have been a feel-good prescription. But it was obvious that nothing would make today feel better. He drew in a breath of pine-scented evening air and exhaled slowly, trying to diffuse the gut-churning disappointment.

He wasn't a tissue match for his mother. Not even close, according to the percentages and science-speak accompanying the HLA results. *"Even with a parent or sibling, it's only a one in four chance of being a marrow donor, at best."* His mother's words on the day he'd had the blood drawn. She'd tried to warn him, but Fletcher had been confident he would beat those odds as handily as he'd aced his firearms qualifications. If his mother needed a marrow transplant, it would come from him. But there it was, in black-and-white: no match.

The waiter set his coffee in front of him, steam rising in the cool air.

"Thanks."

The letter had been waiting for him when he arrived home from Macy's place—couldn't have been lousier timing. Not only had he failed a major opportunity to save his mother's life; his girlfriend's money manager was trying to place a wager on her early death.

Fletcher closed his eyes against an image of Macy's face, the reaction when he confronted her about Rush's viatical brochure. She had looked confused, then horrified. Genuinely. He wanted to believe it, but he kept remembering what she'd said about the "acting lessons" from her mother. How she'd survived when they were forced to live on the streets. From homeless orphan to a trust fund millionaire? How was he supposed to take that in? And reconcile it with the woman he'd come to . . . *love?* Had he really been headed down that path?

Fletcher didn't know anything for sure anymore. Except that . . . *I don't belong here.* He turned to look out across the deep-blue expanse of Lake Tahoe, to the snow-topped peaks beyond, still visible in the waning light. The chill breeze lifted his hair. June, and it wasn't much over forty degrees. And so dry a spark had arced from his finger when he reached out to close the door of his Jeep. It was foreign . . . No, *he* was the foreigner here. Homesick. And after today, he only wanted—

His phone signaled a call. Jessica.

"Hey," Fletcher said, cell against his ear.

"Well now, if this isn't a for-sure miracle," she laughed, the honeyed sound so very familiar. "What are the odds? Me thinking of you. And you actually picking up."

"I'm here." Fletcher glanced toward the snow. "Where are you, exactly?"

"Not where I want to be. I'm at work. On my break— at the tables outside Houston Grace. By the ER. You remember."

Fletcher swore he could hear the thrum of summer cicadas. "I remember."

"I was thinking of that time I got an itch to run the beach on Galveston Island. After my p.m. shift. And you insisted on driving me. Insufferable, overprotective bully that you are," Jessica teased. "Picked me up right here."

At nearly midnight. Because the thought of her driving there alone made him crazy with worry. And because it had been one more chance to—

"We had such a great time, Fletcher. Running down that beach, watching the stars, laughing at your stupid jokes . . ."

It hadn't been that way at all. Not even close. Jessica had been desperately sad then, scattered, fragile—riding a self-destructive roller coaster that threatened her life. Fletcher was the only constant, the one person she trusted. He'd done everything he could to keep her safe, and accomplished it. The same summer he'd rescued a child from a storm-damaged house. But now, when it was his own mother who needed help, he couldn't make it happen.

Why, Lord? Where are you?

"It was July, I think. Sweltering, anyway." Her voice sounded wistful. "The air was so thick you could spoon it up. It smelled like pink popcorn . . . and a bucket of those fat, grilled Gulf shrimp. Except that they'd already closed the restaurants." She sighed with obvious regret. "And we missed the live music up on Pleasure Pier. My bad timing, of course. But it was still so great having the whole beach to ourselves . . ."

Fletcher closed his eyes, letting the soft-taffy pull of Jessica's voice transport him across the miles. *Home . . .*

"Do you remember that time, Fletcher?"

"Kind of." He turned his collar up against the frigid Sierra breeze. "Feels like a long time ago."

"And it sounds like I'm keeping you from something important. Sorry." A distant siren replaced the drone of cicadas. "I just needed to hear your voice, that's all. My break's almost over, so I should—"

"Wait." Fletcher's fingers tightened on the phone like it was a last vestige of hope. "How much time's left on your break?"

"I don't know. Three or four minutes maybe."

"Good." He released the breath he'd been holding. "Remind me of that time in Galveston. And anything else you can think of. Just keep talking, Jessica. I need to hear your voice too."

———

The Buick was parked not twenty feet below him. In the garage, directly beneath where he lay now—on his belly on the floor of the master bedroom. An empty, echoing space, cold and dark. As black as the unseeing eyes of his first deer kill. It was his father's bedroom. And being here felt good . . . right. Especially tonight. This last night.

He propped himself up on one elbow, ran a palm over the familiar gold shag carpet. It smelled like his father's cigarettes. Lucky Strikes. And like dog—there had always been a dog sleeping at the foot of his father's bed. But the last dog was gone. And so was his father, three weeks tomorrow. It was for the best. He'd never belonged in that nursing home. Never would have wanted to see it all come to this.

He reached for the old, tasseled couch pillow he'd snagged from the Buick, comforted by its lingering scents of gasoline and gun oil. He thought of the last time he'd seen his father's face, the only time he'd ever been glad not to find recognition there. He folded the couch pillow to his chest, closed his eyes. The bed pillows at the nursing home stank the way those places always did: adult diapers, soured Ensure . . . and hopelessness. Even a flea-infested jack-rabbit deserved better than that. His father should never have gone there.

He crawled across the carpet, raised himself just high enough to peer over the windowsill and across the driveway to the neighbor's roof. He knew it like the back of his hand; he'd nailed every one of those shingles in place himself fifteen years back, when he was between jobs. And he'd plinked a few BB gun shots off that same roof maybe twelve years before that. He smiled, enjoying the thought.

Then he crawled back across the carpet, bunched the couch pillow under his head. Tomorrow it would finally be over.

39

"IT'S A LITTLE RED," Macy told Taylor, shifting the phone as she leaned down to lift the Band-Aid away from her ankle. The tattoo was laser-zapped and gone as of two hours ago. "I probably shouldn't have done the bike miles. My sock rubbed it. They said to expect some swelling."

"Sounds painful."

"Not too bad." Macy sat back up. She'd forgotten the appointment until the reminder popped up on her phone this morning, then raced to the dermatologist's office after only a few hours of fitful sleep. She'd been kept awake by a merciless flood of should-haves, regrets, and achy-sweet memories. Fletcher had never answered her texts. Or the pitiful "Call me?" voice mail she'd left around eleven o'clock last night.

"My ankle's okay," Macy added with a sigh. "I've had things that hurt a lot worse."

"I hear you." There was empathy in Taylor's voice. "Did you get tired of people asking if you'd tattooed pinto beans on your leg?"

"Just . . . not a ballerina." Pain jabbed that had nothing to do with the laser procedure. Nonni had been wrong about that, too.

"But you're almost a homeowner."

"Yes." Macy glanced at the brass door set she'd polished during those sleepless hours. If the contractor agreed to install it, she wanted it shiny. "I'm meeting the Realtor there this afternoon. To take a thousand pictures."

"I can't wait to see them. You're at work tomorrow, too, right?"

"Bright and early."

"Good. I need to get to that dentist appointment, but we'll talk in the morning. I . . ." Taylor seemed to hesitate. "I want to run something by you. A new life plan, I guess you'd call it."

"Wow. Sure, I want to hear it. I'm all about making a new plan . . ." Macy stopped herself before she told the volunteer chaplain the rest of her thought: *Because it's not like God's working on one.* She wasn't going to dump any of this on Taylor.

———

"Yes, ma'am," Fletcher told the thirtysomething jogger who apparently managed—determination over exhaustion, no doubt—to do her daily run behind a stroller carrying chubby twins. "That's a good, detailed description. And you've never seen this man before?"

"Never." She peered down the quiet, tree-lined street, well outside what the FBI believed was the target area. "And that's what made me suspicious," she explained. "Even if it wasn't that car they showed in the *Bee*."

Not even close. Fletcher would make a sizable bet the shooter would be smarter than to trade the nondescript Buick for a pumpkin-orange muscle car. Or even to risk being seen in daylight since the police sketch went national. There had been no reliable sightings since the night Fletcher followed the Buick off Macy's street. The shooter either had successfully fled the area or was lying low somewhere.

"I didn't like the way he was sort of checking out the neighborhood," the jogger finished, jostling the stroller as one of her twins began to fuss. "And there are still a few foreclosures in here. One of them has been vacant for at least a year; the bank sees to it that the front lawn's reasonably kept up, but who knows what's going on inside? It's not even on the market right now. Someone could easily hide in there. You know?"

"Yes, ma'am." Between the Feds and local law enforcement, it had probably been checked off the list of vacant homes already. "If you know the address, I'll drive by there right now. Give it a look. And I'll pass on the information about the suspicious car to the deputies who work this area."

"Thank you." A flicker of anxiety crossed her face. "That bank manager, she was only two years older than I am. I don't know how my husband would cope if he had to manage the boys without me, and . . . I just want this whole thing to be over with."

"Keeping citizens safe is our top priority," he told her,

reminding himself that it was why he'd chosen law enforcement. For the chance to keep that promise. *Service with Concern*—it was painted right on his car.

Fletcher took down the address, then gave the young mother a card with the phone numbers for making reports. Then watched as she and her twin boys continued their jog through the neighborhood. His cell phone buzzed the instant he slid back into his patrol car.

"Bad time?" his mother asked.

"No. No problem." Unless she'd been Macy. Fletcher almost called her after that voice message last night, but he still hadn't figured out how to handle it. "What's up?"

"Spaghetti," she told him. "With Spanish olives and the last of that ground venison you brought us. And I wanted to be sure you're not beating yourself up about the HLA test."

"Maybe I should get a second opinion."

"Maybe you should stop worrying and remember who's in charge of this. Way bigger than both of us—even with Texas factored in."

"Ma . . ." Fletcher didn't know what to say, how to say it. Every time he closed his eyes, he saw that viatical brochure on his mother's kitchen table. And the horrible truth hit him like a fist in the gut: maybe, in the end, that self-serving weasel, Rush, could offer his parents more peace than he could. "It's hard not to be doing something about this myself. I came here to do something. Help you. Not stand by and watch."

"I know. But that's the thing about faith." Her voice was as gentle as when she used to purse her lips and blow a kiss onto his skin scrapes. "You have to wait. Hang in there."

There was the barest of chuckles. "Faith isn't like a carton of milk. There's no expiration date."

"Right." He frowned, scrolling through the updates on the car's MDT computer.

"I forgot to ask when I invited you for dinner," his mother added. "Are you seeing Macy tonight? She's more than welcome to come for—"

"No. Macy's busy. I'll be there for dinner. And . . ."

"And?"

"I talked to Jessica last night. I was thinking maybe I'd try to take a couple days off and fly home. See some friends, check on the house—" He stopped short as dispatch voiced a pending prowler call. He scanned the text of the call on his MDT, put the patrol car in gear. "Gotta go. I've got a call. See you tonight."

He keyed the mic and told the dispatcher, "94-Boy-1. I'll take the 910 on Atwood. I'm about four away."

"Copy, 94-Boy."

Fletcher checked his mirrors and pulled away from the curb, stepped on the gas.

Possible prowler at a vacant house. Reported by a neighbor. He'd check it out. It would probably amount to nothing. But it wasn't a pumpkin-orange muscle car, and it was within the shooter's target area.

———

Macy balanced on the porch rail and stretched up precariously—Band-Aid pulling against the laser blister—to get her phone close enough to snap a photo of the nest. She smiled as another round of insistent and hungry peeps rose.

A nest and baby birds. Tucked, somehow, into the porch overhang, only a few feet above the door of . . . *our house. Our nest.* Goose bumps rose. She couldn't wait to show Leah. What could be a better sign of good luck than—?

"Swallows," the perspiring middle-aged man told Macy, appearing at the edge of the porch.

"Oh, hi." Macy rebalanced her footing and peered down at him. He'd been working in the yard next door, watching covertly as she waited for the Realtor. "It's a swallow nest up there?"

"That's right. Here." He raised his metal rake and stepped closer, rubber thong sandals slapping. "Use the handle to knock it down. Couple of good pokes should do it."

She stared at him. "There are babies in that nest. Can't you hear them?"

"Junk birds—you don't want to let them get a foothold. They always latch on right over the door." He gave her a cursory once-over as she climbed down from the rail, brushed at her blouse. "You showing the place?"

"Meeting the Realtor." Macy decided against telling him more. She worked during the day. Hopefully she'd rarely see this obnoxious neighbor.

A siren sounded in the distance, and the baby birds began another round of hopeful cheeps.

"Folks will tell you all kinds of things about how to discourage 'em," the man continued, frowning at the nest. "Paint the overhang blue, squirt shaving cream up there, hang plastic owls, install those wire spikes . . ." He seemed to enjoy her grimace. "Doesn't work. They're stubborn little cusses. Knock them down when you first see them and then keep at it. That's the only way they'll get that they don't belong there. Trust me." He shrugged, glanced toward his house. "Well, I'd better get back to work."

Macy watched as he ambled back to his yard. If she'd had some decent sleep, she wouldn't let this guy get under her skin. *"Junk birds . . . stubborn little cusses . . . don't belong there . . ."* If that man thought these little birds were stubborn, wait until he met his new neighbors. Maybe she'd ask the Realtor if the contractor could install wire spikes to keep *him* from being a nuisance.

She chuckled aloud, then glanced at the time display on her cell phone. If the Realtor ever got here, that is. Fifteen minutes late now. She'd left a voice mail, but he hadn't called back. No one was returning calls, it seemed. Only a short all-okay text from Leah after her doctor's appointment today; they'd had a cancellation and squeezed her in early. There were no return messages from Elliot . . . or Fletcher. Still no word from Fletcher.

Stop it. I'm moving forward.

Macy stooped down to pick up the brass door set and crossed to the red-lacquered door. She eyed the cheap, temporary latch the bank had installed after the previous owner removed the original. Doubt crept in—would Nonni's set fit this door? Were these measurements standard? She had no clue. Her learning curve as a homeowner was going to be as steep as the face of El Capitan.

"Macy."

She turned, dropping a screw from the door set.

"Elliot. You scared me."

———

Two blocks from the address of the prowler call, Fletcher's radio squawked with an update. "94-Boy-1, be advised: Neighbor reports possible smoke from windows at the Atwood Court address. Fire has been dispatched. Unknown if suspect is still on scene."

"94-Boy. Copy. Be there in two." Fletcher slid the lever for the siren and lights. "I'll be going code."

Arson?

40

THE BRANCHES OVERHANGING THE ROOF provided shade—and cover. He'd counted on that. He let himself remember, as he hunkered into position on the shingles, the carving he'd done in the trunk of his neighbor's old tree all those years ago. Not his initials or some girl's name. Just five simple gouge marks in the thick bark: four in a row, one slashed diagonally across them—the toughest segment to cut. He'd sliced his finger doing it. Even left a little blood behind.

Five marks. For each of his neighbors' missing cats. His father wouldn't have liked it. And he would have hated the rest of this . . .

He looked back toward the house, saw smoke escaping from the windows on the driveway side now. It wouldn't be long before flames were visible. Before his father's home was fully engulfed—gone before they could slam down the gavel, take it away like they had everything else. At least his father hadn't lived to see it all play out.

He closed his eyes, remembering his father's age-lined face again, his milky-blue eyes. The way he'd looked on that last day. Had Abe Archer smiled, just a little, when his son kissed his forehead? And when he finally dozed off, did he dream of the times they'd shared . . . the dogs, bedrolls, campfires, that old canoe? And . . . He took a slow breath. *Did he know it was me holding the pillow over his face?*

No. It didn't matter now. It would all be over soon.

Ned Archer lifted the Browning .270 from the shingles, balanced it expertly in his hands. He sighted down the driveway. The sirens were close. It would only be a matter of minutes now. If he'd cut tally marks on that tree for this new hunt, it would have been only two kills so far. The woman and the dog.

Today there would be more. And he'd leave some of his own blood behind again.

———

"I'm surprised to see you, that's all," Macy explained as she walked ahead of Elliot into the empty house. Her footfalls echoed on the hardwood floor like a sound effect in a low-budget horror movie. She looked for a spot to lay the brass door set down and finally put it on the ledge of the small pass-through window that connected the dining room with the kitchen. Then she turned to look at him, feeling strangely uncomfortable. But it was bound to feel awkward, considering their recent history. "Stan wasn't available after all?"

Elliot's prolonged silence did nothing to put Macy at ease. "Stan had several appointments," he said finally. "I told him I would handle this."

This? For some reason, Macy thought of the neighbor with the rake.

"I brought the copies of your agreement with the contractor," he added, resting his briefcase against the dining room wall.

"Good. I appreciate it." Macy cleared her throat, determined to retrieve that happy feeling she'd had when she first found the good-omen bird nest. The questions she had regarding Charly Holt could wait a bit; right now she wanted to savor her future. Elliot wasn't going to spoil it for her.

"I told Stan I wanted to take some photos," she said, reaching up to admire the wood trim framing the pass-through window. "Mostly for my sister. But also to get some ideas for carpet, paint colors, and decorating. Stan said he knew a contractor with contacts at discount places. I won't spend a lot, but I want to make it feel homey. For us and for when people come to visit us here. So—"

"He's wrong for you, Macy."

She thought for a moment that Elliot was talking about the contractor, but the look on his face warned of the same dialogue he'd pressed in his office. He stepped closer and Macy suspected he'd been drinking this time too. Reddened eyes and his breath—"I'm not going to have this conversation, Elliot."

"Don't talk; listen." His eyes darted back and forth. "Whatever Holt told you is a lie," he sputtered. "I don't know how he ever got past the psychological exam. He's paranoid, dangerous, and—"

"Did you do that?" Macy forced Elliot to meet her gaze but kept her voice calm. "Did you send his mother information about selling her life insurance policy? Without her request? And then imply I had something to do with it?"

"The brochure had our address stamped on it. He didn't have the envelope. Holt could have picked it up anywhere." Elliot swept his fingers through his thinning hair, his agitation mounting. "Don't you see what he's doing? He's trying to drive a wedge between us, Macy. He can't handle that our relationship has spanned *years* and has grown into something—"

"You told him about the trust money," Macy blurted. The last thing she wanted was to taint this hopeful house with bitter accusations but . . . "You compromised my privacy. You had no right to do that."

Elliot's eyes narrowed. "And what exactly do you think *he* wants to compromise? What do you think that street cop's sniffing after? He only wants one thing. He doesn't see you like I do, Macy. He doesn't admire you for all you've accomplished, for who you are. Fletcher Holt couldn't care less that you're intelligent and savvy . . . and yes, a person of substantial means because of that. And because of *me*. Holt looks at you the way he looks at every conquest. He only sees a very desirable woman with amazing eyes, long legs . . ." His gaze fixed on her blouse. "And such beautiful—"

"Stop it," Macy demanded, repulsed. "What *is* this? Don't say another word. This is making me ill." Her eyes widened as he grasped her arm. She pulled back, but his grip tightened. "Let go of me, Elliot. Right now."

"Please," he begged, loosening his grip only slightly. "Can't you see that I'm only trying to protect you? I've been doing that since you were a kid. I know you better than anyone does. You know me. I would do anything for you, *anything*. Please, listen to—"

"Let *go*."

"There!" He dropped her arm, then leaned so close that saliva speckled her face as he continued his rant. "You know, you should be a lot more grateful. Where do you think you'd be without me? Maybe living like your mother did? Turning tricks out on the—"

"Don't!" Macy stepped back, anger giving way to disbelief. Then horror as he lurched forward again, making her stumble backward until her spine smacked against the dining room wall. He pressed closer still, grunting. Pinning her. Macy shoved against his chest. "No . . . stop."

"You should be a *lot* more grateful," Elliot growled, grabbing at her hair. Macy thrashed, turned her head as his mouth connected with her cheek, then slid under her jaw to her throat. "Macy . . ."

Kick him!

"No!" Macy fought as Elliot's hands tore at her blouse, sweaty fingers fumbling with her bra. "Get off me!"

"C'mon . . . relax . . ." Elliot's mouth sought hers again.

Macy shoved back, tried to bring her knee up between his legs.

"Don't you dare, you little—"

Elliot's obscenity dissolved in a guttural growl as he

wrenched her left wrist, hard. There was a pop, pain so intense it made her gag. He slammed Macy against the wall again, yanking her injured arm over her head. But her right hand remained mercifully free, and she stretched it out, searching for . . . hoping . . . *Please, please.*

There.

Elliot began pulling her down to the floor.

She raised the brass door set high and slammed it hard against his skull. He cried out, staggered backward, and fell.

Macy sprinted for the door.

———

"Barricades in place," the volunteer firefighter reported, wiping a beefy hand across his brow. He glanced toward the house, a scant ten yards up the driveway. They'd pulled the water tender in, parked close to the garage. Flames licked at the windows of a room on the second story. "We're keeping the looky-loos back. Neighbors. You know."

"Yeah." Fletcher had been on scene barely seven minutes and had already escorted an elderly woman home twice, but she'd pushed her way back through the hedge. She was the next-door neighbor who'd first reported the possible prowler and the subsequent smoke. She wanted to make certain Fletcher recorded all of her observations— along with some extraneous and long-winded history about a man with Alzheimer's and his very nice son who'd tried so hard to hold on to the house. Fletcher squinted toward the porch, thinking he'd been here before. Not on any call he could remember but . . .

"Arson team is on the way," the firefighter added, raising

his voice over the insistent chug of the tender truck. "You didn't see anybody when you looked around?"

"No." It had been a cursory inspection; the firefighters needed to get in. But Fletcher would buy the arson idea—it fit from the 911 sequence—except that the neighbor woman said the house was bank owned and scheduled for auction. It wasn't like a foreclosed homeowner could collect on insurance. The house hadn't been sitting empty as long as some, from the looks of it. But long enough for the back lawn to grow weeds and thistles knee-high; Fletcher could vouch for that. And it had been vacant enough time for its windows to be shattered by vandals. The garage windows were covered with plywood.

"Let's get some hoses in here!" a firefighter shouted as smoke billowed out from the open garage. "And we better roll this old car out."

Car?

Fletcher squinted, pulse quickening. Couldn't be . . . *Is it?* He broke into a jog, one hand on his radio. Ready to—

A sharp crack split the air.

The firefighter dropped in the driveway, bleeding.

God . . . no.

"Down, down! Everybody, down!" Fletcher drew his weapon and hunkered low, scuttling for cover. "94-Boy—shots fired! Firefighter down," he radioed as he attempted to gauge the trajectory of the shot. "Be advised: vehicle in garage fits description of—"

Shouts rose. "On the roof, up there. Next door!"

Fletcher whirled, gun raised, saw the muzzle flash—and was blown instantly backward, his thigh exploding in pain.

He collapsed onto the driveway, blood gushing beneath him.

"Officer down!"

Another crack. The cement pulverized mere inches away.

"94-Boy . . . I've been shot. . . ." Fletcher groaned and rolled to his side, slipping in pooled blood as he positioned himself to take aim again. His heart was as loud as gunfire in his ears. He risked a glance at his leg. Too much blood. Pumping, red . . . an artery? He was dizzy, faint . . . Couldn't pass out. Had to stop the shooter before he killed someone else. *God . . . help me do this.*

It was an effort to lift his gun. . . . *Weak, too weak.* And the pain . . . Fletcher held his breath, searched the roof— *there. He's there.* He fought a surge of nausea as the man met his gaze directly, lowered the rifle a few inches, and continued to stare. Fletcher blinked as his vision dimmed. Sweat dripped down his face; he was cold, dizzy. *Bleeding out . . . got to stop it. Get a shot, before . . .*

The shooter began to raise his rifle again.

Fletcher snatched at his bloody pant leg, found the bullet hole. Gritted his teeth and jammed his thumb in, burying it deep enough to feel the weak pulsing of his severed vessel. He pressed down hard, sucked in a breath, then aimed his weapon and fired until the slide locked back—clip emptied.

41

Sirens . . . Did they need so many sirens?

Fletcher's head pounded . . . then floated. He wanted to vomit. He needed to sit up. It felt like there was a block of cement sitting on his leg. And what was this thing tied over his—?

"Easy, Deputy Holt. That's an oxygen mask. In the ambulance, remember?" A man's face loomed over his. Young, stethoscope around his neck. "Your heart's pumping more IV fluids than blood right now. You need all the oxygen you can get. Trust me." He shook his head. "That bullet got some major vessels."

Bullet. Fletcher's groan fogged the mask as the images rushed back. The house fire, the Buick . . . "The shooter?"

"You got him." The medic leaned over him again. "Someday you're gonna show me how you did that with one thumb buried in your femoral artery. But right now I just want to keep your BP over 70 until I can hand you over to a trauma surgeon." He steadied the IV bags as the ambulance jolted around a turn. "We're taking you to Sacramento Hope."

Macy. Fletcher closed his eyes, saw her beautiful face. An ache crowded his heart. The oxygen mask wasn't giving him enough air.

"Almost to the ER," the paramedic reported, frowning at the numbers on the monitor displays. "You hang in there. Don't let me down now, hear?"

Fletcher nodded, tried to lift his hand for a thumbs-up, but it was more than he could do. Even breathing was sapping his strength. His head was floating, bobbing like a buoy out on Galveston Bay. The pain was hardly there anymore. Was that a good thing or—? Fletcher's vision went fuzzy dim as he tried to sit up.

"What's wrong?" The paramedic loomed overhead again.

"My parents . . ." Fletcher swallowed, mouth dry. "They've had a lot to deal with. If I die—"

"No way." The paramedic clamped a hand on Fletcher's shoulder. "We're pulling up to the ER now, buddy. No dying on my watch."

Please, Lord, don't take me . . . not yet.

———

"Do you believe Mr. Rush's intent was to rape you?"

Macy's stomach lurched. If she had anything left in it, she'd probably heave again. Even close to two hours afterward, it was still impossible to accept. "I'm not sure."

The older female deputy leaned forward in the clinic's chair, her tone gentle but firm. "You told the doctor that Mr. Rush tore your blouse and touched your breast."

Macy nodded, glanced down at her left arm—in a purple fiberglass cast. Elliot had twisted her wrist hard enough to fracture it. Her voice emerged in a hoarse whisper. "I was afraid he might . . . force it further. He wouldn't let go of me. That's why I hit him."

"With that brass . . ." The deputy scanned her notes.

"Door set. I was hoping to have it installed on the house." Nonni's door set. In a police evidence locker now. Macy shivered despite the warmed blanket the nurse had given her. She'd driven to an urgent care a few blocks from the hospital, too embarrassed to go to the ER where everyone knew her. And where they knew—"How badly did I hurt Elliot?"

"I can't really answer that. I mean I don't know," the deputy amended. "I only know that he's in custody. His arrest was without incident."

Arrested. Macy struggled to take it in. How could all of this be possible? It was a nightmare. A new thought made her breath catch. "Will I need a lawyer? Will there be—?"

The deputy's cell phone buzzed and she held up a finger. "Excuse me one minute." She stood and walked a few steps away.

Macy took a sip of water, hiked up the blanket. She wouldn't confide any of this to Leah. It would be such an unwelcome reminder of—

"I'm sorry for the interruption," the deputy said, taking her chair again. "Crazy out there after we took down the freeway sniper."

Macy's jaw sagged. "I didn't hear. I haven't seen the TV or . . . You got him?"

"About forty-five minutes ago. He was pronounced dead on scene. The media's having a field day trying to ferret out the details, of course." The deputy's brows puckered. "That call was an update on our deputy who was shot in the confrontation. He's in surgery. Such a great guy. And his mother's a Crisis Care chaplain."

Macy's heart stalled. "Wait . . . Fletcher Holt?"

"That's right. You know him?"

———

Taylor pressed Charly's doorbell a second time, glanced at Seth. She was still reeling. The shooter was Ned Archer. She and Charly had attempted a chaplain visit at that house— Seth too. The man had been a patient at the ER; Taylor had talked to him. And now . . . Her stomach knotted. "Charly hasn't answered our calls either. Maybe—"

"Ring it again." Seth's expression said he knew what she was thinking: chaplains on the doorstep meant bad news. They were bringing it to a friend this time. "Charly could have been showering, having quiet time with her Bible," he explained. "She should hear this from us first."

Taylor pressed the doorbell again. Took a slow breath— and it stuck in her chest as Charly opened the door.

"Oh, my goodness, what a treat," she said, her lovely eyes lighting. She wore an apron and a spongy set of vintage earphones draped around her neck. "I hope you weren't standing there long. I was cooking venison spaghetti and listening to music on my—" Her gaze met Taylor's, and the light went out of her eyes. Charly pressed a hand over her heart. "Is something wrong? Oh, dear God . . . is it Fletcher?"

———

Macy stood outside the ICU doors, trying to work up the nerve to phone the unit's clinical coordinator. She'd changed into scrubs, hung her hospital ID badge around her neck, and made her way into Sacramento Hope, satisfying security. Though she had no official reason to be here. And no credible relational reason either. *Would Fletcher even want me here?*

He'd been out of surgery for five hours. Macy had waited—watching TV news, pacing the house—until the hospital night shift arrived. The nurse in charge was a friend. She'd confided that Fletcher's condition was critical but stable; his initial lab work was . . . *so bad.* Macy's heart cramped. They were infusing blood.

She tapped her phone.

"You're here?" the nurse asked her.

"Right outside—in scrubs. Okay to come in?"

"There's family in there. His father just got in from Alaska."

"I won't even go to the bedside. I . . . need to see him with my own eyes. That's all."

"You know the door code. He's in 15."

Macy stepped inside, blinking as her eyes adjusted to the dim lighting. The familiar *whoosh-sigh* of ventilators and dinging of alarms welcomed her. Staff hustled in all directions. Her friend, desk phone to her ear, gave Macy a discreet nod. Room 15 was right over there. She told herself he'd probably be asleep, certainly in no shape to converse. Not that she would even try to . . .

Macy stopped a few feet from the door, shocked as she caught sight of Fletcher through the glass. Eyes closed, oxygen mask over his face, skin so sallow and pale that . . . *he looks dead.* Macy forced herself to remember that critical blood loss always looked that way. Fletcher was still under the effects of anesthesia, and he was receiving transfusions. Her gaze swept the IV poles: near-empty blood bag, a fresh one at the ready. Liters of normal saline and Ringer's solution . . . Macy took a slow breath. It was only then that her tunnel vision widened enough to see Fletcher's visitors.

His father—she'd have known it without the charge nurse's remark. Tall, darker hair than his son's, but the same angular jaw and wide shoulders, hunched over now as he sat in a chair pulled close to the bed. Near him was a woman who looked something like Fletcher's mother, same coloring but shorter probably. She had a spiral notebook in her lap. Macy's gaze shifted to the other side of the bed. Someone there, too. She took a few steps closer to see better.

The young woman, pale blonde, slid her chair forward, angling it to bring herself as close as possible to the bed. She stretched out a bare, willowy arm to smooth the sheet over Fletcher's chest. Then she grasped his hand and kissed it lightly. She tipped her head, saying something to the family on the other side of the bed.

A piece of rolling equipment clattered behind Macy, and the blonde glanced up. Spotted her standing there.

"Did y'all need to get in here?" she asked, stunning gray

eyes connecting with Macy's. "Just say the word and we'll scoot out of the—"

"No," Macy muttered quickly. "No problem. You're fine there. I . . . I have the wrong room." She made herself smile, backed away, and then forced herself to walk, not run, out the ICU doors.

She leaned against the corridor wall and closed her eyes.

Jessica. Of course she would come. It was clear she was incredibly close to the Holt family. A childhood neighbor to Fletcher, a dear friend. Macy tried to push the image aside: the beautiful woman clasping his hand. Kissing it. There had been concern on her face. And love. Anyone could see that. Even . . . *a fool like me.*

Macy lifted her cast, supported it with her other hand. Her fingers were swollen; she'd left it hanging down too long. It ached. Like everything else today. She needed to find some ice. And get away from here.

She approached the ICU waiting room on her way down the corridor—and caught a glimpse of someone in there: Charly Holt, alone, hands clasped and head bowed. The poor woman. Macy told herself she should go in there, see if there was anything Charly needed. She should tell Fletcher's mother how very sorry she was that this awful, incomprehensible thing had happened and . . .

Apologize for my part in sending that viatical brochure? For trying to "profit" from her cancer? Did Fletcher say that to Charly, too? Would she really believe I'm capable of that?

Macy hugged her cast to her chest and jogged toward the exit to the parking lot.

42

"You okay in there?"

What? Where . . . ? I'm in the car?

"Everything okay?" There was another tap on the darkened window.

"Yes, we . . ." Macy fumbled with the ignition, confused, wrist throbbing. She lowered the window halfway and found a smile. "Fine, Officer. We were just—" She stopped, stared. Not a police officer. Hospital security.

"Macy Wynn?" The elderly guard smiled back at her. "I thought that was your car. But I told myself you don't usually work nights." He chuckled. "We've been friends how many years now? You don't have to call me officer."

Macy managed a laugh; she'd almost told him her uncle Bob was a police officer in Wyoming. The clinic's pain pill had made her fuzzy. She'd been waiting to peek in on

Fletcher one more time, but . . . "I had a little accident," she told him, lifting her cast. "I thought I shouldn't drive until the medication wore off."

"Well, my goodness. Sorry to see that." He glanced toward the hospital doors, his heavy ring of keys jingling with the movement. "You don't want to come inside? The surgeons' lounge is empty. I could grab you some coffee while you wait."

"Thank you," Macy told him, touched by the kindness. "But no. I'll just sit here a little longer. If that's okay."

"More than okay." The guard winked. "Take as long as you like—sleep if you need to. Make yourself at home, Macy. I'll look out for you."

——

Fletcher shifted in the bed, prompting a flash of pain that seared deep into his thigh. He groaned, opened his eyes.

Jessica raised her head from where she'd been resting it on the edge of the mattress. The blanket had left a small imprint on her cheek.

"You're still here?" he asked her.

"Of course." Her hair was sleep tossed, smile as warm as Houston. "Where else would I be? Neiman Marcus?"

Fletcher shook his head. "I won't kid myself—it's closed." Her fingers found his. "Hey, seriously. Thanks for being here."

"Least I could do. You always gave me half your Halloween candy." Her eyes rolled. "Okay. You never gave me a hard time for stealing all the good stuff."

"You're . . . the good stuff," Fletcher told her, embarrassed by a rush of emotion. Too much medication . . . too much of everything. He glanced toward the door. "Mom and Dad?"

"I made them go get some sleep. Aunt Thena's been here too." Jessica smiled. "The reporters will have their hands full if they try to get past her. By the way, you should expect a 'Sorry You Got Shot' poem."

Fletcher chuckled. "Lots of news coverage?"

"To put it mildly. You're a national hero. Promise you'll let me pick out your clothes for the White House lunch—I can't trust you with something that critical." Her eyes filled with sudden tears. "Thank God you're okay, Fletcher. Don't *ever* do this to me again."

"I won't." He squeezed her hand. "Any more word on the firefighter?"

"Holding his own, last I heard. They said fifty firemen volunteered to donate blood—almost as many as the cops who rolled up sleeves for you." Her lips quirked. "Of course, we'd have twice as many in H-Town."

Fletcher glanced up at the IV poles and the blood transfusion bag. It all seemed surreal. Seeing the Buick, hearing the shot. The shooter up on the roof. *And the way he stared at me. Like he was daring me to kill him.*

"I guess he left a note—more of a book, sounds like." Jessica met Fletcher's gaze. "That sniper, Ned Archer. He wrote one of those manifestos. About how he didn't trust the US government. Or this city. How they caused his father's dementia, poisoned his dog, stole their house. He said it was all a plot involving the Chinese . . . Pretty crazy stuff."

"Sounds crazy." Fletcher grimaced against a wave of pain. "Aagh."

"Hurting?" Jessica leaned close. "Want me to push the button on the med pump?"

Fletcher nodded. "Thanks."

"There."

He glanced toward the door again, squinting at the distant blur of scrubs. "Has anybody else come to visit?"

"A guy name Seth. But you were asleep. I think they're limiting visitors. He's a chaplain?"

"Yeah." Fletcher blinked, feeling the medication's effects.

"You were expecting another visitor?"

"Not really, I guess."

"A gorgeous dark-haired nurse . . . sort of exotic-looking?"

His breath stalled. "Why are you asking that?"

"Because she's peeked into this room at least three times and said she had the wrong room when I asked. But she doesn't look like someone who gets lost." Jessica smiled. "She looks like she could lead a trek across the Andes without a map. Who *is* she?"

"Sounds like Macy Wynn."

Jessica was quiet for a moment. "And who is she to you?"

"We were sort of seeing each other. But not anymore."

She tilted her head. "I don't believe you, Fletcher."

"What do you mean?"

"I mean that look on your face just now. When you said her name. Like even if you've taken a bullet to a major artery, you could trust everything will be okay as long as you have her."

"It's . . . complicated."

"Do you want to talk about it?"

No. He tried to shake his head, but the morphine whispered, *"Relax. It's all good now . . ."*

"You don't want to tell me about Macy?"

"No. But I think . . ." He told himself it was the narcotic effect, that after twenty years there was no point in—"I think we should talk about us, Jessica. You and me."

———

The best part of this day—yesterday now; it was after midnight—was that Macy arrived home to a mercifully empty house. Sally was working nights at UCD Medical Center, and her other roommate had left a note to say she was bunking with her sister tonight. And not to worry; she'd taken Dood with her. Worrying about the goofy Labradoodle would have been comparative bliss.

Macy shifted the ice-filled ziplock on her wrist, and a frigid rivulet found her stomach. She sighed. In a single day, she'd been lasered, assaulted by a longtime friend, and told that the man she'd come to care for had been felled by a sniper— only to land in another woman's arms. Macy squeezed her eyes shut against an image of Jessica's lips brushing Fletcher's hand. That incredible-looking blonde. With stunning eyes, a sugary drawl, and a heart-level connection to Fletcher that . . . *I'll never have a chance at now.* The shooting incident—its role in bringing Jessica from Houston—had been horrifically dramatic, but it was only a final blow. Macy's relationship with Fletcher had already been fatally wounded. Even without a rifle. Elliot had seen to that.

Macy ran a thumb over her cell phone screen, frowning. She'd received two frantic texts from Ricki Rush, the first one along the lines of **You ungrateful snot, what did you do?** followed by a much more contrite **Please, please . . . we can fix this.** Fortunately, the police must have forced Elliot to surrender his cell phone. She shuddered, remembering how his face had twisted with anger as he raged about Fletcher, how he clumsily attempted to kiss her, and how he'd torn at her clothes, groped her.

Macy groaned aloud, sickened—and angry with herself. Not because she thought she'd encouraged Elliot in any way; she wasn't going to fall into that victim trap. But . . . *why didn't I protect myself better? Block his first grab, get a defensive blow in sooner?* She was a kickboxer, not a ballerina. Elliot shouldn't have been able to take advantage like that. But the ugly incident had taken her so much by surprise. Confused her and seemed too impossible because . . . *I trusted him.*

Macy squeezed her eyes shut, refusing to cry at the sad, pathetic truth: the only person she'd come close to completely trusting—in her whole life—was Elliot Rush. And she'd had to bash him in the skull to stop him from violating her.

Macy lifted her cast from the pillow on her lap, trying to find a more comfortable position on the couch. She was stiff and achy from sleeping in the Audi. She shook her head, recalling her confusion when the guard awakened her; she'd thought for a moment that she was with her mother in that old car in San Francisco. Homeless and being told to move along by local law enforcement, much the same way that neighbor got rid of nesting swallows—babies and all—with the handle of his rake. *"Couple of good pokes . . . the only way they'll get that they don't belong there."*

He was wrong. The same way Elliot was wrong when he said that hateful thing about her mother. Her mother had simply made the same mistake Macy did: trusting the wrong person. Macy should never have risked that. And she wouldn't anymore. She wouldn't let anyone tell her that she couldn't make it on her own. She wouldn't let losing what fragile hope she'd had of a relationship with Fletcher stop her from moving ahead. The broken wrist would heal. She'd get Nonni's door set back, polish it up again. Transfer the trust money to a safer place. She'd keep that contractor working and close escrow on the house. She had to. It was all that mattered now. Making a home for—

Her phone rang. Leah . . . at this hour?

"I know it's late," she told Macy. "I hope I didn't wake you."

"No. No problem. Is something wrong?" Macy grimaced at a jab of pain from her swollen wrist. "The baby?"

"No. All good there. The nurse said they'd have to watch things, but that the drugs I took probably wouldn't have harmed my baby."

"Good. I know you must be relieved." Macy closed her eyes, seeing Leah in that beanbag chair, running her fingertips across her belly. She wished she'd been able to get those pictures of the house so Leah could choose a room for a nursery.

"I'm five weeks and five days." There was awe in Leah's voice. "They did an ultrasound. I saw our baby's heart beating, Macy."

Our baby. Auntie Macy. She smiled. Could anything be

more perfect? She and Leah and the baby would have a home and—

"Sean wants me to marry him."

Macy's throat closed.

"I told him about the baby, how I saw the heartbeat. He *cried*, Macy. He's so happy about this. And—"

"Leah. Wait." Macy raised her cast, shushing her sister as if she were in the room. This could *not* happen. "We talked about that. Remember? Sean's in no position to—"

"That's the other miracle. They're counting his rehab as time served. He's coming home!"

Home?

"Sean's boss at the shipping company says he can start back next week. We'll just squeak by on the rent with his first paycheck, but we'll make it. His mom wanted to help, but he told her we need to make it on our own. Be responsible, start off right. Getting married is first."

"But . . . the house." Macy's whisper was hoarse. "We're set to close by the end of next month. And we planned—"

"I know. I told you I might come out there and stay for a while. You were so sweet to offer. I can't tell you how much I appreciate your being there for me during rehab and . . ." Leah's voice cracked. "I'll always be grateful. You've been like a real sister to me during the hardest times of my life. And by my side these last few weeks. I'll always love you. But . . . Sean and this baby . . . they're my family now. My home is with them."

They'd said good night—at least Macy thought she'd said it too, though her voice had been choked by gathering tears.

She'd been too stunned. Heartsick. And now, half an hour later, she was still hearing Leah's voice saying, *"You've been like a real sister to me . . ."*

Macy hugged the couch pillow close, struggling to make sense of pain that was far beyond disappointment. She'd never considered the concept of "real" when it came to how she felt about Leah. The little girl she'd met at Nonni's house had been her sister from that first day. Macy never thought of it any other way.

"Sean and this baby . . . they're my family now. My home is with them."

Leah wasn't coming. Nonni's brass door set was in an evidence locker. And Macy's determination to put it all together—finally make things right—had, in the end, sent Fletcher away. Accomplished nothing. Except to point out, once and for all, the essential truths: Macy didn't belong anywhere. She was as much a "junk bird" as the swallows on the porch of that house. She wasn't a credible ballerina or kickboxer. When it came to trust, her judgment was dangerously flawed.

A sob rose. She was a fool to ever, *ever* hope for a chance at love. After all that had happened, even remembering the warmth of Nonni's home didn't help anymore. But . . . Macy brushed at a tear. But for the first time she wished, really wished, that what Nonni had said about God was true. That no matter what else had happened—or would happen—nothing could change the beautiful fact that she was a child of God. Known before she was born. Loved unconditionally.

She thought of Fletcher, that day when they summited

the Mist Trail at Yosemite and looked out at the breath-taking view. He'd said he was sure God had been up there first, the deep certainty evident in his voice. Right this min-ute, Macy needed to believe it was so—that the power who created all that . . . *is the Father who will always love me.*

"God . . . ," Macy whispered, bowing her head. There was no way to stop her trembling. She was weak, but being strong didn't seem so important now. "I can't do this alone anymore. I need to belong somewhere. . . . I need you in my life. Please help me."

43

"Hɪ. Remember me?"

"Hello." Taylor paused outside the radiology suite and smiled at the little girl, trying to place her. Sober-sweet expression, big eyes, pigtails, and patent-leather shoes. Her small hands clasped a tote bag stenciled with a stick-figure ballerina.

"You saw Annie a few weeks back," the older woman sitting next to the girl explained. Leaning against her, on the opposite side, was a second youngster. A boy with a Mason Allen splint on one hand and a banana in the other. The woman smiled at Taylor and traced a finger gently over Annie's forehead. "We had some stitches. After . . . a car accident."

The school van. That first incident with the sniper. The woman was a foster mother.

"Of course. Annie Sims," Taylor recalled as the girl slid down from her chair and clattered forward in the shiny shoes. She chuckled. "I'd never forget a pretty little girl in tap shoes."

"Hard to." The woman shook her head. "We changed to sneakers after dance class but . . ."

"These floors are perfect for tapping." Annie shuffled her feet to prove it, pigtails bouncing. "Is Macy here?"

"No. I'm sorry. Not today." Macy's early morning text said she'd injured her wrist.

"I wanted to tell her something. Something really good." A grin lit Annie's face. "My mom is all better. She's coming tomorrow to take me home."

The foster mother smiled. "It's a big day. A happy one."

"Will you tell Macy for me?" Annie peered at Taylor, great certainty on her face. "She would want to know."

Taylor promised to relay the news, then continued on toward the cafeteria. She'd planned to meet Seth on her break. She stopped, scanned the room—large, bustling, and sausage-scented—and saw that he'd somehow managed to snag a small table in a virtual sea of hospital staff and visitors. It was an impressive accomplishment, since several tables had been commandeered by human resources to showcase retirement information. Surprisingly, Elliot Rush wasn't manning the display today. Taylor grabbed her coffee and joined Seth.

"Decaf," he told her, pointing to his coffee mug as she sat. "I'm being good. Even with bacon whispering my name." His eyes met hers. "How're *you* doing?"

"Better than if that horde of reporters outside was waiting

for me." Taylor shook her head. "I hope Charly wore those big Texas sunglasses." There was no use trying to evade this bighearted chaplain. Truth was the only option. "I didn't sleep much. I kept thinking about how I'd actually met Ned Archer, here in the hospital. And how Charly and I walked right up that driveway trying to find him—while Fletcher was cruising his patrol car down the street, trying to keep her safe. Same man, same house, same driveway. And then yesterday . . ." Taylor's voice dropped to a whisper. "They keep showing those cell phone pictures. Fletcher on the ground and that firefighter . . ."

"It wouldn't be normal if you didn't react to that, Taylor. Very personally."

She wondered what Seth would think if he knew about her reaction to that former flight nurse, Sloane Wilder. It had been a brief and far-from-traumatic encounter, yet Taylor still almost lost control of her emotions. She glanced toward an adjacent table. Sloane was sitting over there now. "I guess I need more good news," she said after taking a sip of her coffee. "Like little tap dancers heading home." She smiled at Seth's raised brow. "You had to be there."

He nodded. "I'd show up anywhere for good news."

And for bad news. He'd show up for that too. Seth would throw his heart in, never doubting he had what it took to help. *That's the difference between us. . . .* Could she tell him that? And about her decision?

"Speaking of good news," he continued, "I ran into Dr. Carlyle's husband. He said they'd had some hopeful reports on their baby. He was planning to stop by the ER and tell the staff."

"I'll have to pass that along to Macy."

"Have you talked with her today?"

"I texted her to see why she called in sick. She said she injured her wrist—a small fracture." Taylor's brows scrunched. "I assumed it happened on her bike. Or during some kickboxing move. But it happened after she climbed up on a porch railing to take some pictures of a bird nest."

"She said that?"

"Yes. Why?"

"I think you should call Macy when you get a chance. See how she's doing."

"I will." She tried to read Seth's expression. "Is there something I should know?"

"I . . . really can't say."

"Right." Taylor glanced toward Sloane's table again, saw the nurse looking their way.

"I arranged for a visit with Fletcher." Seth glanced at his watch. "I should get up there." He stood. "You and I are set for a debriefing on that incident, but if you want to talk with me—even in the middle of the night if you can't sleep—you'll call?"

"I will."

And she'd tell him what she'd decided: *I'm taking a job in San Diego.*

———

Macy settled back against the bench, letting her gaze climb the Grizzly Giant.

She remembered her nervous recitation of Google facts to Fletcher: two thousand years old, 209 feet tall, 96 feet around, bark two feet thick, two million pinecones, 700,000 sunsets . . . *thousands and thousands of lightning strikes.*

He'd been amazed the tree was still standing after all that, and she'd told him that these redwoods were flame resistant. That burning actually helped to make the trees stronger. Fletcher called it a "trial by fire" and said he'd heard people were that way too. Macy knew now that it was, oh, so true.

It had taken her all night to even begin to sort it out—her lifetime of lightning strikes—and she knew there was still a long way to go. But when Macy climbed into the Audi this morning, she'd felt a sense of peace she'd never known. So many things made sense now. It had never been about Leah. Or Nonni. Not about a house that smelled of oatmeal cookies or that stolen brass door set. It had always been about feeling safe and loved. *Home* was what Macy had called it; *family* was what she'd struggled so hard to reclaim. And deny . . . But in so many ways, what she needed had always been there.

She smiled, remembering the guard's words last night when she fell asleep in her car. *"Make yourself at home, Macy. I'll look out for you."* Hadn't the hospital always been her shelter? Weren't her teammates—that good-hearted security guard, Taylor, Andi, and so many others—like a family? Didn't this amazing and majestic Sierra valley always stir Macy's senses, speak to her heart in a way she couldn't explain? Fletcher had captured it perfectly: *"God was here first."*

She'd been willing to do almost anything to get that house. It hadn't been for Leah. It had been for herself. A futile dream to fill a hole in her heart by putting a hunk of brass on a front door. It never would have worked. Finding a true sense of home wasn't about a place; it was about feeling safe, loved unconditionally—trusting beyond herself. And that required faith.

Macy's fingers found the strands of hair she'd spent years trying to wish away. She'd succeeded in covering them up, but it never erased the pain she'd allowed them to cause her. And all the time she'd spent on that futile pursuit had kept her from finding what she'd really wanted all along. Nonni had been right about her. Macy *was* loved. Always had been. By a Father who knew her before she was born and who wanted only the best for her life. The idea boggled her mind; it didn't make perfect sense. Maybe it never would. But Macy was going to trust it, feel its promise like that worn brass door latch under her childish fingers. She'd move on with her life in a new way. Starting with—

Her cell phone buzzed. The title company.

"Yes, this is Macy Wynn."

She nodded, listening as the escrow officer recapped the message she'd left early this morning. And then informed her of the ramifications.

"Yes," Macy confirmed, gazing in awe at the huge redwood once again. "I understand I'll lose my earnest money."

"And the contractor's deposit," the officer added with a nervous edge to her voice. "There's a possibility he'll view this as a breach of contract. He could sue."

"Well then . . ." Macy's heart tugged as a marmot clambered up a rock beside the bench, rose on its hind legs to stare at her. "I'll cross that bridge when I come to it."

"You're sure about this, Miss Wynn?"

"Completely sure. Cancel the contract with the bank." That beautiful new sense of peace washed over her, buoying her heart. "I don't want or need that house."

44

"A Twitpic, I heard," Seth told Fletcher. "Crime of opportunity—covert shot uploaded to Twitter from physical therapy. You're still newsworthy, even floundering around on crutches." His teasing smirk crinkled his dark eyes. "Too-tall Texan in a too-short hospital gown. Full color. Or so I heard."

"Great." Fletcher shook his head. "I'll see if my aunt can come up with a haiku in defense of my privacy . . . in 140 characters or less."

Seth slid the visitor's chair a little closer to Fletcher's wheelchair, glanced around the hospital room—on the surgical floor now, after his release from the ICU. His expression sobered. "I saw the film clip. Your press conference."

"For what it was worth."

The media had been relentless. Fletcher finally agreed to talk with reporters this morning, four days after the shooting. He'd kept it brief since so many things were still under investigation by the FBI and the sheriff's department. And because Fletcher was only now beginning to sort things out for himself. He'd tried his best to brush off all that talk of being a hero—it didn't feel right—and had refused to speculate on whether or not the psychotic sniper had committed "suicide by cop." Then Fletcher let his guard down and was gut punched by a reporter quoting Ned Archer's manifesto . . .

"He didn't trust anyone," Fletcher began, remembering the man on that roof. "The government, law enforcement . . . God, either, I guess. Even if he didn't mention him. Archer thought it was all up to him to make things right. He felt all alone in that."

Seth stayed quiet.

"That bullet—" Fletcher pressed his fingers to the blanket covering his thigh—"slowed me down enough to let me do some serious thinking. I'm not so sure I'm any better than him. The man I killed out there."

Seth's brows rose a fraction. No words. Only encouragement in his eyes.

"I've spent a lot of my life thinking things weren't fair," Fletcher admitted. "My sister getting hit by that car. My mother's first cancer . . . and now this second go-round. That whole thing with Jessica." Fletcher half smiled, remembering his recent, very amazing conversation with her. "I always told myself I was trusting God, believing in his plan . . ."

"But?"

"When it came right down to it, I decided I could handle it by myself. Badge, gun, bulletproof vest, justice on my side. My plan. My timing. My heroics." Fletcher shook his head. "My ego . . . my fear."

Seth nodded. "Trust me, I've been there, friend. And now?"

"Now I'm looking at things differently. I'm putting my trust where it belongs." Fletcher glanced toward his well-worn Bible, brought in by his father early this morning. "And I'm trying to set things right."

"That's why you asked Macy to come by?"

"Yeah." According to the hospital grapevine, she'd been out of state visiting her sister again. "I couldn't leave things the way they ended with us and—"

"Fletcher?" A tap on the door beyond the privacy curtain separating his bed from the door. Macy's voice. "Right room?"

"Yes . . . I'm here." Fletcher's mouth went dry.

"I'll be sending a prayer up," Seth said quietly, rising from his chair. "I'll check back later, too. Count on it."

"Thank you."

There was a murmured exchange of greetings at the doorway; then Macy peeked around the curtain. Her gaze flicked over Fletcher—wheelchair, injured leg extended—and her expression showed concern despite her polite smile.

Fletcher reminded himself to breathe. "Hi."

"Hi."

She was dressed in a faded denim skirt, green T-shirt, sandals . . . and a purple fiberglass cast. *Rush.* Fletcher's gut tensed. He'd heard the story about the man's arrest and about what he'd done to Macy. Sexual battery—he'd be looking at serious prison time. The assault was part of the reason Fletcher asked Macy to visit. To see how she was and to tell her how awful he felt. About everything.

"I'm sorry, Fletcher," she said, settling on the edge of the bed across from him. She tipped forward, met his gaze. "I hate that this happened to you. I was so scared when I heard you'd been shot. Everyone was. I wanted to come see you right away." Macy shook her head, dark hair brushing her shoulders. "But after what happened with your mother and the viatical brochure . . ." Her eyes shone with sudden tears. "That's a big part of why I said I'd come today. To apologize for what Elliot—"

"No. You don't have to take the blame for what that lying, twisted—" A curse rose, but Fletcher stopped himself. "You don't need to apologize."

"I do." Macy pressed the cast to her chest. "I should never have had any conversation with Elliot about your mother. I swear I never gave him confidential medical information. But even expressing my concern for her was a breach of privacy. Wrong. And you were right when you said those things about gambling with lives and betting against hope. About it being unfair and—"

"Wait. Please," Fletcher insisted as Macy made a clumsy attempt to wipe at a tear with her casted arm. "I had no right to accuse you and come off so . . . almighty self-righteous." He shook his head. "'Self-righteous street cop'—Rush's wife had me pegged from the get-go."

"Fletcher . . . hey . . ."

"No. She was right. Lying around with a bullet hole in my leg's given me time to sort things out. I've been pulling the 'unfair' card for way too long. My sister's death, my mom's health, my relationships . . . Maybe even that I got stuck with a Maine coon."

"Who was supposed to be a hunting dog." Macy offered a small smile.

"Yeah, total smackdown on my idiot pride," Fletcher admitted, grateful for his honest conversations with Seth. In the ICU and then again a few minutes ago. He was thankful, too, that the morphine had let him risk confiding his long-held and confusing feelings to Jessica. She'd been great about it. And not all that surprised apparently. *Of course you love me . . . and kept tryin' to save me all those years. I stepped into your little sister's Mary Janes. You are the brother I never had. That's a double blessing. And a forever kind of love . . .*" It had felt good to get it off his chest. Even better to finally understand that she was absolutely right. Fletcher would always love Jessica as a sister. And then he told her about Macy . . .

"Somehow I made myself the judge of what's fair," Fletcher continued. "Maybe I even stopped believing that God had a better plan for my family . . . my life. You know?"

"Yes." Macy's beautiful eyes held his. "I think I do."

Fletcher scraped his fingers through his hair, groaning at a bitter irony. "I just killed somebody whose mental illness kept him from trusting anyone. And I was the better man for insisting I could handle things all by myself? Like some kind of self-appointed . . . savior? Then when I couldn't pull my sister out from under that car, be a match if my mother needs a transplant . . ." Fletcher's voice almost cracked. "I blamed God for not giving the right answer to my prayers. *Self-righteous* doesn't even cover it. I know that now."

Macy slid down from the edge of the bed to kneel beside Fletcher's wheelchair. Her heart ached at the raw honesty in his eyes. "I've made big mistakes too. With Elliot—" she expected Fletcher's reaction and raised her hand to stop him from speaking—"but most of all by thinking I shouldn't really count on anybody but myself. I don't want to live like that anymore. And even if you've been beating yourself up about your doubts, it was *you* who got me thinking like this, Fletcher."

"Thinking about what?"

"Trusting God." She smiled at the look on his face. "It's a learning curve like the Yosemite Mist Trail. But I'm determined to give it a go."

Fletcher took hold of her hand.

"There's a lot of things I want to catch you up on," Macy explained. "About Elliot, that trust fund, my sister, and—" she wrinkled her nose—"the fact that I just dumped the dream house I was buying . . . and I could get sued. But if you're not going to stick around, you probably don't care about any of that."

"I'm going somewhere?"

"Back to Houston. To convalesce and because things have changed with Jessica. It's what I heard."

"Leave it to the hospital rumor mill."

Macy's heart climbed to her throat. "Is it true . . . about Jessica?"

"Yeah, things have changed for her." Fletcher smiled. "She's in love . . . with a youth pastor in Houston. Some ex-jock named Ben. Turns out he's a decent guy." His eyes held hers. "There's nothing romantic between Jessica and me. Never was."

"So . . ." Relief made Macy's voice quaver. "You're staying here for a while—as planned?"

"Yep." He raised her hand to his lips. "But not exactly *here*, I hope." He frowned. "Hospital gown, leg all bandaged, and my rear in this wheelchair. It's awkward. Especially if, say . . ." Fletcher's smile spread slowly. "I wanted to kiss you."

"Do you?"

"From the second you walked through the door."

Macy's face warmed. "I think we could . . ." She stood, stooped down again, then leaned in as he pushed up with his good leg, tried to meet her halfway, and—"Oops," she said as she thumped Fletcher's jaw with her cast. He laughed, reached for her.

"Oh, hey . . ." Macy's skin tingled. "Yes. That could definitely work."

"C'mere then," Fletcher whispered, taking her face in his hands. He kissed the corner of her mouth. "Mmm. Yes. Medical miracle."

"I'm all about that," she whispered back, slipping an arm around his neck. She chuckled as his lips nibbled the pulse spot under her jaw. Then quieted as his mouth found hers for a quick kiss . . . and a second, much longer one. She buried her fingers in his hair, kissing him back and—

"Mr. Holt?" A disembodied voice beyond the curtain. "Ready for some physical therapy?"

Macy laughed. Fletcher groaned. "One minute, ma'am."

"Yes, sir."

Fletcher brushed Macy's hair back. "Marmots, room-mates, Labradoodles, therapists," he protested, his voice a husky whisper. The blue eyes held hers. "Will *you* stick around?"

"Absolutely."

"Good. I'm going to find a thousand places we can be alone without the world crowding in." His lips touched the tip of her nose. "Count on it."

"I'll hold you to that."

"Mr. Holt . . . ?"

"Ready," Fletcher called out to the therapist. "Bring on the crutches—I've got a thousand places I need to get to."

EPILOGUE

LATE AUGUST, THE FOLLOWING SUMMER

"Welcome to the top of the world!"

The young and very sun-bronzed hiker greeted Fletcher as he clambered onto the granite summit, breathless and perspiring. The man raised his voice over the rush of the falls below, obviously eager to share his thrill. "Prepare to be blown away, my friend. First hike up the Mist Trail?"

"Second," Fletcher answered, reaching for his water bottle. "I crawled up here last June." *More than a year ago now . . . incredible.* He slid his sunglasses to the top of his head, swept his gaze over the clumps of hikers spread across the summit.

"That accent," the hiker noted. "Southern?"

"Houston."

The young man laughed. "Thick air there. No wonder you're breathing hard. Hiking Yosemite by yourself?"

"Nope. With a California native—half–mountain antelope." Fletcher scanned the distance again. "She would have passed you a couple of minutes ago. Sooner if she wasn't tired today. She's tall, wearing black biking tights, a bright-pink shirt . . ."

"Right. Yeah," the hiker confirmed. "Gorgeous lady. Long black hair with this crazy-cool white stripe in it."

Fletcher laughed. "That would be my wife."

"You actually talked her into leaving all this?" the young man asked, incredulous. "Moving to the flatlands?"

"We're back to California a lot—just closed on a condo near Tahoe. My wife heads up a studio for kids in Sacramento."

"Studio?"

"Two, actually. One there and one in Houston. Part of the YMCA," Fletcher explained, thinking of the shiny, child-high brass hardware she'd installed on the door leading into the Nonni's Place location. Macy had named the studio in Houston after Fletcher's sister. "Both are completely free of cost to underprivileged children. Dance classes."

"That's cool. So like . . . ballet?"

"And tap dancing." Fletcher chuckled. "Plus, they're hiring instructors for Christian martial arts. Macy likes the idea of a child finding confidence in both—she's a ballet dancer *and* a kickboxer." He slid his sunglasses back down. "Did you happen to see which way she went?"

"Yeah." The young man pointed. "Right over there. See?"

"I do."

Fletcher's heart pounded—nothing to do with thinner air or the hike up the Mist Trail. Seeing Macy, knowing she was his wife, always affected him that way. When he stopped by the Houston Grace ER during his patrol shift to see her, when they helped his parents unpack boxes and get resettled in Texas, when she sat beside him at church . . . and whenever the pale morning light offered his first glimpse of her beautiful face on the pillow next to him. *My wife . . .*

Their marriage, four months ago, hadn't seemed too fast to either of them. Maybe the traumas they'd survived the year before taught them life was fragile and time on this earth too uncertain. Maybe—though they'd never discussed it this way—his mother's illness had added to their decision. But mostly, it had come down to a matter of trust. In the deep love they had for each other and in the plan God had for their lives. It was a foundation as solid as the granite under their feet right now.

———

"Hey." Macy smiled as her husband came close. She patted the space beside her. "Pull up a rock."

"You're okay being seen with a 'flatlander'—" Fletcher's gaze swept the breathtaking vista as he sat—"way up here?"

"Anywhere," she told him, heart skittering as he brushed a kiss on her cheek. "And especially today."

"Yeah. Nothing finer than that view. Unless it's my view following *you* on a trail. I figured that out on my first hike up here." Fletcher grinned. "You're right; it's been a great trip—fast, but great. Though it's too bad Taylor couldn't make it up to Sacramento after all. I know you wanted to see her."

"Next time," Macy told him, determined not to let one little disappointment cloud this special time with Fletcher. She'd waited, planned, hiked up that long trail, and—

"You found a wireless connection?" he asked, pointing to the cell phone in her lap.

"Didn't try." The diamond in Macy's engagement ring sparkled as she tapped the screen. Butterflies fluttered in her stomach. "I was looking at the photos we took at Sean and Leah's. I can't believe our niece has her first tooth. Of course Andi's little guy has two now. And he's maybe five pounds heavier. Hard to imagine they ever called him an elf. That's a future linebacker if I ever saw one." She was chattering; she knew that. Macy took a deep breath. "When we get home to Houston, I think we should make a dinner reservation. Maybe Danton's—I've been craving their blackened catfish enchiladas."

Fletcher laughed. "Why am I not surprised by that?"

Hang on . . . you will be.

"Sure," he told her, tucking a finger under her chin. He kissed her nose. "You got it, Mrs. Holt. Reservation for two at Danton's."

"I think we should invite your parents." She smiled at him, happiness besting the butterflies in a move worthy of martial arts.

"Great idea. We can celebrate Mom's first year in remission. And that Aunt Thena can hang on to her poetic bone marrow for now." Fletcher nodded. "I'm on it. Reservation for four."

"Make it for five." Happy tears filled Macy's eyes. "It will be . . . five of us for dinner."

"Five?" Fletcher's brows scrunched.

"A double celebration," Macy explained. "We're having a baby, Fletcher."

"What?" His blue eyes widened. "You're pregnant?"

"Test at home, confirmed yesterday by my lab pals at Sacramento Hope." Macy reached up, stroked her husband's face. "We're going to be a family."

"Macy . . ." Fletcher drew her into his arms, hugging her so close that she felt his heart beating against hers. "I love you. I can't say it right. Except that I'm the happiest man in the world."

"That's perfect," she breathed against her husband's ear. "And I love you too. So much." Her eyes swept the view and she sighed. "I wanted to tell you about it here, at Yosemite, where everything started for us."

And where God was first . . . with a beautiful design for our lives.

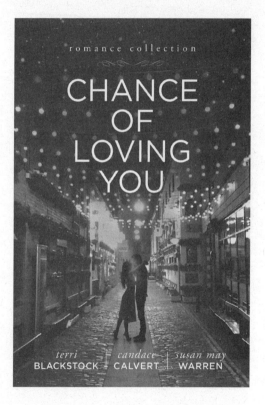

1

LUCAS MARCHAL fully expected his grandmother to show no interest in her hospital dinner tray; her appetite had dwindled to almost nothing. But in his wildest dreams he didn't imagine that her dour, no-nonsense nurse's aide would lift the dish cover, scream, then stumble backward and fall to the floor.

He bolted toward her to help, vaguely aware of other San Diego Hope rehab staff filing through the door.

His grandmother's roommate, chubby and childlike despite middle age, pitched forward in her bed to utter a lisping litany of concern. "Oh . . . my . . . goodnethh. Oh, my!"

"Here." Lucas offered a hand to the downed nurse's aide. "Let me help you up, Mrs.—"

"No need," she sputtered, waving him and one of the other aides away. "I'm all right. Weak ankle. Lost my balance, that's all. After I saw that . . . *horrid* thing." Revulsion flickered across her age-lined face. "On your grandmother's plate."

What?

Lucas's gaze darted to the remaining staff now gathering around his grandmother's tray table. They stared like curious looky-loos at a crime scene. Lucas was all too familiar with that phenomenon, though as an evidence technician, he operated on the other side of the yellow police tape. He turned back to the nurse's aide—Wanda Clay, according to her name badge—who'd managed to stand. "What's wrong with my grandmother's dinner plate?"

"It was on the rice," Wanda explained, gingerly testing her ankle. It was hard to tell if her grimace was from an injury or from what she was struggling to explain. "Sitting there on the food, bold as brass." She crossed her arms, tried to still a shudder. "Black, huge, with those awful legs. I haven't seen one of those vile bugs since I left Florida."

A cockroach? On his grandmother's food? It could snuff what little was left of her appetite—and his hope that she'd finally regain her strength.

"It's probably scurried away by now." The nurse's aide rubbed an elbow. "That's what they do in the light. But I saw it, plain as can be. And you can bet I'll be reporting it to—"

"You mean *this*?" A young, bearded tech in blue scrubs pointed at the plate. Then made no attempt to hide his smirk. "Is this what freaked you out, Wanda?"

"I wasn't scared," the woman denied, paling as she stared at the tray. "Startled maybe. Because no one expects to see—"

"A black olive?" the tech crowed, pointing again. "Ooooh. Horrifying."

Someone else tittered. "Yep, that's an olive—was an

olive. Sort of cut up in pieces and stuck on the rice. A decoration, maybe?"

"Oh, goody." The roommate clapped her hands, expression morphing from concern to delight. "Can I see? Is it pretty? Can I have a party decoration too?"

"Hey, Wanda," the tech teased, "what form do we use to report an olive to—?"

"I think that's enough," Lucas advised, raising his hands. "No harm, no foul. Okay?" He reminded himself that law enforcement saw its own share of clowning. But . . . "We have two ladies who need to eat."

"Yes, sir." The technician nodded, his expression sheepish. "Just kidding around. I'll get your grandma some fresh water."

"Thank you." Lucas glanced toward Wanda. "You're not hurt?"

"Only a bump." She rubbed her elbow again, lips pinching tight. "Some decoration."

"Yeah."

Lucas watched for a moment as Wanda helped the chattering roommate with her tray; then he glanced toward the window beyond—the hospital's peaceful ocean view—before returning to his grandmother's bedside. He slid his chair close, his heart heavy at the sight of her now. Asleep on her pillow and far too thin, with her stroke-damaged right arm lying useless across her chest. For the first time ever, Rosslyn Marchal actually appeared her age of seventy-six. So different from the strong, vibrant woman who'd essentially been his mother. A woman whose unbridled laughter turned heads in more than a few fancy restaurants, who shouldered a skeet rifle like she intended to stop a charging rhino. A still-lovely senior equally at home in a gown and diamonds for a charity event or wearing faded jeans and a sun hat to dig in her wildly beautiful garden high above the Pacific Ocean. She was an acclaimed painter, a deeply devoted believer. And a new widow. That inconsolable heartbreak had brought her to this point . . . *of no return?*

No.

Lucas watched her doze, torn between the mercy of letting her dream of far better times and the absolute fact that if she didn't eat, drink, move, breathe, she'd succeed in what she'd recently told her pastor and her grandson: *"I'm okay with leaving this earthly world."* Lucas couldn't let that happen even if his grandmother's advance medical directive, her legal living will, required he honor her wishes regarding life support. She'd beaten the pneumonia that brought her to the hospital this time, and the therapists said she still had enough physical strength to regain some mobility, as long as she mustered the will to take nourishment.

"Here's that water," the technician said, setting a pitcher beside the food tray. He cleared his throat. "I'm sorry about that kidding around earlier. It wasn't professional."

"No harm done . . . Edward," Lucas told him after glancing at his ID badge. "I appreciate the help all of you give my grandmother."

"Pretty special lady, huh?"

"The most."

"If you need to get going, I can help feed her tonight," Edward offered. "I know she's on Wanda's list, but I don't mind. I have the time." He shrugged. "And after all that joking around, I'm probably on her list too. Wanda Clay's ever-growing—" The young man's gaze came to rest on the Bible on the bedside table, and he appeared to swallow his intended word. "Her hit list."

Lucas smiled. His grandmother's powerful influence for good. Even in sleep. "Thanks, but I can stay tonight. Things look pretty decent out on the streets."

"You're a cop, right?"

"Evidence tech—CSI," Lucas added, using the TV term everyone recognized.

"Cool."

"Sometimes. Mostly it's like being a Molly Maid. With gloves, tweezers, and a camera. Not as exciting as TV."

"Still sounds cool to me." The tech moved the dinner tray closer. He pointed to the tepid mound of boiled rice. "I guess I can see how someone might think that thing was a bug."

Lucas inspected the offensive olive. "You think it's supposed to be a garnish?"

"Yeah." Edward smiled. "Some bored dietary assistant getting her cutesy on."

———

"It's not like I'm sous-chef at Avant or Puesto," Aimee Curran told her cousin, citing top-ten local restaurants. She tucked a tendril of light-auburn hair behind an ear and sighed. "Or that I even get much of a chance to be food-creative here. But . . ." She raised her voice over the mix of staff and visitor chatter in the San Diego Hope hospital cafeteria so that Taylor Cabot could hear. "At least working in a dietary department will look good on my application to the culinary institute."

"You're serious about it. I can see it in your eyes," Taylor observed, mercifully offering no reference to Aimee's failed and costly past career paths. Nursing, right up to the moment she panicked, then passed out and hit the floor during a surgery rotation, followed by early childhood education that . . . just didn't fit. "Aunt Miranda would love it, of course." Taylor slid an extra package of saltines into the pocket of her ER scrub top. "She was such an awesome cook."

"She was." Aimee's mother had been a school nurse, but her kitchen was her beating heart. "Apron time" with her only daughter had meant the world to her. And to Aimee.

"If I win the Vegan Valentine Bake-Off, it will be enough money to pay for the culinary institute," Aimee explained. "I can't qualify for more student loans. So this is it."

"I didn't know you'd gone vegan."

"I haven't. Not even close, though Mom taught me to respect organic and local foods. It's just that there won't be so many entries in a vegan contest. It's a calculated risk. And I need to win, Taylor." Aimee's pulse quickened. "It's my last chance to honor my mother with a choice I'm making for my life—my *whole* life. I've got to do that. I can't bear it if I don't."

"I think . . ." Taylor's voice was warm, gentle. "I think that your mother would be proud of you, regardless."

"I know. But it just seems that everyone else has found their calling, you know? You've got your career in the ER. My brother's starting medical school up in Portland, and

Dad's found Nancy." Aimee smiled, so very happy for him. "Now they've adopted those two little rascals from Haiti . . ." Her eyes met Taylor's. "The contest is being held on Valentine's Day."

"Your birthday. And also . . ."

"Ten years from the day Mom passed away." Aimee sighed. "I'm going to be twenty-six, Taylor. It's high time I got myself together and moved on."

"I understand that."

"I know you do." Taylor's husband, a Sacramento firefighter, had been killed in an accident almost three years ago. Taking a job in San Diego was part of Taylor's plan to move on.

"So what are you going to wow those bake-off judges with?" Taylor asked after carefully tapping the meal's calorie count into her cell phone. The old familiar spark of fun warmed her eyes. "Some sort of soybean cheesecake?"

"Not a tofu fan," Aimee admitted, her nose wrinkling. "I thought I'd go through Mom's old recipe tin and adapt something—you know, ban the chickens and cows, but keep the sugar."

"And all the love. Aunt Miranda was all about 'stirring in the love.' I think I asked my mom once if you could buy that at Walmart in a five-pound sack like flour."

Aimee smiled. "The first phase is tomorrow. I've got to pass that. The bake-off finals will be televised. Professional kitchen, top-grade tools . . . ticking time clock." She grimaced. "Nothing like pressure. But at least the hospital dietary kitchen gives me a chance to handle more equipment than I have at my apartment and practice my chopping and slicing techniques." She shook her head. "Mostly when nobody's looking, since the biggest part of my job is tray delivery. But I've been known to add a few artistic, signature Aimee touches and—"

"Hey, Curran!"

Aimee turned and saw a familiar young man in scrubs cruising toward them. Beard, husky build. That rehab tech, Edward.

"Hey there," he said, plunking a hand on the edge of their table. He grinned at Aimee, raised a brow. "Was it you?"

"Was *what* me?"

"That cutesy olive on Mrs. Marchal's rice."

"I don't know what you mean," Aimee told him, afraid she did. Why was he making a big deal out of—?

"A black olive, cut up like some kind of decoration? I think someone got pictures of it."

"Really?" She hesitated. Was he flattering her? Or . . .

"Wanda thought it was a cockroach. She screamed like a banshee and fell down on her—"

"What?" Aimee's heart stalled. *No . . .* This had to be a bad joke.

"Anyway," he said, waving at a passing student nurse, "Wanda's probably gunning for your department. Thought you should know." He winked, smacked his hand on the table. "But thank 'em for me, would ya? Highlight of my day."

Aimee closed her eyes as he sauntered away. *Please . . .*

"Aimee?" Taylor leaned over the table, touched her hand. "You okay?"

"I . . ." She met her cousin's gaze and groaned.

"Oh, dear." Taylor winced. "A 'signature Aimee touch'?"

"It was a *daisy*. I snipped all those little black petals really carefully. I didn't even know whose tray it was. But I thought it was sort of cheery." Another thought made her breath catch. "Wanda's pretty old. Do you think she got hurt? Broke a hip or—?"

"I doubt it," Taylor interrupted, her expression reassuring. "But I do think you should go over there and explain. Apologize to this Wanda. And to the patient, too, if she was upset by it."

"Oh, great. I just thought of something else." Aimee squeezed her eyes shut again. "I think Mrs. Marchal's grandson works for the police department. Can this get any worse?"

TURN THE PAGE FOR
A PREVIEW FROM THE
NEXT CRISIS TEAM NOVEL

CRISIS

STEP BY STEP

TEAM

AVAILABLE IN STORES
AND ONLINE SPRING 2016

1

"YOU TOOK YOUR RINGS OFF."

"I . . . did." Taylor Cabot glanced at her hand resting on the weathered boardwalk railing and found the small indent on her third finger. She refused to accept her stomach's reflexive quiver. Her younger cousin Aimee Curran was right: the wedding band and engagement ring had finally come off, after migrating from her left to right hand in a painfully slow march through grief—like a turtle navigating broken glass. But two days ago she'd soaped her finger, twisted the rings off, and tucked them back into their original Grebitus & Sons box—along with a creased and well-worn love poem. The only poetry her firefighter husband ever attempted in his too-short life. *My life . . . my wife . . . I love you more . . ."*

Taylor drew a deep breath of salty-cool March air, grateful there was no fresh stab of pain. Almost three years after the horrific accident that snuffed Greg's life, his death was a scar, not a tender scab now. All as it should be. She swept aside a breeze-tossed strand of her coppery hair and met her cousin's gaze. "It was time."

Aimee's eyes, nearly the exact Curran green as her own, held Taylor's for a moment. "I'm proud of you."

"Thanks. I'm . . ." Taylor raised her voice over the lively thrum from the busy boardwalk and beach below: music, loudspeakers, carnival rides, childish squeals, and the amazing syncopated flap-flutter of hundreds upon hundreds of colorful and wildly fanciful kites surfing the sea breeze—the Kiwanis Club's annual kite festival in its full glory. She smiled, new certainty buoying her as well. "I'm kind of proud of myself, actually."

"You should be." Aimee returned her smile. "And I'm selfish enough to think that moving back home was a big part of that."

"It was."

In fact, it was at the top of the survival list Taylor had drafted—edited, rewritten, lain awake night after night getting straight in her head and in her heart—during the last edgy, anxious months in Sacramento. Those long months she'd been so frustrated with herself, uncomfortably angry, and so completely sick of being a widow, an unwilling member of a select club no one ever wanted to belong to. Moving away had seemed like a good way to move on. It had been a tough decision, finally made easier when she was asked out on her first new-widow date—by the husband of a close friend. When Taylor's skin stopped crawling, and after she'd hurled her cell phone against the kitchen wall, she sat down and drafted her list.

She hadn't shared it with anyone, but accomplishing

every last item, regardless of how difficult, had become Taylor's biggest goal. She was determined to move on, step by shaky step.

Transfer to a nursing position at San Diego Hope ER
Start jogging again
Lose the Krispy Kremes—and fifteen pounds
Find a good vet for Hooper
Take off wedding rings
Go through the last of Greg's things

And—

"So . . ." Aimee's brows rose a fraction. "Did the gorgeous Dr. Halston have anything to do with the timing?"

"Timing?"

"Taking off your rings. You know, that you've been seeing him?"

"Not exactly . . . maybe," Taylor conceded, unable to deny the confusing mix of feelings the surgeon managed to inspire. If you asked anyone at San Diego Hope hospital, they'd say Taylor Cabot and Rob Halston were a couple. Typical grapevine speculation. And not true. Though, lately, each step forward in Taylor's life did seem to be headed closer and closer to—"It's really more of a friendship thing."

Her cousin's lips quirked ever so slightly. "Always a good place to start."

"I guess." Taylor tried her best for a casual shrug. "I'm not sure I'm ready for anything more than that. Not quite yet."

It was the last item on her checklist: *Fall in love again.*

"I'm sorry." Aimee touched her arm. "I didn't mean to put you on the spot. It's just so good to see you looking happier. More hopeful."

"I know." Taylor smiled at her cousin. "And I am. Really . . ."

Her gaze swept the vista beyond the railing, a long stretch of beach and tranquil green ocean dotted with palm trees and pastel clusters of beachfront bungalows. The sun shone on red clay roofs of far grander homes on the cliffs above. Today's cloudless blue sky boasted a joyful rainbow of kites. Like hope . . . on a Southern California breeze. It was starting to feel that way now. Hopeful. She was back home, part of a skilled, tight-knit ER team at the same hospital where her favorite cousin worked in the dietary department. It wasn't perfect; Taylor didn't expect that. But it did seem promising, as if peace and healing were really possible. A new beginning. No more painful detours after unimaginable tragedy.

"Look." Aimee jabbed her finger toward the distance. "See? Between the big purple dragon and the SpongeBob that keeps going into a spin. It's a plane. I'm surprised they let the pilot fly in that close with all that's going on here. Maybe it belongs to a news team."

"Don't think so," Taylor said, locating the small plane. "There's a privately owned airstrip a few miles from here. Greg had a pilot friend who got permission to use it a couple of times when we flew in to visit the folks . . ." She hesitated, prepared for a pang, but the memory came painlessly: Greg sitting beside his buddy at the controls of the rented plane, then turning back to grin at Taylor with boyish excitement on his handsome face—so full of life. The sun glittering like diamonds on the surface of the sea, that breathtaking view of Coronado Island from high above, and the roller-coaster dip in her stomach when the plane tilted into a turn . . .

"He'll probably be directed to another approach," Taylor guessed, buoyed once again by the certainty that removing her rings had been good timing. Not because of what might or might not be on the horizon with Rob Halston, or even that the rings had been looming large on her checklist, but because she really was past the worst now. She thought of what she'd just said to her cousin, that the pilot would be directed to another approach. Maybe Taylor was being redirected too. A giddy laugh rose. She tapped her cousin's shoulder. "You know what we need?"

"Kettle corn?"

"No way. I've only logged 11,000 steps today." Taylor touched her activity-tracking bracelet. "It won't work in my calorie budget."

"That evil thing." Aimee groaned. "I keep telling you: Curran women are born to be curvy. You're coming dangerously close to losing your membership." She feigned a childish pout. "Okay, what else do we need?"

"Kites!" Taylor pointed down the crowded boardwalk. "Just past the face-painting booth, there's a tent where we can make our own. All different kinds of options: diamond kites, rollers, deltas, sleds. Crazy colors and even glitter. C'mon, we haven't flown one together since we were Girl Scouts."

"Wait, hold on." Aimee squinted, staring toward the ocean. "That plane . . . I swear its wing just skimmed the water. Some kind of air show? But it seems too reckless even for that."

"Where?" Taylor turned to look at the same moment the crowd around them exploded with shouts.

"What's he doing?" someone yelled.

"Oh no, that plane's in trouble!"

"Pull up, dude!" a young man yelled. "Stop clowning—"

"There . . . ," a women offered with breathless relief. "He's back up in the air again and turning toward—"

No.

Taylor's heart stuttered as the small plane banked errati-cally, dropped far too close to the water again, then hurtled, out of control, across the sand, and—

She grabbed her cousin's arm. "He's coming right at us!"

"Look out," someone screamed. "He's gonna hit the boardwalk! Run; get away from here!"

There was a tidal wave of screams, drowned by a deaf-ening engine roar. Then a horrifying overhead shadow, a rush of wind that nearly knocked Taylor to her knees, the acrid and eye-watering scent of airplane fuel—and finally a thunderous, earth-jolting crash.

"Aimee!"

ACKNOWLEDGMENTS

HEARTFELT APPRECIATION TO:

Literary agent Natasha Kern—you are a blessing, always.

The incredible Tyndale House publishing team, especially editors Jan Stob, Sarah Mason, and Erin Smith—it's a joy to work with you.

Critique partner and author Nancy Herriman—I'm so grateful for you.

My Sacramento resources:

Chaplain Mindi Russell, executive director of Law Enforcement Chaplaincy, and David Vincent, director of US Crisis Care—for the hope you bring to so many and for your gracious help with this story.

Detective Brian Meux, Sacramento County Sheriff's Department—for your generous and invaluable assistance with the law enforcement components of this story.

Any inaccuracies, or changes to accommodate fictional portrayals, are mine alone.

Daughter Brooklynn, trail name Landmark—your knowledge of and appreciation for Yosemite National Park put my characters (and readers) "right there."

JoAnn Shiley—for your gracious gift of time in helping me capture the hopeful theme of this story: trusting God.

Thena Cullen, real-life poet—for volunteering to be our hero's favorite aunt.

Fellow authors and medical comrades Dr. Richard Mabry and Laurie Kingery—for your input regarding hospital scenes.

My wonderful family, especially husband and real-life hero, Andy—I am so very blessed to have you "by my side."

And with deep appreciation to my readers—it is a joy and a privilege to bring you these hopeful stories.

ABOUT THE AUTHOR

CANDACE CALVERT is a former ER nurse and author of the Mercy Hospital series—*Critical Care, Disaster Status,* and *Code Triage*—and the Grace Medical series—*Trauma Plan, Rescue Team,* and *Life Support*. Her medical dramas offer readers a chance to "scrub in" on the exciting world of emergency medicine. Wife, mother, and very proud grandmother, Candace makes her home in northern California. Visit her website at www.candacecalvert.com.

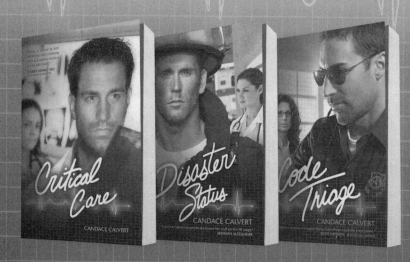